REAL*

FROZEN SEA

Invader Bay

WITHDRAWN

izard Head

Chalk Cliffs

Firehole R.

Fortress Rock

Marisa Pines Camp

Marisa Pines Pass

Way Camp

Hunter's Camp

Queen Court

Alyssa Plateau

The Harlot

Spiritgate

Delphi

North Rd.

KINGDOM of ARDEN

Heartfang Mtns.

Middlesea

Temple Church

Ardenswater

Bittersweet Keep

Ardenscourt

East Rd.

Baston Bay

THE IND OCEA

Ardenswater

Heartfang R.

Bright Stone Keep

Bitter Springs R.

Watergate

Gryphon P

The Cla

The Wastes

WE'ENHAVEN

Hidden Bay

Northern Islands

Demon's Wounds

JARTHIS

Deepwater Court

Salt Sea

The Indio Ocean

Dragonback Mountains

Tarvos River

Scorched Lands

Guardians

Tarvos

Endru

FLAMECASTER

Also by Cinda Williams Chima

THE HEIR CHRONICLES
The Warrior Heir
The Wizard Heir
The Dragon Heir
The Enchanter Heir
The Sorcerer Heir

THE SEVEN REALMS SERIES
The Demon King
The Exiled Queen
The Gray Wolf Throne
The Crimson Crown

FLAME

CINDA
WILLIAMS CHIMA

CASTER
A SHATTERED REALMS NOVEL

HARPER TEEN
An Imprint of HarperCollins Publishers

To all of those writers who opened their veins and wrote the incredible books that made me fall in love with reading. You are the ones who kindled the hope that I might one day be a writer.

Library of Congress Control Number: 2015938988
ISBN 978-0-06-238094-4 (hardcover)
ISBN 978-0-06-245490-4 (international edition)

Typography by Erin Fitzsimmons
16 17 18 19 20   PC/RRDH   10 9 8 7 6 5 4 3 2 1

First Edition

HEALER

Compared to the freezing weather outside, the stable was warm and steamy and alive with the sleepy murmurings of horses.

Adrian sul'Han pulled off his fleece-lined gloves and stuffed them into his pockets. He went first to see if his father's pony, the latest in a long line of Raggers, was still in his stall.

He was, poking his head over the stall door, looking for a handout as usual. So his father hadn't left the city. Not yet, anyway. Adrian needed to talk to him before he did.

He walked on down the line of stalls to look in on the piebald mare. She came forward to meet him, lipping hopefully at his hand. Adrian studied her critically. Her eyes were bright, ears pricked forward, and when he ran his hand over her shoulder, he could tell that the muscles of her withers were filling in.

Sliding his free hand under his coat, he gripped his amulet and sent a tendril of power into the mare, looking for trouble. To his relief, the white-hot focus of infection was nearly gone.

"You'll be all right," he murmured, stroking her head, proud that it was true.

He heard Mancy's step-and-drag footsteps behind him. "I thought that was you, boy," she said, coming up next to him. "Here to see my Priscilly? It's amazing, what you've done. I thought I had lost her, and now she's like a brand-new horse."

"Actually, I'm looking for my da, and I thought I'd look in on Priscilly while I'm here," Adrian said. "Have you seen him?"

She shook her head. "Not today, no." Worry flickered across her face. "You don't think the High Wizard will come here, do you? See, I'm moving slow this morning, and I only just got the front stalls mucked out. I need to—"

"Don't worry," Adrian said, raising both hands. "I just thought he might have stopped by."

Mancy was a soldier who'd been assigned to the stables while she recovered from a nasty leg wound courtesy of one of the kingdom of Arden's collared mages. Now her wound drew Adrian's attention like a poke in the eye. It wasn't healing properly, he could tell, and he wanted to know why.

In fact, Mancy had the smell of death on her.

"Hey! Did you hear me?"

That was when Adrian realized that Mancy had asked a question. "I'm sorry," he said, wrenching his attention back to the conversation. "What was that?"

"I *said*, is it all right if I put her back on her regular feed?" Mancy said, a little huffily.

"Oh. Ah. Two more days of the mash, and then she can go back," he said. Grain was hard to find after a quarter century of war. Nobody was getting fat in Fellsmarch these days.

"I was telling Hughes at West Gate about you," Mancy said. "I told him you was just a lýtling, but you can work miracles with horses."

I'm not a lýtling, Adrian thought. Maybe I don't have my growth, but I'm already thirteen.

"He's got a moonblind horse that an't getting any better, and he asked me to ask you if you might come by and take a look."

The West Gate was two days' ride away. And Adrian was hoping to leave town in a week.

"I can't go out there right now, but I'll send over an ointment that might help," he said. He paused, clearing his throat. A lýtling healer might be good enough for horses, but . . . "How's the leg?"

Mancy grimaced. "It's all right, I guess. It's closed over, but it's still giving me a lot of pain. Plus, I can't seem to get my strength back. I been back to the healing halls three different times, but they don't want to see me."

Mancy's collarbones stuck out more than before, and Adrian noticed that she leaned on the stall door for support. "Mind if I take a look?"

Mancy blinked at him. "At me? You do people, too?"

Adrian bit back the first response that came to mind. "Sometimes."

"All right then. Be my guest." Mancy sat down on an overturned bucket, and rolled back her uniform breeches. When he went to touch her leg, though, she flinched back. "You an't going to—do anything, are you?"

"Like?"

"Hex it or something?" Valefolk were wary of wizards, for good reason.

"I'm just going to take a look, all right?" The wound was closed, the skin tight and hot, the leg puffy all the way into the ankle. Adrian brushed his fingers over it, murmuring a charm, and saw that the infection had gone into the bone. He'd seen it before, in horses, and they always had to be put down.

Adrian looked up at Mancy, chewing his lower lip. The leg would have to come off, but he knew she wouldn't take that verdict from a thirteen-year-old untrained wizard.

"Mancy," he said, "your leg needs to be seen right away. Go back to the healing halls, and ask for Titus Gryphon. Don't get shuffled off to anyone else, and don't take no for an answer. Tell him I sent you, that he needs to look at your leg. Do it now."

Mancy blinked at him, her brow furrowed. "Now? But right now I need to muck out the—"

"That can keep," Adrian said. "If you want, I'll put in a word with Jarrett." The stable master owed him a favor.

"You don't need to do that," Mancy said. She swallowed hard. "I'll just let him know where I am. If you really think I need to go now."

"You do." Adrian put a hand on her shoulder, soothing her. "You'll be all right."

With Mancy on her way to Gryphon, Adrian continued his search for his father. Outside again, it seemed even colder than before. The wind howled down from the Spirits, sending bits of greenery from the recent Solstice celebration spinning down the street.

He really, really needed to get a yes from his father before his mother the queen found out what he was up to. His father, the High Wizard, was a little more flexible when it came to rules. Like the one that said that wizards weren't supposed to receive their amulets until they turned sixteen.

Adrian reached for his amulet now, as he did a dozen times a day, feeling the usual flow of energy from wizard to amulet. Wizards continually produced flash, a magical energy. Amulets stored flash until enough accumulated to do something worthwhile. Without an amulet, flash leaked away, and was of no use to anyone.

His father had given him this hand-me-down amulet two years ago, on his eleventh name day, along with a lecture on all the bad things that would happen if he abused or misused it.

Adrian had worn the amulet—carved in the shape of a hunter—on a chain around his neck ever since. He'd trained hard in the use of magic—most often with his father, when he was home; elsewise with some of his father's handpicked friends. Yet it had made no difference. His older sister, Hana, was dead, and his little sister, Lyss, was heartbroken. And Adrian needed to get out of town.

If his da wasn't in the castle close, and if he hadn't ridden out, he'd be somewhere in the city. Likely Ragmarket or Southbridge. Adrian headed for the markets.

To call them "markets" these days was being generous. With Solstice just over, the shelves had been cleared of what little food there was. There was nothing on offer but some tired-looking root vegetables that had been held back till now so as to fetch the best prices. His father said it reminded him of the hard times during the reign of Queen Marianna, when there was never enough to eat. Or during Arden's siege of Fellsmarch Castle, when they had contests to come up with new recipes for barley.

Hard times are back, Adrian thought, if they ever left. For Solstice, the royal family had dined on venison, courtesy of their upland clan relations. Otherwise, it would have been ham and barley pies (light on ham, heavy on barley).

Not that it mattered. None of them had much of an appetite. It was the first midwinter since Hana died.

Around him, the market was waking up: first, the bakers, produce sellers, and fishmongers. Then the secondhand shops selling hard-worn, picked-over goods (all claimed to be clan-made). This was his father's home ground. He'd once ruled this neighborhood as the notorious streetlord of the Ragger gang.

Adrian always drew attention, too, when he walked the markets. He was too easy to pick out as Han Alister's son, with his red hair and wizard's glow. Today it seemed worse than usual—he felt the pressure of eyes upon him wherever he went, the prickle on the back of his neck that meant he was being watched. He guessed it was because he'd been in the camps in the mountains when Hana died, and he hadn't been down to the markets since.

He asked after his da in several of the market stalls.

Nobody had seen him, but they all sent their good wishes for a brighter new year.

Adrian had nearly given up when he walked into the flower market, where the merchants were just unpacking their wares. There was his father, his back to Adrian, bargaining with one of the vendors, a young girl in beaded Demonai garb.

His da was dressed in the nondescript clothing he wore when he walked the city streets, but there was no mistaking the broad shoulders and deceptively slouchy stance. His sword slanted across his back, which was nothing unusual in a city filled with soldiers.

His hair glinted in the frail winter light, more silver than gold these days. His amulet was hidden, but he wore the aura that other wizards recognized. He was known, especially here, on his home ground, as Han "Cuffs" Alister, the lowborn hero who'd become High Wizard. The strategist who continually outfoxed the Ardenine king. He was a former street thief—*their* former street thief—who'd married a queen.

The flower vendor was flushed and fluttering at having such royalty in her shop, bringing blossoms forward and arranging them in a copper bucket to show them off.

Adrian edged closer, listening as his father bantered with the vendor. In the end, he chose red foxflowers, white lilies, and blue trueheart, along with a few stems of bog marigold and maiden's kiss.

The girl wrapped them in paper and handed them over. When he tipped a handful of coins into her palm, she tried to give it back. "Oh, no, my lord, I couldn't. I'm so very sorry for your loss. I used to see the princess in the mountain camps sometimes. Running Wolf was . . . was always kind to me."

Running Wolf was Hana's clan name.

His father closed her fingers over the money, looking her straight in the eyes. "Thank you," he said. "We all miss her. But you still need to make a living." He bowed and turned away, cloak kiting behind him. The girl looked after him, blinking back tears, clutching her hair in her fist to keep it from flying in the bone-chilling wind.

That was when his father spotted Adrian lurking nearby. "Ash! This is a surprise," he said, using the nickname he favored. A-S-H, for Adrian sul'Han. Striding toward him, he extended the flowers. "What do you think?" he said, almost shyly. "Will your mother like them?"

"That depends on how much trouble you're in," Adrian said, extracting a faint smile from his father. They both understood what the flowers were for, and why his father was in the market on this particular day.

Adrian's older sister, Hanalea ana'Raisa, the princess heir, had died six months ago, at the summer solstice, in a skirmish along the border with Tamron. From the looks of things, she'd been the last one standing, taking down six Ardenine mudbacks before she went down herself. Her bound captain, Simon Byrne, had died at her side.

The Ardenine general, Marin Karn, had severed her head and carried it back to his king. King Gerard had ordered it paraded through the captive realms, then sent it back to her mother the queen in an ornate casket.

Hana was only twenty years old. She'd been the golden child who combined her father's good looks and street-savvy charm and her mother's ability to bring people together and lead. She was one who could walk into a room and command it within minutes. She'd been a symbol of hope, the promise that the Gray Wolf line would survive.

If the Maker is good, and all-powerful, Adrian thought, then why would this be allowed to happen? What cruel twist of fate sent a large Ardenine company into the borderlands in an area that hadn't seen fighting for nearly a year? Most importantly, why Hana? Why not Adrian? She was the heir; he was in every way the spare.

"What brings you to the markets?" his father said, draping an arm around Adrian's shoulders. He was never afraid to show affection in public. "Are you buying or selling?"

"I wanted to talk to you. Privately."

His father eyed him keenly. "You're selling then, I believe," he said. "I have some time right now. Come to breakfast, and we'll talk."

A CRUEL FROST

They chose a place called the Drovers' Inn, a hostelry on market square that Adrian had never been to. Everyone knew his father, of course; the server led them to the very best table, near the hearth, and clunked steaming mugs of cider down in front of them. "I'm so sorry, Lord Alister," she said, her cheeks pink with embarrassment. "All we got is porridge and a wee bit of ham, but the bread is fresh this morning."

"I was hoping for porridge," his father said, signaling for her to bring two bowls. Setting the bouquet carefully aside, he leaned his sword against the wall and slung his cloak over the back of a chair and sat. He always sat facing the door, a throwback to his streetlord days.

He looked tired, the dark circles under his eyes still visible against his sun-kissed skin. He'd lost weight, too, during the long marching season. Adrian resisted the temptation to reach out and grip his father's hand so he could look for damage. "Da," he said. "Are you . . . ?"

"I'm all right," his father said, taking a deep swallow of cider. "It's been a hard season for all of us."

"But now you're leaving again." Adrian had promised himself that he wouldn't sulk like a child, but he came close.

At that, his father hunched his shoulders and darted a guilty look his way. "Your mother's seen wolves every day for the last week. Something bad is about to happen, and I need to figure out what it is, and how to prevent it."

Visions of gray wolves appeared to descendants of the Gray Wolf line of queens in times of trouble and change. They were actually the dead queens—ancestors of the living queens of the Fells, come back as a warning.

"How can you figure out how to prevent something when you don't know what it is?" Wolves had appeared in the days before Hana died, but it had happened anyway. To Adrian, a vague warning was worse than none at all.

The porridge arrived, steaming, with the promised bits of ham arranged on top for show.

When the server left again, his father said, "I think that the attack on Hana's triple was more than very bad luck. I think she was the target."

"How would they know it was her?" Adrian asked. "How would they know where she was?"

His father leaned across the table. "I think someone told them. I think Arden has a spy on the inside."

"No," Adrian said, with conviction. "Who would do that? Everyone loved her. And why would Arden target Hana in particular? She's the heir—I know that—but wouldn't it have made more sense to go after General Dunedain?"

"Not if the goal is to break your mother's heart," his father said. "Captain Byrne and Shilo Trailblazer have been over the killing field dozens of times. From the looks of things, it wasn't just a platoon—it was an entire company. Hana was smart, and a strong fighter, but it's unlikely she would take down a half dozen Ardenines before they killed her—unless they were holding back, trying to take her alive." He paused, glancing around for eavesdroppers. "There's more," he said. "It appears that her death wound was self-inflicted. We believe that when she realized that she was about to be captured, she shoved her own dagger through her heart."

Adrian felt like he'd been daggered himself. "She killed herself?"

"What would you have done, in her place?" his father asked.

Adrian shuddered. On this one point, they all agreed— it had been a blessing that Hana hadn't been taken alive to

Ardenscourt, to the dungeons of the monstrous king of Arden, Gerard Montaigne. It was one thing to break their hearts; it would have been worse if he'd held their hearts in his hands.

His father pushed bits of ham around his bowl with his spoon. "Montaigne is under considerable pressure from his thanes to finish this thing. They've been spending men and treasure for a quarter century with little to no results. Perhaps the king of Arden has hit on a new tactic—targeting the royal line, the queen's family. This is a grudge match, remember. Your mother rejected him in a very public way."

Adrian knew that story. The queen had refused to sign over her queendom in exchange for the king of Arden's hand in marriage. "But that was twenty-five years ago," he protested, not wanting it to be true. "He got married eventually, didn't he, to somebody else?"

"Don't expect it to make sense, Ash. Montaigne is a proud, nasty brute who's used to getting his own way. My biggest regret is that I didn't shiv the bastard when I had the chance."

Looking into his father's face, Adrian saw a rare glimpse of the ruthless streetlord he'd once been. Until his father ran a hand over his face, as if to wipe that person away.

Adrian's skin prickled. It was like he felt the hand of the Maker touch the delicate thread that connected life and death. "So what can we do?"

"If we can identify who betrayed Hana, that would be a start," his father said. "One of our eyes and ears has an informant who claims to know something. I'm supposed to meet with them in Southbridge in a little while."

The temple church in the market sounded the quarter hour, reminding them both that time was passing. "Now," his father said, placing his hands flat on the table. "What was it you wanted to talk to me about?"

Adrian took a gulp of cider for courage. "You know I've been working as a healer with the clans the past two summers. And I've been helping with the Highlander cavalry string when I can."

"So I've heard. If Willo had her way, she'd like you to apprentice with her year-round. She's not as young as she used to be, and there's never enough healers available during the marching season. General Dunedain wouldn't hold still for it, though. She'd like to put you in charge of the military stables full-time. Everywhere I go, all I hear about is how you can work magic with horses. It's too bad there's only one of you."

Right, Adrian thought. It's too bad. So he hurried on. "I've also spent time in the healing halls in the city."

"Ah," his father said, his face hardening. "Lord Vega's domain. I keep hoping he'll retire." Harriman Vega was the wizard who oversaw the healing halls in the capital, the ones wizards and most Valefolk patronized.

"That's the problem," Adrian said. "Willo can't help

me with high magic, and Lord Vega has no interest in clan treatments and green magic. He still thinks it's witchery for the gullible masses. And until I graduate from Mystwerk, he won't let me do more than make beds and do the washing up." Mystwerk was the school for wizards at Oden's Ford.

"And you can't go to Mystwerk until after your sixteenth name day."

"Right." Adrian took a deep breath and plunged on. "I can't get into Mystwerk at thirteen, but Spiritas accepts novices at eleven, just like Wien House."

"Spiritas?"

"That's the healers' academy at Oden's Ford. You wouldn't remember it—it's just three years old. They're combining green magic, music and art therapies, clan remedies, and, eventually, wizardry."

"Eventually?" His father raised an eyebrow.

"That's the goal, but from what I hear, the deans at Mystwerk haven't been eager to join in so far."

His father snorted. "Why am I not surprised?"

"My thought was, I could go to Spiritas now, then move over to Mystwerk when I'm eligible. That way I won't waste time watching people die who might have lived if I only had the skills." Despite his best efforts, his voice shook.

"That's the thing about guilt," his father said. "It always seems like there's enough to go around. The only ones who don't take a share are the ones who are actually guilty." He paused, lines of pain etched deeply into his face. "I lost my mother and sister when I wasn't much older than you. I did my best, but my best wasn't good enough." He ran his fingers over his serpent amulet. "I never angled to be High Wizard. All I've ever wanted is to protect the people I care about. And now I've lost Hana, too."

"It's not your fault, what happened to Hana," Adrian said. It was odd to be in the position of consoling his father. "Hana was a good fighter, and Mama is, too, and Lyss—I guess Lyss will be, when she gets older." His younger sister, Alyssa, was only eleven.

"It's not your fault, either," his father said, reaching across the table and gripping Adrian's hand. "We don't protect them because they're weak. We protect them because they are strong, and strong people make enemies. We just need to do our best—whatever it takes—to protect your mother and sister—the Gray Wolf line. And pray that it's enough."

"My best can be better," Adrian said, looking his father in the eyes.

His father got the point. He tilted his head. "How do you know they would take you on at Spiritas?"

"The dean of Spiritas is a Voyageur healer named Taliesin Beaugarde." The Voyageurs were a nomadic tribe of sheepherders from the Heartfang Mountains who traveled the flatlands in colorful caravans. Flatlanders claimed they were witches. Like that was a bad thing.

"Taliesin spent some time at Marisa Pines while I was there, and we got along. I've been in touch with her, and she's hot to make this happen. I would be the first wizard to attend. They're hoping that if the deans at Mystwerk see what's possible, then maybe they'll come around."

His father laughed. "You're too much like your mother—always two steps ahead of me." After a beat, he went on, "Speaking of the queen, what does she say?"

Adrian cleared his throat. "I haven't talked to her about it."

"Ah," his father said, rubbing his chin. "Trying to slide in the back gate, are you? You know she won't be eager to let you out of her sight after what happened to Hana."

"I was hoping you might help me persuade her."

His father fiddled with the flowers, knocking a few petals loose. "As you know, she's not happy with me right now. I might not be your best advocate. Maybe if we waited a bit . . ."

"Taliesin's here now. She came to visit family for Solstice. If I can get permission, I can go back with her."

"So you're in a hurry for an answer." His father looked down at his hands and picked at a scab on his knuckles. "It sounds like a sensible plan," he said finally. "A good use of your talents, and close to your heart. I think you should go. I'll do whatever I can to make it happen. See if you can arrange time with your mother tonight, and I'll be there, ready to deploy my meager weapons in your defense."

"Thank you," Adrian said simply. He knew his da would understand. He somehow always did.

The bells bonged out the hour.

"I'd better go," his father said. "It's already ten, and I don't want to be late. I'll see you tonight." He swept his cloak around his shoulders, strapped on his baldric, and slid his sword into place. Every eye in the room followed him as he went out the door.

Adrian gazed after him, his gut in turmoil. His father's theory about Hana had unsettled him. What if it were true? He'd thought of her death as tragic bad luck, a matter of being in the wrong place at the wrong time, part of the senseless carnage of the war. But now . . .

There was something he was missing, some pattern that he wasn't seeing. Hana had died at midsummer, an event the wolves foretold. Now it was midwinter, and the wolves were back, and his father was heading to a meeting with an unknown informant.

His father's words came back to him. Perhaps the king of Arden has hit on a new tactic.

No. Oh, no.

"Da!" Lurching to his feet, Adrian careened out the door of the tavern. Breathlessly, he scanned the market square, but he didn't see his father. Which street would he take to Southbridge? Since he was late, he'd probably take the most direct path, down the Way of the Queens to the river.

Fighting through the market day crowds, Adrian turned

onto the Way and ran, dodging carriages and families out for a stroll. The cobbled pavement was perilous, and layered with snow and ice. It was like one of those dreams, when you try to run and your feet seem to be glued to the ground. Several times he nearly fell, and once he was nearly run down by a teamster, who swore at him as he streaked past.

Now he was almost to the river, and he still didn't see his father. If he'd turned off into one of the side streets or alleys, Adrian would never find him in time.

When Adrian finally spotted him, far ahead, he was nearly to the bridge, the bouquet of flowers still in his hand. Adrian put on speed, already working on what he would say. *I know you're street-savvy and all, but I think you're walking into a trap.*

He was so focused on his father that he scarcely resisted when somebody grabbed him from behind and clapped a hand over his mouth. His attacker pulled a hood over his head, and began dragging him backward. Adrian could feel magic buzzing into him, no doubt an immobilization charm. But Adrian was wearing a clan talisman alongside his amulet—a pendant that absorbed attack magic.

He pretended to go limp, and when his captor adjusted his grip, Adrian came up off the balls of his feet, hearing a crunch and a screech of pain as his head smashed into cartilage.

When the grip on him loosened, Adrian twisted free

and tried to dodge into the alley, but plowed straight into someone who held him tightly against his body, so Adrian couldn't reach his amulet or yank away the hood.

Learn to use all your senses, his father always said. That way, if you're blind, you can use your ears and your nose and your hands instead.

From the feel of the man's body and the angle at which he held him, Adrian could tell that he was tall, spare, and gifted. He could also feel something metallic and jingling that hung at his waist under his robes. Not an amulet. But what?

"Don't let him touch the jinxpiece," one of them growled.

"I'm not an idiot," Alley Man snarled. "Take the boy. Our agreement was that I wouldn't be personally involved in this." The voice seemed familiar, and there was a scent about him—a familiar scent—that Adrian couldn't place.

As they made the handoff, Adrian managed to strip back the hood. He was surrounded by cloaked and hooded men. He saw his father in the distance, already midway across the bridge. "Da! Help!"

His father heard, and turned. The flowers fell to the bridge deck like jewels scattered on the pavement as he drew his sword in one fluid movement and charged at them.

All around Adrian, swords hissed free. While his captor was distracted, Adrian brought both feet down on his instep.

The wizard howled, something smashed down on Adrian's head, and he landed flat on his face on the icy cobblestones, twisting his ankle.

"Careful," somebody growled. "Don't hit the mageling too hard. We want him alive."

Mage. That was what they called wizards in Arden.

Close by, Adrian heard the clatter and clash of swordplay, smelled the acrid scent of wizard flame, heard somebody scream as a blade hit home. Black spots swarmed in Adrian's vision as he tried and failed to prop himself up. Tried not to spew onto the stones.

Finally, he rolled onto his back. His vision cleared enough that he saw his father, surrounded by six or eight swordsmen, fighting like a fury in the stories with flame and sword. He was backing toward him, trying to get close to Adrian, but he hadn't escaped the bite of the blades. His cloak was already sliced through in several places and spotted with blood.

It took everything Adrian had to sit up, then straighten to a standing position. He swayed, then shouted, "Leave him alone!" Gripping his amulet, he stood up next to his father and launched a flaming volley of his own, putting all of his frustration and fury into it, driving the assassins back.

"No, Ash! Run! Get to the river if you can," his father shouted, pivoting and cutting down another swordsman. "Get into the river and dive."

"I'm not leaving you. We can win this."

That was when his father staggered, the tip of his sword drooping a little. He looked at the assassins, tried to lift his sword again, but it was as if it was too heavy.

"Da? What's wrong?" Adrian stepped in closer, but his father shook his head, reached for his amulet, then dropped his hand away, swearing softly. His body shuddered, and despite the cold, a sheen of sweat gilded his face.

That's when Adrian knew. It was poison. His father was poisoned. He followed his father's gaze, and saw that the assassins' blades were stained blue-gray with it.

His father stumbled to his knees, his sword clattering free on the stones. His face was pale, as if the blood were called to other places.

"That one's done," the leader said. He pointed at Adrian with his poison-daubed blade. "Bring the mageling, and let's go."

Howling with rage, Adrian turned and charged toward the assassins, sending a deluge of flame out ahead. But, somehow, his father tripped him, and he went down hard on his face in the snow. His father crawled forward and covered his body with his own. He felt warm breath in his ear.

"Lay still," he said. "Play dead, buy some time. The bluejackets will come. These ones will run. They don't want to be caught and questioned."

Adrian struggled to get up, but his father had him pinned. He heard what sounded like an army of running feet and somebody shouting, "The High Wizard! The bastards have killed the High Wizard!"

A mob of people hurtled past. Adrian heard screams and blows landing, shouts of rage and despair.

Finally wriggling free, he gripped his amulet with one hand, pressing the other hand into his father's chest. He sent power in, seeking to isolate the poison. But it was everywhere, and already the spark of life was all but extinguished. He ripped his father's cloak and shirt away, exposing wounds that should have been minor. He sent flash in directly, desperately trying to draw the poison out. It hit him like a runaway cart, and he reeled back.

"Don't," his father whispered, twisting away from Adrian's hand. "You don't want to risk it. You're not strong enough, on your own. Wait for help."

Adrian understood. Wizard healers took on the ailments of their patients, and so healing a gravely sick patient was always risky. Even more so for someone who didn't know what he was doing. But there would be no waiting, because waiting meant that his father would die.

"I am going to save you," Adrian growled. "I don't care what it costs. You're important. You need to live."

"Ash. Please listen. I have been saved so many times," his father said. "First your mother saved me, and then you and your sisters. I'm not the one who needs saving now." His body shuddered again. "Save yourself, and the Line. Your mother will take this hard, and she's had enough grief in her life already. Tell her . . . tell her that having her . . . that being with her . . . that loving her . . . it was worth it. It was worth it. Will you tell her that?"

"No!" Adrian cried. "You can tell her yourself. I'm not letting you go."

"Sometimes . . . you have to . . . let go." His father took both his hands and closed them over the serpent amulet. "This is yours. I want you to go to Oden's Ford and learn how to use it."

And then he was gone, the spiritas departing like a whisper on the wind, or a gray wolf on the snow. And, with it, Adrian's childhood.

A fierce anger ignited inside him, mingled with guilt and pain. His father had survived a lifetime of fighting— until Adrian lured him into a fight he couldn't win. He'd failed him in every way possible. He bowed his head over their joined hands and prayed to whatever god was listening, "Take me. Take me instead. Spare him. Please."

The gods, it seemed, were occupied elsewhere.

Adrian was no use in a fight, and he was no use as a healer. He was no use to anyone. He couldn't bear the thought of facing his mother and sister and telling them what had happened. How could he live in a world that claimed the good and left the bad alone?

He lifted the serpent amulet from around his father's neck and hung it around his own. He didn't much care where he went, as long as it was away from there. So he ran, limping badly, until he lost himself in the tangle of streets.

3

RILEY

The day Jenna's friend Riley died began as they all did—
at three in the morning with the long, bone-jarring ride
up the mountain to the mine. It was sleeting when Jenna
trudged up the hill to the pickup place, so she was shivering and soaked through by the time she got there. The
wagon was waiting, the horses steaming and stomping in
the cold, the driver yelling at her to hurry up, he didn't
want to get fined for being late.

Jenna shook off the ice as best she could and climbed
in, squeezing in next to Riley as the wagon lurched into
motion. She always sat next to Riley if there was room,
with little Maggi on her other side. He'd put his arm
around their shoulders, their bodies pressed tight together.

That way, they'd all three stay warm, and she could sleep, which made the workday seem shorter.

On the way home, if they could stay awake, she and Riley would talk about what they wanted to be when they grew up, even though Riley was fifteen and already grown, and Jenna twelve and nearly grown. They'd made a pact that they would get out of the mines one day.

Today, Riley had this smug look on his face, like he was hiding a great big secret. As soon as Jenna got settled, he draped a bright-red cloak over the two of them, pulling it up over their heads to keep off the sleet.

The cloak smelled of wet sheep, and it was scratchy, but it was big enough to cover them both, even leaving a corner for Maggi, and it was rum warm. Jenna fingered the wool, snuggling down inside it. "Riley! Where'd you get such a fine cloak?"

"There was an explosion at the ironworks two days ago, and three of the colliers was killed. So the foreman, he give me one of their cloaks."

"You got a cloak off a dead man?" Jenna stared at him, horrified.

Riley shrugged. "He won't be needing it."

"But . . . but that's bad luck," Jenna said. "Everybody knows that."

"Me, I think it's good luck, 'cause we're warmer for it. Also 'cause it's like a cave to hide in." He leaned close, his lashy brown eyes meeting hers. She knew he wanted to kiss her—he'd done it before—but was a little shy, with Maggi there. Jenna pulled his head down toward hers, and he kissed her on the lips.

Her cheeks burned, but she felt a pleasant tingle deep in her belly. She didn't know what to say, so she changed the subject. "I have a surprise for you, too." She patted her lunch bucket. "In here."

He eyed the bucket. "If I guess, will you tell me?"

"Maybe."

"It's a meat pie. Isn't it?" Riley was big and strong and he always seemed to be hungry. Jenna ate better than most because her father owned a tavern. She'd brought Riley a meat pie once before.

Maggi overheard. "A meat pie! Can I have a bite?" Maggi was probably seven years old, scrawny as a baby bird. She was an orphan, so she was always hungry, too. There were lots of hungry orphans in town, though lots had died. If Jenna'd had a sister, she would want her to be just like Maggi. Except better fed and living somewhere other than Delphi.

Jenna shook her head. "Sorry, Maggi. It's not a meat pie. It's a book."

"A book?" Riley looked away and cleared his throat. "But you know I can't read. I'm fixing to learn, but—"

"I'll teach you," Jenna said. "I'll read it to you on the way home."

"You will?" Riley's eyes widened.

"Can I listen, too?" Maggi said. "You tell the best stories."

Jenna nodded. "You can listen. And here." Digging in her pocket, she pulled out a small, wrinkled apple and handed it to Maggi. "I found this on my way up to the ride. You can eat it now or save it for the midday."

Maggi had already bitten into it. She knew better than to save things for later. The juice ran down her chin, making trails in the dirt on her face. Once she'd finished the apple, she tossed the core and snuggled down to sleep, her head in Jenna's lap. Jenna stroked her hair, working out some of the tangles.

"Most of my stories come from books," Jenna said to Riley. "I used to read all the time before I went into the mines. My da taught me how. I liked to pretend I was one of the characters."

Riley wrapped their cloak tighter to keep out the wet and looked over the packed-in bodies around them. He blotted rain from the end of his nose with his sleeve. Riley was usually a cheerful sort, but on this morning he seemed a little downcast. Maybe because the bosses were working him harder than anybody else. "If I was a character in a book, I'd want to be in a different story."

"You will be," Jenna said, leaning closer so she could speak into his ear. "You can be in my story." And then, for reasons she couldn't explain, she leaned toward him and shared the secret she'd kept forever. "See, I'm magemarked."

"Magemarked?" His eyebrows came together. "What's that?"

"Shhh," she said, clapping her hand over his mouth and glaring around the packed wagon. From what she could tell, everyone else was asleep. It was amazing how alone you could be in the middle of a crowd. "Nobody can know." She took his hand and placed it over the raised emblem on the back of her neck, the spiderweb of metal, the smooth stone at the center.

His eyes widened as he brushed his fingers over the surface. "What's it mean?" he whispered.

"It means I'm powerful."

"Well," Riley said, swallowing hard, "maybe *you* are. But I don't have a mark."

Jenna was instantly sorry she'd brought the whole thing up. She'd kept it to herself for this long. Why had she chosen to blurt it out now?

"That doesn't matter," she said. "We are chosen, you and I. We'll write our own story, you'll see." Putting her hands on Riley's shoulders, she looked into his eyes. "When I look at a person, I can see who they really are."

"You can't," Riley said.

"I can." That was a stretcher. She'd see pictures or hear fragments, was all, but it wasn't easy figuring out what they meant. Sometimes it was the person as they were, only clearer, truer, like when somebody lets their guard down. And sometimes it was the person they were going to be.

Other people she knew by their scent. For instance, Riley smelled of sweat and hard work and kindness and honesty.

"Who'm I?" Riley asked, lifting his chin and striking a pose.

Jenna stared at him. She saw him just as he was. Beyond that, nothing at all.

"What? What is it?" Riley swiped at his face like he was afraid it was dirty.

"Why, Riley, I think you're going to be a king," Jenna said finally.

"A king. What do you mean?"

"I keep seeing you, and a crown, and a sword. That must mean you're meant for great things, right?" She leaned in close and whispered, "In our story, the king of Arden gets eaten by wolves in Chapter One."

Riley laughed softly, but he still looked around to make sure nobody could overhear. "For now, I'd be glad to hear the story you brought. It'll give me something to look forward to, while we're down in the mine." He sighed. "I wish it was the end of the day right now."

But it wasn't the end of the day. They were just pulling up in front of the Number Two mine, which meant that the end of the day was twelve hours away. They called it the Number Two because a year ago there'd been an explosion at the Number One mine that buried the entrance under tons of rubble, shutting it down.

The colliers said it was firedamp, the explosive gas that built up in the mine. The Ardenine bosses claimed it was sabotage, because it happened at change of shift, when there were few miners underground. The king of Arden was furious when he heard, because he needed coal and steel to put weapons into the hands of his army. So they cut a new shaft into the mountain. Most of the able-bodied men and women in Delphi had been forced into the mines already. So King Gerard issued orders to herd up every lýtling in Delphi and send them into the mines to make up for lost time. That was a year ago.

The youngest lýtlings died the first month. They'd be carried from the mine at the end of each shift, piled in a wagon, and driven back down to town so their parents could claim them. Jenna was just eleven when she went into the mine, but she was wiry and strong, and healthier than most. Plus, she was too stubborn to die, and leave her da all alone.

"Keep your head down, now," Jenna said, when they parted at the crossroads at the bottom of the shaft.

"Keep your head down," Riley said back. It was a ritual with them, like a charm of protection before he trudged off, toward the deepest part of the mine. More and more, they'd put him on the coal face as a hewer, digging with a pick and shovel with the other men. By the end of the day he was so tired that he slept all the way home. He'd been in the mines for three years. He'd started when he was a twelve-year, being big even then. The more often he worked the coal face, the more he coughed.

When Jenna first went into the mine, Riley was a "hurrier"—he wore a leather strap around his waist and pulled heavy carts of coal up the ramp to the cage. Jenna worked as a "thruster," pushing the carts from behind. Or sometimes as a "trapper," opening trapdoors so the carts could rattle through. You had to look sharp if you were a trapper—if a cart came up and you weren't ready, you'd get run over. Or you'd open up a trap, and the firedamp would roar out like a dragon and burn you right up.

Jenna had a knack for knowing when firedamp was lurking behind the trap. It was like she could feel the seething heat of it, her heart beating with the pulse of the flame. Once, she pulled Maggi off right as she was about to open the trap. One of the bosses swung his club at her for slowing down production. Then he opened the trap and was charred to a crisp.

People liked to work with Riley, because he was so strong that it made it easy on the thrusters, and he was always careful of the trappers, especially at the end of the shift, when everyone was tired.

Riley also had a way of getting between the bosses and the lýtlings when they were handing out beatings. And showing up when this particular wormy-lipped guard tried to drag a little girl into a side tunnel. He didn't say anything, he'd just be there until the guard let her go.

The bosses didn't like Riley because of what he said and did, and because the other miners looked up to him, even though he was only fifteen.

Jenna was sorry that Riley was in the mine. At the same time, having him there made her life bearable.

When the end of the shift finally came, they rode up in the cage together, holding hands. They walked out into the twilight, blinking like cave creatures, joining a jostling crowd of miners just outside.

The wagons were not lined up as usual, but had been pulled over to one side. A tented pavilion had been set up a short distance from the mine, and the red hawk of Arden flew from the tent poles. There were armed soldiers everywhere—surrounding the pavilion and keeping a close watch on the collected miners. The soldiers wore black coats marked with the red hawk, too. The usual name for them was blackbirds.

"What's going on?" Riley asked Brit Fletcher, who always seemed to know.

"It seems we're about to hear some scummer from His Majesty, King Gerard." Fletcher spat on the ground.

"He's here?" Jenna shrank back a little. "What's he doing here?"

"It seems that he and the missus are promenading around the empire, showing how they an't scairt of a few Patriots."

"What do you mean?"

"An't you heard? There's been riots in Tamron Seat, and rebels took over the keep at Baston Bay a few months ago. Didn't hold it long, but still. Word is that some of the thanes is getting restless 'cause they're tired of war." Fletcher smiled, like he approved.

"Shhh," Riley said, glancing around. "Somebody might hear."

Fletcher made no secret that he hated the king of Arden. Some whispered that he was an actual Patriot—one of those who fought back against the king and his blackbird guards. His family had died when Arden took the city, so he didn't have a lot to lose. He was old—near to forty, some said—so he'd be dead before long anyway.

"That must be him," Jenna murmured, pointing.

A small group of people had emerged from the pavilion amid a crowd of soldiers. Jenna recognized Delphi's greasy mayor, Willett Peters, along with Ned Shively, the Big Boss at the mine. Swiving Shively, the miners called him.

With them was a finely dressed pair. It was hard to get a good look from that distance.

"Let's move up closer," Jenna said, thinking it might be her one chance to see a king or a queen in person.

"I don't think that's a good idea," Riley began, but she was already sliding through the crowd to the front so she could get a better view. Still murmuring protests, Riley followed after, pulling his new red cloak closer around himself.

Now at the front, Jenna got a good look at the king. He was a narrow man of medium height with nearly colorless blue eyes and a thin, cruel mouth. He wore a slate-gray velvet jacket with a fine blue cape over top, already spotted from the sleet. The wind that blew down out of the mountains ruffled his mouse-brown hair.

The woman with him was taller than the king, but she hunched down a little, maybe so people wouldn't notice. She looked to be a foreigner, with her tawny skin and brown eyes and a mouth as full as the king's was stingy. She wore a pale yellow dress with a white fur wrap, yellow silk slippers, and white gloves.

"Who's that lady?" Maggi asked Fletcher, pointing. She'd wormed her way up front, too.

"That's Queen Marina, poor thing," Fletcher said. "She was a princess in Tamron, daughter of the king. Gerard murdered her whole family, took over the kingdom, and married her."

"She's beautiful," Maggi whispered.

Fletcher snorted. "Did you ever see anything like it? Little fancy shoes and white gloves—in Delphi? They won't be white for long."

The king of Arden moved to the front of the pavilion, his queen a foot behind him, and looked down at the collected miners.

"Miners of Delphi!" he said in a carrying voice. "Queen Marina and I have come north to thank you for your hard work this past year. I know it hasn't always been easy, but I'm pleased to announce that coal and steel production is at an all-time high."

Mayor Peters and Boss Shively clapped like mad, but the miners just stood in stony silence.

"Now is not the time to pull back, however," the king said. "Indeed, we must redouble our efforts to put weapons into the hands of our soldiers. I have advised Mayor Peters and Master Shively that production goals for next year will be increased by ten percent."

This was met by a rumble of protest. The queen looked from the miners to the king, frowning and biting her lower lip, as if this was bad news to her, too. Then her face went back to blank.

"I know this is an ambitious goal. But with Saint Malthus's help, we will defeat the witch queen in the north and bring peace and prosperity to the Empire."

Nobody in Delphi looked for much help from Saint Malthus. Although Arden had sent Malthusian missionaries into Delphi, they hadn't made much headway in converting people to the state church.

"How about you send old Saint Malthus down into the mine?" somebody shouted. "We could use the help."

The soldiers moved forward, scanning the crowd, trying to identify whoever had spoken up. Meanwhile, the queen knelt at the edge of the stage to speak to Maggi. Jenna was right there, so she heard everything that was said.

"I have a little girl at home," the queen said softly, in Common, "only she's younger than you. Her name is Madeleine."

Maggi looked up at her, her eyes a startling blue in her coal-smirched face. She reached out her hand, as if to touch the queen's dress, then jerked it back, as if realizing that her grubby hand wouldn't do the queen's dress any good.

The queen didn't seem worried. "What's your name?" she said.

"Maggi."

"Do your mommy and daddy work in the mine?" she asked.

"No'm," Maggi said, looking puzzled. "They're dead." She jabbed a thumb into her chest. "I work in the mine. Since I was six."

The queen reared back as if she'd been slapped, her eyes widening with horror. "Oh, no," she whispered, shaking her head. "You must be mistaken." But the queen must have seen that Maggi was telling the truth, because she took a quick look over her shoulder to see where the king was. Jenna looked, too, just in time to see an object fly through the air and splat at Gerard's feet, spattering his clothing all the way to his waist.

Jenna knew right away what it was—steaming dung, dropped by the horses that pulled the coal wagons. She had to pick her way around it on a daily basis.

"Scummer," Fletcher muttered. "There'll be hell to pay

now. If they was going to do anything, they should of gone ahead and shot him, and done us all some good."

Jenna took a step away from him. Fletcher was like a plague you might catch if you got too close.

Things moved fast after that. Black-jacketed guards closed in around the king, leaving the queen on her own at the edge of the stage until two soldiers hustled her to safety. Other blackbirds formed a ring around the gathered miners, so none of them could slip away. Shively's club-wielding thugs swarmed to the front of the stage.

Jenna shrank back, suddenly sorry she'd pushed to the front. Riley wrapped an arm around her, sheltering her.

"All right," Shively snarled, slapping his club against his other hand. "Who did that?"

Nobody made eye contact. Nobody said anything. Nobody dared to move, afraid to call attention to themselves.

"I'm warning you, give him up, or you'll be sorry."

Nothing.

That's when the king of Arden broke free from his guards and strode to the edge of the stage.

"These people have no imagination, Shively," the king said, his voice like melted ice. "You have to make the consequences very clear." As he spoke the last word, he reached down, gripped Maggi by the arm, and hauled her up onto the stage. Wrapping one arm around her, he lifted her up high while she wriggled and whimpered in fear.

"Now. The guilty party had better step forward, or I'll kill the ratling."

Everyone stood and stared at the king of Arden and the struggling Maggi, frozen with shock. Jenna wanted to turn away, but she couldn't. It was like she was hypnotized, like the king had cast some kind of monstrous spell.

"Your Majesty, please! Have mercy! She's just a child." The queen lunged toward him, but the blackbirds grabbed her arms, holding her fast.

Maybe the dung-thrower would have stepped forward, but the king didn't give him much of a chance. With a quick, vicious move, he snapped Maggi's neck. Tossing the small body aside, Gerard looked out across the crowd. "Let's just keep doing this, shall we, until somebody confesses. Now then. Who's next?"

PATRIOT

Jenna couldn't remember deciding to kill the king of Arden. It was like everybody else was frozen—even the blackbirds—and she was moving. Before she put two thoughts together, she had vaulted up and over the edge of the stage and smashed right into him, putting him flat on his back. Looking down into his startled eyes, she rammed her fist into his blueblood nose, wishing it was a knife between the ribs instead.

The king's royal nose spouted blood like a fountain. It smelled like anybody else's blood, and it wasn't really blue. Gerard was stronger than she expected, though, and flipped her over, pinning her with his knee in her chest. He wrapped his blood-slick hands around her neck and began to squeeze. The strength drained out of her arms and legs and she knew she was dying.

"No!" Somebody smashed into them, sending the king of Arden sprawling. Jenna sucked in air through her bruised throat. Hands grabbed hold of her, and she kicked and struggled, but it wasn't the blackbirds, it was the miners, dragging her off the stage and pushing her toward the rear of the crowd. "Stay down!" Brit Fletcher said into her ear.

But Jenna didn't stay down, because she knew who had come to her rescue. She worked her way to a place where she could see the stage.

The king of Arden was back on his feet, behind a wall of blackbirds, trying to plug his nose with a snowy handkerchief. Blackbirds stood all along the edge of the stage, their crossbows aimed into the crowd. Riley stood nearby, his arms pinioned, his face battered almost beyond recognition. The queen sat forgotten, cradling Maggi's body in her arms.

When he'd got the bleeding stopped, King Gerard crossed the stage to where Riley stood.

"Who are you?" Gerard said. "Another hero?"

Riley shook his head. "No, sir. It was me. I was the one that done it. I threw the scummer at you. I did it, and I'm sorry."

"Did you now?" The king stood, hands on hips, gazing at Riley.

"No!" Jenna tried to fight her way toward the front of the crowd, but Brit Fletcher held her fast. He was rum strong for an old man.

"Look here," he growled. "Don't make that boy throw away his life for nothing. We both know he didn't do it, but he's a goner now anyway. Nobody jumps the king and lives to brag about it."

"No," Jenna whispered, tears rolling down her face. But she smelled the truth on Fletcher, so she no longer struggled to get away.

The king of Arden scanned the crowd, searching the sea of faces. Jenna held very still. Finally, heaving a sigh, he turned back to Riley. "I'm not sure I believe you, but you'll do, I suppose. Hold him." He drew his sword, turned, and rammed it into Riley's stomach, all the way to the hilt, then twisted it. Riley made a sound, a kind of grunt, his eyes going wide.

The king yanked free his blade with a wet pop, then stuck it in again, in a slightly different spot. Now blood bubbled from Riley's mouth. Somehow, miraculously, his eyes met Jenna's and held.

"Finish him, you murderous bastard," Fletcher muttered.

But clearly the king of Arden meant to take his time. He pulled out his blade, chose another spot, and stabbed Riley again.

By now, black spots were swimming in front of Jenna's eyes, but Riley's eyes were still locked with hers, and she refused to faint and leave him on his own. Just then, she heard a sound, a kind of *thwack* from above and behind her. Riley's body jerked, and suddenly a feathered shaft stuck out of his throat, just below his chin. It was an arrow, and just like that, Riley was gone.

After that, it was bedlam. The king and queen disappeared in a hurry, and Shively's thugs waded into the crowd, swinging their clubs. Jenna turned and tried to run, but something smashed into the back of her head and she went down.

When she awoke, she could hear people talking in low voices. It was dark, and it was cold, even though she was wrapped up in something that smelled like wet sheep.

It was Riley's cloak. She rubbed the fabric against her cheek, sniffling, her shoulders shaking with sobs. Her head hurt like fury, but her heart hurt even more, being broken.

She sat up, put her feet down. Loose rock shifted under her feet.

"You're awake," somebody said in a gruff voice. "Good. I thought maybe you was out for keeps."

It was Brit Fletcher. He set an oil lamp on the floor next to the bench she was lying on and thrust a steaming mug at her. It was barley coffee laced with something that just about lifted her scalp right off her head. Jenna drank it all.

Fletcher watched her, his eyebrows lifting higher and higher until she clunked the cup down.

"You're a tough scrapper, an't you." He rubbed his chin.

"How old are you? Ten?"

"Twelve." She looked around. Stone, as far as she could see in the flickering light from the lamp. "Are we in the mine?"

"Sort of. We're in the old Number One. We've dug out some of the tunnels so's we can get in and out."

"Why?"

"Makes a good hiding place, don't it?"

"For who?"

Fletcher snorted. "You, for one."

"What day is it? What's happened?"

"It's the day after the king's visit. He's already hightailing it back to the city."

"And . . . and how many are dead?"

"That's the thing. They can't afford to kill too many of us, 'cause they need us to work the mines. There's just four dead, counting Riley and little Maggi. Four too many. Five, counting you."

"Me?" Jenna's hand closed on a large rock. "What do you mean?"

Fletcher snorted. He sure snorted a lot. "Don't look at me like that. I an't going to hurt you. What I mean, is, as far as anyone knows, you're dead. You was killed in the riot."

"I'm dead?" She thought of her da, with his care-lined face and haunted eyes. "But—what about my da?"

"We got word to him that you're safe. So. You have a choice. Would you rather stay dead and leave town? Or go back and take your chances?" He held up a hand. "Before you decide, you should know that the king an't forgot about you. The blackbirds is looking for you on the quiet. Asking questions, trying to find out who you are. Nobody knows nothing, of course."

Jenna's middle hardened like iron slag. "Delphi's my home. I'm not going to leave my da behind."

"Wouldn't he go with you? To save your life?"

"He'd have to leave the inn behind," Jenna said. "It's not that easy to make a living these days. He's too old to start over. I don't want to ask him to do that."

Fletcher sighed. "I figured you'd say that. What if you come back as somebody else? Somebody brand-new to town, with a different name?"

Jenna thought about it. Could she really pull it off? She'd always liked pretending to be somebody else.

"I know it's a risk, if you're found out," Fletcher said. "I just don't want that boy Riley to have died for nothing."

Me neither, Jenna thought, her fingers finding the raised emblem on the back of her neck. It was all her fault. First, she'd drawn the attention of the Breaker by laying claim to a power she didn't have, a destiny rooted in witchery and fairy tales. Then she'd jumped the king with no thought to what might happen to those around her.

She wasn't a child—she couldn't afford to be a child anymore. This was real life, not a fairy story, and she wouldn't forget that again. She'd come back as someone whose feet were planted firmly on the ground.

"All right, we'll try it," she said, blotting tears away

with her forearm. "Could I ask you something?"

"Ask away," Fletcher said. "I don't know that I'll have the answer."

"Is it true, what they say? That you're one of those Patriots?"

"Why do you want to know?"

"Because I want to join up," Jenna said. "I mean to make Arden pay for what they've done." By "Arden" she really meant the king of Arden, but he was far away already. So she'd start close to home.

Jenna thought he would say no, would tell her she was too young, that it was too dangerous. Instead, he gave her a long, studying look. "You know what happens if you get caught," he said.

Jenna thought about Riley, about how he died, and tried to ignore the shiver of fear that went through her. "If not for you, I'd be dead already."

"True enough," Fletcher said, rubbing his chin. "We'll see." It wasn't a yes, but it wasn't a no, either.

"There's one thing I just don't get," Jenna said. "The bad times really started after the explosion last year. What makes the king think we blew up the mine on purpose?"

"What makes you think that we didn't?" Brit Fletcher said.

Their eyes met, and held. "Good," Jenna said. "I'm going to help you burn Arden to the ground."

THE VOYAGEUR

Adrian lay on his belly on a rooftop in the city of Delphi, peering down at the shop below. A gnarled walking staff hung next to the door, the sign of the Voyageur. Over the doorframe, a wooden sign had weathered to a whisper. La Ancienne. The Old One. Voyageur children with stick-straight black hair, flat noses, and thick, embroidered sheepswool coats herded goats around the yard.

It was two weeks since his father had died, ten days since he'd slipped across the border onto enemy ground. Since his stays at Marisa Pines lodge in the high country, Adrian knew how to survive in the mountains and navigate off-trail. The border was porous to a single rider in a white winter cloak—even a rider with a bad ankle, a stolen pony, and a broken heart.

Riding into Delphi was like descending into a fuming, sulfurous hell—if hell happened to be bitterly cold. The air was thick enough to chew, but almost impossible to breathe. It stung Adrian's eyes and set him to coughing. Everything was covered with a layer of soot and coal dust thick enough to kill what little color there was. The people were thin and haggard and hollow-eyed, so worn out and weary that they took little notice of a stable boy with mud-brown hair (the result of a night spent rubbing black walnut paste and strong tea into it).

He'd come here hoping to intercept the healer Taliesin Beaugarde on her way to Oden's Ford. She'd told Adrian that she planned to visit relatives in Delphi who owned a shop that sold herbs and remedies. This was the only one in town, so it had to be the place. He'd been watching it for a week, and there'd been no sign of Taliesin so far. It was risky to stay here, but he had nowhere else to go.

The ankle was worrisome—swollen twice its size, purple and green. Maybe he deserved whatever pain he was in, but he wouldn't seek healing from someone he didn't know. A wizard can't use his gift to heal himself, and incompetence would only make matters worse. So he kept it wrapped and hoped for the best.

Despite the ankle, he'd found bed and board in a stable in exchange for mucking out stalls. It seemed that help was hard to come by in Delphi, since every able-bodied person had been sent into the mines. To call it "board" was being generous, even by Fellsian standards. Neither he nor his pony was living high.

The herb shop stood in a Delphian neighborhood so desperate that the toughest streetlord from Ragmarket would think twice before moving in. First off, there was nothing worthwhile to steal. He'd already seen a knife fight break out over a warm pair of gloves.

Second, the king of Arden's blackbird guards were thick as crows on a carcass. Black was a good color choice for Delphi—a mountain town that resembled a Fellsmarch gone horribly wrong.

Adrian shivered. The heat from his body had melted the snow underneath him, and now he was soaked to the skin. Since he'd come to Delphi, he'd developed a cough and a fever that wouldn't go away. It was either camp fever from the wells or winter fever from exposure. It would be another day wasted, but he needed to get off the roof and out of the cold.

Hearing voices below, he slid forward again, far enough so he could see over the gutter tiles. A wagon had pulled up in front of the shop, and the children who had been playing in the street clustered around it, chattering excitedly.

The wagon was painted in Voyageur style, and the ponies were sturdy, shaggy, mountain-bred. Adrian's heart beat faster. He slid back, out of sight, as a clutch of mounted blackbirds appeared, shouting at the driver to move the wagon out of the way. The blackbirds seemed bent on emptying the streets, using clubs and short swords to encourage those who didn't move fast enough. The wagon lurched into motion, turning down the alleyway next to the shop so it could park behind.

"Getting your eyes full, boy?" The voice came from behind and above him. Before he could turn to look, the speaker delivered a vicious kick to the ribs, connecting with a crackling sound. Adrian rolled and came up on his knees, gasping, groping for his amulet until he remembered where he was, and let his hand drop away. Not a good idea to draw attention to himself with magical displays in a place where they burned the gifted.

The speaker was a blackbird, dressed head to toe in black, down to his shiny black boots. He was totally bald, with a slash of a mouth and officer's braid on his shoulders. He reached down, gripped Adrian by the front of his cloak, and dragged him to his feet. With his other hand, he pawed him all over, looking for weapons, but thankfully missing the amulet. He found nothing else, because Adrian, of course, had nothing.

"What's your name?" the blackbird demanded in Common.

"Ash Hanson." The name spilled out before Adrian could edit it.

"Ash Hanson, sir," the blackbird said. "Waiting for someone?"

"No, sir."

The blackbird shook him, hard. Adrian's weight came down on his ankle, and he smothered a cry of pain that evolved into a fit of coughing.

"Don't lie to me," the blackbird said, pulling him in close, so close Adrian could have spat in his face. "I'm going to ask you one more time. What are you doing up here?"

Adrian cleared his throat. His fingers twitched, eager to take hold of his magic. "It's just—the air's clearer up here. I've got this awful cough, and lately it's all blood." Adrian coughed into his sleeve, then extended it for the blackbird's inspection. "See?"

The blackbird recoiled from the offer. "Keep your distance, you consumptive Delphian whelpling. If you lot didn't live like vermin, you wouldn't catch the fever. I want you down off this roof and away from here. Now!" he roared, giving Adrian a push. "If I see you again, I won't be so gracious."

"Yes, sir," Adrian said, backing away. "Thank you, sir."

Back on the ground, Adrian circled around in back of the Voyageur shop. He needed to get out of sight, but he didn't want to leave and come back and find the wagon gone. The rear courtyard was deserted, the wagon's owner having gone inside. He boosted himself up and into the bed of the wagon.

It was a typical vagabond wagon, with a pallet in the front corner and cooking pots hanging from hooks. It was lined floor to ceiling with bins and containers of goods.

Adrian knew he was in the right place when he breathed in the familiar scents of ginger and sage and peppermint. It brought back memories of nights in the upland lodges, Willo and Taliesin telling stories, their faces bronzed by firelight and inscribed by time and wisdom.

Bunches of herbs hung from the ceiling—black cohosh and blessed thistle and mistletoe. Jars and bottles were jammed into net bags on all sides. It was an apothecary on wheels. Many of the containers were marked, but he didn't know what the marks meant. He began opening bins and jars, sniffing the contents, kindling light on the tips of his fingers in order to see.

Finally he found it, in the back corner, hidden behind two rows of bins. As soon as he sniffed it, he recognized the potent odor of death. Gedden weed—insurance against an uncertain future. Emptying peppercorns out of a cloth bag, he scooped a few tablespoons of weed into it and slipped it into his breeches pocket.

Adrian knew he should leave and find some less compromising place to wait and watch, but this bit of thievery had exhausted him. He was shaking with chills, and knew that his fever was rising again. He scrounged around until he found a packet of willow bark and a tin cup. Scooping the cleanest snow he could find into the cup, he melted it with flash from his hands until the water was steaming. Dirty or not, it was likely to be safer than water from the wells.

Back in the wagon, he steeped the willow bark into a

murky tea and drank it down. Still shivering, he found the pile of blankets and crawled underneath, planning to rest a bit until the willow bark took hold.

The next thing he knew, somebody was shaking him awake and thrusting a lantern in his face. "Come on now, you, climb down out of there before you freeze to death. If you're looking for syrup of poppy, it's locked up."

She spoke in Common, but Adrian recognized the voice.

"Taliesin," he said, blinking, shading his eyes against the light. He heard a quick intake of breath as the lantern slipped from her hand, then a clunk as it hit the bed of the wagon.

Taliesin usually didn't startle easily, but now she stared at him like she'd seen a ghost. "Blood and demons," she whispered. "Mageling?"

"It's me," Adrian said.

"What are you doing here?" she demanded. "They said you were dead."

"Not quite," he said.

"Well, you will be, or worse, if the blackbirds find you here."

"I need to talk to you."

She reached out and gripped his chin, leaning in to take a good look, then pressed the back of her hand against his forehead. The witch had a way of pinning a person with her narrow black eyes. She could tell more with a look than Adrian could with an hour of hands-on.

"How long have you been sick?" she asked.

"I'm all right," he mumbled, trying to pull free.

"Wait here," she said. "I'll be right back."

It took a while, but she returned with a heavy sheeps-wool coat. "Put this on," she said. "It's my nephew's, but I think it's about the right size."

Adrian was still shivering, so he pulled it on.

"Now, come inside, where it's warm," she said. "Nobody will see you. I've cleared everyone out of the back."

Before he knew it, he was sitting in the back room of the shop, and Taliesin was sitting between him and the door, pouring hot water over crushed leaves in a kettle. She'd made up a makeshift bed on the floor by the hearth.

While the leaves steeped, she shook some black, wrinkled beans from a cloth bag onto a stone and added some dried brown root and a pinch of yellow powder. "Tell me what happened."

"What have you heard?"

"It doesn't matter what I heard, I asked you to tell me what happened." She set the stone in Adrian's lap and handed him a pestle. "Crush these fine as you can."

Adrian weighed the heavy pestle in his hand. He didn't know what to say.

"I'm guessing you're here because you want my help," Taliesin said. "If you want my help, you're going to have to talk to me."

Adrian sighed. Maybe once Taliesin knew what had

happened, she'd give him what he wanted.

"My father is dead," he said, smashing the pestle down. *Crunch.*

"So I've heard. The whole town was in mourning when I left. For both of you." Her voice softened. "I'm sorry, Mageling."

"It's my fault he's dead." *Crunch.*

"You killed your own father?"

"No!"

"Then I suspect it's someone else's fault."

"But it was my fault he couldn't get away. I lured him into a trap."

"Ah." Taliesin nodded, her beads clattering together. "So *you* were in on the conspiracy."

"No!" Adrian struggled to organize his feverish thoughts. "They—some people—grabbed me on the street. My father came to help me. And they killed him."

"Then I suspect someone else used you to lure him into a trap."

"It doesn't change the fact that if I hadn't been there, he'd still be alive. I was useless. Worse than useless." Despite his best efforts, tears welled up in his eyes. *Crunch.*

Taking the ground herbs from Adrian, Taliesin brushed them into a mug and added the steaming contents of the kettle. She held it out to him. "Careful," she said. "It's hot."

He blew on the tea, and the aroma boiled up into his

nose. Glaring at Taliesin, he banged the mug down on the hearth. "If you think you're going to drug me and ship me back home, you're wrong," he said.

Taliesin sighed. "You're going to want that for pain, because I'm going to need to work on your ankle."

Taliesin should be queen of something, Adrian thought, since she was so good at giving orders and having them obeyed. He picked up the mug and sipped at the tea.

Taliesin unbuckled his boot and slid it off. His ankle had not improved. The healer rolled her eyes.

"You've been walking around on a broken ankle? Did you forget everything I taught you?"

"I should be dead by now," Adrian said. "Then it wouldn't matter. It's just—*blood and bones*!"

With a quick, expert snap, Taliesin had realigned the bone. The pain nearly put Adrian through the roof.

"You could've warned me," he said.

"You're the one that didn't want to drink the tea," Taliesin said without sympathy. She began wrapping the ankle with long strips of cloth. "Why are you here?"

"I want to come with you to Oden's Ford," Adrian said. "You said you could get me into Spiritas. I'll study with you, then transfer to Mystwerk when I'm old enough."

"I *can* get you into Spiritas. But right now you should go home to your mother. You can't let her go on thinking you're dead or kidnapped. She needs you right now."

"She doesn't need me. She doesn't need anyone. If not

for her, my da would still be alive." Even as he said it, Adrian knew that it was wrong, and unfair. But he was sick and tired, and in no mood to be reasonable.

"Ah," Taliesin said, sipping at her own tea. "Then *she* was in on the conspiracy. I suppose she didn't love him?"

"Just stop it!" Adrian shouted. A young girl poked her head between the curtains that divided the back of the shop from the front. Taliesin waved her off without taking her eyes off Adrian.

"That's not what I mean, and you bloody well know it," Adrian hissed. "Yes, she loved him. He's dead because he loved her back, and because he loved me, and he shouldn't have had to pay that price for love."

"Aye, there's something we agree on." Taliesin set her cup down. "He shouldn't have had to pay that price. Love is the root of so much suffering and misery, so much loss. It's the worst thing in the world, to risk yourself by loving someone. At the same time, it's the best thing in the world—and worth the risk. I don't know your mother and sister—but I know you, and I'd wager that they want you back." That was as close to a compliment as he'd ever get from Taliesin.

"I have to go to Oden's Ford," Adrian said. "The . . . the last thing my da said to me . . . he gave me his amulet and he said, 'I want you to go to Oden's Ford and learn how to use it.' But there's no way my mother would let me go now, after what's happened. It was bad enough after Hana."

"Tell the queen what your father said. I'm sure she'll want to honor that. If not this year, you can come to Spiritas next year. I'll hold a place for you."

"You don't understand," Adrian whispered, his voice catching. "It's not just that."

Taliesin gripped his hands, leaning in toward him. "Tell me what I don't understand."

"I can't go back. I—I just can't go back, and have to tell my mother and sister how he died. They deserve to know, but—I don't want to have to see their faces, and know that I should have done something to prevent it. I can't go anywhere in Fellsmarch without noticing the big hole he left behind. Every time I turn a corner, I'll remember something he said, or did, or a story he told. He was like the beating heart of the city, and the king of Arden put a blade right through it. And people will look at me, and know I'm the one responsible."

"Do you really think they'll blame you, Mageling?"

"Why shouldn't they? I blame myself. I'll think they're looking at me that way, and every time, I'll die a little bit. I'd rather just get it over with." He was shaking again, whether from grief, or fever, or what, he didn't know.

"Have some more tea," Taliesin said softly. "It's not a cure for a broken heart, but it does take the edge off."

This time, Adrian drank deeply. "I'm not looking for sympathy. I'm not even looking for you to agree with me. I just want a way out. I just want the pain to stop. If I can't

come with you, I'll find a way to end this on my own."
His gaze met hers, and his fingers found the shape of the
packet of gedden weed in his breeches pocket.

Adrian could tell that Taliesin understood his meaning
immediately, and believed him. She always took him seriously, always treated him like a grown-up even when he
didn't deserve it. It was one of the things he liked about
her.

"What if you know something that might help to catch
the killers?" she said. "Do you want that knowledge to die
with you?"

That was like a punch to the gut. What if?

"What if you might be able to prevent another murder?"

Or at least avenge the ones that have already happened.

That idea, once kindled, was hard to put out. Once at
Oden's Ford, he'd be closer to the enemy. And yet—that
would mean there would be no escape from the pain any-
time soon.

He tried to think back, to recall if he'd seen or heard
anything that might help. But it was like the memory was
walled off, too painful to poke at. He reached up and fingered the knot on his head. Had someone hit him over the
head? Or had he fallen? Maybe both? He looked down at
his hands, picked at his scabbed palms.

She sighed. "About Oden's Ford. School is hard work
under the best of circumstances. I want you to have the
best chance to succeed. I need you to succeed, if I'm going

to persuade the deans at Mystwerk to cooperate with me."

"I *will* work hard," Adrian said. "I won't disappoint you."

For a long moment, Taliesin studied him. "Do you really think that would help—to be somewhere else, for a while, anyway?"

"I don't know," Adrian said. "Maybe. Probably." The tea was kicking in, and his thoughts had become clumsy, aimlessly stumbling into each other.

"If you feel guilty about your father's death, one way to heal is to help others." She seemed to be trying to convince herself. "There are so many people dying needlessly that want to go on living. Saving a life can offset the taking of life." The Voyageur noticed his drooping eyelids. "Come," she said. "Sit down on the bed before you topple over."

He moved to the pallet on the floor, then eased into a lying-down position.

Taliesin sat on a stool next to him. "In truth, it may be safer for you to go south with me and let everyone here think you're dead. You can heal yourself by healing others. Perhaps that's what the Maker intends for you."

"I don't understand," Adrian said. "How does it make sense that the Maker would take my father and Hana and leave me behind?"

"It's easy to die, Mageling," Taliesin said, stroking his hair. "It's staying alive that's hard work."

A LONG FUSE

It had been a long time since Jenna Bandelow had been up the road that led to the Number Two mine. As that one played out, new ones had opened, farther west and lower down.

There had been changes since four years ago, when Maggi and Riley had died. Most of the trees were gone now, burned for charcoal to feed the hungry steel mills, or cut down so there wouldn't be cover for ambushes along the road to the garrison house. The Ardenine regulars (everyone called them mudbacks because of their uniforms) had moved the headquarters up here so the soldiers coming and going wouldn't have to pass through the dangerous streets of the city, where soldiers disappeared on a regular basis.

Four years ago, it had been a miserable March day, with the sleet pelting down, and the wind howling out of the witchy north. Today, it was a clear cold night in October, but the wind still blew, carrying the promise of winter from the fresh snowfalls in the Spirit Mountains.

Last time, Jenna had been packed into the wagon with Riley and Maggi, who were about to die, but none of them knew it. This time, she sat high in the driver's seat, with a slightly older boy named Byram beside her. A younger boy rode in the back with the barrels. He called himself Mick.

They shouldn't have much to say to each other, but that didn't keep Byram from talking all the way from town.

Byram wouldn't be his real name—not if he was smart. He knew Jenna as a boy named Flamecaster. Sometimes she went by Sparks instead. That was just easier, all the way around. It had been so long since she'd been a girl that she wasn't sure she remembered the ins and outs of it.

Jenna preferred to keep her mouth shut and play her cards close. That way, if any of them was caught, they wouldn't have much to say to the blackbirds, either.

When she wasn't on Patriot business, Jenna answered to the name of Riley Collier, a skilled blaster from the Heart-fangs. She rotated from mine to mine, boring the blasting holes, packing them with powder and setting them off, moving rock off the coal seams so the miners could get at them.

It was a good job, for a mining job, if you had steady hands and the nerve to do it. Unlike some of the other jobs, it didn't require a lot of muscle. It also wasn't so strenuous that you were fit for nothing else when you went off shift. Her days were shorter, with nobody looking over her shoulder, because none of the bosses was eager to go down there with her. It allowed more time in the fresh air, less underground, and she'd learned useful skills—skills she would be using tonight.

They were nearing the turnoff to the garrison house when Byram said, "Hold up." Jenna reined in, and he stuffed some papers into her hand. "Here's your paperwork, in case we get stopped. We got flour and oil for the kitchens, see? If it's clear when we get to the bridge, turn the wagon around and pull onto the shoulder. Soon as you come to a stop, me and Mick will roll the barrels under the bridge and light it up. Once it blows, we'll hop on and hit the road. Take it nice and easy, though, 'cause we don't want to get noticed. Got that?" For some reason, Byram fancied that he was in charge.

Jenna got it, but she didn't like it. The upside of traveling at darkman's hour was that there wasn't much traffic on the road. The downside was that once the bridge blew, they'd be prime suspects to any soldiers who happened to be on that side of the bridge. Especially since they'd be driving away, when any other person would head for the noise, to see what happened.

"We'll be the only ones on the road except for mud-backs and blackbirds. Once the bridge goes up, they'll be all over us, with no place to hide."

Byram snorted. "What's the chance there'll be mud-backs this side of the bridge in the middle of the night?"

"Not mudbacks so much as blackbirds. From what I hear, that new commander is mean as a snake. I want to be far away when it blows."

"If you're scared, you should've stayed at home," Byram said.

"If you're not scared, you're stupid."

"Look," Byram said, in the manner of someone instructing a small child. "Somebody's got to light the thing; after that we got no more'n a couple minutes." His eyes narrowed. "Or are you thinking me or Mick should stay behind while you beat it back to town?"

Jenna shook her head. "I brought this." She pulled a long, thin tube out of her carry bag. It was made of cotton, coated with pitch, and stuffed with black powder.

"What's that?" Byram poked it warily with his forefinger.

"Something new. Blasters in the Heartfangs are beginning to use them in the deeper shafts. Light one end, and it takes as long as a half hour to burn through."

"I never heard of that," Byram said, as if that was that.

It would help if you talked less and listened more, Jenna thought. "I heard about it from a collier who was passing through town on his way north," she said vaguely. She didn't care to reveal her sources to anyone who might spill.

"How do we know it'll actually work?" Byram said. "We don't even know how to use it."

"You don't, I do. You get the kegs down there, I'll handle it," Jenna said. She slapped the reins and they rolled forward again. Her heart was beginning to hammer as it always did during this kind of job. She tried not to think about what would happen if they got caught. Instead, she thought about Riley and Maggi, who were dead, and her da, and everyone else in Delphi, squirming under Arden's thumb.

She thought of Arden going up in flames, leaving nothing but a charred skeleton behind. That always gave her the heart to do what she did.

They turned off the main road toward the garrison headquarters. It was in a manor house the army had taken over when they moved out of the town. Now the army encampment spread on both sides of the road, and squat, ugly warehouses had been raised behind the stables and the manor kitchen. There were still bits of what must have been a garden around the building, but it had been trampled into mud by men and horses. A few winter-blasted shrubs still framed the house. All of this was encircled by a high stone wall.

The wall was new. It seemed that the garrison's young

commander, Halston Matelon, had grown tired of hit-and-run attacks.

The military road crossed the river midway between the main road and the wall. Jenna drove across the bridge, found a wide place to turn around, crossed back, and pulled over.

Mick and Byram wrestled four kegs of powder off the back of the wagon. They hauled them down to the water's edge. Jenna set the brake on the wagon and scrambled down after them, her carry bag slung over her shoulder. "Mick, you go up and keep a lookout," she said, though she'd have rather sent Byram. With him looking on, smirking and rolling his eyes, she was more fumble-fingered than usual, so it took longer than she expected to get everything tied together—two kegs on either end of the bridge, each with its own fuse.

Kindling a spark, she lit both fuses. "These should go off at about the same time," she said. "I just don't know how long we have."

"Maybe we should wait and see if it actually works," Byram said.

"You can wait if you want," Jenna said, beginning the climb back to the road. "I'm the one with the wagon, and I'm heading back to town." After a moment, she heard Byram following after her.

They scrambled back up the bank to where Mick waited with the wagon. Back in the driver's seat, Jenna released the brake and flicked the reins, and they began their descent toward the main road. The horses knew they were heading back home, so it was hard to keep them reined in. Before they reached the intersection, they saw a dozen riders galloping toward them from the main road.

"Scummer," Mick muttered. Mick never said much, and when he did it was usually "scummer."

As the riders drew closer, Jenna could see that they rode black horses with silver fittings and wore black capes over their black tunics and gray breeches.

"Blackbirds," Jenna muttered, and thought, Scummer.

"Blackbirds?" Byram squinted at them. "There's no way you can tell, that far away, in the dark."

"My eyes are better than yours," Jenna said. "You wait."

Before long, there was no question who was riding hot toward them.

Jenna would have preferred mudbacks, who'd leave you alone if you didn't get in their way. Most of them were reluctant recruits from the down realms or mercenaries with no ax to grind. They just wanted to survive their time in the north and go back home.

Blackbirds were the king's personal enforcers in the empire, known to be as cruel and ruthless as the king himself. Meanwhile, behind them was a bridge that might blow up any minute.

Jenna's heart had been beating fast before, but now it was thumping so hard it seemed the blackbirds couldn't help but hear it.

Byram shifted on the seat beside Jenna as if he might launch himself into the dirt at the side of the road.

"Don't you move," Jenna said, gripping Byram's forearm, digging in her nails for emphasis. "You can't outrun them, and there's nothing looks guiltier than running away. And keep your mouth shut." Byram bobbed his head, his face pasty in the moonlight. He seemed more than willing to shut up now.

The troop of blackbirds surrounded their wagon, blocking the way. One of them nudged his horse in closer, so that when Jenna looked sideways, his black boots were all that she could see. She looked straight forward, gripping the reins hard, trying to keep her teeth from chattering.

There was one thing in their favor: being scared of the King's Guard wasn't unusual—it would have been more suspicious if they hadn't been nervous.

"It's late to be out on the road," the blackbird said. Something about his velvet voice made Jenna's hair stand up on the back of her neck.

"Yes, sir," she said.

"Would you care to explain it?"

"We—we was bringing dry goods to the kitchens yonder." Jenna nodded toward the garrison house.

"In the middle of the night?"

Jenna nodded, her gaze fixed on the wagon team.

"Look at me, boy."

Jenna looked up at the blackbird. His eyes were like

twin coals set into his skull, or maybe more like marbles set over a straight nose and an almost lipless mouth. He was completely hairless—no brows or lashes, and his head was smooth as a billiard ball. He wore the signia of an officer.

Scummer, Jenna thought. It's Clermont.

Marc Clermont was the commander of the King's Guard in Delphi, the spider that maintained the king's web of control here in the north. He was rumored to have a knack for torture. Once you came into Clermont's hands, you would talk. And when you'd spilled everything, then you would die. Slowly.

At least he's not a mage, so he can't spell me, to make me tell the truth. Jenna could always tell a mage—they had this peculiar glow about them, to her eyes, though others said they didn't see it. Very few mages ever came to Delphi, and those who did were all in the army or the King's Guard.

Jenna suddenly realized that the commander had said something, and she'd missed it. "I'm—I'm sorry, sir. What was that?"

"There's no reason to be frightened," Clermont said with a smile. He put his hand on her shoulder. When she flinched, he tightened his grip. She didn't like him touching her, but didn't dare fight back. Now she was the one who was tempted to bolt blindly, without a plan.

"What's your name?" Clermont said.

"Munroe, sir." To Jenna's surprise, the lie spilled right

out. So you *could* tell lies to the Breaker after all.

"Munroe. That's an unusual name." His voice had an odd, soothing quality. Byram was staring at him, like a rabbit at a hawk. Jenna kicked his shin to bring him back to his senses.

"Tell the truth now—why are you really out here in the middle of the night?" Clermont said.

She tried another lie. "We had to come late, 'cause we work in the mine in the daytime. And then there was nobody around, so we had to unload it our own selves. That made us late heading back." Remembering Byram's papers, she pulled them out and thrust them toward him. "Here's our papers."

Clermont made no move to take them. "Doesn't day shift in the mines start in just a few hours?"

"That's why we're in a hurry," Jenna said. "Elsewise, we won't get any sleep at all."

Clermont gave her a long, searching look, then released her shoulder, settling back into his saddle, frowning, as if he didn't know what to make of her.

"What about you?" Clermont said to Byram. "Do you have anything to say?"

"Nossir," Byram croaked.

Turning to the other blackbirds, Clermont said, "Search the wagon."

That didn't take long, because there wasn't much to see except Mick, huddled in a corner, ready to piss himself.

Still, it seemed like a lifetime to Jenna, who sat, shoulders hunched, waiting for the blast that would signal the end of the world.

Finally, the blackbirds jumped down from the wagon. "There's nothing, sir," one said.

Clermont rubbed his chin, squinting at her like he was fascinated. "Your eyes," he said, "are an unusual color. Like old gold, or candlelight through honey." The way he said it gave her the crawls. She didn't like him noticing anything about her. It made her glad she was dressed as a boy.

"Sir?" one of the blackbirds said. "You want to bring them along, and see what the garrison commander says?"

Clermont hesitated, then shook his head. "No. We've wasted enough time here." When Jenna still sat frozen, afraid to move, he snapped, "Are you deaf? Go on, then." He waved them on down the road.

Jenna loosened the reins and slapped them across the broad backs of the horses, and they rattled into motion. Behind her, she heard one of the blackbirds make a rude joke, and the rest of them laughing.

Her ears were sharp as her hawk's eyes. Her da claimed she could hear candy rattle into a jar from a mile away.

She heard the horses moving, slowly at first, accelerating into a drumbeat that dwindled as the distance between them grew.

"Scummer," Mick whispered.

Beside her, Byram let out a long, shuddering sigh. All of his cockiness had drained away.

As they mounted a small rise, Jenna reined in the horses and looked back. The moon had risen yet higher, and the riders cast long shadows behind them as they reached the bridge. Even at that distance, Jenna could hear the faint clatter of hooves as they hit the decking.

Byram stirred beside her. "Well," he said, clearing his throat. "That was a close call. Guess it's just as well it didn't work. If that bridge had blown, we'd be on our way to gaol."

"Hang on." Jenna watched as the last of the blackbirds rode onto the bridge. She saw a glare of light, oddly silent, followed by a distant boom, and then another right on its heels. The bridge crumbled, pitching men and horses into the gorge, leaving a jagged hole where the span had been. A plume of dust rose, glittering. On the far side of the bridge, a small cluster of survivors spurred forward, collecting at the edge of the cliff.

A primitive joy filled the void inside Jenna that had opened when Maggi and Riley died. Jenna tried not to think too hard about why she liked to blow things up and watch them burn.

Byram hooted and pounded Jenna on the back, his skepticism forgotten. "Did ya see that, Flamecaster? Did ya see it?" Even Mick was grinning broadly.

Jenna was glad the surviving blackbirds were on the

far side of the bridge. She couldn't tell whether Clermont was among them, but she had a feeling he was. He'd seen them—he'd seen all three of them, and now he'd be looking for them.

With any luck, though, he'd be looking for a boy named Munroe.

7

ODEN'S FORD

"You never come to see me these days unless you're on your way to kill someone," Taliesin said.

That was close enough to the truth that Ash didn't dispute it.

The Voyageur had her back to him, had not so much as looked at him, but she always seemed to know him by his step, or the smell of him, or because he was so simple and she so clever that she could tell what he was likely to do on any given day.

"I'm a second-year at Mystwerk now," Ash said. "There's much more work than last year. The masters and the deans keep us busy."

"I see," Taliesin said. She squatted barefoot between the

rows of carrots, expertly lifting them with her digging fork and sliding them into her carry bag. Taliesin Beaugarde might be dean of Spiritas, but she never put on airs. The contrast between the healer and the humblest master at Mystwerk was striking. Wizards were arrogant by nature, and Taliesin had her feet planted firmly in the earth.

Ash had been fighting his private war on Arden every summer since his father's murder. Every marching season he traveled the south, working as an itinerant farrier. Farriers were welcome everywhere they went—in army camps, in cities, at every farm along the way, in the stables of the highest-ranking thanes—everywhere there were horses.

Farriers didn't excite suspicion like other strangers did. Most had to travel from place to place in order to find work. It was a natural fit for Adam Freeman, a native of Tamron. Young as he was, his work was top of the line, and so his services were in great demand. He was good with horses, after all.

He was also good with poisons, garrotes, and the small daggers known as shivs. Poisons were his weapons of choice. Courtesy of Taliesin, he used compounds no one had ever heard of, that no southern healer would ever detect. It helped that green magic was considered witchery in Arden, and so was forbidden.

Even if his poisons were identified, it was always too late, anyway. Once he got to someone, they were already dead. By then, young Adam Freeman would be on his way somewhere else, trailing death and misery in his wake.

Often it was one of the nobility—perhaps a thane who supported the king. It might be a commander or a general, or a blackbird who was known to be especially cruel. Sometimes an entire column of mercenaries took sick and were unable to march north for weeks. The Summer Sickness, they called it, guessing that it might be caused by mosquitoes.

An encampment of recruits would break out with pustules that drove them absolutely mad with itching. Or a severe dysentery that had them in the privy for days. That was attributed to bad water. When all else failed, Adrian resorted to his array of blades. He preferred to avoid bloodshed, because that left no doubt that there'd been an enemy in their midst.

He rarely took the life of a line soldier if it could be avoided, since many were unwilling recruits from the captive realms. It wouldn't make much of a difference strategically, anyway. The king of Arden viewed them as expendable.

He never targeted the horses, either. For one thing, it would draw attention to his work as a farrier. For another, he preferred horses to most people.

"This is not your usual hunting season," Taliesin said.

"I thought I'd try something new. In the summertime, the southerners I want to kill are all in the Fells, killing northerners. In autumn, I might find them at home."

She finally turned to face him, shading her eyes against the declining sun. The sun was at his back, and his long shadow slanted across the rows. "You've grown so tall, Mageling, in these four years," she said, as if she hadn't really looked at him for a while. "And handsome. Are you taller than your father was?"

"I don't know. It's hard for me to remember now." That was a lie. He remembered—exactly—the measure of his father's arm around his shoulders, the distance between them when he leaned down to speak at Ash's level, even the scent of him—leather and sweat and fresh mountain air.

"Other young men your age come to me seeking love potions." She looked him up and down again. "I suppose you're not in need of those."

"No," he said, shifting from foot to foot. Taliesin still had the power to put him off balance. She was the closest he'd had to a mother since coming south. A mother who was nobody's fool.

"Quit fondling that jinxpiece," Taliesin snapped. "It makes me edgy." Witches had no use for amulets. She wiped sweat from her brow with her forearm, leaving a smear of dirt, then tossed a digging stick at him and pointed with her fork. "Here. Finish that row."

Idle hands made her edgy, too. Ash squatted next to her. He was in a hurry, but he knew better than to rush his longtime teacher. There was a price to be paid for access to Taliesin's vast inventory of plants and expertise in poisons.

"Where are you off to this time?" Taliesin said. She seemed to have a talent for breaking into his black moods.

"Me? I'll be in the Southern Islands, studying in the library of the arcane and collecting herbs for the healing halls."

"Where will you be, really?"

"It's better if you don't know," Ash said. Though she'd never admit it, he knew that she worried whenever he was away.

"They killed your father, and now you're killing them. What makes you different from them?"

It was part of their bargain that he would listen to these lectures now and then.

"They fired the first bolt," Ash said. "If they'd stayed in the south and left us alone, I'd have no quarrel with them."

"Poison is such a scattershot technique," Taliesin said. "You never know where your bolt will land."

"I know that, but I'm careful. And I'm good at what I do. I had the best teacher."

If he'd thought he was offering an olive branch, she slapped it away. "I did not teach you to travel about, leaving death in your wake," she snapped. "I thought you intended to heal yourself by healing others."

"I do heal others—three seasons of the year. As for the rest, that's a public health measure. Consider how many premature deaths I'm preventing. The lives I take are balanced by those I save."

"You should stay here and work with me," Taliesin said. "You may not think it, but you still have much to learn." She paused for a response, but he said nothing. "The time will come when you will wish that you were a better healer."

Ash thrust his stick into the soil with vicious jabs. "Teach me how to bring the dead back to life. Then I'll stay and listen."

That shut her up for a while. Finally, she said, "I may be gone when you return."

"Really?" Ash frowned at her, thinking she must be bluffing, trying to persuade him to stay at school. "Where are you going?"

"It's better if you don't know," Taliesin said, getting her own poke in. "A better question is why."

"All right, *why* are you going away?" Ash said, gritting his teeth, knowing that Taliesin was right—she always had something to teach him, even when she was giving him a hard time. *Especially* when she was giving him a hard time.

Taliesin sat back on her heels, resting her forearms on her knees. "Something has changed. There's danger here, like a noose tightening around us."

"Not here at the academy," Ash said.

"Yes, here. I don't know that the gifted will be safe here for too much longer."

"Really." Ash found this hard to believe. With Arden on one side, and the vassal state of Tamron on the other, the academy at Oden's Ford remained an oasis of neutrality—a real sanctuary from the ongoing wars. No doubt Mystwerk, the wizard school, presented a tempting target to Arden's mage-handlers. And the Temple School had never toed the Ardenine line when it came to history and religion.

The reputation of the faculty kept outsiders away. The most powerful wizards, the fiercest, best-trained warriors, the cleverest engineers, the most skilled healers—many returned to the Ford to teach. The academic houses didn't agree on much, but they all took a dim view of any attack on its sovereignty.

The Peace of Oden's Ford had persisted for five hundred years. The war in the north barely merited a footnote in its history.

"Would you like some advice?" Taliesin said, lancing into his thoughts again.

"No."

Like usual, she ignored him. "You have a rare talent, sul'Han, especially for a mage. I've never seen the likes of it. It's a shame to waste it this way. This is not what I had in mind when I agreed to teach you."

This is not what I had in mind for a life, Ash thought. Oh, well.

But Taliesin wasn't finished. "Some creatures were

made for murder—" Her hand shot out, into the row of carrots, and came up gripping a wriggling adder. She broke its neck and tossed it into the carry bag, too. "You were not. You cannot stand astride the line between good and evil, life and death, for long. It will destroy you."

"Isn't that what a healer does?" Ash said, drawn into the debate in spite of himself. "We follow our patients into those borderlands, where life and death meet."

"Aye, we do," Taliesin said. "And then we either turn them around, or gently help them across." Her eyes narrowed and her voice sharpened. "We do *not* give them a push."

"Aren't you the one who always says that it's easier to prevent a problem than to treat it?"

"I have said that," Taliesin admitted. "But—"

"I was right there when my father was murdered," Ash said. "I was *right there*, and yet there was nothing I could do. What I learned that day was that healing has its limits."

"There is never a shortage of killers. Any brute with a club in his hand will do. But a good healer is hard to find." Taliesin rose gracefully to her feet, settling the bag of vegetables on her ample hip. "You need to find a way to let go of your anger. Leave Oden's Ford while you still can. Go home and be the healer that you were meant to be."

"Right now there are advantages to being dead. No expectations, no obligations, no restrictions. It gives me the freedom to do what I have to do."

"You don't stop being who you are just because you've run away."

"I'll go home eventually."

"If you live that long. Now. What is it you've run out of this time?"

Finally, the lecture was over. Ash had his list ready. "Gedden weed. Black adder. Sweet misery. Dollseyes and wolfsbane. Sweet forgetting."

"Sweet forgetting?"

"For witnesses," Ash said. "Despite what you think of me, I try to keep bloodshed to a minimum."

"I don't know why you always come to me," Taliesin grumbled. "Your decoctions, infusions, and tisanes are as good as mine."

"They're good," Ash allowed. "Just not *as* good. Besides, I'm in a hurry."

"You are always in a hurry these days," Taliesin said. But she'd already surrendered. "All right, then. Come with me."

Ash handed her his carry bag and followed her into her cabin, breathing in the fumes from the pots that simmered on her wood stove all year round.

He wrinkled his nose at something new, a foul stench that made his eyes water. "Did something die in here?"

"Those are the eels I'm having for supper," Taliesin said. "You're welcome to stay."

It didn't take long for her to put Ash's kit together,

once she quit stalling. Still, by the time he left her cabin in Tamron Wood, following the road back to school, it was nearly dark. Though the weather was still warm, the sunny southern days were growing shorter. The scent of night-flowering spice lily hung like lust in the air, just one more sign that the season was turning.

This is the dying time, Ash thought, morbid to the bone.

You've got to stop thinking so much. It's the end of term, after all.

In fact, he'd been through a series of grueling exams that day. He was magically depleted and bone-weary, and he wanted to make an early start the next day. Still, he knew from experience that it might not be easy to escape into the oblivion of sleep.

He entered the academy by the postern gate, treading the well-worn path through the park, used by countless students on their way to and from mischief. Just past the gate, he turned down the path toward Stokes, the proficients' dormitory, which housed senior-level students from several academic houses. He was considered a fourth-year, having spent two years at Spiritas, the healers' academy, and two at Mystwerk.

His father and mother had schooled together here, back before the war. His mother had spent a year at Wien House, the school that drew would-be warriors from throughout the Seven Realms. His father had attended Mystwerk, the school for wizards, or mages as they were called in the south (usually coupled with fear and loathing).

The entire campus, with its green lawns and time-buffed stone buildings, had the look of a Temple School at home if you overlooked the gritty bits, such as the taverns and inns on Bridge Street. The Bridge would already be crowded with students, eager to celebrate the end of term and the beginning of the Interregnum.

What would his parents have been like, back then, before they'd suffered so many losses? Ash guessed it must have been a carefree time.

It was just then that he felt a presence, like cold water trickling between his shoulder blades, or a cadaver's hand on the back of his neck. He instinctively turned sideways, to present a smaller target, gripped his amulet, and looked back along the path.

The academy grounds were heavily wooded, and the moon shrouded in clouds. He could barely make out the darker shapes of the trees on either side of the gray strip of flagstone path. The gloomy undergrowth beneath could hide an army. It was probably not an army, but someone was definitely out there, watching him. Several someones.

They weren't gifted, Ash guessed, or they would show up better in the dark. It was his own gift, and their need, that told him they were there. It was only when he closed his eyes that he could see them, like deeper holes in the shadows. Ash had been trained to discern disorder in others. Had they not been so hungry, he might not have noticed them. They were like lanterns with no light inside.

Ash was more curious than worried. He wasn't the most powerful wizard, or the most skilled fighter at the Ford, but when it came to predators, he was likely near the top of the local food chain.

Ash took two steps back toward the shadowed border of the trees, meaning to take a closer look. Then froze as he sensed the excitement rippling through the watchers. Not fear, but greed and anticipation, as if they were a pack of high-country wolves with the scent of blood in their noses.

The hairs on the back of his neck stood up.

The breeze freshened and the leaves shivered. The moon freed itself from its wrapping of clouds and light cascaded onto the path. Nearby, an owl spoke and then its blunt shape passed silently overhead. Still the watchers waited in the woods. A small group of students passed by them on the path, and they didn't stir from their hiding places.

Holes in the darkness. Lanterns. Or wolves. Right. Taliesin had him seeing ghosts and monsters. One thing for sure: there were fewer ghosts and monsters at the Ford than where he was headed.

HELLO AND
GOOD-BYE

Reaching Stokes Hall, Ash trudged up the well-worn stone steps to the second floor. From all appearances, the dormitory was deserted. Everyone would be at the Bridge by now.

He pushed open his door and pointed at the reading lamp, and it blazed into light. He frowned, rocked on his heels, and scanned the room.

Someone's been in here.

It was hard to explain. The furnishings were simple: a bed, a dry sink with a pitcher, a desk and chair, the table by the door, a bookcase lined with precious books, a battered chest for his clothes. Although the arrangement of objects appeared to be random, there was a design and power in it, a charm of protection that gently redirected an intruder, turning him away without his realizing it. Ash always placed the spell instinctively. It was something he'd done since he was a boy, since his father had taught it to him. Back then it served to keep his younger sister out of his private things. But now the pattern was disturbed. Items had been picked up and shifted in subtle ways.

Doors in the student quarters were rarely kept locked. No one had much worth stealing, though borrowing was common, as long as you left a note. There was no note, but then nothing seemed to be missing. What was most disturbing was that his charm hadn't worked to keep them out.

He couldn't help thinking about Taliesin's warning. *I don't know that the gifted will be safe here for too much longer.*

But there were plenty of gifted at Oden's Ford— prominent teachers and practitioners. There was no reason anyone would target him. As far as students and faculty at the Ford knew, he was Ash Hanson, son of a minor landowner in the borders. The only person at the Ford who knew his real identity was Taliesin.

Still, he went back to the door and locked it. Then crossed to the hearth, lifted a loose stone, and retrieved the leather case, locked with charms, whose padded pockets and compartments were filled with vials, bottles, and pouches of death. Everything was just as he'd left it. He released a sigh of relief.

Maybe it was good he was leaving tomorrow. The Voyageur had made him jumpy.

He replenished his supplies with the herbs Taliesin had given him, working quickly and methodically, like a warrior arming himself for battle.

Ash pulled his drawer out from under his bed and laid out his travel gear. Weapons—his bow, arrows, small sword, the small daggers called shivs that his father had favored. The kit bag with an array of medicinals, surgical tools, dressings, and the like. Another bag containing tools for his work as a traveling farrier and healer of horses. His bedroll, cooking pots, small packets of upland teas, herbs, and seasonings for the road.

The mingled scents brought the usual rush of memory. Another year gone.

Though he'd told Taliesin that he preferred being off the map, he couldn't help thinking about the family he had left. Lyss would be fifteen, preparing for her name day on her sixteenth birthday. They'd been close—the gulf between eleven and thirteen wasn't so large, and they were both spares in the royal hierarchy. Did she still miss him the way he missed her? Four years is a long time when you're eleven years old. Especially when you carry the weight of the world on your shoulders.

Would she have boys buzzing around her by now, the way Hana always did? What kind of queen would she be? From what he remembered, she'd be happier playing the basilka or the harpsichord.

After Hana died, he'd promised Lyss he'd help her. That he'd be there for her when she came to the throne. That she wouldn't have to manage on her own. That promise still sat heavily on his conscience.

He could still keep his promise, he told himself. There was still time. She wasn't queen yet. But there was no telling how he would be received. He wouldn't blame her if she slammed the door in his face.

As far as he knew, his mother had not remarried, though he guessed there would be pressure to do so. An unmarried queen was an opportunity for alliances, something the Fells desperately needed. He preferred not to think about it.

Still, more and more, he longed for home. He wanted to climb out of the cloying sweet southern air into the clean, pine-scented mountains—a place where the northern winds needled the nose and cleared the head for thinking. A place that, even now, would be filling with snow.

If wishes were horses even beggars would ride. It was something his paternal grandmother used to say. The one who burned to death in a stable, long before Ash was born. His father often told stories about life on the streets of Fellsmarch, trying to make that piece of his heritage real to him.

"I never knew my da," he'd said. "I want you to know yours."

Ash sorted quickly through his single trunk of clothing.

He'd leave behind his heavy winter cloak, woven of upland sheepswool spun in the grease to turn the rain and snow. He'd bring his warm weather rain gear, beaded and stitched with clan charms. Clan goods were treasured throughout the Seven Realms, so that wouldn't mark him out as a northerner.

Studying his shelves of books, Ash chose two. One was Tisdale's, the green magic handbook he'd used since his arrival in Oden's Ford. The other was a small, battered volume bound in leather. A guide to poisons.

Taliesin had given it to him, but not without making her opinions known.

With everything assembled, he quickly stowed his supplies in two panniers, distributing the weight as evenly as he could.

When all was ready, Ash considered taking advantage of the deserted dormitory to carry his panniers to the stables and stow them there. In the end, he returned them to the drawer under the bed. He didn't want to risk their being discovered in the unlikely event the stable boys mucked out the stalls again before he left.

Just as he got his gear stowed away, there came a knock at the door.

"Ash! It's Lila." That would be Lila Barrowhill, a Southern Islander cadet from Wien House, the military school.

"It's open," Ash said.

"No, it's not."

"Oh." Ash unlocked the door and swung it open.

Lila stalked past him and dropped into a chair like she owned the place. In fact, he might not have recognized her without an introduction. She'd replaced her dun-colored Wien House uniform with a long blue skirt and a close-fitting blouse that exposed her shoulders and set off her dark skin. Her tangle of curls was pinned up and she'd rouged her lips.

"How come your door was locked?"

"I didn't realize it was," Ash said, sitting down on the bed.

Lila was one of a handful of Southern Islanders at Wien House. Most attended either the Temple School or Isenwerk, the engineering school. She looked to be of mixed blood, actually, and she spoke several languages fluently, including Fellsian.

Up to this year, they'd rarely crossed paths. Wien House was on the opposite side of the river from Mystwerk. Lila also seemed to spend considerable time away from school. He'd heard that she'd been expelled several times, but always talked her way back in.

Lila spent every spare moment in the dining halls, the taverns, the gymnasium—anywhere people gathered, played cards and darts, drank, ate, gossiped, and flirted. Ash had no idea when she got her studying done, but she seemed to do middling well in her classes with very little effort.

Ash had little time for socializing, between his doubled class schedule and the time he spent in the healing halls and studying with Taliesin. Besides, he was a loner at heart.

Now that Ash was a proficient, and Lila a cadet in Wien House, they'd ended up in the same dormitory. Though they saw more of each other than before, they mixed like oil and water. If anything, Lila seemed to dislike him for some reason. It perplexed him. Granted, he was no charmer, but he got along with most people.

He stole another look at Lila, still distracted by the sudden transformation and wondering what had brought her to his door.

Lila caught him staring and said, "No, Hanson, this is not the scene where the girl puts on a skirt and some paint and her schoolmate, who's a little thick, suddenly realizes that she is his true love."

"Oh," Ash said. "Good to know."

"Just because you're on the market doesn't mean that I am."

"What makes you think I'm on the market?"

"I saw Suze on Bridge Street earlier. The end-of-term party started mid-afternoon. She wondered where you were."

Oh. So that's what this is about. Suze was a plebe at Isenwerk. She and Ash had walked out together for a few months, but had recently called it quits. At least he had.

"I went to see Taliesin, to say good-bye. It took longer than I expected."

"I think Suze was hoping to give you a reason not to go." When Ash said nothing, Lila growled, "You broke her heart, you know. The least you can do is talk to her."

"I *have* talked to her. I tried, anyway. I told her up front that I wasn't looking for a long-term sweetheart. I thought we both agreed to that."

"Did you make her sign a bloody contract?" Lila laughed, but there was a bitter edge to it. "'I promise that I won't fall in love with the moody, mysterious Ash Hanson. I will enjoy his rangy body, his broad shoulders, and shapely leg, all the while knowing it's a lease, not a buy.'"

"Shapely leg?" Ash thrust out his leg, pretending to examine it, hoping to interrupt the litany of his physical gifts.

But Lila was on a roll. "'I will not fall into those blue-green eyes, deep as twin mountain pools, nor succumb to the lure of his full lips. Well, I will succumb, but for a limited time only. And the stubble—have I mentioned the stubble?'"

Ash's patience had run out. Lila was far too fluent in Fellsian for his liking. "Shut up, Lila."

"Isn't there anyone who meets your standards?"

"At least I *have* standards." He raised an eyebrow.

"Ouch!" Lila clutched her shoulder. "A fair hit, sir. A fair hit." Her smile faded. "The problem is, hope is the thing that can't be reined in by rules or pinned down by bitter experience. It's a blessing and curse."

For a long moment, Ash stared at her. He would have been less surprised to hear his pony reciting poetry.

"Who knew you were a philosopher?" he said finally. "Now. If you're staying, let's talk about something else. Where's your posting this term?"

"I'm going back to the Shivering Fens," Lila said, "where the taverns are as rare as a day without rain. Where you have to keep moving or grow a crop of moss on your ass."

Good-bye, poetry, Ash thought. "Sounds lovely. You can't get a better posting?"

"Not with my record," Lila said, not meeting his eyes. "But you—you have a choice, and you're going back to Freetown? There aren't enough dusty old libraries and indecipherable manuscripts for you here?"

"There's plenty," Ash said, "but they have different dusty old libraries and indecipherable manuscripts in the Southern Islands. Anyway, I need a change of scenery."

"How will you get there? I hear that Arden has stepped up patrols along the river all the way to Deepwater."

"I'll go via Sand Harbor," Ash said. "It's a little out of the way, but I want to go to the market there, anyway." He schooled his face to display nothing. Drunk or sober, Lila didn't miss much.

He shouldn't have worried. Lila was already restless, shifting in her seat, on to the next thing. "Listen," she said.

"Renard Tourant is hosting an after-hours party over at the Turtle and Fish. Everything's bound to be top-shelf. Want to come?"

Ash stared at her, surprised. Lila had long since given up inviting him to parties. "Not if it means spending time with Tourant."

"Aw, c'mon," Lila said. "It's not that late, and you've scarcely come out with us all term."

"I've been busy." Ash slid a sideways look at Lila, wondering if Suze would happen to be at this party, too. "Anyway, given Tourant's reputation, I'm surprised you'd want to go."

"I can take care of myself," Lila said, which was certainly true. "It might be my last chance to spend an evening with drunken Ardenine swine—for a while. Besides, Tourant insists on introducing me to some rising star in the Ardenine army."

"If he's a rising star, then what's he doing here?"

Lila shrugged. "Maybe he wants to recruit me. Wait till he finds out I don't have the right equipment."

"What do you mean?"

Lila slapped at the front of her skirt. "In here. I'm not a man."

Ash rolled his eyes. "If I didn't know better, I'd think you preferred the company of swine." At this point, he was being just about as disagreeable as he knew how.

"A girl can learn a lot from a drunken southerner," Lila

said, bestowing that familiar tight-lipped smile that could mean anything at all.

"Well, I've got better things to do. Like sleep."

"You should come," Lila persisted. "Tourant's invited everyone from Brocker and Stokes, so it won't be a totally Ardenine crowd. At least it'll be diluted a bit."

"You're welcome to stay here with me," Ash said, knowing what her answer would be. "We could read Askell and Byrne and discuss military campaigns during the Wizard Wars."

"Um. No," Lila said, making a face. "I'm done with textbooks for now."

"Give my regards to Tourant then," Ash said. "Tell him I hope he's less of a bunghole next year."

"Suit yourself," Lila said. "But don't say I didn't warn you—it'll be a graveyard here at Stokes tonight."

TOURANT'S PARTY

The coin was still piling up—Fellsian girlies and Tamric double eagles and Ardenine steelies, so-called because people doubted there was really any silver in them these days. Even a few coppers from those unwilling to put real money on the table.

There were two piles—some bet on Lila Barrowhill, others on Renard Tourant, the class commander. Lila noticed with some satisfaction that her pile was bigger. She spent a lot of time in the Turtle and Fish, and the regulars knew better than to bet against her. She was known to have a high tolerance for intoxicants and a lot of demons to drown.

Those who bet on Tourant were only brownnosing, and they stood to lose.

Tourant had secured a table next to the kegs so he could play the gracious host. His father was a high-up in the Ardenine army, which meant he had a paved road to the top. All of the high-ups in the Ardenine army were men, because in Arden, apparently, there were no competent women.

The class commander fancied himself a ladies' man. Lila suspected he took his standard-issue Wien House uniforms to a tailor, because they always had a custom fit. He also sported one of those ridiculous tiny mustaches that probably take hours to achieve, but that look like a shaving mistake.

Around them seethed a sea of dun-colored uniforms just like her own, save the markings of rank. It was nearly all Wien House, nearly all Arden with just a splash of Mystwerk black here and there. No Temple white at all. Which was probably a good thing.

"Is everything on the table?" Lila said, looking around for more takers. "All right, then. You ready?" she said, looking across the table at Tourant.

The commander nodded, his face shiny with sweat, his knuckles whitening as he gripped his ale.

"Hey, now," Lila said, grinning. "No worries. I'll cover your tab out of my winnings."

He flushed russet. "Go!" he said, tipping back his head, gulping noisily.

Lila shook back her hair, opened her throat, and poured

the ale down. She thunked down her glass moments before Tourant did. "You lose," she said, scooping up her share of the money, leaving enough on the table to cover the drinks. This was timely, at least. She'd been thinking she'd need some traveling money.

Tourant slammed his hands down on the table, going white with fury. Funny how he could change colors like that.

"You—you—you—" Turning away, he scooped up a fresh tankard, drew off some ale from a smallish keg, then thrust it into Lila's face. "Try this one. Lieutenant Rochefort brought it all the way from Ardenscourt."

"Did he, now? Does he have his own brewery? Raising a little money for the war effort?" Lila accepted the tankard with the exaggerated care of someone who's a bit lushy already. Peering into it, she saw a muddy brown brew, with a rather musty nose to it. Not as top-shelf as she'd expected.

She looked up to find Tourant watching her. "Where is this Lieutenant Rochefort, anyway?" she said. "I'm eager to meet him."

"He'll be here," Tourant said. "Soon. He had some business to attend to." He gestured toward the ale. "What do you think?"

Lila made a show of gulping some down, then wiped her mouth with her sleeve. "It's quite . . . complex, isn't it?" she said.

"Indeed," Tourant said, smirking. "It's not the usual Tamric swill." His gaze shifted so that he was looking over Lila's shoulder. "Here's Rochefort now. You can thank him in person."

Lila swung around, coming face-to-face with the newcomer. In contrast to Tourant's plumage, the visitor's clothing was finely made but subdued, without the markings of rank. He had a lean, sinuous build and fine-boned, artist's hands. His skin was pale and unmarked, as if it had never seen sunlight. His eyes were hazel—oddly pale under thick dark lashes, and his hair was the same color as his ale.

Blood and bones, she thought. Destin Karn. What are you doing here?

"Lila Barrowhill, may I introduce Lieutenant Denis Rochefort," Tourant said, seeming eager to make it a three-way. "Lieutenant, this is Cadet Barrowhill. The one I told you about." His eye twitched, and Lila realized that Tourant was trying to wink and not quite succeeding.

Lila had been working with Destin Karn for two years now—long enough to know that the younger Karn was a chameleon of a man, who could play any part, who could take on the colors of his surroundings. Just as he was doing at that very moment. She just wasn't sure who the real Karn was.

Destin's father, Marin Karn, was commander of the Ardenine army and of the military campaigns against

Tamron, Delphi, and the Fells. He was the architect of Arden's captive mage program, in which they used flash-craft collars to force wizards to fight alongside them. Both Karns were wizards who had found a way to survive and thrive in a land that despised magic. Naturally, they'd managed to avoid taking the collar themselves.

"Pleased to meet you, Lieutenant Rochefort," Lila said, putting on a fierce, brilliant smile that said she wasn't pleased at all. Setting her ale on the table, she extended her hand. Destin hesitated, as if worried about her intentions, then took it. His palm was smooth, uncalloused, and delivered a definite sting of wizardry. Magic was the weapon he wielded on behalf of his king.

Destin kept hold of her hand, his eyes fixed on Lila. "Tourant was right," he murmured, his lips twitching with amusement. "You are quite lovely—such an exotic mingling of races. We don't have officers like you at home."

Lila bit back the first retort that came to mind. "No," Lila said, withdrawing her hand. "You don't." Destin was having fun at Tourant's expense—always a good thing—but that didn't excuse his showing up here like this. She needed to get rid of Tourant, so they could have a heart-to-heart.

"While we're on the subject of physical gifts," Lila said loudly, "I must point out Proficient Tourant's very impressive ass. Nobody fills his breeches like he does. Turn around, Tourant, and give the lieutenant a look."

Lila described a circle in the air with her forefinger and raised her eyebrows.

Horror and rage chased embarrassment across Tourant's face.

"And did you notice his skin—it's the color of roasted beets."

The commander backed away, spluttering, unable to manage a suitable retort.

"You forgot your ale!" Lila thrust a mug at him. Tourant took it and slunk away.

Destin's eyes followed Tourant's retreat, then he looked back at Lila, grimacing. "Is it politically astute to antagonize your class commander?" Meaning Tourant.

"I've never been accused of being politically astute," Lila said.

"Tourant should know better than to engage with you."

"He should, but he does not," Lila said, "just as you should know better than to come here." She added loudly, "So what brings you to Oden's Ford, Lieutenant? Is the marching season really over in Arden?"

"It's always the marching season in Arden," Destin said, cradling his mug of ale but not drinking from it. "The king is a demanding master."

Lila leaned toward him, so their faces were inches apart. "If you're here to see me, you're wasting your time."

"I'm here on other business," Destin said, looking away.

Which raised the question—what other business?

"But as long as I'm here," he went on, "it seemed like a good opportunity to convey a message from our quartermaster. We have an urgent need for as many—"

"I thought I made myself clear. I don't do business here. Never ever. If you want to talk, I'll be heading east in another week or so. You can leave me a message at the Seven Horses on the West Road, or Chauncey's in the city. Let me know how to get in touch with you."

Destin's hand stole to his neckline, then dropped away as he remembered himself. "Hear me out, at least. The king has made a proposal that I think you'll find—"

"I said no. Is there something you don't understand about no?"

"Is there a problem?" Somebody's foul breath washed over her, and Lila looked up to find that Tourant was back, like a bad dream, and pulling up a chair. He all but fell into it, clunking his mug down on the table. It was nearly empty.

"Tourant," Destin said in a low, vicious voice. "Go away. The lady and I were having a private discussion."

"Lady?" Tourant snorted. "You must be joking. I can tell you stories about Barrowhill that would—"

"It's all right," Lila said heartily. "We were done with our discussion anyway. How are you feeling, Tourant?" She propped her chin on her fist. "You look a little under the weather."

"Me?" Tourant blinked his bleary eyes as if unable to

focus. "You! You're the one who . . . how are you feeling?"

Lila shrugged. "I'm fine. But it looks like maybe you should call it a night."

"You're drunk, Tourant," Destin said icily. "Why don't you do as she says and go somewhere and sleep it off?"

Tourant ran his tongue over his lips. Did it again. Frowned. Pulled his tankard toward him, and sniffed at it. He reached for Lila's, and she pulled it back, out of reach.

"Keep your hands off my ale!" she said. "Go lay down before you fall down."

Tourant pointed a shaking finger at Lila. "You—you—you switched drinks on me." He turned to Destin, a wounded look on his face. "Lieutenant Karn, I—"

Karn. It was as if the room had gone silent around them, leaving that one name ringing off the walls. Destin Karn might keep a low profile, but his father's name was known throughout the Realms.

Karn planted both hands on the table and leaned in toward Tourant. "Imbecile. Have you lost your mind?"

Lila saw death in Destin's face, and wondered how far her own usually reliable sharp's face had slipped. "Ease up, Lieutenant Rochefort," she said. "Tourant's just a little confused is all. He gets that way when he's drinking. No harm done."

"But . . . she switched drinks on me," Tourant persisted. "See for yourself." The cadet shoved his tankard toward Rochefort/Karn. The lieutenant snatched it up and hurled it into the fireplace, where it shattered, sending shards of glass flying everywhere.

Temper, temper, Lila thought, picking a sliver of glass out of her arm. Destin seemed to keep a lot of anger bottled within his sleek skin. "I don't know what you're talking about," she said. "Why would I want to switch drinks? And why would it matter, anyway, since it all came from the same—"

Tourant swayed in his seat, wilting before her eyes. Then slammed facedown on the table.

Really, Tourant? Lila thought. Did you think I'd actually fall for the turtled ale trick?

Tourant snored on, drool pooling on the table beneath his open mouth.

Lila took a quick look around, what she should have been doing all along. All around the room, people were slumped over tables, snoring in corners, sprawled on the floor. With the exception of a dozen Ardenine cadets, hard-faced and totally sober. And they all stood between Lila and the door.

Yeah, you're clever, Lila, she thought, panic flickering through her. You were so focused on the turtleweed trap that you didn't notice the other one closing around you.

"Well, Rochefort," she said casually as cold sweat trickled down between her shoulder blades. "Who knew that Tourant can't hold his ale?"

"Who knew?" Destin said evenly.

Pushing to her feet, Lila crossed to the row of kegs, scanning the room for a way out. Saw none. She turned back toward Destin. "All this talk makes me thirsty. Would you like another?"

He shook his head.

Lila filled a new cup and set it down on the table, her mind working furiously. It didn't make sense. Arden wouldn't break the Peace of Oden's Ford in order to dispose of a black sheep cadet who'd become a valuable Ardenine spy and an important black market supplier.

Could they really have nailed her this quickly? If so, she'd underestimated them.

Unless she wasn't really the target. Unless they just wanted to keep her—and everybody else—out of the way long enough to—

Bones. Bloody, bloody bones. Ash. Ash was the target.

Destin was watching her, still as a coiled snake.

"Watch my ale," she said. "I'll be right back."

Destin's hand shot out and gripped her wrist. "Sit down, Lila," he said. "Please. Stay a little longer."

Let go of me, Karn, or lose the hand. "I said I'll be right back."

"Where are you going?"

"To the privy," Lila said. "Now let go, unless you want me to piss in your lap."

Lila could see the indecision in Destin's eyes. She guessed that he and his crew wanted to do whatever they'd come to do and get out without being noticed. She was banking on that.

"All right," he said, releasing her wrist. "Hurry back. We're not done talking yet."

Maybe you're not, Lila thought. But I am. I just hope I'm not too late.

BLOOD HUNGER

Ash awoke from a nightmare into a nightmare. It was the weight on his chest that aroused him, as if someone had placed an anvil there. He opened his eyes to find a man smiling down at him, a man who might have been a demon out of the old stories. His face was framed in the cowl of his rough-woven robe, his pale skin stretched across the bones around the caverns of his eyes and the slash of his mouth. A pendant dangled free at his neck, some kind of amulet. No, it was a tiny gold cup, like the kind used to dose medicines. Something in the man's face reminded Ash of the cannis fungus addicts who lived in caves in the Spirit Mountains, growing their hallucinatory mushrooms in the dark.

Ash tried to lift his hand to move the weight off his chest and found he couldn't move, not one finger. When he looked down the length of his body, he saw nothing to explain it.

He sought his gift, and could touch nothing. It was like pumping from a dry well. Nor could he touch the shivs under his pillow or behind the headboard or hidden in the book on his bedside table.

The robed man gripped the chain of Ash's serpent amulet, lifted it over his head, and tucked the pendant into his carry bag. Then he brought out a knife, a wickedly sharp thin blade, the hilt inscribed with runes and symbols. He waved it before Ash's eyes, making sure he got a good look at it.

The man spoke softly, a cadenced Malthusian prayer in Ardenine. Then he switched to the Common speech. "Rejoice, mage, for I am a priest of the true church come to cleanse you of the taint of sorcery."

Ash felt the cold metal of the blade against his arm. A stinging pain told him he'd been sliced. Then, horribly, his attacker lifted Ash's arm to his lips and sucked the blood from the wound. The man shivered, closing his eyes, as if it were syrup of poppy. Blood was smeared all around his mouth, until he wiped it away with one hand. He uncorked a small bottle and poured something burning into the gash. Ash screamed, but made no sound, struggled and thrashed, but moved not a bit. Sweat pooled beneath the small of his back, soaking the linens under him.

The blade man raked a hand through Ash's hair, then lifted the bloody knife. Cut a lock away, tied it with a thread, and put it into a little bag at his belt. A trophy. Ash struggled again to move, to raise a wizard flame, to cry for help. Nothing. That was when he realized that he was going to die.

The priest drank from the wound again and smiled a beatific smile, his teeth rimed with blood. "I do so wish that we had more time, and a private place, to do this properly," he said, running his cold fingers along Ash's collarbone, seeking the pulse point. "I would take you up in small sips, slowly draining you of sin and substance until the mana'in slips away like a whisper in the dark. With a healthy young demon such as yourself, the cleansing ceremony can last for hours." He sighed. "It's a lovely ritual, and a peaceful end." He sighed again. "But my brothers will be here soon, and then, I'm afraid, it will be something of a feeding frenzy."

As if on cue, Ash heard the door to his room slam open. The priest muttered a curse, and his movements now became quick and purposeful. He grasped Ash's chin and shoved it back and up. Ash closed his eyes and sent up a prayer to the Maker, expecting the touch of steel at the base of his neck, where the great vein comes close to the surface.

The assassin made a new sound, a cross between a grunt of surprise and a gurgle. Something warm and wet splashed across Ash's bare chest, and his chin was suddenly released. He opened his eyes just as his attacker slid sideways onto the bed, his own knife sticking out of his throat.

"Ash." Lila's voice was soft and urgent. "Are you all right? Did he stick you?" Her face appeared within his field of vision, eyes narrowed with worry.

Ash could only stare at her helplessly. Lila sucked in her breath and ran her hands over him, looking for a point of entry. Her hand stopped over his heart. "What's this?"

The suffocating weight was gone. Ash pushed up on his elbows.

Lila was holding something on her palm, like a dark spot. When she passed it under the light from the window, Ash could see it was a stone, a burnt-sugar color, veined with crystal.

"It's magic," Ash gasped. "I couldn't move, not a twitch. And . . . and it sucked all the magic out of me."

Lila weighed the stone in her hand, then tucked it into her pocket. "Are you hurt otherwise?"

Ash shook his head. "Just my arm. It's nothing."

"Nothing? Where's all the blood coming from then?" Lila's voice tremored a bit.

Ash looked. The sheets where his arm had rested were sodden with blood, and the flesh was ripped from his wrist halfway to his elbow. It was the sort of a wound a person *might* have made a fuss over, in normal circumstances. But just now it seemed unimportant, next to his life. He flexed his fingers and found the tendons and nerves intact. Blood still ran freely down his arm, and he pressed it tightly to his side to stanch the bleeding. An anticoagulant, he thought, his training kicking in. They use an anticoagulant to keep the blood flowing.

"He took my amulet," Ash said hoarsely. "It's in his bag. On the floor. There." He pointed. Can you . . . get it for me?"

"You mages and your amulets," Lila said, the relief in her voice unmistakable. She turned away from Ash, knelt on the floor, and rooted in the assassin's carry bag.

Ash saw a flash of movement over Lila's shoulder, someone flying through the doorway, heading his way.

"Lila!" Ash shouted, using the body of the dead assassin as a shield so that the newcomer buried his blade in the corpse. The newcomer was still trying to free it when Lila slammed into him, sending him flying. He landed, hard, his head striking the washstand.

Instantly, Lila was on him. She gripped the hilt of her knife with both hands, raised it and—

"Wait!" Ash shouted.

The blade was already on its way down, with all Lila's weight behind it, but she somehow managed to turn it so it stuck in the floor next to the man's throat. She swore and yanked the point free, then let it drop until it rested just above the assassin's collarbone. He didn't stir. Lila looked back at Ash.

"What?" She sounded wild, bloodthirsty, and completely unfamiliar.

Ash shoved the body of the first assassin aside and stood up unsteadily. "Maybe we should try to find out who they are and why they're trying to kill me."

Lila stared at him a moment, and then brushed a hand absently across her face, as if to wipe something away. Then nodded. "Right."

"Why don't you go fetch the dorm masters and provosts and I'll search these two for clues."

"Fair enough." She produced another dagger from some hiding place and slapped it into Ash's hand. "I'll be right back. If he moves, stick him."

Ash stared at the dagger in his hand. "Actually, I have my own—" he began, but she was gone.

First things first. He pulled on his breeches, then stuck Lila's dagger into the sheath hidden in the waistline. Dropping to his knees, he dug in the first assassin's bag and retrieved his amulet, sliding the chain back around his neck. He palmed the jinxpiece, feeling the welcome flow of the magical energy called flash. All he had was what was stored in the pendant—he'd been completely stripped of power. It would take a while to recover.

Using his amulet, Ash kindled the lamp next to his bed. He pulled a cloth bandage from his healer's kit and wrapped it snugly around his arm, using his teeth in place of a second hand. A more thorough search of the assassin's carry bag turned up a traveler's edition of the *Book of Malthus*, a few religious charms, two more runed blades, a stoppered bottle, and a wadded-up cloth.

Ash spread the cloth out on his washstand, thinking it might be a map or something. It was a handkerchief, made of white We'enhaven cotton, but stained brown with old blood. It was the plain, utilitarian style used at Oden's Ford. In fact, the school's laundry mark was faintly visible in one corner.

Ash looked from the handkerchief in his one hand to the pinkish scar that ran across the meat of his thumb on the other. He'd cut himself badly, chopping betony herb, a month before. He'd stopped the bleeding with a handkerchief just like this one.

It was not a random attack, then. But why had they come after him? Could Ardenine spies have discovered what he'd been doing with his school vacations? Or, worse, had they somehow figured out his true identity?

Lila was back, slipping in through the door like a wraith, her sword in her hand. She locked the door behind her, then pulled the window shutters closed and latched them.

"There were three more in the hall," she said, turning toward Ash. Her hands were covered with blood. Her face was splattered with it as well, like a dark rash, and perhaps the whole front of her, although it was hard to tell with her back to the lamp.

"Three more?" Ash stared at her. "What did you—?"

"I killed them," she said, rubbing her neck. "What a mess. It's so hard to find that sweet spot between the . . . anyway. Sorry. So let's hope this one has something to say." She nudged the man on the floor with her boot. He groaned.

"I thought you went to get the dorm masters and provosts."

"The dorm masters are dead," Lila said wearily. "Here at Stokes, anyway. They must've killed them on their way in. Two provosts as well."

The news was like a punch in the gut. After four years, it was hard to let go of the notion that this was a place of safety, with rules, and people to enforce them. He'd become accustomed to being the predator, not the prey.

Taking in his reaction, Lila said, "Look, the provosts are used to dealing with drunken students and domestic squabbles. Not professional killers."

Ash was learning things about Lila Barrowhill that he had never known before, things he wasn't sure he wanted to know. His hard-drinking dorm mate had just dispatched multiple armed men without making a sound.

Ash had his secrets, and so, apparently, did she.

"By the way, thanks for saving my life," Ash said. "Good that you came home early."

Lila snorted. "Don't thank me just yet."

Ash extended the handkerchief toward her. "He was carrying this in his bag."

Lila took it, examined it under the lamp, and handed it back. "I don't get it," she said.

"I think they follow a blood scent," Ash said, wadding the cloth in his fist. "This is my blood. Somebody here at school must have given it to them." He stopped then, realizing that he had nothing to say about why they might do that.

"Yeah," Lila said, scowling. "Somebody must have." Her expression suggested she had a candidate in mind. She leaned against the wall, where she could watch both the man on the floor and the door. "Well? What are you waiting for? Interrogate him."

"Me?" Ash's brain wasn't working as well as it usually did.

"No, one of the other mages in the room." She pointed her chin at the assassin on the floor. "Time is wasting. We've got to get out of here."

His subject was as pallid and gaunt as the dead man on the bed. Ash gripped his amulet with one hand and pressed the other into the assassin's chest. Then he concentrated and forced the assassin into consciousness, using the direct magical pressure called persuasion. Being a flatlander, the man would likely have little knowledge of or defense against wizard interrogation techniques.

The priest opened his eyes and fixed them on Ash. His hands scrabbled on the floor like claws trying to gain purchase. Ash flinched backward, then took a deep breath to calm himself.

"Who are you?" Ash asked in Common, his voice cold and hard. "What is your name?"

The man squirmed, as if to avoid the wizard mind pressing down on him, but there was no place to hide. "My name is Usepia," he said hoarsely, in Ardenine-accented Common. "I am of the Darian Guild."

"Darian Guild," Ash repeated. "What's that?"

"Redeemers of mages," Usepia replied. He had stopped squirming and was staring at Ash, his eyes shining with desire. "We are the Blades of Malthus, who cleanse the world of sorcery."

"There are lots of mages here. How did you choose me?"

"We smelled your blood. We tasted it when we were given the kill."

"Somebody gave you the kill? Who told you to kill me?"

"A mage," Usepia said, eyes slitted against the wizard light, as if it hurt his eyes.

"A mage? What mage?" Ash leaned closer. "What was his name?"

Usepia shrugged, as if mages were mages. "He said there were many mages here, but you were the one to be redeemed."

"You heard him say that?" Ash pressed. "You spoke with him?"

The Darian shook his head. "The mage spoke to our master, and our master spoke to us. It seems that this mage is a man of faith."

"What faith?"

Annoyance flickered over Usepia's face. "The *true* faith. The Church of Malthus. Don't pretend that you . . ."

Usepia's voice trailed off as his attention was diverted. He eagerly extended a hand, palm cupped. Ash followed his eyes. Blood had soaked through the bandage on his arm and was again dripping onto the floor. The Darian brother was trying to catch the drops. Ash jerked his arm away, and Lila slammed Usepia's wrist to the floor with a booted foot.

The Darian screeched like he was being tortured. "Aiiieee! That hurts!"

"Then stop that!" Lila said. Maybe it was the light, but her face looked to be a strange, gray-green color. The Darian brother went limp, and Lila removed her foot.

Ash pushed with his mind again. "Did he tell you why I was to be killed?"

"You are Adrian sul'Han, the get of an unholy union between a powerful mage, Han sul'Alger, and the witch queen in the north."

Ash heard Lila's quick intake of breath. He looked up, met her narrow-eyed gaze, and looked away.

Scummer. Never ask a question without considering what the answer might be.

Well, there was no jamming that cat back into the bag. After four years at Oden's Ford, he'd been outed.

It also confirmed what he'd suspected. It was not a random kill.

"What if you're wrong? What if I'm not the mage you're looking for?"

The man smiled an awful smile. "Ah, but you are. And even if you were not, we have our own reasons to kill mages. We free mages from the sin of sorcery by drinking their blood." Usepia seemed all too willing to share the good news.

Ash recalled the little goblet that hung around the blade man's neck, and shuddered.

Lila held something between her thumb and forefinger in front of the man's face. "What is this?" It was the stone that had paralyzed Ash.

Usepia squeezed the words out, as if they hurt. "That is Darian stone. It keeps mages still so they can be cleansed. It takes up the mana'in, the taint of sorcery, so it can be used for the good of all."

Ash had never heard of Darian stone. Maybe it worked in the same way as an amulet—by storing flash, the magical energy wizards constantly produced. Only in this case, a wizard wouldn't get it back.

"We've seen five of you," Ash said. "Are there more?"

"There are many brothers in the guild, and we've all tasted your scent," Usepia whispered. "You are a dead man, mage. We are the best, and we never give up. If you submit, I will take you quickly and painlessly. I am . . . quite skilled . . . with a knife." Still flat on his back, he reached up with both arms, as if to embrace Ash. Light reflected off metal.

Ash jerked backward as the blade slashed past his throat. Then instinct took over. In one movement, he'd drawn his borrowed dagger and pinned the Darian brother to the floor with the blade through his chest. Lila all but impaled him a second time.

"Blood and bones!" Lila looked from the dead priest on the floor to Ash and back again, then shook her head in disgust. "I didn't even search the bloodsucking crow. I'm too stupid to live."

"I didn't search him, either," Ash said.

Lila pulled her blade free, using her foot to stabilize the body. "I'm sorry, Hanson, or sul'Han, or whoever the hell you are. He gave me the all-over crawls."

Ash couldn't argue with that. Usepia's eyes were open, and it still seemed like they followed him around the room. Finally, he dropped his bloody handkerchief over the Darian's face. Enjoy, he thought.

"Come on." Lila spoke briskly, breaking the spell of indecision. "Let's bind up your arm again so you don't bleed to death. We need to change clothes, pack up, and get out of here."

Ash stared at her, his thoughts muddled by loss of blood. "What are you talking about?"

Lila wiped her dagger on the assassin's robe and shoved her sword back into its scabbard. She worked quickly, but spoke slowly, as if to the dim-witted. "The Peace of Oden's Ford is broken. Clearly, princeling, Arden knows you're here, and wants to cleanse the world of you. Unless you're good with that, we need to go."

I'm not a princeling, Ash thought, but didn't say it out loud.

Lila crossed to the window, threw open the shutters, and scanned the empty, moonlit yard. Then pulled them closed again and latched them.

"I'll be right back," she said. "Don't open the door to anyone but me." And she was gone again.

Ash was beginning to feel dizzy and weak from loss of blood. He needed to do something about that before he was too far gone. He sat down on the hearth, his healer's kit next to him. Look on the bright side, he thought. At least poison's not a worry. It would have been washed out long ago.

Ash cleaned the wound one-handed, then packed a poultice of herbs over it. He was in the process of trying to wrap it again when there came a tapping at the door.

It was Lila, dressed in clean, nondescript clothing, saddle-bags over her shoulder. She'd scrubbed the blood off her face and hands, too.

Dropping her bags by the door, she gripped Ash's elbow and led him back to the hearth. "Here, let me help with that. We've got to hurry, and I can't have you falling off your horse."

She sat next to Ash and began wrapping, but not without wrinkling her nose at the smell of the herbs. "At least maybe the stink will keep those bloodhounds off your scent," she said.

"Are you sure Arden's in on this?" Ash asked, leaning his head back against the fireplace. "Odd that it was a wizard who ordered the kill. Our family has enemies at home. It could have been one of them."

"Maybe," Lila said, clearly humoring him, "but I don't think so. I think Renard Tourant found out who you were somehow, and sent word to Arden, along with your handkerchief. Somebody set up the kill with the Darian brothers. Tourant threw a party to empty out the dorms, but he knew you wouldn't come, so you'd be here alone." She gave him a hard eye. "That's what you get for being boring."

"What tipped you off?"

"They turtled my ale. I knew something was up, so I hurried back here."

"If they were in on it, why didn't they stop you?"

"I swapped ales with Tourant, so he was down for the count," Lila said. "Arden doesn't want the academy on their necks, and I'm sure they'd like to keep training soldiers at the Ford. They were likely hoping that if things went wrong, the Darian brothers would take the blame for breaking the peace and not them."

Ash knew Lila had edited something out, something she didn't want him to know. "Why would your turtled ale send you rushing back to the dorm to check on me?"

The cadet shrugged. "I came back here for weapons," she said, "not to check on you. When I saw blood in the hallway, I thought I'd better take a look around. You're lucky I did."

"It's an interesting theory, but there's quite a few maybes and mights," Ash said. "I'm not in line for the throne in the Fells. They had no reason to target me." Unless his secret life had somehow become public.

Lila shrugged. "Maybe they don't understand the Fellsian rules of succession. Or maybe they just don't care."

"Or maybe King Gerard is still working his plan to destroy my mother's family and eliminate the Gray Wolf line for good. He finally found one of us that he could get at." The anger that always smoldered in him flamed up again. "That means that the queen and the princess heir may be next." Assuming it hasn't happened already. That thought was like a knife to the gut.

"I'm sure they've been targets all along," Lila said. "There's nothing you can do about that."

Yes, there is, Ash thought. Something I should have done, or tried to do, before now. For four years, I've been lopping legs off the spider when I should have gone straight for the heart.

"Ash? Are you listening to me?"

Ash looked up to find Lila scowling at him. "Oh. Sorry. What did you say?"

"What we do know is that they know you're here. So

it's not safe here, not anymore. If it ever was. Which means we've got to get out of here."

We? A traveling companion did not fit into Ash's plans.

"Lila, listen," Ash said. "I don't want you to change your plans. Go to your posting in the Fens. I'll just go on to Freetown tonight. Problem solved."

Lila looked pointedly at the body on the floor, then the body on the bed. "Right," she said with a sour grin. "How many people here know about your plans to go to Freetown? How long before those bloodsuckers are hunting you there?"

"I can take care of myself," Ash said stiffly. "They won't catch me by surprise again."

"No." Lila shook her head. "Now that your secret is out, the safest place for you is back in Fellsmarch. And that's where I'm going to take you." She gave him a sideways look. "It's worth it to stay out of the swiving Fens."

"So what's your interest in this? What makes you think we should partner up?"

"I'm not talking about being partners," Lila said. "I'm hoping there'll be a reward in it for me. As soon as I collect, I'm gone." She rubbed her fingers and thumb together. "Now change your breeches. We won't get far if you look like you've been the guest of honor at a blood-bath." Lila folded her arms and stood, tapping her foot, like she planned on supervising.

She had saved his life. Now it seemed there would be a

price to be paid for it. Until he got his game going, as his father would say, it was better not to leave this loose end hanging.

"Turn your back, at least," Ash said.

Lila heaved a great sigh, but she turned and faced the door. "I can't believe you're making a fuss about this, after everything that's happened."

Stripping quickly, Ash dropped his bloody clothes on the floor and yanked on clean smallclothes, a fresh set of breeches, and a linen shirt.

"Can I at least help pack your things while you're busy being shy?" Lila said to the ceiling.

"I'm already packed," Ash said, pulling his panniers from under the bed. "Let's go."

GOING EAST ON THE WEST ROAD

Either Ash Hanson sul'Han didn't want to be rescued, or he had no common sense. It wasn't like Lila expected a medal, but still—a little cooperation would be damned nice. She hadn't planned on spending a month or two nannying a blueblood mage. She had business of her own to attend to. Pressing business.

Leaving the bodies where they lay, Lila and Ash carried their gear down to the first floor. The guards that were usually posted in the doorways were gone, and the corridors yawned, empty and sinister.

The kitchen yard, so busy during the day, was tenanted only by moonlight and by Scraps, the Mistress of Kitchens' battle-scarred tomcat. The lock on the kitchen door easily gave to Lila's practiced hand. Scraps watched bale-fully from the doorway as they gathered as much travelers' food as they could carry: salted meat, bread and cheese and dried fruit, two skins of wine. Given the carnage in the dormitory, a raid on the kitchen would receive little attention in the morning.

While they worked, they argued, debating which road to take.

Lila favored the Tamron Road, which would get them into friendly territory quicker and keep them away from Ardenscourt. She didn't feel it necessary to mention that it would also make it less likely that they would run into someone she knew. The last thing she needed was to be seen with Princeling sul'Han.

Ash pushed riding east to Ardenscourt, then north through Delphi. "The Tamron Road is the logical choice, which means they'll be watching it," he said. "Only an idiot would head straight for Ardenscourt."

"Exactly," Lila said. "Only an idiot would try that. I don't like it. That road is heavily traveled, always crawling with southerners."

"We *are* in the south," Ash said, rolling his eyes. "More traffic means we'll be easier to overlook."

"Unless we run into more of those bloodsucking crows of Malthus." Or some other people I'd just as soon avoid, Lila thought.

"Let's split up, then," Ash suggested. "I'll go via

Ardenscourt and you go via Tamron. We'll lay bets on who gets there first."

You're trying to get rid of me, Lila thought, so you can go south to Freetown, like you planned. Well, I'm not going to let you. But that meant giving in.

Once that was decided, they hurried on to the stables, where Ash insisted that they pick out horses to steal, arguing that they couldn't take their own if they wanted to play dead. Ash chose Maribel, a spirited piebald mare that had belonged to the messenger service, so she'd been exercised more than most of the students' personal mounts. Lila picked Brady, a bay military gelding newly arrived from Arden with a student at Wien House.

Less than an hour after the last man died, they rode away from Oden's Ford. At least Lila convinced Ash not to leave a note for Taliesin, dean of Spiritas, the healing academy. She was determined to win that one.

"I don't want her to worry about me," Ash said, looking down at his hands.

"Maybe she's the one that outed you," Lila suggested. "She knows you better than anyone, right?"

Ash flinched when she said that, but then he shook his head. "If she wanted me dead, I would be dead," he said.

"That's an odd thing to say about a healer," Lila said. "Anyway, she won't worry if she thinks you're dead. And it's probably best for now if that's what everyone thinks. Especially while we're traveling through Arden."

So far, the princeling had met all of her admittedly low expectations. He was a major pain in the ass. Still—she couldn't get the image of the bloodsucking crows out of her mind.

They rode first in the moonlight, and then in the darkness after the moon had set, and finally in the mist of the early morning, climbing the long, gradual slope away from the river. As the light grew, the great trees of Tamron Forest gradually became visible on either side, like rooted ranks of soldiers. Their horses moved at a brisk pace, their hooves flinging up the mud of the road, splashing through the puddles of a recent rain. They didn't have much to say to each other.

"I wonder how wide a net they'll cast," Ash said, after an hour's silent riding.

"Who knows?" Lila said. "Depends on how committed they are to killing you." She studied him critically. "Your size and that copper head of yours make you stand out."

Ash reached up, fingering his hair, as if he'd forgotten what color it was.

"Too bad the weather's not colder," Lila said. "Once it's light out, it would be best if you kept your hood up."

As the day came on, the landscape around them began to emerge, the colors muted and grayed. The autumn mist clung low to the ground, filled the ditches on either side of the road, and shifted and swam as the horses moved through it. Now and then the dense forest was punctured by a clearing along the road, centered on a farmhouse and other buildings. The shapes of people drifted through the yards like ghosts. Farmers rose early.

Tamron Forest crowded close to the road, as if anxious to reclaim it, and Lila found herself startling at every sound. The roots of great trees broke through at the berm, and the canopy often met overhead, shutting out the frail light. Any assassin hidden along the road would be but an arm's length away. Lila imagined a rush from the undergrowth, sinewy hands reaching up to drag Ash from his horse and slam him to the cold earth, a circle of pale faces within dark cowls.

Once, they heard hooves behind them on the packed surface, horses coming fast. They shoved off through the small growth that fringed the road and hid behind the massive trunk of a moss-covered oak. A dozen black-clad men on dun-colored horses thundered past, ringmail glittering. Among them, Destin Karn, the only one unarmored, eyes fixed forward, slitted against the wind and dust.

"The King of Arden's Guard," Ash murmured when they had gone. "They're in a hurry, aren't they?"

Bones, Lila thought. Destin Karn, of everyone, might expect me to take this road. I told him I was going to, after all. Is he hunting me after I ditched him on Bridge Street? Or is he hunting Ash? Does he suspect that I helped him escape?

Maybe he's just hurrying home to report the bad news.

Now they proceeded more cautiously than before, aware that the soldiers they'd seen might double back when the trail grew cold. When they began to see traffic upon the road, Lila led the way back into the woods, penetrating several hundred yards before she chose a camping place, a defensible spot with a low hill at their backs. They built no fire; it wasn't worth the risk. They left their horses saddled, fed them, and tethered them to a long lead to allow them to browse. Then they threw their blanket rolls on the ground in a grove of trees.

They sat up for a bit, eating cheese and bread, passing one of the wineskins back and forth until it was empty. Lila ached all over, courtesy of the rough and tumble in Stokes and from riding horseback cross-country for the first time that season. Ash sat with his back against the trunk of a tree, one knee bent, the other leg straight. He said little, though she noticed he was favoring his arm.

By the time they'd finished the wine, Lila could scarcely keep her eyes open.

"I'll take first watch," Ash offered.

Lila shook her head. "I'll be fine," she mumbled, her lips oddly numb. "You've got to be exhausted from loss of blood and having the flash sucked out of you and all. Let me just get up and walk around a bit. That'll wake me up."

"Hey," Ash said, putting a hand on her arm. "Go to sleep. You don't have to be the hero every single time."

"All right." Lila yawned. "But wake me up at midday and I'll take over." She slid into her bedroll and was immediately asleep.

When Lila awoke, shivering, the sun was low on the horizon, the light nearly gone. It took her two tries to sit up, and then her head spun so that she had to brace herself with her hands. She was stiff and sore from lying too long on the ground, half-covered in leaves, and her mouth tasted like the floor of an unmucked stall.

"Ash?" She looked around the clearing, and the motion nearly put her flat on her back again. "Ash!" she said, a little louder. Brady stood a short distance away, looking at her, ears pricked forward, still chewing. The other horse was gone. A scrap of chamois was pinned to a nearby stump with Lila's own knife. It bore a single word. *Sorry.*

That's when she knew. "Bones," she muttered. "You two-faced, conniving, sneaky bastard."

Lila rose shakily to her feet. The empty wineskin lay nearby. She kicked it, and it went sailing into the brush.

Really, Hanson? Did you think I'd fall for the turtled wine trick? I guess so. I am too stupid to live.

He'd probably left as soon as she had fallen asleep, took a chance by traveling in daylight. Nobody would expect to find him riding back toward Oden's Ford. He could be halfway to Freetown by now. Or on his way to the dungeon in Ardenscourt. Or dead at the hands of the bloodsucking priests.

That was the thing. Lila had secrets, but Ash had proven that he had secrets of his own. Now there was no telling where the princeling was headed or what he really intended to do.

IN THE KING'S GARDEN

Destin Karn dressed for his meeting with King Gerard Montaigne of Arden, knowing that he might not survive it. He knew the price of failing to meet the king's expectations, and he had failed at Oden's Ford.

It wasn't for lack of effort. Destin had it on good authority that ten bodies had been found in and around Stokes Hall—but none were students. Five were Darians and five were school officials—provosts and dorm masters. They'd all been killed with conventional means—if throat-cutting could be considered conventional. None had been killed with conjury, so they hadn't been done by the witch queen's son. That fit with what Tourant had said—that the boy had been training as a healer, and so would be an easy mark.

According to the academy, two students had gone missing: Lila Barrowhill, a cadet in Wien House, and Ash Hanson, a northern student who was a proficient in Mystwerk. It appeared that a great deal of killing had happened in Hanson's room—it was awash in blood. But the two bodies in there were both Darian brothers.

Had the Darians and provosts killed each other? Had Lila intervened? Why would she? From what Tourant had said, she and sul'Han weren't particularly close at school. Nor was she the hero type. Anyway, Destin found it hard to believe that a woman could be responsible for so much bloodshed. The king had ordered him to keep Lila away from the killing field as a precaution. Montaigne had no intention of risking one of his most promising operatives in case a sudden attack of citizenship prompted her to intervene.

The irony was that Destin was the one who had recruited Lila—he'd been her handler for the past two years. But now, more and more, she interacted directly with the king. Destin didn't like losing control of that relationship.

He never should have allowed her to leave the party—he knew that now. If Lila and sul'Han were both dead, Destin had failed. If they were both alive, Destin had failed.

There had been just one verified student casualty. Renard Tourant, an Ardenine cadet, went missing that night and was found floating in the Tamron River a few days later, apparently drowned. Destin wished he'd been able to take a little more time dispatching that blundering fool, but he'd been in a bit of a hurry to get out of town before anyone thought to question Denis Rochefort, a visitor from Arden.

It was possible that the scheme had succeeded. It was possible that there had been more than five Darians, and that the survivors had carried the bodies of Barrowhill and sul'Han away for one of their ghastly rituals. They were blood-hungry bastards, always fighting like jackals over who got to do the deed. Destin preferred a more dispassionate approach to killing. It was sometimes necessary, but Destin didn't enjoy it as a rule.

It was *possible*, but Destin didn't believe it. He'd been promised proof of the kill that he could take back with him to Ardenscourt, but had not received it. According to his sources, the two missing students had not surfaced, alive or dead, in Arden or the Fells, in the weeks since.

Destin suspected that it was only that bit of hopeful ambiguity that had kept him alive this long. That, and the fact that the deans at Oden's Ford had been unable to prove that Arden was behind it.

Oh, they suspected plenty. The Darian Guild was tied to the Church of Malthus, the state church of the Ardenine Empire. The king of Arden had long claimed the right to search the academy campus for saboteurs, spies, and contraband, though he'd never before tried to exercise that right. The administration at Oden's Ford sent stern letters to the king and to the principia of the Church of Malthus, demanding to know what, if anything, they knew about the violation of the peace. Since it appeared that those responsible had fled into Arden, they further demanded that the culprits be apprehended and returned to the academy for trial.

Agents of the church and the empire denied any knowledge of the attack at the academy. They pointed out that Arden had no reason to attack students at Oden's Ford, assuming that the school was not harboring enemies of the state. They suggested that they look to the north for the guilty parties. After all, one of the victims was a citizen of Arden. Perhaps the two missing students were responsible for the killings. The king of Arden offered to station soldiers at Oden's Ford to protect students and faculty if the academy requested it.

The academy declined.

The king had made his displeasure known since that day. Though just eighteen, Destin had been considered a rising star and a favorite of the king's—until Oden's Ford. He hadn't had an audience with Montaigne or an assignment from him since. Destin had little to do but worry that the king might show his displeasure in a more concrete way. Some nights, as he lay awake in the stifling heat of the season they called autumn in the south, he considered fleeing the country.

His father had anticipated that he might run, and issued a preemptive warning. "There's no going back from that.

The king has a long memory, and Arden has a long reach. It won't be long before the king controls all of the Seven Realms. What are you going to do then—try your luck in Carthis?" The look in his father's eyes was a threat and a warning and a dare all in one.

And so, finally—this meeting, after weeks of silence. Why now? Destin guessed that the king had reached a decision about his future.

So—what's proper dress for one's own execution? Destin wasn't prone to elaborate attire. If he had been, his father would have beaten it out of him long ago. Still, he knew how to present himself well when the occasion demanded it. Black was always in good taste. He dressed head to toe in fine black wool with leather trim. His shirt bore lace at the collar and cuffs. His boots and sword-belt were plain, but made of the finest leather. His amulet was tucked discreetly inside his shirt, where it wouldn't be seen, but it would absorb mana'in, the demonic energy that oozed from him, day and night, like the seepage from a sulfurous spring. Best not to fling that in the king's face, on top of everything else.

Being gifted was a double-edged sword in the south. It made Destin and his father useful to the king, but it also made them vulnerable. The Church of Malthus had a habit of burning uncollared wizards, and the king had a habit of letting them do it. Montaigne viewed the gifted in his employ as a necessary evil.

Destin studied his image in the glass inside his wardrobe, and was satisfied. This will do to be buried in, he thought. Assuming there is enough left to be buried. With that, he went to find his father, who, for once, would be in his apartments.

Marin Karn might be general of the Ardenine armies, with quarters in the palace itself, and estates on Ardenswater and at Baston Bay, but when he was in the capital, he could often be found playing cards and drinking in the common room of the barracks, where Destin always felt out of place.

Destin saluted the brace of soldiers in front of his father's door. "Can you let the general know I'm here?"

That word was conveyed, and Destin was duly admitted to the first waiting room—the first circle in the maze that would eventually lead to his father.

When he was finally ushered into his father's privy chamber, he found the general half-dressed, in the process of stripping off his linen shirt. "Fetch me another," he ordered, dropping the shirt on the floor. "I've sweated through two of these already. All of this traveling from the arse-puckering borderlands to the ovens of Bruinswallow will be the death of me."

Promises, promises. Destin crossed to the wardrobe and chose another shirt, then played valet, helping Karn into it. Fetching a towel, he blotted sweat from his father's face and neck. Karn slapped the towel away.

"Stop that," he said. "A man sweats. But maybe you wouldn't know that."

Destin could tell that his father was nervous because he was being nastier than usual. Which meant he was worried about this meeting between his son and the king. Worried that his own position was precarious enough without collateral damage from the failures of his son.

At last, the general was committed, laced into his final choice of shirts. Destin handed him his uniform tunic.

"Belt first. Then the jacket," Karn said through gritted teeth. "Are you ever going to get that straight?"

"I'm sorry, sir," Destin said stiffly. "I don't often wear a uniform myself, so—"

"Oh, that's right," Karn said, as if it had just occurred to him. "You don't."

Destin clenched his teeth. They could never seem to have a conversation without a dig from his father. Instead of the army, Destin had chosen the clandestine service, which reported directly to the king. Though his rank was lieutenant, he wasn't a real soldier in his father's eyes. Plus, his father didn't like Destin being out from under his direct supervision.

Destin, on the other hand, liked it very much.

The bells of the cathedral church bonged the quarter hour.

"It's nearly time to go," Destin said. "Do you have any advice?" That, in fact, was why he'd come. Somehow, his father had managed to survive thirty years in service to this king. He must have developed some sort of strategy.

"Stop quaking like a girl," Karn said, his usual disappointment plain on his face.

"You are mistaken, General," Destin said evenly. "I am not quaking. Merely concerned."

Karn snorted. "If the king means to kill you, you'll never see it coming. So relax."

That wasn't exactly helpful.

"Second thing, whatever the king asks you to do, say yes. If he asks you to dig up your mother and hang her body from the ramparts, say yes. If he wants you to make him a coat from the carcasses of kittens, your answer is yes. If he wants you to kiss his royal ass, say yes. Am I clear?"

"Yes," Destin said. Then couldn't help adding, "And if he asks me to kill you? Should I say yes to that as well?"

Their eyes met. Held. Then Karn barked out a bitter laugh. "By all means, boy, do the deed if you think you can pull it off. If you say no, the king will find someone else to kill us both. One of us may as well come out of it alive."

Destin and the king were to meet in the royal gardens. King Gerard liked the garden for discussing what he called "delicate matters," like assassinations, kidnappings, betrayals, and the like. When it came to keeping secrets, there were fewer eyes and ears in the garden than in the palace.

It was also a good place for *acting* on delicate matters. There was always a risk that if you went into the garden, you wouldn't come out again.

Destin awaited the king in the private courtyard that led out to the royal gardens. A raw wind from the north brought the promise of the season they called winter in the south. He shivered, regretting that he hadn't dressed more warmly.

Finally, a half hour past their meeting time, Montaigne descended the steps from the terrace, wearing a nondescript woolen cloak, a hood covering his damp-sand hair. He was accompanied by a tall, rangy girl in prim scribe blue.

It was Lila Barrowhill.

For a long moment all Destin could do was gape. Until he remembered himself, closed his mouth, and went down on one knee.

Well. That answered one question, at least—she was still alive.

"Lieutenant Karn," Montaigne said, waving him to his feet. His cold gaze flicked over Destin, stinging his skin like tiny needles. "Lila and I were just talking about you."

"Karn!" Lila said heartily. "I've wondered where you've been. How are you?"

Destin swallowed hard. "Never better," he lied. He met Lila's gaze. "It's good to see you looking so well." No lie there.

She raised an eyebrow. "As opposed to dead?"

"As opposed to dead, yes," Destin said. "When you disappeared after that unfortunate incident in your dormitory, I feared the worst."

"As I told His Majesty, I feared the worst as well," Lila said.

"As you know, the son of one of our military officers died that night," Montaigne said. "Colonel Tourant has been pressing for an inquiry. Lila agreed to answer some of his questions about what happened."

Destin stared into Lila's face, trying to read it. So there had been a meeting—one he had not been invited to. That was never a good sign.

"Wonderful," Destin said. "I stand ready to be enlightened." He fought the temptation to locate the dagger hidden under the black wool of his tunic or bolt like a deer through the garden.

What had she told the king? Was he dead or alive?

Lila leaned against the courtyard pillar. "I think you already know part of the story," she said, "so I'll make it short. When I returned to the dormitory, there were dead bodies all over, and Hanson was missing. I worried that he might be out hunting for me."

"For you?" Destin stared at her.

"I blame myself. I knew he was high-strung and entitled, but I thought he understood that there would never be anything between us." She sighed. "It's not like we had anything in common—no chemistry at all. He was all, study study study, talk talk talk, and, as you know, I like to have a good time."

"Yes," Destin said, like a dolt.

"He fancied himself a theologian." Lila rolled her eyes. "Always ranting about the evil Church of Malthus and how somebody ought to keep the crows—the Malthusian priests, I mean—away from the Ford. He kept nagging me to join his little band of fanatics and blow up churches and such."

She slid an apologetic look at the king. "I know you are a man of faith, Your Majesty," she said, without a hint of irony, "but I'm just not interested in religious debates. Besides, I can't afford to get into any more trouble at school."

"Of course," King Gerard said, his face all sympathetic understanding.

Destin cleared his throat. "Young Hanson sounds . . . tiresome."

Lila nodded. "That's what I thought—he was tiresome, but all talk and no action. Lately, he'd been chewing a lot of razorleaf so he could stay awake to study, and he got to acting crazy again. So I finally told him off—the night of Tourant's party. I knew he was pissed. But I never expected this." She shook her head sadly.

Destin was lost. "You never expected—?"

"I never expected him to start massacring priests," Lila said.

Blood of the martyrs. She thinks sul'Han did the killings? Seriously? Destin studied her face. He saw no evidence of deceit, but he was beginning to realize that Lila was a master liar.

Well, he wasn't going to call her on it in front of the king. Especially since Montaigne seemed willing to go along.

"So," Destin said, rubbing his chin. "It was Hanson that did it?"

Lila shrugged. "That's my guess, though I don't know how he would have lured priests to the dormitory. I was confused, at first, because he didn't use sorcery to kill them. But I think maybe he was trying to prove something—that he could get things done without magic."

"Because—?" Destin cocked his head.

She flushed. "Because, well, I told him that I don't really, you know, consort with mages—no offense, Lieutenant."

"None taken," Destin said. "So. Hanson wasn't among the bodies, then . . . ?"

"I didn't see him, but I didn't do a thorough search," Lila said. "Like I said, I was worried he might come after me. Plus, I had other plans, and I was afraid I'd be stuck there till Solstice, answering questions. So I left. Hopefully it'll all blow over before next term."

"We share that hope," Destin said. He was still trying to get his arms around the fact that Lila Barrowhill had, in all likelihood, saved his life by surviving. Even better, she had deflected blame from Arden by suggesting that "Ash Hanson" had been responsible for the killing. The only way this disaster could have a better outcome would be if she'd shown up carrying the mageling's head and an apology from the academy.

Destin cast about for something to say, some way to repay the favor. "I look forward to working with you again this winter," he said. "As I told you the last time we met, there are—"

"Actually, I have other plans for you," the king broke in, sending Destin's gut into turmoil once again. "That will be all, Lila. I need to speak with the lieutenant in private."

They both watched her as she walked away.

"That was a remarkable story," King Gerard said, when she was out of earshot. "Do you think she really believes any of it?"

"It's a plausible story, at least," Destin said. "The mage, sul'Han, was a loner at school, which makes sense for a person trying to hide his real identity. He spent a lot of time with a Voyageur, a hedge witch named Taliesin Beaugarde."

Montaigne's mouth twisted. "Voyageurs are like rats. Despite all of our efforts to exterminate them, they keep coming back. They are impossible to civilize."

Impossible to control, you mean, Destin thought. "We tried to find Beaugarde after the killings so we could question her, but she's disappeared as well. That seems suspicious. I'd not heard sul'Han was a zealot, but maybe he picked up some radical ideas from the witch. If so, that's good for us."

"The deans at the academy don't seem to be aware of any of this," the king said. "At least, they're not following that line of investigation."

"I think they decided up front that Arden was responsible and so they haven't looked further. Besides, apparently Lila didn't report any of this history before she left." He paused. "I would advise against sharing it with the school authorities. If she's to be of use to us, it's best if she isn't connected to us in any way."

The king considered this for a moment. "I agree," he said. "The deans have their suspicions, but they can't prove anything. As long as they continue to accept and train our cadets, I don't care what they think."

"Yes, Your Majesty," Destin said, beginning to hope that he might have dodged the heavy hand of the king's justice.

"What do you think of Lila?" the king asked abruptly.

That was a loaded question if Destin ever heard one. "She's been reliable so far," he said. "She knows everyone at Oden's Ford, and nothing happens that escapes her notice."

"The war will not be won at Oden's Ford."

"Maybe not," Destin said, "but the academy is a crossroads. Lila travels all over the Seven Realms, she speaks multiple languages, she fits in everywhere, and thus far the information she's provided has been on the mark."

"What is her reputation at school? Was she really as poor a student as she would have us believe?"

"She's in Wien House, as you know. Tourant was her class commander, and he had nothing good to say about her. She's been brought up before the deans several times.

Tourant claimed that it's only the drop in enrollment at the academy that has kept her from being expelled permanently."

"Perhaps the girl cannot help it," the king mused. "I've never believed that women are well suited for the military. But she also could be playing a part for our benefit. What do you think?"

"The military is all about rules, and that's not a good fit for Lila. Besides, I think Tourant was a fool. We're better off that he fell into the river before he could reproduce."

The king threw back his head and laughed. "Ah, Karn, I have missed our conversations. It's just that there are so many claims on my time."

"Of course, Your Majesty."

"What's the girl's background?"

Destin realized that this was more than an interest in Lila—it was a test of his investigative skills.

"She's a war orphan. She grew up in the Southern Islands, raised by an aunt. Then joined another aunt in a smuggling operation along the east coast. It's a family business."

"What is a smuggler doing at Oden's Ford?"

"It seems that her family keeps sending her back there, hoping she can make good connections with high-ups in the military."

"And so she has," Montaigne said, "on your recommendation."

"I interrogated her under persuasion when I brought

her on," Destin said. "The story she told checks out."

"I do enjoy having her at court," the king said. "She came to dinner last night, and had the entire table in stitches. Even Lord Matelon."

"Lila is a reckless wit," Destin said. "She says things other people think but don't say out loud." That was always a risk around the king. Montaigne found that kind of candor amusing—until he didn't.

"I'll need convincing that she can come through with the magecraft we're needing. I don't want an army of uncollared mages running amok in the empire."

"I have people in Baston Bay, at Watergate, and in the Southern Islands," Destin said. "I'll see what else I can find out."

Maybe Lila will be the king's new protégée, Destin thought. The king had a habit of elevating commoners to positions of power at court. They tended to be more beholden and compliant than the nobility, who were used to wielding power on their own.

But would he choose a woman for his inner circle? That would be unprecedented.

The king had a habit of playing courtiers against each other. Perhaps it was nothing more than that. Destin liked Lila, too, but he didn't trust her.

"Come, walk with me." Montaigne led him out along the low stone wall that divided the formal plantings from the woods beyond. The trees blazed with color against the brilliant sky. The gardens were still overblown with flowers, their scent rank and overpowering, like the smell of decay.

The king walked on, moving delicately, like a deer picking its way over rough terrain. "Asters," he said, sweeping an elegant hand toward some ragged pink and purple flowers along the flagstone path. He picked a few and handed them to Destin, who let them slip from his hand as soon as he could do so surreptitiously.

Destin had never known the royal gardens at Ardenscourt to be out of bloom. Violas had been his mother's favorites. They were the only flowers he could remember the name of, though Montaigne always repeatedly pointed out and named the others.

Perhaps it was because Destin was always distracted in the garden, waiting to find out whom it was he had to kill.

By now they'd reached one of the many pavilions that studded the garden, overlooking a pool of stagnant water overgrown with grotesque plants.

"Sit with me," the king said, settling onto a bench next to the wall.

Destin sat. And waited.

"You've been to Carthis, haven't you?"

It was good that Destin was sitting down. The question came like a blow to the head, so unexpected that Destin might have stumbled on the path.

That the king had asked it meant that he already knew

the answer. But how would he know? It seemed unlikely that Destin's father would have told him.

"Yes, Your Majesty. I lived there for a time as a boy." My mother and I were so eager to get away from my father that we sailed across the ocean, Destin thought. As it turned out, that wasn't far enough.

"Tell me about it," the king said.

As always, there was no telling what the king already knew, and what lay behind his questions.

"Well. It's mostly sand and rock," Destin said. "Though it's pretty far north, the ocean currents keep it warm. It's nearly impossible to grow anything, so people are desperately poor. That is why so many have turned to piracy."

Destin was ambushed by memories of the cottage by the sea that he'd shared with his mother, the village where he'd run barefoot through dusty streets. Those had been some of the happiest times of his life.

"Yet, I understand that they have very powerful magic there," Gerard said. "They say that's where the mages came from originally."

"That's true in a way, Your Majesty," Destin said. "Mages originated in the Northern Islands, which as you know were once one of the original Seven Realms. After the Breaking, the islands joined with Carthis. They . . . ah . . . they are still loosely connected, I believe."

"Have you been to the islands?"

"No, my lord."

"Do you speak the language?"

Destin shook his head. "I used to. I don't really remember it now."

Abruptly, the king changed the subject. "So. Another marching season over, and we are still no closer to our goal," Montaigne said. "I had such high hopes that this would be our breakthrough summer."

Destin didn't risk a reply.

"And yet, we have gained no ground," Montaigne said. "I am losing patience. I'm wondering if we need a new strategy."

Does he expect me to defend my father? Actually, my life would be immeasurably improved if he were dead.

But Destin knew better than to fall into that trap. "I wouldn't hazard an opinion on that, Your Majesty. I am no expert on military strategy. I have no doubt that we will prevail in the end, given our superior military and your creative leadership."

"I will do whatever it takes to win this war," the king said, his voice low and vicious. "I will break their spirit and I will break their hearts until the witch in the north kneels to me and begs for mercy. She'll beg, but will receive none."

"Yes, Your Majesty."

"I need you to find a girl for me."

This time, Destin managed to navigate the conversational curve. "I'll find a dozen for you, Your Majesty," he replied. "What's your pleasure?"

Montaigne laughed. "Do you take me for a fool? If I send a young man like yourself out hunting, you'll keep the best for yourself."

"Your Majesty, I know better than that," Destin said. "I would be poor competition for a man like yourself." That, at least, was true.

Montaigne snorted, shaking his head. "No, there's a particular girl I need you to find, if indeed she exists. If she does, she may be in Delphi."

"Delphi!" Destin struggled to hide his dismay. He'd been to Delphi, too, and his memories of that time were horrifying. He had no desire to go back. "You want me to go to Delphi?"

"That stands to reason, Lieutenant, if I want you to find this girl, and she is there."

"I see," Destin said. "I wonder if there might be . . ." He trailed off, remembering his father's advice. *Whatever he asks of you, the answer is yes.* He swallowed down his protests and said, "Thank you for your confidence in me, Your Majesty. I am eager to serve."

The king smiled a thin-lipped smile that said he wasn't fooled. "She would be about sixteen years old, and she bears a rune, like so, on the back of her neck." Montaigne handed Destin a piece of paper with a symbol sketched on it, a spiderweb of lines framing an arrangement of triangles, like a faceted gem.

Destin stared at it, ambushed for a second time. His heart began to thud, and he felt strangled, as if he couldn't get his breath. He brushed it with his forefinger, as if he could read it by touch. The symbol was familiar, and yet—unfamiliar.

He swiveled away from the king, staring across the bog to where the meticulously clipped hedgerows ran into the trees. He was glad that it was nearly dark, so that the king could not read his face. "Your Majesty," he said hoarsely. "If I may ask . . . who is this girl, and why is she important?"

"She's important to somebody," Montaigne replied. "A potential ally from the Northern Islands."

"The Northern Islands," Destin repeated, the truth slamming home like a punch to the gut. He turned back toward the king. "But . . . is that wise, Your Majesty? To engage with sorcerers, idolators, and the like in a place that has spawned so much evil?"

Annoyance flickered across the king's face, and Destin knew he'd made a mistake. "Where do you suggest that I draw the line, mage?" The king's voice crackled with menace. "You wouldn't want to find yourself on the wrong side of it."

"No, Your Majesty, I would not," Destin said hastily. "Every day I thank the great saint for your gracious tolerance."

And every day I curse this king's ability to dance on

both sides of that line, taking whatever position suits his agenda at the moment.

"The fact of the matter is that the thanes are restive and holding tighter to their purses and their bannermen than in the past. I am tired of crawling to them, begging them to meet their obligations. I need to find a powerful ally—someone who will enable me to field an army that can bring us a decisive win. Finding this girl just might be the key to ending the war in our favor."

"We will hope and pray that's the case, Your Majesty," Destin said. "How did you learn that the girl is in Delphi?"

"We don't know for a fact that she is still there," the king said. "We know she lived there as a child. It's exceedingly important that no one knows who you are looking for. We don't know what the girl knows. There are a hundred holes to hide in, in Delphi. We don't want her to dive into one of them."

"Yes, Your Majesty," Destin said, trying to focus his turbulent mind.

"One more thing—we need her alive and unharmed, understand?"

"So, we're not being asked to assassinate this girl?"

"Precisely."

Things were looking bleaker and bleaker. Destin knew from experience that it was much simpler to kill a person than to capture and transport him without damage.

Destin wasn't sure just how far he could push, but he

needed all the information he could get. "Do you know what the symbol signifies? Or what she looks like? That might make it easier to—"

"I have no idea," Montaigne said and shrugged, as if this omission were inconsequential. "If you find the girl, we'll get some answers directly from her."

"Of course, sire," Destin said, his mind racing. It was either a blessing or a curse that the king had chosen him for this task. He just wasn't sure which.

"You'll be working with Marc Clermont, the captain of my guard in Delphi. He's a man who's willing to take decisive action when it's required, and yet, still that town has never been entirely subdued. There are uprisings every month or two, trouble in the mines, sabotage, smuggling across the border with the Fells. Recently, there was a direct attack on a squadron of guards, killing several. I want you to find out what's going on."

So you want me to spy on your commander in Delphi, Destin thought. And, he, in turn, will be spying on me. There's something to look forward to.

"I'm just wondering. This girl. Does she have a name, at least?" That last sarcastic sentence was out before he could clap his mouth shut.

Montaigne fixed his glacial eyes on Destin. "Her birth name was Jenna Bandelow. Perhaps she's still using it. Her parents were Bill and Erien. They were old when she was born. They would be quite old now, if they're still alive."

He paused. "The girl may have been born in Ardenscourt. At least her birth was recorded here, but her parents took her to Delphi when she was still a baby."

The Malthusian friars at Ardenscourt kept meticulous records of births, of people of all stations, complete with birth measurements and identifying marks. That must be how the girl had been discovered.

"Why would anyone move to Delphi?" Destin muttered.

"Perhaps they were looking for a place to hide," Montaigne said. "And Delphi would do nicely, don't you think?"

13

THE WAY-FARRIER

It was a nasty trick Ash had pulled on Lila, and he knew it. It was an especially low blow after she'd saved his life at Oden's Ford. The truth was, he didn't trust Lila Barrowhill. There was something about the story she'd told that hit his ear wrong, and he'd learned to trust his instincts. She'd seemed overly eager to join up with him and drag him back to the Fells. Maybe she was looking for a reward, maybe not. Ash had other plans.

It seemed that Gerard Montaigne was bent on murdering the entire royal family of the Fells, whether they were in the royal line or not. That meant that his mother and sister were in danger, and he knew of no sure way to protect them, save one.

He was on his way to Ardenscourt, aiming for the heart of the beast. He planned to stay until Gerard Montaigne was dead. Or Ash was dead. Or they were both dead. He tried to shut down the voice in his head that said neither his mother nor his sister Lyss would make that trade.

Well, then. He'd make no promises, but he'd survive if he could.

He rode into Ardenscourt one morning two weeks after he'd left Lila sleeping in the woods. Unlike the mountain towns of the Fells, tucked into valleys, framed by the uplands, Ardenscourt sprawled for miles across the plains of Arden like a Tamric lady's lurid skirt. Ash always found that featureless flatness disorienting.

He planned to apply to work with the healing service in the palace. Hopefully that would bring him close enough to the king for his purposes. Since most itinerant healers would not arrive astride a military mount, Ash left his horse in a livery stable on the outskirts of town. It took him half a day to walk from the edge of town to Citadel Hill, Gerard Montaigne's stronghold overlooking the Arden River.

As Ash navigated through the twisted, crowded streets, he assessed conditions in the enemy capital with a practiced eye. Soldiers were everywhere, in uniforms of every color, bulling their way through throngs of people, clustering on street corners, spilling from inns and hostelries. Members of the King's Guard were thick, too, in their black uniforms, hands on the hilts of their swords, eyeing the crowds for signs of trouble.

And, everywhere, the Church of Malthus, its crow-like priests swishing through the streets, the keys to the kingdom swinging at their waists. The city bristled with temple towers, grim and forbidding.

Pickings were slim in the street markets he passed, and prices high, though it was harvest season and the flatlands of Arden and Tamron had once been the breadbasket of the Seven Realms. Street urchins were everywhere, shaking their begging cups, crying out to passersby. Ash knew better than to give them his coin—they wouldn't be allowed to keep any of it. Besides, any traveler with coin in his pockets became a target for footpads and slide-hands.

Ash had no stomach for killing thieves. He was hunting bigger game.

The blackbirds grew thicker as he neared the citadel gate. A line had formed there, seeking admission to the castle close. Ash merged into it. The southern sun was hot, even in this season, and Ash was grateful for the broad-brimmed hat he'd bought to cover his newly mud-dyed hair. The line crept along, processed through by a clutch of blackbirds and a long-nosed steward who checked off names on a list. Most people were being turned away.

When Ash reached the front of the line, the officer in charge demanded his name and business.

Ash kept his eyes on the ground so that his hat shaded

his face. "Adam Freeman, healer, seeking work in the royal service, sir." Ash touched the brim of his hat.

The steward scanned his list. "There's no Adam Freeman on here," he said. "As for the infirmaries, Master Merrill prefers to choose his own apprentices."

"Of course," Ash said. "If I could just speak with Master Merrill, perhaps he—"

"Do you have a letter of recommendation?" the steward demanded. "A diploma from the Temple School?"

"I've attended Spiritas, the healer's school at Oden's Ford," Ash said, thinking that Taliesin would be unlikely to give him a recommendation just now. "I've not graduated yet, but I do have some skill with—"

"Merrill is a busy man," the steward snapped, eyeing Ash's bulging bags. "He does not have time to entertain every traveling herbalist who wants to see the big city. Perhaps one of the country estates would be better suited to your credentials. Or lack thereof." He looked over Ash's shoulder. "Next?"

One of the blackbirds gripped his arm, meaning to hustle him on, but Ash set his feet. He was not about to be turned away when he'd waited in line for so long. "What about the stables?" he blurted.

The steward shifted his eyes back to Ash. "What about them?" he asked in the manner of a man who had lost patience a long time ago.

"I meant, do you need help in the stables?"

"Make up your mind, boy," the steward said. "Are you a healer or a muck-shoveler? Or both?" The blackbirds all snickered.

"I'm a healer of horses as well as people, and a farrier, too." Ash patted his carry bag. "I do have a letter of recommendation from the stable master at Fetters Ford."

The steward was already shaking his head, but one of the blackbirds spoke up.

"Lord Pettyman," he said. "Marshall Bellamy was complaining last night that the regular farrier got kicked by a horse and now he's got nobody until the man wakes up. If he ever does. Might be this one could fill in."

Pettyman took another look at Ash. "What was your name again?"

"Adam Freeman."

"Where are you from?"

"Tamron. But I've traveled to all parts of the Seven—of the empire."

The steward heaved a great sigh. "Well," he said in a foot-dragging way, "I suppose it couldn't do any harm to let you talk to Bellamy. But if he says no, you will be on your way, understood?"

"Of course."

The blackbird who spoke up was detailed to lead Ash to the stables. And, presumably, to boot him back out of the gate if the master of horse said no. As Ash passed through the outer gate into the bailey, the back of his neck prickled.

He'd come there on purpose, but still—he couldn't help but feel like a trap was closing around him.

As soon as he set foot in the stables, Ash could tell that it was well managed. The bedding was fresh, and the horses well fed, bright-eyed and alert, poking their heads out of their stalls as he passed by. The horse marshall was outside the granary, arguing with a tradesman.

"This is not what we agreed on," Bellamy said. He opened his fist, displaying a handful of oats crawling with weevils. "You told me this shipment would be clean and free of chaff and straw and dirt. This looks like you scraped it off the floor."

"This is the best I could find," the broker whined. "You try and find quality feed anywhere in the empire. The army swallows it all up."

"It's your job to find it, not mine," the marshall replied. "I paid a quality price, I should get quality grain. I wouldn't feed this to my worst enemy's dogs. Now take it away."

The broker turned away, still muttering excuses.

"Lord Marshall," Ash's blackbird said, giving Ash a push forward. "This boy says he's a farrier."

"Does he now?" Bellamy looked Ash up and down. "Where have you worked before?"

"Oden's Ford and Tamron, sir," Ash said. Digging in his bag, he produced his letter of recommendation.

Bellamy scanned the page, then handed it back. "It sounds like you're some kind of miracle worker," he said drily. "If so, can you conjure up some good grain?"

Ash shook his head. "I wish I could, sir."

"Well," the marshall said. "Let's have a look at your work. Come with me."

When the blackbird made as if to follow, Bellamy put up his hand. "I'll nanny this one," he said. "I promise I'll toss him back if he doesn't suit me."

He led Ash to a box stall in the rear. As they drew near, a horse poked his head out, ears flat, eyes wide and rolling, snorting his distrust. He was a rich blue roan with black points, not the standard dun color typical of Ardenine military mounts.

Ash stopped a short distance away, setting down his bags. He could smell infection from where he stood. "What's going on?" he murmured, more to the horse than to Bellamy. But Bellamy answered.

"He's a three-year-old, and he's been out on campaign all summer," Bellamy said. "Came back in a foul mood that's just gotten worse. He's favoring his right front leg, but nobody can get near enough to take a look. My farrier was the last one that tried, and he got kicked in the head for his trouble. Now he's off his feed, and I'm worried he'll go down for good."

The farrier or the horse? Ash thought of saying, but didn't. "What was he like before he left in the spring?"

"He's a good horse," Bellamy said, a bit defensively. "He was always willing if you knew how to manage him. Oh, you know, like most horses, he'd get away with whatever he could, but he was never mean-tempered. Not like this."

Ash liked the fact that Bellamy stood up for his horse. "How long has he been off his feed?"

"Couple weeks."

"What's his name?"

"Crusher."

Ash raised an eyebrow. "*Crusher*?" At the sound of his name, the gelding's ears pricked forward.

Bellamy grimaced. "He's a warhorse, all right? Man doesn't want to ride into battle on a horse named Daisy."

"You have a point." Ash stood, hands on hips, studying the horse, noting his prominent backbone and ribs. "He's lost weight?"

Bellamy nodded. "I'd say so."

"Has anyone checked his teeth?"

Bellamy rubbed the bridge of his nose. "Be my guest."

Ash laughed. He liked the horse marshall—he couldn't help it. "Maybe later, after we've gotten to know each other."

"Anyway, like I told you, the problem seems to be in his foreleg."

Ash squatted and rooted through his carry bag, finally coming up with an apple he'd picked along the road. He crossed to the stall, moving slowly and deliberately, avoiding eye contact with the gelding. Still, the ears went back again and the roan showed his teeth. When he shied back,

Ash could see how he favored his right foreleg.

"Hey, now," Ash murmured, keeping the apple out of sight. "Something's hurting you, isn't it? No wonder you're snarly. But you know we're just trying to help." The ears flicked forward again and the gelding's nostrils flared as he caught the scent of the apple. It was a good sign that he was still interested in food.

Ash just kept talking, keeping up a gentle one-way conversation as he watched the gelding's neck muscles relax. Finally, he extended his flat hand, the apple centered on his palm, and Crusher lipped it up and crunched it between his teeth, his whiskers tickling a little.

Behind him, Bellamy released a long breath he'd been holding.

Ash let Crusher snuffle the back of his hand, then scratched him all along his neck and withers, trickling soothing power through his fingers, relieving the white-hot pain that coursed through the horse. Before long, the roan was pushing with his nose, wanting more. After a few minutes, Ash unbolted the lower stall door, pulled it open, and stepped into the stall.

Crusher's tail clamped down, ears back again. "It's just me," Ash murmured. "You know me, don't you?" Another ten minutes of work, and Ash had the halter on him and his head secured. After that it was a matter of persuading the gelding that it was a good idea to allow Ash to pick up his foot. It helped that he could all but eliminate the pain.

Unfortunately, that required that he take it on himself.

Fortunately, Ash had a high threshold for pain.

He examined the hoof, which badly needed picking out. The shoes were nearly worn through. This horse had been ridden hard. The hoof was hot, the pulse fever-fast above the fetlock. Puss oozed from a crack along the white line and around one of the nails.

Ash looked up at Bellamy. "It's an abscess," he said. "I'm going to drain it. If you look in my carry bag, you'll find—not that one!" he all but shouted. Bellamy looked up, startled.

That's all I need, Ash thought, to have the king's horse marshall pull an array of shivs and poisons out of my travel bag.

"The other one. Look for a white bag labeled 'horse mustard.' Measure out a cup, thoroughly wet it with water, then bring it to me."

By the time he'd finished with the roan, Ash had a job in the stables and a cozy room next to Bellamy's. He'd hoped to be housed inside the keep, and he'd rather it wasn't next to Bellamy's, but he could hardly complain.

"It's just a shame," Ash said as he repacked his supplies. "This has been festering for a long while. If it had been caught early, it could have been handled and this horse spared a lot of pain. Now he'll be out of commission for months. I intend to give the owner an earful about taking better care of his horse on the road."

"Well," Bellamy said, a peculiar expression on his face. "It's up to you, but I wouldn't do that."

Ash stared at the marshall, surprised. He didn't seem like the kind of person who'd shy away from a hard conversation. "Why not?"

"This horse belongs to His Majesty, the king of Arden."

EXILED IN DELPHI

Destin Karn was tired of looking for Jenna Bandelow. After a month in this hellhole of Delphi, he was no closer to finding her than when he'd arrived. He understood the price of failure; he'd claimed it often enough on behalf of the crown. The worst of it was, there was no guarantee success was even possible. There was no way to know if the girl was still alive, or still in Delphi.

It occurred to him that the king had set him an impossible task on purpose, like in that old ballad where the elfin knight asks a maid to make him a shirt without thread or needle. Then Montaigne had sent him to do it in the most miserable place in the empire.

And if he found the girl, what then? What would it

mean for his own future—for the hope he still carried in his heart?

Destin drained his tankard of ale and slammed it down on the table, the noise lost in the din of the room. The metal left a raw gash in the battered wood.

Marc Clermont, the captain of the King's Guard, laughed and signaled to the server to bring another round. "This place grows on you, boy," he said, "like a nasty boil. The only thing that helps is ale and stingo." He shoved his chair back and rested his hand suggestively on the hilt of his sword. "When things get really bad, I just kill a few Delphian rats. That never fails to raise my spirits."

An impossible task in a miserable place with despicable help.

The only thing that might raise Destin's spirits was to find a way to get rid of Clermont. Delphi was a dangerous place, after all. The thought made him smile, drawing a wary look from the captain of the guard. Destin raised his refilled tankard and winked at him. His mood was so black that getting murdered was beginning to seem appealing.

He and Clermont were seated at a table in a corner of a crowded tavern, but there was a cushion of space about them, an invisible boundary no one cared to cross. The tavern was called the Mug and Mutton, and it drew a mixed crowd: miners and soldiers intent on heavy drinking, furnacemen and ironworkers having a night out. Plus, a sprinkling of travelers who, against all reason, had actually chosen to come to Delphi.

Destin's father had been posted here a few years ago to put down yet another revolt. Destin had come along, unwilling then as now, to serve as the general's squire and punching bag. It wasn't long after he and his mother had been dragged back from their refuge in Carthis.

"It's time we got to know each other, boy," his father had growled. "Your mother's done her best to ruin you, but I'll make a man of you yet."

His memories of Delphi were nightmarish. Aside from the absence of his father, it was even worse now than he remembered. Much of it had to do with the commander of the King's Guard.

Clermont never reined in his blackbirds, who roamed the city like predators, picking off the vulnerable. They used the search for the rune-marked girl as an excuse to drag women into back alleys in order to "examine" them.

When Destin argued that this was counterproductive, Clermont just laughed. "It's cold up here, Lieutenant. The men need to stay warm somehow."

It would do no good to report it to the king. King Gerard was unlikely to buy Destin's theory—that the city seethed with rebellion because Clermont was too cruel as opposed to not cruel enough. Meanwhile, Ardenine assets blew up and burned on a regular basis. Miners had ready access to explosives and they seemed to know how to use them.

Montaigne didn't care about process—he valued results, and so far Destin had nothing to show. If he was ever to get out of Delphi, he had to work smarter. He knew he'd been going about his mission in a haphazard manner, but he couldn't think of a way to put a method in it. He'd called in a whole series of Delphians: miners and shopkeepers, smelters and serving girls and government officials. He'd questioned them all.

Destin was a gifted interrogator, a valuable resource at Montaigne's disposal. That made torture unnecessary for the most part, unless he was dealing with other mages, who could resist his mind magic. People talked to Destin, and they told the truth. And then he wiped their minds, and they didn't remember what he had asked, or what they had revealed. That singular talent had been the key to his rapid rise in the clandestine service.

Yet, so far, his talent for interrogation had turned up nothing of value in Delphi save the odd black marketeer or other small-time schemer. If the rune-marked girl was known, it was only to a few. No one could recall a family named Bandelow, and no one seemed to know anything about a girl with a birthmark on her neck.

It didn't help that it was the custom in Delphi for women to wear their hair long, and most wore heavy black scarves to keep the coal dust out while they worked in the mines or walked the streets. That made any casual survey impossible. Why couldn't this girl have a magemark on her nose?

Sleet rattled against the tin roof of the building. Destin had just finished his fourth ale, and soon he would have to go out into the storm again.

"It could be worse," Clermont said, scratching his crotch. "You could be in the Fells, fighting monsters and demons. They say a man might as well fall on his sword as march into those cursed mountains." He snorted. "The stripers are just as terrified as the recruits. 'Course stripers couldn't find their manhood with both hands in their breeches and a map. Those black-robed crows of Malthus can prattle on about martyrdom and Paradise all they want. I'm not signing on."

Destin shrugged, the safest response. He couldn't decide which was worse: listening to Clermont or going out to the freezing privy. Difficult choice.

"The devil of it is, the Fells is ruled by a woman! They say she wears armor and plays soldier. The northerners spend their days picking wildflowers and dreaming and their nights fornicating under the stars. They're just a bunch of pretenders and mystics."

"So why aren't we in Fellsmarch by now?" Destin said bluntly, thinking dreaming and fornicating sounded a hell of a lot more appealing than where he was now. "We've got to stop believing our own propaganda and take the witch queen seriously."

"Cheer up," Clermont said. "This girl you're looking for probably died years ago. If she was ever here."

"Keep your voice down," Destin hissed, looking around to make sure no one had overheard. The more Clermont drank, the louder he talked.

Still, he had a point. Children died in droves in Delphi.

"I don't know why it's such a secret," Clermont said. "All you do is, you post up notices all over town, demanding her surrender. Then execute the vermin, one a day, until she turns up. Or we run out of vermin. Either way, we win."

Destin became aware that someone was standing silently before him. One of the servers had finally dared approach, but could not bring herself to interrupt.

"Yes, what is it?" he snapped. And then, when he really looked at her, he realized she was young, with silken blond hair and frightened blue eyes. He'd never seen her before, so she must be new.

"I wondered if you all would be wanting more ale," she said nervously, in the soft cadence of the borderlands. "Or perhaps some supper, now or later on?" She set their empty tankards on the tray she carried.

Destin smiled at her, trying to reassure her. "I've had enough ale," he said. He turned toward Clermont in time to see him push to his feet, grasp a handful of the server's hair, and force her to her knees. The tankards slid off the tray and onto the wooden floor as the tray went vertical.

"Here's an idea, Lieutenant," Clermont said. Still holding on to her scalp, he drew his knife with his other hand.

The girl saw the blade and let out a little cry of fright. She closed her eyes, her lips moving in a silent prayer.

Destin half-rose from his chair. "Clermont! Have you lost your bloody mind?"

Clermont wrapped the hair around his hand, the knife swept across, and then he opened his fist and allowed the golden hair to slide to the floor. Two more quick cuts, and she was left with a ragged helmet of hair, like some knight's unkempt page. He shoved her head forward, almost to the floor, so he could examine her neck. Nothing there. "Guess she an't the one," he said, shrugging. "Oh well." He sat down again, resheathing his blade.

The server remained on her knees, tears streaking through the paint on her face, her shoulders shaking with sobs, not making a sound. The tavern had gone remarkably silent around them.

Destin looked from the terrified girl to Clermont, and back again, speechless with mingled relief and disgust. It was just as well he was speechless, since Clermont technically outranked him. After a moment, he leaned forward and put two fingers under the server's chin so that she opened her eyes. "You're all right," he muttered. "It's just hair." He jerked his head, giving her permission to go.

The girl picked up the tray and the tankards. "Thank you, my lord," she murmured, her lip quivering. She didn't look grateful, though. And she moved away quickly. Her hair remained, like pale gold threads scattered on the battered plank floor.

"Maybe I shouldn't have done that," Clermont mused. "We'll be lucky if we get another drink all night."

"You're right," Destin said. "You shouldn't have done that. And I shouldn't have to remind you that the marked girl is not to be harmed in any way."

Still, the episode of the hair had given him an idea. Not foolproof, but better than the strategy so far, which was none. And less dangerous than turning the blackbirds loose on the populace.

"Clermont, could you set up a meeting with the mayor—tomorrow, if possible?"

"Why?" Clermont's eyes narrowed. "What do you want me to tell him?"

"Let's surprise him, shall we?"

A DEAL WITH
THE DEVIL

Lila dressed carefully in her cellar room. It was small, but at least she had it to herself.

Suitable attire was always a challenge at Ardenscourt. Because other women at court were either fine ladies or maidservants, Lila had no template to follow. She'd finally hit on a kind of uniform—an overdress in the same sober blue that court scribes wore. She laced it over a long-sleeved linen shirt and black underskirt. The result was a prim, schoolteacher look, like a dedicate in one of the more lenient churches. Having hit on that, she had several made.

Her dark skin helped her blend into a servant class that was mostly made up of races from the conquered lands to the south. With any luck, her Ardenine colleagues would forget she was a woman at all.

To the nobility, she was a trader and smuggler. They had come to rely on her as a person who could, despite the war, procure most anything desired by people in the south who were used to getting what they wanted: clan-made jewelry, remedies, perfumes, tack and leather goods, the scrying balls that allowed bored Ardenine ladies to look ahead and see their boring futures.

She evaluated herself in the looking glass by the door, careful to tuck her serpent's tooth talisman into the neckline of her shirt. Crafted of rowan, ebony, and ivory, it had been given to her by her clan friend and sometime partner, Shadow Dancer. It had proven itself once again when Destin cornered her and questioned her with persuasion soon after the meeting in the garden.

Then he'd disappeared. Try as she might, she hadn't been able to learn anything about his whereabouts. She hoped he still lived. She'd stuck out her neck to save him, after all. Though, truth be told, she *had* enjoyed his flustered reaction to her story about the princeling's fit of crazy.

Hearing the temple bell mark the quarter hour, Lila knew it was time to go. Slinging her carry bag over her shoulder, she bolted out the door.

She'd been called to a meeting with the king and Marin Karn, the general of the southern armies and the architect of the war against the Fells. She'd not met the general before, since Lila usually came to Ardenscourt during the marching season, when General Karn was in the field. She tried to tell herself that this was what she'd wanted all along—to be allowed the kind of access that would enable her to play the big game. But she missed having the insulation of Destin Karn between her and the king.

She moved through the corridors at a trot, afraid she'd taken too much time primping, worried she'd be late. She climbed the stairs from the cellar and passed swiftly through the labyrinth of echoing, marble-faced hallways, intentionally confusing to the untutored, until she reached the unmarked entrance to the king's apartments.

The blackbirds at the door were familiar. Fleury and DeJardin. Though Lila was taller than many, Fleury could have made three of her. He wore a wicked-looking sword strapped to his waist and the black of the King's Guard. DeJardin was a collared mage, pinch-faced and wary. A slave. Lila tucked her carry bag more securely under her arm.

"What's in the bag, girl?" Fleury demanded. He knew her name, but never used it.

Lila thrust her carry bag toward him, knowing there was no getting out of it. "Have a look," she said, avoiding DeJardin's eyes.

Fleury poked through the bag, smirked at DeJardin, and handed it back. "Search her," he said to DeJardin.

The wizard patted her down thoroughly. He found

nothing, of course. Lila had brought no weapons, knowing they'd only be taken away from her.

Gripping Lila's wrists, he sent a tendril of power in. "Tell the truth," he said softly. "Why are you here?"

"I'm here to meet with the king," Lila said. "We have business."

"Do you intend harm to His Majesty or any close to him?"

"No," Lila said, "I do not." Not today, anyway.

"Are you carrying any weapons or poisons that I did not discover?"

"No," Lila said, her fingers going numb from the pressure of the mage's hands. The talisman at her neck sizzled against her skin. Protection against magic.

DeJardin turned to Fleury. "Is there anything else?" he asked.

Fleury shook his head, and DeJardin released her. Fleury gestured to Greenberry, the chamberlain, who disappeared inside. A moment later, he returned, saying, "The king will see you now." He shoved open the door, and Lila proceeded into the king's apartments.

A map of the kingdom and surrounding territories covered one wall. Large, arched windows at either end of the room were designed to catch any breeze during the stifling heat of the southern summer. It had been a warm day for the time of year, and the shutters stood open, admitting the failing light.

The room was furnished sparingly. A small conference table was set up next to the fireplace, with three men ranged around it, bottles and glasses in front of them, though it was just mid-morning. There were no servants in evidence, only the usual flock of blackbirds by the door. It was to be a very small meeting, then.

One of the men at the table was Michel Botetort, a thane Lila had worked with in the past. A thane whose unflinching loyalty to the king had won him lands and titles at the expense of less pliant nobles. The other, a stocky, middle-aged man, must be Marin Karn—the Butcher, as he was affectionately known. The third man was Gerard Montaigne, King of Arden.

Lila crossed to within twenty feet, then assumed the position. The king waved her to her feet. "Please," he said. "Let's keep it informal. Be at ease."

As if that were possible in the presence of this king.

This morning the king wore an elegant pearl-gray doublet over a shirt and charcoal trousers. His hands were manicured, the nails buffed to a soft shine. The heavy gold chain around his neck bore his device of office.

It would be a mistake to think of the king as an easy mark. An ornate blade leaned against the wall behind him, and even at a distance, Lila could tell that it had seen heavy use. She'd heard from reliable sources that the king was a deadly swordsman and he rarely went unarmed. Which, considering his history, was no doubt a good idea.

Next to the elegant king, Marin Karn was a stocky plug of a man with snuff-colored eyes. His uniform was a poor fit, straining across his back and shoulders. Perhaps he was getting fleshy in his middle age, but Lila guessed it was mostly muscle. He'd still be deadly in a fight, especially since he wore the glow that said he was gifted.

She couldn't help comparing him with Destin. The only resemblance Lila could see between father and son was that they shared the same tawny brown hair color. At least she guessed they did: the general's was clipped so short that it might have been a stain on the top of his head.

Destin had the lithe strength of an acrobat or dancer. He reminded Lila of the clan runners who could cover miles without stopping. Put him in students' robes, and he would look bookish. Dress him in finery, and he would break hearts at court. In peasant garb, he would blend into any crowd.

You have no idea who he is, Lila thought. He's a role-player, just like you. Never forget that. With some effort, Lila forced herself to focus on the Karn in front of her, Marin.

That Karn had been taking his own long look at Lila, and it seemed he was not impressed. "This is your smuggler, Botetort?" Lila noticed that he directed his skepticism to the thane rather than to his king.

"I've been working with Lila for three years," Botetort said, "and she's never disappointed me."

"Really?" Karn said, snorting. "Women disappoint me all the time."

"Perhaps the fault isn't in the women, but in you, General," Lila thought. But somehow it came out of her mouth.

They all froze, staring at her. Several of the blackbirds put their hands on the hilts of their swords, their eyes sliding to Karn to see what he would do.

Karn moved fast, for a large man. Erupting from his chair, he gripped the front of Lila's blues and yanked her close, so they were nose to nose. "What did you say?"

Well, that's a good start, Lila thought. The only thing more frightening than Marin Karn at a distance was Karn up close.

Don't show fear don't show fear don't show fear. She looked into Karn's tobacco eyes and said, "Forgive me, General, if I've offended. I only meant that it would be a rare woman who could hope to be a suitable match for you." She snapped her mouth shut, unsure whether she'd made things better or worse. Stop spilling scummer, Lila, or you're the one will be knee-deep in it.

After what seemed like a lifetime of silence, the king of Arden began to laugh. Once started, he laughed so hard that tears leaked from his eyes. Just like that, the cord of tension snapped.

"You have to admit, Karn, she has a point," he said, swiping his eyes with his sleeves.

But Karn wasn't admitting anything. "The bitch has a

mouth on her that's going to cost her if she isn't careful." He'd gotten the message, though. Releasing his grip on Lila, he stalked back to the table and dropped into his chair.

"Botetort." Montaigne nodded toward the door. "Leave us. We'll talk later."

Botetort wanted to stay, Lila could tell. But he seemed to know better than to object. He bowed out of the room.

They must have decided that Lila posed no threat, because Karn sent the blackbirds out, too.

There was an empty chair now, but nobody invited Lila to sit. She was tempted to sit down, anyway, but wasn't sure how far she could push these two. So she stood behind it, resting her hands on the back. Anyway, she thought better on her feet.

With no further ceremony, the king nodded to Karn to proceed.

"Where are you from, girl?" Karn studied her through heavy-lidded eyes.

"I grew up in the Southern Islands, General."

"And yet, I believe you're of mixed blood."

"Aye. My father was a soldier. He wasn't around much."

"Ah," Karn said, nodding as if he understood, which he didn't. "A sell-sword, then. Who did he fight for?"

Lila met his gaze. "The Fells. That is one reason I am fluent in that language. But I work for myself. You could call me a sell-sword, although I believe my talents would be wasted on a battlefield."

Montaigne and Karn looked at each other. "Well, then," the king said. "Did you bring the collar that you mentioned?"

"Aye, Your Majesty. As you know, I've been able to source magical tools from time to time in the past, but it's very hard to get. The clans are wary of letting go of flashcraft these days, since they worry that it might make its way to Arden. But I do have a piece to show you. With your permission?" Lila patted her carry bag.

"Please."

Unfastening the flap, Lila reached inside and pulled out a collar made of beaten silver, its dull finish inscribed with blackened runes. She extended it toward the king, but he yanked his hands back and shook his head. "Have a look, Karn."

He's a cautious bastard, Lila thought, for about the hundredth time.

Karn took the collar and turned it in his hands, examining it on all sides. It took on a glow as he sent power into it, testing it. "It is flashcraft, Your Majesty. Copperhead made. But it looks old—like a vintage piece."

"It is," Lila said. "It dates from the Wizard Wars. It's more than a thousand years old."

Karn looked up sharply. "Is it, now? Where did you get this?"

Lila shifted her eyes away. "I have a contact who can supply flashcraft now and then. Not just collars. Talismans, magical armor, and amulets."

Karn unfastened the catch and opened the collar, snapped it shut again, tried the connection. "Who is this contact and where does he get the merchandise?"

"I don't know," Lila said. "But he is trustworthy."

"Trustworthy?" Montaigne said, raising an eyebrow. "Is there really such a person?"

"What I mean is, he knows better than to cross me."

Karn rolled his eyes, as if he found that hard to believe. "We would rather work directly with your contact," he said.

"First of all, this person doesn't want to meet either of you," Lila said, feeling sweat trickling down between her shoulder blades. "Second of all, if he traveled south, people would wonder why. As a student and a soldier, I have an excuse."

"He's a swiving copperhead," Karn said, like a trout striking a fly. "Isn't he? That's why he can't come to us."

Lila hesitated just long enough to confirm it. "Understand his position. He's taking a huge risk as it is."

Montaigne splashed more whiskey into his glass. "Well, Karn? What do you think?"

The general fixed Lila with his muddy eyes. "I think a trickle of flashcraft doesn't do us any good. We need a source who can supply a large number of collars right now. If you're as good as you think you are, you will find a way to make that happen. Otherwise, we're not interested."

"How many collars were you thinking of?"

"Five hundred to start."

"Five hundred!" Lila stared at him. "It's not like we're running a factory. And if we divert that number of collars, people will notice."

"Let them notice," Karn said, "as long as we get the collars first. If you come through on this, it won't matter. If you don't—" He bared his teeth in a feral smile that was scarier than any scowl Lila had ever seen. "Consider this a test, girl. A demonstration of your abilities."

Lila took a breath, then let it out slowly before answering. "It'll be pricey. I'll need to be compensated for the loss of future business from this source."

"I have no doubt we can meet your price," Montaigne said.

That's odd, Lila thought, given that I've heard your coffers are empty.

Of course, there's no need to pay a dead person.

"It will take me a while to make arrangements," Lila said, her mind racing. She needed to reach Shadow Dancer, and she needed to do it without risking being traced or followed.

"Just don't take too long," Karn said. "Or we'll find somebody else."

"No worries, General," Lila said, reaching for the collar he was still toying with.

Karn yanked it back. "I'll keep this," he said. "I want to study it more carefully."

You'll have it wrapped around some poor wizard's neck before the day is out, Lila thought.

"As you wish," Lila said. "I will keep you up to date on my progress."

As she took her leave, the king and his general already had their heads together, talking. This meeting had spawned more questions than answers. What could they possibly want with five hundred collars? Where did they expect to find that many wizards to enslave? Was this a piece of a plan to invade the Fells? She had no idea.

There was one thing she did know: she'd made a deal with the devil—something she might regret.

16

OFFICER OF
THE CROWN

When Jenna shouldered her way into Fletcher's Tack and Harness, Fletcher was at his workbench, buffing a pair of boots. Three old men clustered around the coal stove, clawlike hands extended, staying warm. A young man leaned against the counter, waiting for a pickup. She stole a second look. Yes. He was a mage, which meant he must be in the army or the Guard.

The harness shop was one of the few businesses in Delphi that catered to everybody—citizens, miners, travelers, blackbirds, and dirtbacks. Anybody who needed any kind of leather goods—shoes, scabbards, gloves, and harness passed through there. It was usually repair, because most people couldn't afford to buy new. Aside from the inns and taverns, it was one of the best places to get the news. Since Brit Fletcher took it over three years ago, it had also become headquarters for the Patriots.

"Riley!" Fletcher said, looking up and smiling. "I never see enough of you these days."

"'Cause every time I come in here, it costs me money," Jenna said in her gruff boy voice. She held up a leather pouch, the kind she used to carry blasting powder. "Can you fix this? I burned two holes in it on accident."

"Sure thing," Fletcher said. "I'll write it up soon as I finish up with the lieutenant here."

Lieutenant! Jenna slid another look at the young man at the counter. He was young for a lieutenant, if that's what he was—not much older than she was. He was dressed for the weather, but his heavy coat had no insignia on it that she could see. It looked new, and finely made. The bit of fur around the hood said it cost real money.

"Take your time," Jenna said, turning away from the lieutenant and toward the stove, where the three idlers sat stiffly, pretending not to pay attention to the officer but all of them stealing looks when they could.

Fletcher clunked the boots on the counter. "Here you go, Lieutenant. I think you'll find these is warmer than the ones you had. And the soles'll be better on the snow."

"I hope so," the lieutenant said, pulling out his purse. "What do I owe you?"

Jenna couldn't help herself. She turned to gape.

Fletcher snorted. "Clermont didn't tell you? The King's Guard don't pay for nothing here in town."

"What?" The lieutenant looked up sharply. "Why not? Do you run a tab or—"

"You're here for our protection, an't that so?" Fletcher drawled. "So you just take whatever you want for the good of us all."

"I don't," the young lieutenant said flatly. "What do I owe you?"

Fletcher's eyebrows shot up in surprise. He thought a moment. "Ten steelies," he said.

While the officer counted out the coins, Fletcher leaned his elbows on the counter and said, "So you're an officer of the crown, huh? You must be the Lieutenant Karn on this notice here that's in charge of this hygiene thing. The one that'll be approving all the coming and going from town." Fletcher jerked his thumb at a placard on the wall just inside the door. Jenna hadn't noticed it when she walked in. She could read the headline from where she stood.

By Order of the Health Minister
HEALTH AND HYGIENE MEASURES

"I am," the officer said. He didn't seem all that eager to own up to it.

"Glad to hear that the king is takin' an interest in our health and hygiene," Fletcher said.

The lieutenant smiled—at least his lips did, but the rest of his face was blank as any stone wall. "Good day," he said, and walked out of the shop.

When Jenna was sure he was gone, she crossed to where she could read the whole notice.

Due to a recent outbreak of plague among soldiers of His Majesty's army, and for protection of the citizens of Delphi, the ministry has ordered the following:

Item One: The gates to the city have been closed and will remain closed until the outbreak has been contained. All travelers and citizens leaving the city will be required to show proof of medical treatment prior to departure. All permissions will be issued by Lieutenant Destin Karn, Officer of the Crown.

Item Two: Because the plague is thought to be carried by fleas that dwell in ladies' hair, all female citizens of Delphi, ages twelve and up, are hereby ordered to report to hygiene stations that have been set up throughout the city. Their hair will be shorn, washed with a medical soap, and examined for vermin. Each woman so treated will be affixed with silver earrings to signify that she has complied.

Item Three: Any man with hair longer than four inches will be similarly treated.

Item Four: Treatments are to commence immediately and are to be completed before the Solstice holiday.

OFFICER OF THE CROWN

Item Five: Any woman in the city who has not completed treatment by then will be subject to fines and imprisonment.

"Scummer," Jenna muttered. "Plague? You know anybody that's got the plague?"

"Nah," Fletcher growled. "They're looking for somethin' or someone. Just don't know what. Now what you got for me, Riley?"

Jenna leaned across the counter, the powder bag between them. "How long will it take to fix this?" she said loudly. Then whispered, "There's two mudback wagons coming up the South Road day after tomorrow. About suppertime."

"Cargo?" Fletcher's voice was terse.

"Powder, weapons, dry goods," Jenna murmured. "Heard two soldiers talking about it in the Mug and Mutton earlier today."

"I don't know that this is worth fixin'," Fletcher said, "but if you insist, I'd say in a week."

"A week?"

"D'you want me to write it up or not?"

"Never mind," Jenna grumbled, picked up the sack, and turned to go. Message delivered. That wagon would never reach headquarters.

"You be careful now, you hear?" Fletcher called after her.

He always said that when she went out the door.

195

All the way back to the Lady of Grace, Jenna turned over what had happened in the harness shop. At first, she'd just been annoyed at this new intrusion into daily life in Delphi. But now she fingered the magemark on the back of her neck and wondered: after all these years, could somebody be looking for her?

As soon as the idea surfaced, Jenna dismissed it. You've got to stop listening to your da's stories, she thought. There's no need for made-up monsters. We have enough of those in real life.

She had no magical destiny, there was only the here and now. She'd learned that when Riley died.

That night, she bathed and washed her hair, despite the blizzard raging outside. She scrubbed at the back of her neck, like she always did, as if she could wash the magemark off. But all that came off was coal dust.

Her room up under the eaves was poorly insulated, and the wind came through sometimes as if the walls weren't even there. A small stove squatted in one corner of the room, with a pipe through the roof to carry away the smoke. It took the chill off, and allowed her to heat water for tea or bathing. She always tried to end the day clean, and sleep clean. Clean once in a day would have to be enough in Delphi.

Once a day she could leave off the various roles she played all day long—mine blaster, saboteur, spy—and be herself. Whoever that was. It was getting hard to remember. She never saw the girl she really was reflected in someone else's eyes. That girl had disappeared a long time ago.

When Jenna finished with her hair, she lifted the teapot from the stove and poured hot water over the leaves loose in the cup. She never needed a fistful of rags to protect her hands when she stoked the stove, moved pots around, or detonated a charge. Her da said that when she was little she'd pull buns out of the oven with her bare hands and scrape cookies off a hot pan.

Now she curled into a chair and sat, staring out at nothing, the warm cup between her hands. It was a fine china cup; she could trace the designs of blown roses on it. It had belonged to her mother, the woman who mothered her in every way except by blood. Jenna always used the same cup, rinsing it out carefully each night.

She had few things to remember her mother by, and there wasn't much that was beautiful in Delphi.

Jenna heard him knock, a quick, muted, staccato pattern that said he was alone and it was all right to open the door. Sighing, she set the cup aside and moved to the door, her slippered feet making no sound on the wooden floor. She undid the lock and pulled it open so that he could enter.

Her father was carrying a plate of food, sliced chicken and potatoes and carrots with a large hunk of bread alongside. It was a lot of food for anyone in Delphi, one of the benefits of being the daughter of an innkeeper. He set it on the small table next to her chair and kissed her on the forehead. He held her tight for a moment, and then stepped back so he could look at her. He looked tired, and his face was creased with worry lines. They were permanent by now.

Jenna drew in a quick breath. Her father would soon be gone and she would be alone. She shook her head fiercely, dismissing the thought, and he stared at her, puzzled.

She summoned a smile. "You always bring too much food, Da. Who do you think you're feeding up here, two strapping sons?" She spoke quietly, so the sound wouldn't carry beyond the walls of the room. She sat back down in the chair and began to eat. She didn't believe in wasting food, even though her stomach was tied up in a knot. Her father sat in the other chair, the one reserved for him. No one else ever came to visit.

"You need to put some flesh on your bones, girl," he said. "If your mother could see you, she'd say I've neglected you."

"She would say no such thing!" She snorted. This was one of their rituals. She cut the chicken into bite-size pieces and lifted one of them to her mouth.

He watched her eat in silence for a while. When she slowed to picking, he reached inside his jacket and withdrew a folded sheet of paper. He unfolded it and handed it to her.

She scanned it and handed it back, nodding. "I saw it. Who knew that we had a health minister in Delphi? And I wonder who's paying for all that silver? Us, probably."

He didn't say anything for a moment, as if saying it aloud would call the demon. "Do you think this has anything to do with you?"

She looked down at her hands. "I don't have vermin," she said, misunderstanding on purpose.

"What if they're looking for the magemark?" He leaned forward, his face prepared for pain.

"You're never going to get past that old witch and her stories, are you, Father? We've been living scared all our lives because of her. Why did you even listen to her?"

Her father made a sign to avert evil. "She was your grandmother, Jenna."

"So she said."

"I believed her," her father said. "I am convinced that she was truly trying to protect you. She cared about you, if I'm any judge, and she seemed . . . she seemed to be scared to death. She said your father was dead, that he had enemies who would come looking for you, and they would know you by the mark on the back of your neck. That's why she gave you up. That's why she warned us."

"For all we know, she stole me from my birth parents and didn't want them to find me. You are my father, and my mother is buried here in the graveyard. That's who I honor on the Day of the Dead!" Jenna realized her voice was rising, and stopped speaking for a moment. "You are all I need," she continued quietly.

He sighed. "We should never have allowed the monks to record your birth. We were just so anxious to have you officially ours, afraid you'd be taken away from us. And Delphi seemed so far away from Arden at the time."

It was an old story. They lived their lives in little circles, always rounding back to the same fears, the same conversations.

"Da," she said softly. "I don't have time to worry about bogeys and witchmarks. If somebody's looking for me, it won't be because of some age-old curse. It'll be because I've been betrayed, because somebody tipped off the blackbirds."

"That's another thing. I wish you wouldn't . . . do the things that you do. That's surely a job for someone else. You're getting to an age that you should be thinking about marriage and family."

"How'm I supposed to walk out with anybody when I'm dressed like a boy all the time?" Jenna snapped. "Anyway, why would I bring a child into a world like this?"

"This can't last forever," her father said. "Things will change. The Maker—"

"The Maker helps those who help themselves, isn't that what you always said? Things will change if we change them."

"Still. Nobody else takes the risks that you take. Sooner

or later, the blackbirds will put two and two together."

Jenna sighed. She'd tried to keep her father in the dark about some of her activities, at least.

"Everything's a risk," she said. "Is it less risky for a woman to walk down any street in the city? Is it less risky to work the mines every day, laying charges and setting them off? If not for Riley, I'd be dead already."

"That's why every day is a gift from the Maker," her father said. "Don't waste them in a futile cause. It won't bring Riley back."

"I'm not just doing this for Riley. I'm doing this for me, for you, and for everyone who's suffered at the hands of King Gerard. I don't have time to worry about made-up demons when there's a real one sitting on the throne."

"Please, Jenna. At least stay out of the taverns."

"I grew up in a tavern," Jenna said, "and I learn a lot, spending time in taverns—information that can help save lives."

"Why is that your job, girl?"

"The work I do is important, and I'm better at it than anyone else in town, least since Bowman got blown up. I'm not going to huddle in a garret while others do my fighting for me."

"If you can't stay hidden, maybe you should leave Delphi for a while," her father said. "I have friends in Tamron Seat, at least I think they're still there. I don't want you going through this inspection, whatever it's for."

"You read the notice. The city gates are locked until the inspections are over. Anyone who wants to leave has to get approval. And the storms have started, and they say there are wolves already running outside of the town." What she really meant, was: I'm not going to run away.

She remembered what she'd said to Riley four years ago. We are chosen, you and I, and we're destined for great things. We'll write our own story, you'll see.

She'd never considered that it could be a short story with a sad ending. The fact was, she didn't believe in destiny, or miracles, or magemarks—not anymore.

"I'll be careful, Da," she said. "I'll be fine. I promise."

Her father looked at her, chewing on his lower lip. "I have something to show you," he said finally. He lay on the floor next to her bed and pulled out a small chest that was underneath. It had always been there, as long as Jenna could remember, and it was always kept locked. But this time, he drew a key out of his pocket and unlocked it. He opened it and lifted out a bundle wrapped in many layers of cloth. He unwound the cloth, and spread the contents on the bed.

Jenna's hand went first to the dagger. It caught her eye, as shiny things always did. Its hilt was twin dragons, twined together, and layered with red stones—rubies and garnets, she guessed, though she'd never seen real ones up close.

With her free hand, she reached for the magemark

under her hair, brushing her fingers over the stone that centered it. The magemark hummed with power.

"Yes," her father said. "The stones are the same."

When she withdrew it from its sheath, the blade was bright and razor-sharp, as if it had not lain under her bed for more than a decade. And along the blade, runes glowed red against bluish steel—letters in a language she didn't know.

There was a fitted leather breastplate, also covered in runes, and clearly made to fit a woman, and a pair of finely made leather gloves. Not the kind meant to keep your hands warm—the kind that ladies wore to go riding. She pulled them on, and they fit perfectly, extending partway up her arms. She extended her hands, admiring them, then pulled the gloves off and laid them back on the bed. Not very practical for a coal miner in Delphi.

Finally, there was a broken pendant on a chain, a fragment of an instrument that reminded her of a spoked wheel, but not quite. It looked to be made of gold (likely brass) with markings all along the edge and a kind of spinner anchored at the center. It tingled a bit in her palm, meaning it was flashcraft.

When Jenna looked up at her father he said, "That's part of a mariner's astrolabe, or made to look like one, at least." He took it from her and slipped the chain over her head so that it rested just below her collarbone. "It may help you find your way."

Not if it's broken, she thought. "Where did all this come from?"

"Your grandmother left it for you. The pendant was your birth father's. I don't know about the dagger and the rest. Maybe it was your birth mother's."

Jenna stroked the leather armor again. People said that northern women rode into battle shrieking like banshees. "Was she a—a warrior?"

"I don't know," her father said with a wistful smile. "A warrior. I suppose that suits you, in a way."

No, Jenna thought. I'm the kind of warrior who slips down alleys and hides in the dark places. Not the kind who rides into battle.

Jenna scooped up the dagger again, turning it this way and that, so it caught the light. Her mother's. It felt strangely balanced, like it belonged in her hand. She struck a pose, like she'd seen young mudback officers do with their swords. Of course, this wasn't a sword. This was a weapon that was meant to be hidden and used on the sly.

Maybe it suited her after all.

She quickly pushed it back into its sheath. There was no point in falling in love with a thing that could put food on the table and a roof over their heads.

"You should've sold this," she said. "We could have gone anywhere. We still can. You won't have to worry about leaving the tavern behind. We can start over, somewhere else, and build a finer place than this. On the ocean, maybe."

The ocean called to her, even though she'd only seen it in stories.

"No. It's your legacy, and I'll not sell it. I should have given it to you long before now. I know how you love beautiful things, and you've had little enough beauty in your life. Keep it with you, and maybe it will somehow keep you safe if they . . ." He shook his head, blotting at his eyes with the back of his hand. "I don't know what else to do."

Jenna allowed herself to be persuaded. She hung the dagger on a hook on the wall, next to her clothes. When she reached up to adjust her collar, her fingers lingered on the magemark. She traced it, a hot spiderweb of metal centered by cool stone. As much as she tried to dismiss it, there was a weight and importance to it. She had to resist the urge to touch it whenever her mind wandered.

With some effort, Jenna pulled her hand away. "I don't care what my grandmother said. There couldn't be anything powerful about me—nothing someone would hunt me down for, anyway."

"How do you know?"

"Because if there were, the king of Arden would be dead."

THE KING GOES A-HUNTING

Ash pivoted in the center of the arena, cueing the king's roan to shift from a walk to a trot. His paces were smooth, unbroken, with no sign that he was favoring his front leg. Ash had him on a lunge line and a halter, not the best means of control for a high-spirited horse, but Crusher was fast becoming the best-mannered horse in the barn—at least when Ash was handling him. When he called "Whoa!" the gelding trotted over and lowered his head for a scratch, snuffling into his hand.

"Good job," Ash murmured. "Don't get too comfortable. I'll be back after lunch for another go." That had become their routine, an hour-long workout on a lunge line in the mornings and afternoons.

"I can't believe what you've done with that horse. It's like you put a spell on him."

Ash turned, startled. It was Bellamy.

"Nothing to do with spellcraft," Ash said. "He's not in pain anymore, and that makes all the difference."

"Maybe so, but he's still unpredictable around anyone else."

"He's got a lot of bad habits to unlearn," Ash said. "I'll work on that. Nobody should be riding him now, anyway, and he needs to stay on soft ground. Another couple of weeks, we can begin putting him under saddle. Rolley can take over lunging him, once I've given him some pointers." Rolley was one of the grooms, the best of the lot in Ash's opinion.

"And here I thought I was the one in charge," Bellamy said wryly. He held up his hand when Ash opened his mouth to apologize. "Never mind. Skill and talent give a man a certain authority. Now there's a mare in the army livery I'd like you to take a look at."

After just a few weeks with Bellamy, Ash's role had changed from that of farrier to that of consulting healer to the royal stables, the army paddocks, and the kennels. He might prefer to be working in the healing halls instead of the stables, but there was plenty of work to do here.

Still, he hadn't really come here to find a job. He was no nearer to his goal of killing the king of Arden than when he'd arrived, and he saw no likelihood that would change. He was getting to know grooms, stable hands, and servants of all kinds, but he'd not laid eyes on any member of the royal family since his arrival. Apparently, His Majesty didn't spend much time in the barn. Somehow, Ash needed to work his way into the palace itself.

Patience, he told himself. You knew that it was going to take time. He just wasn't sure how much time he had. For all he knew, an attack on his mother and sister was already in the works.

When Ash returned to work Crusher in late afternoon, his stall was empty. Perplexed, Ash looked down the row, wondering who had moved him, and why. The other box stalls were empty, too. That's when he heard a commotion out in the courtyard, shouts and curses, the snap of a whip, and a horse's scream.

Rolley burst into the barn, a whip in one hand, his face ghostly pale. "Adam! Come quick! It's the roan—I tried to tell him he wasn't fit to be rid, but he wouldn't listen."

Ash bolted from the stable, nearly colliding with a group of bluebloods in hunting attire who huddled to one side, gripping the reins of their horses while a groom struggled to control a pack of leashed mastiffs. And beyond them was Crusher, ears flat, eyes rolling, bucking and crow-hopping, doing his best to fling his rider off his back. Meanwhile, Marshall Bellamy was trying to move in close enough to grab hold of the gelding's reins without being trampled in the process.

The rider was skilled, to have kept his seat for that long, but just as Ash arrived, the gelding slammed against a stone wall and finally succeeded in dislodging him. The man fell, rolling, trying to evade the horse's flying hooves.

Ash's first instinct was to let Crusher trample the fool, but Bellamy was moving in again, stepping between the horse and the fallen rider, desperately trying to drive the gelding back far enough so that the rider could scramble away. Fearing the horse marshall would be trampled instead, Ash came in from the side, managed to snag one of the reins, and pulled the gelding's head around so he circled away from the other two. He managed to get a hand on Crusher's withers and pushed soothing magic into him. He kept on turning the horse in a tight circle, repeating "whoa!" until the plunging stopped and the ears came forward and Crusher stood still, shaking and blowing hard. On three legs.

Blood was running down the fourth leg. Not the one with the abscessed hoof. Ash didn't need a close look to tell that the cannon bone was shattered just above the fetlock, the bone poking through the skin. That sometimes happened when a lame horse put too much pressure on his three healthy legs. Ash pressed his fingers between the gelding's eyes, trying to help him with the pain, but it nearly knocked him on his ass.

Bellamy walked toward him. "You all right, Adam?"

Ash shook his head, pointed wordlessly at the broken

leg, and Bellamy's face went gray. "Scummer," the marshall muttered, and looked away.

The rider was on his feet now, brushing himself off, straightening his sleeves. He wore a fine hunting coat, embroidered with red hawks, now besmirched with dirt. A long cut across his cheek oozed blood, and his sandy hair was disheveled.

The rest of the hunting party clustered around him, chattering like sparrows. "Your Majesty? Are you injured? Shall we call Master Merrill? Thank the Maker you weren't killed!"

Your Majesty.

Time seemed to slow to a crawl while Ash's heart accelerated, thumping painfully in his chest. He watched wordlessly as the king of Arden shook off his courtiers, grabbed Rolley by the front of his barn coat, and yanked him close. "Imbecile. I thought you said that beast was improving. He's worse than before." He gave Rolley a shake.

"Y-your Majesty," Rolley croaked, teeth chattering. "I—I'm sorry."

With that, King Gerard backhanded Rolley across the face, sending him staggering.

A red mist collected before Ash's eyes. This was the man who'd tried to bully his mother into marrying him. Who'd been responsible for the murder of his sister and his father. Who'd tried to murder him, and would do so again in a heartbeat.

This was the monster to blame for so many losses. The world would be a better place without him.

Taking hold of his amulet, Ash took a step toward the king, but Bellamy stepped in front of him, gripping his shoulders and glaring into his eyes.

"Don't lose your head, Adam."

"Get out of my way."

"No," the horse marshall said. "It won't do poor Crusher any good, and you'll likely get us all killed. I'm the one that hired you, remember."

"It's worth it," Ash growled, trying to push past him, but Bellamy gripped his arm and held on.

"Not to me and Rolley, it isn't," Bellamy said. "And not to you, either, because you won't touch him, not with magery. He's got a charm against it, or something."

"A charm against magery?" Ash looked past Bellamy to the king, once again surrounded by his anxious crew. "Are you talking about a talisman, or—"

"I wouldn't know about such things." Bellamy made the sign of Malthus. "If you just *have* to give it a go, do it somewhere other than my barn."

The marshall turned toward the king. "I'm sorry about what happened, Your Majesty," he said. "Rolley here was right, the gelding was improving. I don't know what got into him today. Now we'll have to put him down, I'm afraid."

The king slapped his riding gloves across his palm. "Do

it," he said. "The beast is a devil." He turned and walked away without a backward glance. And, with him, Ash's first chance at making good on his promise.

Ash watched him go. Was he being smart, strategic, levelheaded? Or was he simply a coward?

18

LADY OF GRACE

Destin Karn was in a good mood. For the first time since arriving in Delphi, he felt he was making some measurable progress on the hunt for the rune-marked girl. Even if he never found her, he could at least prove he'd been thorough in the attempt. Not that any kind of failure would play well in Ardenscourt.

He'd just supervised the barbering of a hundred women coming off the day shift in the mines. Miners had been especially hard to reach, since it seemed that they were always either working or sleeping. So he'd set up a "hygiene station" at the army camp on the road to the mines, so it wouldn't take them far out of their way.

Over several weeks, Destin had streamlined the haircutting process and handpicked his barbers, choosing the least brutal and the most skillful of Clermont's blackbirds. Each woman treated was fitted with a pair of silver earrings to signify that she had been examined. He'd wrung the silver for the jewelry from the Lord Mayor, who was as corrupt as they come.

He hoped that by making the process as painless as possible, citizens would be encouraged to cooperate. The sooner he got it done, the closer he might be to getting out of Delphi. He only wished he could get shed of Clermont, who insisted on helping. In fact, the captain of the Guard was sticking to him tight as a horse tick.

Destin and his blackbird shadow rode through a blinding snowstorm all the way to town, the sound of their horses' hooves muffled by the thickening blanket. When they finally reached the city gates, they had to hail the guards to be admitted, the result of Destin's order. As they entered the city, Destin realized he was tired of the Mug and Mutton, overfamiliar with all of its marginal fare, and weary of the serving girls who scattered at their approach.

Maybe it would be worth visiting one of the smaller inns, a place they hadn't quartered in. The food might be better, or at least different. He'd heard good reports about the Lady of Grace, in the quiet north end, so he decided to give it a try. Clermont, of course, tagged along.

A painting of a beautiful noblewoman decorated the sign outside. The entrance opened into a large front room with a fireplace at one end and a heating stove at the other. The common room was full. Destin hoped that boded well for the food. Before he chose a table, he walked the length of the room and stuck his head into a smaller room at the back. It had a fireplace, also, and tables for playing nicks and bones.

Destin and Clermont settled themselves in the corner of the main room and ordered up mugs of ale and meat pies. When the pies came, they were enclosed in a tender, flaky crust, fat with meat and vegetables. Destin focused on his food until the edge was off his hunger, and then he once again began to take an interest in his surroundings.

The crowd in the Lady of Grace was more genteel than that which frequented the Mug and Mutton. For one thing, there were women among the customers as well as the help. There were merchants and tradesmen, and travelers complaining about the locking of the gates. A few off-duty officers from the regular army shared a large table at the back. As usual, people kept their distance from Destin and Clermont, but it was less obvious than in the rough-and-tumble atmosphere of the Mug and Mutton.

Some kind of entertainment was going on in the far corner. A crowd had gathered around a table, some standing, some sitting, including soldiers, guardsmen, and travelers. Although Destin couldn't see above the heads of those who were standing, they were all staring down intently, and now and then they broke into laughter, sometimes elbowing each other, as if to say, "Good one." Could be a storyteller, Destin thought, though it was difficult to fathom why a traveling talespinner would visit Delphi this time of the year. The weather and the tips were better farther south.

The party in the corner went on while Destin finished his meat pie and ordered up another mug of ale. Finally, it seemed the show was over. Some people drifted away, reclaiming their own tables again. He could just make out somebody sitting against the wall, and then some more patrons gathered around, blocking his view again.

When his server brought his ale, he asked her what was going on.

"It's a fortuneteller. He reads the cards for people, moves from inn to inn. People seem to like him. Calls himself Lyle Truthteller." She grinned. "Oftimes he tells too much truth, as some have found. But he always draws a crowd."

Destin was mildly curious. When it came to entertainment, a fortuneteller was rarer than a talespinner or musician. True, most of them were frauds—experts at learning a little bit about a person so they could spit it back. Anyone who could truly predict the future wouldn't while his time away in a tavern. Still, they could be amusing, and he had time to kill before the night shift let out at the mines.

When the server returned with Clermont's ale, Destin

put a hand on her arm. "Ask Truthteller to join us." He nodded toward the crowd in the corner. "We wish to talk with him."

She threw a doubtful glance toward where the fortune-teller held court, and a worried look at Destin. "I'll see what I can do, sir," she said.

When she returned, her face was pale, and her eyes large. "He says thank you, but he's more comfortable where he is. Sir," she added, as if mimicking the way the fortune-teller had tacked it on as an afterthought.

Destin straightened, surprised. Most entertainers would jump at the chance to impress someone close to the king. Or would be afraid to refuse, in any case. "Did you tell him who I am?" He turned the mug in his hands.

"I did, sir," the server said, licking her lips. "Maybe the spell is on him. I'm not sure I was getting through, if you know what I mean. I wouldn't take it the wrong way, sir, if I were you."

Clermont gripped the server by the wrist so that she cried out in pain. He jerked her close, so they were eye to eye, and said, "You tell that insolent whey-faced tavern rat to—"

"Let her go, Clermont," Destin growled, his good mood quickly dissipating. "It's not her fault, and it's not that important."

Clermont's eyes narrowed in annoyance. He released the server and she hurried away, rubbing her wrist. Then he leaned across the table. "You're new here, Lieutenant, and you don't know how things work. The thing is, you can't let these Delphian curs think they can get away with—"

Slamming his tankard down, Destin reached across the table and gripped Clermont's wrist. The captain's eyes went wide, and he howled in pain, struggling to pull away.

All around them, the other patrons focused on their meals, pretending not to hear.

Destin leaned in close to the captain. "I'm only going to tell you this once, so I suggest that you listen. I'd like to have a drink in a tavern where the help isn't scared to get near me. I think I'll learn a lot more that way. I don't need you to second-guess my decisions. Keep it up and I might forget that, technically, you outrank me." Then he let go.

Clermont looked down at his charred and blistered wrist, then back up at Destin. "You—you—you're—"

"Yes," Destin said, "I am. Now shut up and stay here." He rose, picked up his ale, and crossed the room to the fortuneteller's table. He didn't look back to see what Clermont did or did not do.

The fortuneteller's clients were a polished young man wearing a fine silk surcoat with a ruffled collar, and a handsome older woman in a well-cut traveling suit. Destin might have thought they were mother and son, except that they were holding hands and smiling at each other like newlyweds or lovers. They did not notice Destin's approach because they were facing the corner, where the truthteller sat. Destin stood just behind the pair so that he had an excellent view of the proceedings. The other spectators took one look at Destin and gradually slipped away, finding things to do in other parts of the tavern.

The seer was a young man, hardly more than a boy, medium tall, with delicate features, dressed in an odd assortment of clothing. He wore a tunic that hung loosely on his spare frame, a surcoat that must have been fine at one time, but now was threadbare and frayed at the edges. The sleeves hung to his fingertips, and bits of tired lace peeked out at the wrist and collar. On his head he wore a large, flat velvet cap of an old-fashioned style, as if he were the scion of an old-money family that had fallen on hard times.

If the truthteller saw Destin approach, he gave no sign of it. He was shuffling cards, and they flashed so quickly under his long fingers that they seemed to appear and disappear. He had the woman cut them, and cut them again. Then he pulled cards from the deck and turned them over, slapping them down on the table in rows. Destin could see that they were not regular playing cards, though they shared some of the same symbols. The boy looked them over, then lifted his gaze to the lady. His eyes were distinctive—a stunning golden color, like a cat's or a raptor's. Destin wondered how he did that—if he used some kind of potion or treatment to get them to look that way. However he achieved it, it certainly gave him an otherworldly look.

"I see a long journey," the boy said. He did look tranced, and his voice had a whispery, mysterious quality, giving the impression that he drew his knowledge from some sacred well within, and not from the cards.

"Well done!" the woman said, smiling. "Garren and I have come all the way from Havensgate this morning." She seemed terribly excited to find out something she already knew.

I could do that well, Destin thought, noting the dust layered on the hem of the lady's skirt, the mud splattered on the gentleman's boots. Garren apparently agreed, because he made a skeptical face and touched his companion's elbow. "Let's go upstairs, Catherine. We need to make an early start in the morning."

"Just a few more minutes, darling," Catherine said. "I want to hear what else he has to say."

The boy picked up another card. This time he looked directly at Garren. "You will lose a great deal of money."

The young man rolled his eyes. "Oh, really," he said. "How horrifying! When exactly will this happen?"

Lyle Truthteller smiled mysteriously. "Soon. Very soon."

"Will I be robbed? Will I have bad luck betting on the horses?" The young man gulped down his drink and signaled for another.

Truthteller turned another card, ran his finger over its surface, and looked up at Catherine. "You are being deceived by someone close to you," he said.

"Really." Catherine glanced at Garren. "Can you tell me who it is?"

"The cards tell us what they will tell us, but not always everything we need to know."

Another easy guess, Destin thought. In his experience, family and friends are always the first to stick a knife in your back. Garren seemed a little rattled, though. He shifted in his seat and looked toward the stairs again.

Truthteller fixed Garren with a penetrating gaze. "I see a letter, addressed to you, from Angelique."

Garren turned white as the snow that was falling outside. "I . . . what do you mean? I don't know any Angelique."

Catherine stared at him in surprise. "Why, Garren, of course you know Angelique, the clerk in my shop in Whitehall?"

Garren planted both hands on the table and pushed to his feet. "Let's go. This is a waste of time."

"It says . . ." The seer frowned, as if trying to make out a hazy script. "It says, 'I'm not going to sleep with you anymore, you faithless bastard.'"

The young man shook his head, his mouth forming a "no" though no sound came out. Catherine was looking alert and interested now. "Excuse me? What's that again?"

"'I think I've caught something from you, Garren,'" the boy went on, eyes half-closed. "'I'm itching where I never itched before. If you're looking for that silk dressing gown, the one with the dragons—'"

"Dragons?" Catherine looked from Garren to Truth-teller, startled recognition on her face.

"'—you left it here, but don't come looking for it, because I threw it in the dustbun . . .'" Truthteller squinted. "I guess that's 'dustbin.' 'If you think you can come back here any time you please and wrap your legs around my—'"

"Enough!" Garren roared, as if trying to drown out the truthteller. "Don't listen to this scummer-tongued devil." He stumbled a bit over "scummer-tongued." "Come, Catherine." He stalked toward the stairs, looking back over his shoulder once to see if the lady was following. She wasn't. She sat staring thoughtfully at Truthteller, who sat relaxed, expressionless, his arms circling the cards on the table, as if protecting them.

Catherine stirred then, seeming to shake off a bit of disappointment. She reached into her handbag, drew out a small pouch, and tossed it onto the table without count-ing the contents. It clanked as it landed, heavily. She didn't look happy, but rather like someone who has had a narrow escape.

"Thank you, Truthteller," she said slowly. "I think you have saved me a great deal of grief." She rose from her chair with great dignity and walked away, back straight, toward the stairs.

The boy swept the cards together and shuffled them again, staring straight out in front of him. The pouch had disappeared. Destin sat down in the chair Garren had vacated.

All of Destin's skepticism had disappeared in the face of the seer's performance. All he had left was a crowd of questions. "How did you do that?" he demanded.

The boy turned his eyes to him. He flinched back a bit, as if startled. Collecting himself, he said, "Foreseeing is an art, not a science. Sometimes you get nothing, and sometimes you get a very . . . clear . . . picture." By now the cards had disappeared into the sleeve of his jacket, and then the boy was standing. "By your leave, my lord." He bowed deeply, and made to turn away.

"Wait!" Destin commanded. "Sit a while. I want to know more about this . . . foreseeing."

The boy shook his head. "I'm sorry, my lord. It is past my time. I need to get some sleep. I work the mines, and we start early." He smiled apologetically. He really did look dead on his feet, drained, in a way.

"You have the day off tomorrow," Destin said evenly. "On my authority. Now sit." Reaching, he gripped the boy about the wrist, careful this time not to grip too hard, or allow any flash to penetrate. The bones were delicate under his fingers, the kind that might be easily broken. Lyle sank back down into his chair. All traces of the trance were gone, and his face had gone pale, as if he suddenly realized his peril.

"Please, my lord," he whispered. "I meant no harm.

Just entertainment, to draw the people, earn a little extra money. I will return the lady's purse, if you like."

Destin kept hold of the boy's arm, studying him. Lyle Truthteller wore no telltale glow of magic, and he could feel no seepage of it through his skin. "I think she got her money's worth. Though not everyone would reward that kind of news."

"Yes, well." Lyle's gaze dropped to the tabletop, and it was as if the lights were dimmed. "That happens. These days, it is not uncommon to be punished for telling the truth."

"Is the magic in the cards?" Destin leaned forward slightly. "Or in you?"

Lyle didn't look up, but shook his head. "Magic, my lord? I want nothing to do with that. The Fathers say that mages are idolaters and devils." Then the boy looked up at him and colored. "I meant no offense to you, sir, I . . ."

"Why would I be offended?" Destin's voice came quiet. "Do you take me for a mage?"

Now Lyle was trembling. "I'm sorry, sir, it was presumptuous of me. I misspoke. You . . . you looked like a mage, that's all."

So the boy was not a mage, but he could spot one. Strange. Was that part of his gift, along with truthtelling? Destin's natural curiosity was piqued. Could this boy be of some help in finding the magemarked girl?

"Lieutenant." A stocky man with a snow-white apron

stood at tableside. A ring of keys at his belt signified that he was the innkeeper. His face was heavily lined with age, and his hair had gone white, but he looked sturdy and deep-rooted, like an old tree. "Is this boy annoying you?" He was looking at Destin's hand fastened about Lyle's wrist. Destin released his grip and sat back.

"No, innkeeper. Not really. I'd like my fortune read, is all. Can we use the back room?"

The innkeeper stiffened, looking from the truthteller to Destin. "I run an honest house here, my lord, and I look after the help. I won't countenance anyone taking advantage of this boy."

Destin raised both hands. "I want my fortune read. That's all. In private. Would you countenance that?"

The innkeeper studied him a moment, as if to be sure, then nodded, as if resigned. "The back room is free," he said, and returned to the bar.

Lyle spoke up then. "Please, sir. I don't think that's such a good idea."

"Why not?" Destin put on his friendliest look, which Lyle didn't see because he was looking down at the table. "Tell my fortune and I'll buy you dinner."

"I . . . I don't trade the truth for dinner. Only for money. And it's dangerous for someone like me to read the cards for someone like yourself."

Destin reached out and lifted the boy's chin until he had to look him in the eye. "And why is that?"

A few freckles stood out against the boy's pallor. He shifted in his chair, ran his tongue over colorless lips. "You . . . you may not like what I have to say. I may be wrong, and you might not like that. Or I may be right and you might not like that, either." His voice faltered. "I don't want to bet my life on figuring out what you want to hear." And then he covered his mouth, as if to take back the words. "I'm sorry, sir," he said in his whispery voice. "I don't always think before I speak."

Destin smiled. "Let's cut to it. I'm not so much interested in my future as interested in you. I'll just ask you a few questions and you can be on your way. How does that sound?"

From the expression on Lyle's face, it didn't sound good at all, but he gave a quick nod and said, "As you wish, my lord."

Destin followed the truthteller into the back room, shutting the door behind them. He motioned to a table by the fire, one with two chairs drawn up. Destin sat, with his back to the hearth, and the boy sat opposite him, watching him warily, the firelight exposing the planes and angles of his face.

"So," Destin said, "let's begin." Without waiting for an answer, he reached across the table and seized both of Lyle's hands, careful not to let any flash penetrate his skin.

If the boy's a mage, I can't sense it in him, Destin thought. And usually there's something . . .

Now Destin released the magic into him, let it flow as if to fill him up, then reached through it to find the boy's mind. And couldn't. He tried again, and it was like searching an empty room.

It was odd, this feeling that the power was flooding into a void, an empty place, not accumulating, but dissipating somehow. Channeling through. He'd tried to charm trained mages in the past, but that was different. In that case, he'd run right into a barrier, a shield that prevented entry altogether. Yet when he looked into the boy's eyes, there was a vacancy there, and his face had relaxed and his breathing slowed. The boy *looked* spelled. He must be. Most people never even knew they'd been had.

"Lyle?" he said softly, experimentally.

"Yes, sir?" His eyes were half-closed, and his head lolled a bit.

"Lyle, what is your real name?"

"Lyle Talbot, sir."

"Not Truthteller?"

"No, sir."

"How long have you been reading the cards?"

"A year, sir."

"I'm looking for something, Lyle. Do you know what it is?"

"Yes, sir."

"What is it?"

"A girl."

"And how do you know that, Lyle?"

"Because you're bringing all the women in and looking at them. There's something you're looking for. It's not plague, sir."

"Do you know where the girl is?"

"No, sir."

"Will we find what we're looking for?"

Lyle frowned. "I don't know, sir."

"Is there magic in you, Lyle?"

Long pause. "No, sir."

"Is there magic in the cards?"

Another long pause. "No, sir. But people like to think so."

Destin blew out his breath, exasperated. "How did you do what you did with Garren and his girlfriend?"

Lyle shifted uncomfortably. His hands became slippery with perspiration. "They . . . I talked to them before, and they agreed to act it out. Sometimes rich people think it's fun to playact. I did it for the crowd. It brings in business. I didn't think you would come and listen."

"So it was an act, Truthteller?" Destin's voice was harsh with disappointment.

"Yes, sir. I'm an entertainer. I don't mean any harm."

Had he really hoped this boy had the gift? Was he really so eager to hear the truth? Destin sat silent for a moment. "What's my mother's given name, Lyle?" he asked softly.

"I don't know, sir." The boy shook his head quickly. Too quickly.

"What's your mother's name?" Destin snapped.

"My mother?" the boy said, seeming flummoxed somehow. "It's Frances. Frances was her name."

"What do you see when you look at me, boy?"

"I—I don't know, I—"

Destin tightened his grip, twisting until Lyle's face went sheet-white and he cried out in pain. "What do you see?"

"I—I see a ship, my lord. You are climbing in the rigging. And a beach. And you're walking on the beach, holding hands with—with—"

"That's enough!" Destin all but shouted. He stopped the flow of power and released Lyle's hands. The boy sat, eyes closed, trembling. Destin regarded him thoughtfully, rubbing his chin, turning over what he'd learned.

"Sir? Did you want to ask me something else? Did I answer any questions?" Lyle seemed agitated, upset, as if afraid he'd made a fatal mistake.

"You did fine, Truthteller. I am satisfied. Go back to your patrons."

Lyle sat for a moment, staring at Destin, looking as if he wanted to say something else.

"I said get out!"

The fortuneteller rose and half-stumbled from the room. Destin watched him go, drumming his fingers on the table.

I spelled him, so he should have been telling the truth. Yet he lied, with bits of truth mingled in.

The truthteller claimed he didn't know Destin's mother's name. But when asked what his own mother's name was, he'd stumbled and said Frances.

Destin's mother's name had been Frances.

He debated. The boy was frightened as it was, and he did respond to pain. He could bring him back in, and lock the door, and it wouldn't take much persuasion to get the truth out of him, if there was more to know.

I see a ship. And a beach . . .

A cold rivulet of fear trickled down Destin's spine. He had his own secrets, after all, and there was no telling what the truthteller would reveal, if pressed. There were some truths Destin didn't want told. He didn't want to have to kill the boy.

The boy wasn't going anywhere, so he had plenty of time to make a decision before he returned to Ardenscourt. Maybe he'd just leave the boy be, let him keep whatever secrets he was holding close.

So. Should he go back to the Mug and Mutton? No. He preferred the Lady of Grace for a variety of reasons, including this private room in the back.

When he returned to the main room, it was still crowded, but Lyle Truthteller was nowhere to be seen. Destin found the innkeeper clearing off some tables. He looked up, and flinched when he saw Destin. "Did the boy read your fortune, my lord? Were you satisfied?"

"I was," Destin said. "He's very impressive. What can

you tell me about him?"

The innkeeper set a tray of glasses on the bar, turned, and faced him. "He works all the inns around here, and he always draws a crowd. He has a rude tongue in his head, though, and some think he crosses a line. If you're concerned, my lord, I won't have him back."

"On the contrary, I believe the boy has a gift. I hope you'll keep him on here. In fact, I insist." Destin made it clear that this was an order and not a request.

The innkeeper nodded, shifting his weight from foot to foot. "If that's your wish, my lord, I'll see it done."

"What is your name, innkeeper?"

"Will Hamlet, at your service."

"Will, I'll be moving in here tomorrow. I'll want one of your best rooms, with a door that locks, and board as well."

"I'm sorry, Lieutenant," Will Hamlet said, licking his lips. "We're full at the present—"

"Then kick someone out," Destin said. "I'll also be needing the use of your back room, for a few weeks, anyway."

"The—the back room? What for?"

Destin forgave the question, since he could tell the innkeeper was terminally nervous. "I intend to cut some hair."

FIRE IN THE HOLE

It was late. So late that the last of the resident stable boys had already burrowed into the straw to sleep. Ash had assisted with a breech foaling of a mare down at the military barns and that had put him behind.

It had been a week since he'd put the king's gelding down. He'd insisted on doing it himself, by using magic to stop the blood as it rushed through the great artery in his neck. It was a painless death, as far as he could tell, but that didn't make it any easier. It was a horse, but that didn't make it less important. It was one more piece of evidence that there was no place to hide, in all of the Seven Realms, where the evil at the top of the Ardenine Empire didn't percolate down.

Ash might try to turn into somebody else—Ash Hanson or Adam Freeman, but the king of Arden would not. He wouldn't stop killing until he'd extinguished the Gray Wolf line.

Ash wished he had let Crusher kill the bastard. And he would have if he'd known who the rider was, and if it hadn't meant risking Bellamy. He couldn't afford to let those kinds of opportunities go by.

Options? He could poison the river, but it was a stinking sewer already. Nobody drew water from the river unless they had no other choice. He might get at the cisterns and wells in the palace, but too many people would die, and still there was no guarantee he'd hit his target. He'd tried to get in to see Merrill, in the healing halls, again, and had been turned away. He'd applied for a job in the kitchens, but in a way he was a victim of his own success. Marshall Bellamy refused to allow a transfer.

Someone else might lie in wait on the rooftops with a bow, but Ash was not that good an archer. He was used to working close. He'd be willing to give his life in a successful attempt, but the last thing he wanted was to hand King Gerard the kill he'd missed at Oden's Ford.

Ash walked out into the yard for a breath of air before finding his bed. It was nearly Solstice, but the oppressive southern heat had scarcely abated. He found himself yearning for the breathless cold of the mountains, where life and death balanced on a knife's edge. Was it snowing at home? Would his mother and sister take the sleigh out on their own?

The stable yard was deserted except for Hamon, the night baker, who sat on the edge of the well, drinking from the flask he carried with him everywhere. Hamon was just starting his shift. He'd be proofing the bread for breakfast in the middle of the night, so it would be ready for baking in just a few hours.

Ash had exchanged just a few words with Hamon, but he felt a kinship with him just the same. They were both solitary individuals, content to work alone.

That's when he saw a slight figure emerge from the keep and cross the yard, heading straight for the stables. When he got closer, Ash realized that it was a boy, maybe ten years old, clad in rough breeches and tunic. He wore a rough jute belt at his waist and sandals on his feet.

Ash knew work coming when he saw it, and he thought of fading back into the shadows before he was spotted but it was already too late.

"You there!" the boy said. "Where can I find Marshall Bellamy's healer?"

"That would be me," Ash said, wishing he could deny it.

"You!" the boy said, looking him up and down with avid curiosity. "What's your name, then?"

"Adam Freeman."

The boy nodded. "You're the one I'm looking for. I'm

Sam, and I work in the kennels. The kennel master sent me here to fetch you."

"Can't it wait until morning? I was just going to clean up and get some dinner."

Sam shrugged his shoulders. "Suit yourself, but if Her Majesty's favorite dog dies before morning, it'll be your fault, not mine."

"Her Majesty's dog?" Ash looked down at his heavy canvas breeches, muck-stained from the stables, and his shirt, covered in bits of straw and horse hair. "If it's that bad, I'll come, but I'll need to clean up before—"

"The dog don't care how you look," the boy said. "If you're going to come, you need to come now. I want to get my own dinner and go on to bed."

Maybe the dog won't care how I look, but he might have an opinion on how I smell.

"All right," Ash said. "Let me get my bag."

When they exited the stable, Ash expected to circle around behind the stables to the royal kennels, but instead Sam led him straight across the paved courtyard to a side door of the palace.

"We're going into the palace?" Ash said, again brushing at his clothes. "I thought we were going to the kennels."

"Her Majesty's dog don't live in the kennels," the boy said, rolling his eyes. "Nobody's going to see us, if that's what you're worried about. We'll go the back way."

His misgivings growing, Ash followed the kennel boy

up and down stairs, through twists and turns where the palace had been added on to. As they hurried down the walkway next to the kitchen, he felt the searing heat from the ovens. Hamon must be in there, getting ready to begin the baking for the next day.

Though Ash tried to keep track of the turns they made, before long he was hopelessly lost. Sam was true to his word, leading him through back hallways and not the main corridors.

Eventually, they descended to the cellar level. That was plain enough, dank and dark and significantly cooler, lined with roughly hewn stones. It was like walking a maze, up and down narrow passages, around barricades and through storage rooms.

"Where, exactly, are we going?" Ash asked, sorry he'd agreed to come. "Don't tell me the queen keeps her dog in the cellar."

"You said you didn't want anybody to see you, right?" Sam said, circling around a puddle on the floor. "This goes under the courtyard and comes out by the queen's apartments. It's a shortcut."

The queen's apartments? Ash's heart quickened. Was there any chance the king would be there?

The air was musty and carried the scent of standing water and old stone. The only light came from torches set into the walls at intervals, but those were few and far between.

After being so chatty at first, Sam said little, except to offer direction now and then. He seemed a little nervous himself, crying out when a rat skittered along the wall, jumping at every little rustling in the dark. Once Ash touched his shoulder, and he flinched away like he'd been burned and made the sign of Malthus. Before long, Ash was jittery, too. He pressed his arm against his side, verifying that his shiv was still in place, and gripped his amulet, feeding it power.

They ended up in a warren of storerooms filled with barrels and casks and sacks piled almost to the low ceiling. There were rows of barrels of the lubricant used to grease wagon axles and carriage wheels, food supplies and kegs of kerosene for the stoves as well. Sam led the way through the storeroom toward a door at the far end.

"I think you're lost," Ash said finally, as they passed a narrow staircase.

"I'm not lost," Sam said stubbornly. "It's just up here a little ways."

"Don't worry," Ash said. "Let's just go back to the main floor and ask someone."

"No, look, I got a map," Sam said, fumbling with a pouch tied to his belt.

"If you have a map, then why haven't you looked at it?" Ash said irritably.

Why, indeed?

Sam turned and swept his hand up toward him, but Ash

was already throwing himself backward, out of danger. Something shimmered in the air, but most of the glittery powder that was meant to hit him full in the face flew past his shoulder. When the trailing edge of it caught him in the face and in the eyes, it was as if someone had taken a torch to him. He screamed and stumbled backward, scrubbing at his face with both hands until his hands were stinging, too. He was nauseous and dizzy and disoriented, his eyes streaming with tears. When he opened them it was like looking into a dense black fog. He could see nothing at all.

"I did it, Father!" Sam shouted. "I threw it in his face, just like you said. Now give me my money and I'll go. I don't need to see any demon-killing."

Ash heard the door at the end of the corridor open and close. The sound of fabric swishing over stone. A muffled cry, cut off, and the sound of a body hitting the floor.

Oh, Sam, Ash thought. You mistook unholy for holy.

He reached out his hands to steady himself and could feel the soft, splintered wood of the doors along the hallway on either side.

"So, mage, I have taken your eyes," a soft voice said. "We'll see how well you do when I hunt you in the dark."

The powder was in Ash's mouth. His tongue and throat burned, and he was choking, his airway constricted so he could scarcely get his breath. He could feel the tears running down his face, but he could see nothing.

Ash kept moving backward, because he could hear the

man advancing, his sandals slapping, somewhere out in front of him. "What . . . what is it? What have you done to me?"

"Lord Darian's stone," the voice replied out of the darkness. "Ground fine."

The same as the assassins had used in Oden's Ford. The stuff that snuffed out magic. That meant this man must be another of the Darian blade men. Ash shuffled backward as he desperately tried to think of a plan.

"I'm going to cut your throat, mage," the Darian said softly, conversationally, in case Ash had any doubt as to his intent. "I'm going to cleanse you of the taint and take the sacrament."

Ash gripped his amulet, extended his other hand, and attempted to send flame roaring down the hallway toward his attacker. He had no idea if it worked or not.

"Is that the best you can do, demon?" The voice was even closer now.

Ash drew his knife.

When Ash could no longer feel the walls on either side, he knew he was in the large storeroom beyond the corridor. He turned and ran, hands stretched out before him, bruising his knees and hips on casks and barrels as he cut a crooked path through the obstacle course that had been laid for him. He moved as quickly as he could, hoping to outdistance the man stalking him, at least temporarily. He knew his only chance was to find his way back to the first floor, but there were not many staircases, and if he took the time to find one, the Darian would get to him first. If the brother followed him onto the main floor, Ash's identity would be discovered for sure.

He turned a corner and slid between what felt like two large barrels, and sank to the floor, hoping he was out of sight.

"Do you think you can hide from me, demon? I can track you by your stench. I caught your scent a few times in the yard, but I could never find you." The owner of the voice was coming closer. "You murdered five of my brothers at Oden's Ford. Now you will feel the blade of Holy Darius."

Keep talking, Ash thought. That way I'll know where you are. But then the assassin fell silent, as if he could read Ash's thoughts.

Ash put his fingers in front of his face and could see nothing. His mouth, his nose, his sinuses were still burning, and he had a raging headache. Every breath he took was like a flame inside his chest. There was no way he could use his power when he couldn't even see his attacker. He would be dead before he knew the man was there. And given the effect of the Darian stone at Oden's Ford, he might not have any power left to use beyond what was already stored in his amulet. He couldn't afford to waste it.

He could hear and see nothing, though he knew the man must be coming closer. He was aware of a rising panic, the smothering onslaught of the dark. His entire body tingled, every nerve screaming, awaiting the cold, intimate touch of the knife. He forced himself to breathe in and out slowly, to think.

Then Ash remembered how he had detected the assassins at Oden's Ford. He couldn't see them in the dark, but he could feel their hunger. He let out a breath and tried to relax. Taking hold of his amulet, he pushed his power outward, seeking the man and his bloodlust. An image appeared in his mind, a bright figure against darkness. The priest was about fifteen feet away, and moving slowly in his direction, turning his head this way and that, as if to sniff the air. Ash couldn't see anything else in the room, but he could roughly place the assassin.

Ash palmed his blade, though he knew he'd fare poorly as a blind man in a knife fight. He would have to hope he could muster enough power to bring the man down. As long as the brother lived, Ash could be identified.

He waited until the bright shape of the man was just opposite him. The assassin would turn in a moment and see him. Gripping his amulet, Ash swept out his arm, flinging out what he hoped was a spray of flames toward the priest. The gloom before his eyes brightened briefly. There was a scream of pain, and then the sound of something heavy falling. Ash didn't wait. He scrambled to his feet again, circling to avoid treading on the man, and staggered across the storeroom. If he were indeed under the kitchen, there should be a staircase off the hallway at the far end.

He heard movement again behind him, and the brother's voice returned, thick with pain and menace. "For that, I'll kill you slowly, mage, and drink your blood many times before you die. This will be our temple for an extended ceremony." The man was still coming after him, but moving more slowly now, as if he were injured. Ash shoved over barrels, rolling them into the path of the hunter behind. He staggered to his left, as far as he could, until he found the wall. Then he followed along it, hoping to find the way to the stairway. In his mind, he could see the shape behind him, mad with rage and need. His groping hand found a small cask, stacked atop a barrel, and he lifted it and tossed it blindly over his shoulder. It smashed on the stone floor, and something splashed against his ankles. He caught the pungent scent of kerosene.

Finally there was vacancy under his questing hand, and he knew he'd found the doorway. He launched himself through it. The stairway should be somewhere along the corridor to the left-hand side. Unless he was completely lost. Then he was a dead man.

At least there were not so many obstacles in the corridor, and he moved along more quickly, trailing his hand along the wall to keep himself oriented. And then, once again, there was an opening. As he turned into it, something sang past his ear and clattered on the stone floor ahead of him. He flinched ineffectively, unsure which way to jump. His questing foot found a step. It was the staircase.

He flung himself upward, half-stumbling, half-crawling up the stairs, afraid a misstep would send him tumbling backward. The blade man was close on his heels, his breath rasping in and out. Something slashed across his ankle and he felt a searing pain. The Darian was trying to cut his tendon to disable him, perhaps still hoping to prolong the kill. Ash kicked wildly, felt his foot crunch into bone, then turned and threw his knife. The priest shrieked, but Ash kept climbing, sucking down painful breaths until he crested the stairs. The darkness before his eyes seemed a little brighter, and he could feel the dry heat from the ovens. He must be in the kitchen.

His hand struck a tall wooden vessel standing at the top of the stairs with a round, indented top. Another barrel. Apparently someone had brought it up the steps, but had not bothered to move it to wherever it was to be used. Ash grabbed its top, lifting and manhandling it into position. He gave it a shove and heard it bumping down the steps. The assassin screamed and then there was the sound of the barrel exploding as it hit the stone floor at the foot of the stairs. Ash sent what he hoped were balls of wizard fire rolling down after it.

He heard a *whoosh!* as if all the air had been sucked away around him. The heat was suddenly blistering, and he staggered away, in what he prayed was the direction of the door.

The door to the outside had been left open to release some of the heat of the kitchens, and the cool draft of air guided him. He crossed the threshold and felt the dirt and stones of the courtyard under his feet. The well would be ahead, at the center. Although he knew he should just keep moving, should try to get as far away from his attacker as possible, he just had to wash the awful dust away and hope. He had heard of blind healers, those who used only the gift, but he didn't want to be one if he had a choice.

He almost stumbled over the low wall around the well. There was always a bucket of water sitting on the ground beside it with a gourd for drinking. He groped for it with both hands. When he found it, he dropped to his knees next to it, grasped each side of the bucket, and plunged his head into the water.

The water was icy cold, and there was almost immediate relief, although his eyes and face still burned. He scrubbed at his face with his hands, rinsing it again and again, opening his eyes to allow the water to sluice the burning powder away. When he lifted his head, the cold water sliding down his neck, he found that his vision was returning. He could see the shapes of the buildings that surrounded the courtyard, the bright bloody haze around the torches in the niches along the wall. Shuddering with relief, he immersed his face once again.

He felt rather than heard a concussion, like an earthquake under his feet, and then another. He sat back on his heels, shaking his head like a dog, flinging water every-where, and looked back toward the palace in time to see one wall of the kitchen slowly collapse into shards of stone. In his panicked state of mind, he thought at first it was the work of the Darian priest, bent on vengeance.

Then he realized what was happening. He could picture all those barrels of lubricant in the basement, the barrel he'd shattered at the foot of the stairs, the wizard fire he'd sent after the assassin. When he saw the bright flicker of flame in the kitchen windows, he knew the conflagration was of his own making.

Then, incredibly, a figure appeared in the doorway of the kitchen, a dark outline against the brightness behind. It can't be, Ash thought desperately. The priest was impos-sible to kill. Ash found a metal rod on the ground next to the well, and wrapped his fingers around it. At least now he could see who was coming after him, and he would have something to turn the knife. He charged toward the man.

The man stumbled and fell on his face, his back in flames. He was wearing cook's whites, not a black robe. It was Hamon, the night baker.

Ash dropped the club and sprang forward. When he reached Hamon, he ducked his face away from the flames and slid his hands under him, heaving him over onto his back. Hamon cried out in agony, but the weight of his body smothered the fire. Ash looked up to see Rolley standing over them, staring in mute shock.

"Bring water from the well, and hurry!" Ash turned the baker back onto his stomach and tore away the charred strips of cloth that covered his back. Hamon's flask rolled out onto the ground. He must have been passed out somewhere in the kitchen when the fire broke out.

There was very little fabric left unburnt, and the flesh beneath was charred as well, with patches of black and pink like poorly roasted meat. Rolley was hovering with a bucket of water, and Ash took it and poured it over Hamon's blistered back. The cook screamed out again, and then went limp and didn't say anything more, which was a blessing. Ash sent Rolley for more water while he struggled with himself.

He wanted more than anything to disappear. He had no idea if the assassin was alive or dead. If he was alive, the Darian priest knew his identity. If he talked, Ash would never leave the city alive.

He didn't know what the baker had seen, either, and might talk about later. But he also knew Hamon would die without treatment, and it was his fault. Rolley had seen him, too, and would ask questions if he disappeared.

It wasn't like he had a real choice.

Ash squatted at Hamon's head and put one hand on his shoulder, where an area of skin was still whole. He grasped his amulet with the other. He hoped the lingering effects of the Darian stone wouldn't interfere with what he had to do. Healing a serious injury was less a matter of expending power than of absorbing Hamon's pain and injury into himself. He closed his eyes, concentrated, searched Hamon for the pain, embraced it, stopped the flow of fluids to where they didn't belong, redirected them, found the discontinuity that heralded an injury, began to reestablish the connections. This was healing at its most basic, healing without tools, reserved to those with the gift.

Time passed. He didn't move. He was vaguely aware of the commotion around him, people shouting, carrying water from the well, fighting the fire. Later, he sensed rather than saw an accumulation of people, watching, but he didn't open his eyes. Hamon was doing his best to cast off his ruined flesh. Ash knew if he became distracted and lost control of his patient, he wouldn't get him back.

Finally, he sensed that there was no more pain and discord to gather, and Hamon seemed securely resettled in his body once more. Ash shuddered, let it go, sat back on his heels, and opened his eyes.

Hamon's back was bright pink, the color of skin that has been too long exposed to the sun, but the blisters and the charring were gone. The cook was breathing, slowly and evenly, like a man asleep.

The light and heat of the fire had diminished, and Ash realized there was still a crowd of people around him. Without raising his eyes, he could see expensive boots, and the well-worn, sturdy boots of soldiers.

"Well done, healer. Miraculous, even." The voice came from behind and above him. "Only I wonder why you and I have never met before." Ash turned and looked up, and found himself gazing into the cold blue eyes of the king of Arden.

ESCAPE FROM DELPHI

Again and again, over more than a month of hunting and haircutting, the king of Arden's words came back to Destin. *Perhaps they were looking for a place to hide, and Delphi would do nicely, don't you think?*

So far, it had done well enough. The month of grace he'd allowed was over. Destin had moved his operation into the Lady of Grace full-time. His guardsmen had scoured the city and now it was exceedingly rare to spot an uncut woman on the street. When they did find someone, she was in for a hard time. No one could claim ignorance, not anymore. Any unshorn woman was intentionally defying the order of the crown.

The house-to-house search had begun. It went slowly.

In some neighborhoods there were five families packed into space meant for one. Tiny houses slouched together, four to a lot: houses where the tenants changed every night, or where people slept in shifts.

The searches went on at all hours, because so many of the people of Delphi worked long hours, night and day. Nighttime raids were often the most effective, because they caught people by surprise, in their beds, and bareheaded, at least if they had heat in their houses. When they found people who needed cutting, they sheared them right then and there. They included the sick (though not with plague), invalids, old women, and the simple. They also gathered up the street people and did them, too. Many of those actually did have vermin in their hair.

Destin didn't care to throw anyone in gaol. The prisons were already bulging, and his goal, after all, was to get everyone inspected and back to work. He made a few examples of people who had avoided inspection because they thought they were exempt. A few days in prison were enough to put fear into anyone, if they survived. Clermont's men even searched the prison itself, because there was no reason why the girl couldn't have gotten herself into trouble. It would have been ironic if he had found her there, but he didn't.

Destin had moved into an upstairs room at the Lady of Grace, which gave him a needed break from Clermont and his blackbirds. Lyle Talbot Truthteller continued to work at the inn one or two nights a week. Destin chose to leave him alone for the time being. The boy avoided Destin when he could, without making it obvious. He seemed pale and withdrawn, nervous as a sparrow.

The weather stayed miserable. The howling wind blew away anything that wasn't strapped down, and the snow drifted, in places swept almost clean away, in other places burying houses to their eaves. The town was running out of places to pile it, even when they shoved it out of the way. It never melted, but only packed down a little, as new layers fell. The snow turned a gritty gray soon after falling, so new snow was only a temporary improvement. Destin cursed the girl roundly, every day, in case she was alive and vulnerable to curses.

Few travelers came to Delphi, or sought approval to leave, either, which was more surprising.

One night Destin was sitting in the common room at the Lady. He'd just finished dinner and begun working on his second ale. It was one of those low moments when he wondered if he was destined to become a permanent resident in Delphi. He needed to find the girl, wherever she was, or make a new plan for the rest of his life. However short that might be.

There were few people in the inn that night. The weather was nasty, and payday was a long way away. Lyle was taking a break from foretelling, and was eating his dinner in a corner, with his back to the room, to discourage any interruptions. When it was crowded, Lyle rarely ate while on duty. He never got a chance. But Will Hamlet sometimes spared the boy a bowl of stew or a meat pie when it was quiet.

Clermont was hanging around, too, in case his men discovered any unshorn women out on the streets. He sulked in the corner, nursing his fourth ale. Two of his men, Hartigan and Virdenne, were sharing a table in the back. They were the best of Destin's barbers.

Destin was just contemplating whether he really needed a third ale when a man bulled through the front door, cursing and complaining loudly about the weather. The stranger stopped just inside with a great stomping of feet to clear them of snow. It melted into slushy gray puddles when it met the heat of the stove. He was wrapped in a huge woolen cloak, and it took him several turns to unwind himself from it and shed hat, gloves, and muffler. He was red-faced and heavy-set, one of those people who create a commotion wherever they are, just by existing. Destin glared at him sourly over his mug of ale. The stranger carried an instrument case that he set carefully aside on a bench.

"Hey, Will Hamlet!" the man said cheerily. "How you be after so many years?"

Will looked up from wiping out tankards behind the bar. "Do I know you, sir?" he asked mildly.

"Why, I'm Hamish Fry. Fiddle player and talespinner of renown. I played an engagement for you maybe ten years ago. I really brought in the customers, if you'll remember. I wondered if you might have need of a little entertainment here again." He looked around the nearly empty room. "Looks like you could use a bit of commerce."

Will shrugged. "We've been pretty steady of late. We have a fortuneteller, and he's popular." He nodded at Lyle, who didn't turn around.

"You don't say so," Hamish Fry said. "He don't look so popular right now," he added loudly, as if that might get a rise out of Lyle, but it didn't. So he bellied up to the bar and ordered an ale.

"I can't say Delphi's improved much," the talespinner went on. He took a long drink and swiped at his mouth with the back of his hand. "In fact, I'd say it was worse than ever. I wouldn't be up here now, but I had some trouble down south."

The man's a fool, Destin thought. He's probably on the run from the law and here he is admitting it for all to hear. He wondered if Hamish Fry had noticed Clermont at his table in the corner. Maybe not. His cloak was buckled over his colors, in a vain attempt to keep warm.

"You know, there's one thing I'm missing that would improve things around here," Fry was saying with a grin. "The best thing in Delphi. Where's that daughter of yours, Will? Pretty little thing, as I remember. She used to sit and listen to my stories, polite, she was. I bet she's turning heads now."

Daughter? Will hadn't mentioned a daughter. Destin looked up to see that the innkeeper was still polishing pewter, but all the blood had drained from his face. After a long pause, Will said, "She died. Four years ago."

"Died?" Fry reared back, surprised. "Well, that's a bloody shame. How'd she die?"

Will darted a glance at Destin, licking his lips, as if his presence made him nervous. "There was some trouble up at the mine," he said finally. "There was several killed, and she was one."

It was odd, the way the innkeeper was reacting. If his daughter had died four years ago, he should be used to answering questions about her. Unless she had been involved in something she shouldn't have been. Had there been some kind of rebellion or riot four years ago?

"What was her name, Will?"

"Her name?" Will had been polishing the same tankard for the entire conversation.

"Your daughter. Usually, I never forget names and faces. It's a gift I have, they tell me. But I just can't—was it Jacie? Janet?" Fry's brow furrowed, suggesting he was thinking hard.

Will stared at him, shaking his head, a stricken look on his face.

"Don't tell me you've forgot your own daughter's name," Fry said, oblivious to the reaction he was getting.

By then, Destin was on his feet and moving toward

the bar. "Will," he said in a friendly way. "I didn't know you had a daughter." He sensed, rather than saw Clermont moving, too, splitting out a little so they were coming at the innkeeper from two different directions.

Will wasn't looking at Hamish Fry anymore. His eyes were riveted on Destin. "I don't like to talk about her. She . . . she was killed," he repeated desperately. "She's dead."

"I'm sorry for your loss," Destin said. "I'd like to hear more about that. Would you mind if I ask you a few questions about her?" He nodded toward the back room. "Let's go in there. We'll talk about it over an ale." He reached out to put a hand on Will's arm, but the innkeeper backed away, keeping the bar between them, shaking his head.

"Jenna! It was Jenna," Fry said triumphantly. "I never forget a name." And then he stared, puzzled, at the three men circling the bar.

"We don't want to hurt her, Will," Destin said. "We just want to find her."

"No!" Will cast about wildly, looking for any route of escape. Destin heard Clermont's sword leave its scabbard.

"No, Clermont, don't hurt him," Destin said quickly. "We need to talk to him." He wanted to get his hands on Will Hamlet in order to spell him. If he could subdue him, they would quickly find out what they needed to know. But Will kept his eyes on Destin. He seemed more frightened of Destin's empty hands than Clermont and his sword.

He knows I'm a mage, Destin thought. He's afraid of being questioned with magic.

Will threw a glance over his shoulder, then bolted for the door. Clermont stepped into his path with his sword, aiming to turn him back. Will hesitated a fraction of a second. Then, with a cry, he sprang forward, seized the surprised guardsman by the shoulders, and impaled himself on Clermont's blade, driving on until there were only inches between them. They stood face-to-face for a moment, innkeeper and guard, and then Will slid to the floor as Clermont, cursing, pulled his sword free.

Then it was bedlam. Someone screamed, Destin and Clermont were both swearing, and Hamish Fry the tale-spinner was shrieking hysterically. The room quickly emptied as people fled madly through the doors.

Except Lyle. The boy stood as if frozen, staring down at the body on the floor, his face a mask of horror.

"Lyle! Quick, boy, find a healer!" Destin ordered, although he could tell by the look of things it was too late for that.

But Lyle didn't go for a healer. Instead, he sank to his knees next to the body of the innkeeper, cradled Will's head in his arms, and lifted a high keening wail, a primitive animal cry of something lost, and lost forever. A voice that seemed wrong, somehow. Then Lyle looked up at

Clermont, golden eyes blazing, mad with pain and rage. He reached under the velvet jacket and came up with something shiny in his hand.

A dagger. The shape of the blade struck a chord in Destin's memory.

Lyle barreled into Clermont, carrying the much larger man all the way to the ground. The blade rose and fell, twice. The truthteller reared back and met Destin's gaze defiantly. He turned the blade, gripped the hilt with both hands, and buried the blade in his own chest.

"Lyle! No!" Destin lunged at the boy, got a grip on his wrists, tightening his hold until the dagger clattered to the floor. The dragon hilt was gaudy with rubies and garnets, the blade dulled with blood.

Destin realized, with a sick recognition, where he had seen that sort of dagger before. He knew that if he wiped off the blood, he'd find runes along the blade.

He pushed Lyle down on his stomach on the floor, straddling him to keep him down. All of this was instinct. His mind was still trying to catch up, to divine why the boy was so distraught over the death of an innkeeper who had treated him with little more than indifference. Why a truthteller would carry a dagger encrusted with jewels, the sort of blade carried by the Carthian bloodsworn guard. Was the truthteller working for Cele, looking for the girl on his own? Did that explain his strange magic?

And then it came to him.

He reached for the hat first, the ridiculous velvet hat, and pulled. It was tightly secured with pins, and he had to yank at it several times before it came away in his hand, exposing a mass of hair pinned underneath. He raked his fingers roughly through it until it came free and tumbled down, pins clattering on the floor. A thick braid that was much too long for anyone in Delphi to be wearing these days.

When he shoved it aside, the neck beneath was nearly black, smudged with dirt or coal dust, artfully so. Spitting into his hand, Destin scrubbed vigorously away at the dirt on the back of the boy's neck. And, gradually, there was revealed, just below the hairline, a shining web of gold, centered by a faceted stone, embedded in his skin. A magemark.

"Clermont!" he shouted hoarsely. "It's her!" When he got no response, he looked over to where the captain lay on his back in a pool of blood.

Hartigan, squatting next to him, shook his head. "He's gone, sir."

That's too bad, Destin thought. I intended to kill the bastard myself.

"Get everyone out of here and lock the doors," he said. Gently, he rolled the girl over. Her breathing was wet and labored, and she kept her golden eyes fixed on Destin's face as if memorizing it. "Go to the Breaker, you heartless bastard," she gasped. "You're too late."

No! Destin ripped open her velvet coat and the linen shirt underneath to get at the wound. The blade had entered just beneath her rib cage. Blood welled from the wound, trickling onto the stones beneath her. He put his ear to her chest, listening for the wet sound that would tell him she had hit a lung. Her breathing was clear, but the flesh around the gash was oddly cold, something only a mage like himself could have detected.

Icy fear channeled through him. The girl was damaged, despite all his efforts to prevent it. Worse, if what he'd heard about this bloodsworn blade was true, she was as good as dead already.

The question was: should he let her die or move heaven and earth to save her? There were things he needed to know before she died.

He gripped the lapels of her coat, lifting her a few inches off the floor. "What does it mean—that magemark on the back of your neck? What does it signify?"

"You tell me," she whispered. "Damned if I know." Her eyelids fluttered, and she slipped into unconsciousness.

"Who are you?" he growled, wanting to shake her. "Why is Celestine hunting you? What does she want with you?" That answer, if he had it, would have helped him decide.

But he didn't have it. Since he couldn't raise the dead, and he had to answer to the king, he'd have to save her if he could.

Though he was a mage, Destin knew nothing about healing. He'd never been encouraged to develop that skill. And he wouldn't trust anyone in Delphi enough to put her into their hands.

He had to get her to Ardenscourt. If anyone could help her, it would be the healers there.

He looked up at Virdenne and Hartigan, who were standing by for orders. "I'll need a carriage and team on the double, and supplies for a week on the road. Also a dozen men ready to travel." He said this, even though he suspected that if it took a week to get to Ardenscourt, he'd be delivering a corpse.

ASH MEETS
THE KING

Ash slumped forward into a bow that put his forehead on the ground. After a moment, he heard Montaigne say something, and then the blackbirds seized his arms and lifted him to his feet, turning him to face the king. He could not have stood unassisted. He was weak and disoriented, nearly overcome by the pain and disorder he'd assumed from the baker. His eyes still burned and his vision swam from the effects of the Darian stone.

Ash had been filthy before he had entered the palace. Now he was acutely aware of his torn and bloody breeches, his hair plastered down with well water, the acrid stink of kerosene. He tried to wipe at his face with his sleeve, but the guardsmen had tight hold of his arms.

The king stood amid a small group of noblemen, dressed as if they had come directly from dinner. They hadn't done any firefighting, since their clothing was pristine. One was a thickset man in an Ardenine army uniform, his hair and eyes the color of razorleaf spit. The braid on his shoulders said he was a high-up.

Marin Karn, Ash guessed, commander of the Ardenine army.

But that wasn't the biggest surprise. That happened when his vision cleared enough that he could look past the king and see Lila Barrowhill, standing behind and a little to the right of Montaigne. Their eyes met, and for a split second, hers widened in shock and alarm. Then she cleared that away, replacing it with a faint, puzzled frown—the appropriate response to a charred scarecrow like Ash. One you'd never seen before in your life.

Bloody bones, Ash thought. What is she doing here, being all chummy with the king of Arden?

He hastily shifted his gaze to the ground, trying to clear his own face of any telltale expression.

"Who are you?" the king asked.

"Adam Freeman," Ash replied softly, keeping his eyes fixed on the stones of the courtyard as thoughts bullied their way into his head. If he weren't so thoroughly wrung out, he could kill the bastard on the spot. In his present condition, he'd be lucky to strangle a gnat. He had no weapons. He'd lost his healing kit somewhere in the cellars, and he'd thrown his only shiv at the bloodsucking priest.

He made a mental note: always carry spare weapons.

"Where did you come from?" the king asked.

"I work in the stables, Your Majesty." He hoped the king wouldn't recognize him and recall his display the day Crusher went down. He guessed in his present state he'd be hard to pick out.

"We have a healer working in the stables?" The king's tone was incredulous. "Are you a healer of horses?"

The rest of the bluebloods chuckled and nudged each other.

Ash shook his head, which was a mistake, since it set his head to spinning again. "When I came here, I applied to work in the healing halls, but they said they didn't need anyone. So Marshall Bellamy took me on." He stole a glance toward the kitchen. It appeared that the fire was entirely out.

"We always have a need for healers, Freeman," Montaigne said. "Especially those who perform miraculous cures. Where did you receive your training?"

Ash looked up, finally able to meet the king's eye and speak without snarling. "My mother was a healer, my lord. She taught me something of it. My father didn't approve, so I am also very good at mucking out stalls."

The nobles chuckled again.

"I see." The king stared at him thoughtfully, stroking

his chin. "It appears you have a gift. In fact, I've never seen anything to match it." He was talking around the issue of sorcery, but it lay there between them, nonetheless.

"I would recommend caution, Your Grace." This was a new voice, and Ash looked up to see that it was one of the king's companions, a tall, spare man in dark religious garb. A great rising sun of Malthus was emblazoned on his tabard, and he wore the keys to the kingdom on a heavy gold chain around his waist.

Bloody bones, Ash thought. It's the principia himself, the spiritual head of the Church of Malthus. Ash racked his brain, trying to recall the man's name. Ah. That's it. Cedric Fosnaught.

Do they all drink the blood of mages? Ash wondered. Or is it just the Darian Guild? He sent up a prayer for the latter.

"This healing could be miraculous," Fosnaught continued, "a manifestation of the Redeemer's mysterious mercy. But the man may not be a true healer." He looked around the circle of bluebloods, his expression grave. Making sure he had his audience. "It is possible he is a sorcerer."

So either Malthus did it, or I'm dead, Ash thought. But he said nothing. He knew he was on very treacherous ground. Malthus could have the credit, as far as he was concerned.

Receiving no response from Ash, the principia gestured toward Hamon. "This healing could be no more than an illusion. The flesh could be corrupt beneath the skin." He produced a thin blade from within the folds of his robe. "Perhaps we should open him up and see."

At this Ash tried to lunge forward, but found himself still restrained by the guards. "Don't lay a hand on him," he said, forgetting himself in his outrage. "He's been through enough tonight. Leave him alone."

"Perhaps the mage fears exposure," the priest said calmly. "Your Grace, for safety's sake, I recommend that he be delivered to my office for examination by the Hand."

The Hand of Malthus was the team of inquisitors maintained by the principia of the church. All priests, and all adept at the art of torture, or so Ash had heard. It was said the Hand could force a confession out of any man, guilty or not. Or, to say it another way, they had never yet interrogated an innocent man. Montaigne often used the red-clad priests of the Hand to punish his enemies, when it suited him politically. At least that was what was said in the Fells.

This church is bound to have my blood, one way or another, Ash thought.

The king shook his head. "Father Fosnaught, I disagree." The note of warning in his voice was unmistakable. "This boy is no sorcerer. I can always sense the taint when it is present."

The principia bowed, his face tight and unhappy. Likely he knew better than to contradict the king.

In one of those ironic twists of fate, the king of Arden had intervened to save the life of someone he'd marked for death.

Odd that nobody suggested that they search him for an amulet. That would have been the most undeniable proof. It was as if they all knew how to play this hypocritical game.

Montaigne turned to his cadre of guards. "Take this boy to the guest quarters. See that he has a bath and a change of clothes. I'll want to see him in the morning." That was said loudly, for the benefit of everyone. And then Montaigne turned and spoke softly to Karn.

Suspicion flared in Ash's muddy mind. What did that mean, the "guest quarters"? Was it code for the dungeon? Had he been recognized after all?

The two guards who had hold of him made as if to escort him away, but Ash dug in his heels. "Am I to be taken prisoner for helping a man, Your Majesty?" he demanded. "Is the practice of the healing arts illegal in Ardenscourt?"

The king looked up, surprised. "No, my boy," he said softly, making it clear his patience was being sorely tried. "Here in Ardenscourt we reward those with talent by washing the filth off them and finding them something useful to do." He nodded to the two guards. "Proceed." He turned with a swirl of his velvet cloak and strode across the courtyard, his courtiers following, like a comet with a long tail. Two blackbirds began sliding the baker onto a litter in order to carry him inside.

The guards had their hands on Ash's arms and he could feel the tingle of magic in them and he knew there was nothing to do but submit. They led him in through the servants' entrance he himself had breached earlier in the evening, slowing their steps to match his stumbling gait, half-supporting him when he faltered. They walked back through the palace, past the staircase where he'd met the Darian brother, and kept going.

Given how the day had gone so far, Ash half-expected the Darian brother to appear at any moment, condemning him by calling out his name. But he saw only the usual servants and scribes, who quickly moved out of the way, staring after them after they had passed. No doubt he looked like a prisoner, towering over his two guards. They were probably wondering what he was guilty of.

Finally, they entered a quiet part of the palace, tastefully appointed, lined with sumptuous suites and apartments. At least this didn't seem to be the way to the dungeon. Windows along the hallway looked out to formal gardens, still blooming with cool weather flowers. They passed libraries and game rooms, all empty of people. At the far end were more modest quarters, maybe meant for ladies and attendants of residents of the guest suites, rows of plain wooden doors, all the same. Ash's escorts stopped in front of one of them, pushed the door open, and stood aside so he could enter.

It was a small, plain room with a stone floor, and brightly woven We'enhaven rugs scattered here and there.

There was a fireplace at one end with a small sitting area, and a bed at the other with a trunk at its foot. There was no window. No way out that he could see.

His two guards stepped outside and closed the door. Ash stood awkwardly in the center of the room, faint with fatigue, unable to put two thoughts together. There was a looking glass on the wall above a pedestal sink. His image in the glass was frightening. His face was reddened, as if sunburned, and his eyes a flaming red from the effects of the Darian stone. He supposed he *looked* like a demon, though the king must have assumed that it was the result of the smoke and the flames.

Ash lowered himself onto the raised stone hearth and nervously shoved his fingers through his filthy hair.

A brisk knock at the door aroused him. Two chambermaids pushed it open without waiting for a response, dragged in a large metal tub, placed it close to the hearth, then left again. They returned moments later with a trolley loaded with buckets of steaming water. These were big, muscular, sturdy girls who lifted the buckets of water easily and poured them into the tub. Then one of them laid a fire in the fireplace, which she lit with a coal from a tin box.

While Ash watched from his seat on the hearth, the servants came and went twice more, bringing more water, and soap and scrub brushes and towels. Then they stood on either side of the tub, as if awaiting further orders.

The hot water in the tub looked wonderful. Ash decided that if he were going to be arrested or knifed to death, it might as well be after a bath. He creaked to his feet, his body remembering every bad thing that had happened to it. "Thank you," he said. "Now, if you don't mind, I'm going to take my bath now."

They moved forward in tandem, like well-matched carriage horses. One of them began untying the cord at the neck of his tunic, and the other fumbled with his trousers.

"Stop that!" Ash stepped back hastily, nearly stumbling over the edge of the hearth, clutching the top of his breeches, which were in danger of falling down. "I can manage on my own," he said firmly. "Although I may not look like it now, I've taken a bath before."

Though Ash had been brought up in a palace, staff at Fellsmarch had more important things to do than bathe him, once he'd left the nursery. That prepared him for his years at Oden's Ford, where students were expected to clean their own rooms, change their own linens, and walk across the commons to the bathhouse. Though it came as quite a shock to some, the school was known as "the great equalizer," humbling the proud and raising up the less fortunate.

After some protest, and with many backward looks, the servants left.

Ash waited a minute or two to make sure they were gone, then stripped off his filthy clothes and dropped them on the floor. Wearing only his amulet, he eased into the hot water gratefully, despite the stinging of the wound on his leg and all his bumps and bruises from the cellar. He sank down to his chin and soaked. Despite his best intentions, he promptly fell asleep.

When he awoke, he noticed to his chagrin that someone had been in and taken his clothes away. New clothes were laid across a chair. He decided he'd better finish up before anyone else intruded. First he washed his face again and rinsed his eyes before he got soap in the water. Then, using the soap and scrub brushes, he scrubbed himself from head to toe, cleaning out the wound on his leg as well as he could. It looked like a clean cut, and not too deep.

It was hard to get out of the water. Despite the fire on the hearth, the room was chilly. He climbed out and wrapped a towel around himself. As if by signal, the bathing girls burst back through the door, bringing warm towels to dry him off with. This time, Ash submitted. He was too tired to resist.

"You look much better, sir, without that layer of dirt," the smaller girl said approvingly. She ran the tips of her fingers over the muscles on his chest, raising gooseflesh. "We don't see many men who work with their backs for a living. It looks well on you. And you've a fine backside, too, if I may say so. It's all muscles, not like them who sit all day."

"He has a nice frontside, too," the bigger girl said,

elbowing the smaller one. "That's a fancy neckpiece you got on," she said, reaching for his amulet.

"Don't touch that!" Ash yanked it out of reach.

"I wasn't going to *steal* it," the girl said, pouting a little.

"How did you cut your leg then?" the small girl asked. "Looks like a bad gash."

"I don't know how that happened," Ash said.

They had a basket of fragrant lotions and ointments that they wanted to use on his burned face and the cut on his leg, but he refused. He thought of asking for his remedy bag from the stables, but then remembered that it was likely either burned up or lying somewhere in the maze of passages in the cellar.

The servants finally left him on his own to get dressed. The clothing that had been left for him consisted of small-clothes and a tunic and trousers in a soft, plain-woven fabric of a dark brown color, like bark. They were comfortable and fit as if they had been made to size. There were soft brown boots, also. He wondered what had happened to his old clothes, in case he was expected to give these back when his audience with the king was over.

He padded barefoot to the door and opened it a crack. The bathing girls were gone, but two blackbirds stood just outside. They both turned and looked at him, hands on the hilts of their swords. He closed the door and sighed. He sat down in one of the chairs by the fire, feeling trapped and helpless and half-sick and hungry and dead tired. It would take a while to recover from healing Hamon, and in the meantime he'd be close to helpless.

Well, sul'Han, he thought, you were hot to get into the palace, and here you are. Maybe when he had a little power on board, he could take advantage of it.

He lay down on the bed and was almost asleep again when he heard voices raised out in the hallway. This went on for a few minutes, some kind of argument, and then the door opened. It was Lila, still wearing the clothes she'd had on in the courtyard—a white blouse, black skirt, and deep blue overdress with a laced bodice.

Ash sat bolt upright and swung his legs over the side of the bed, suddenly wide-awake.

Lila put a finger to her lips, closed the door, waited a minute, and put her ear to it. Then she circled the room, poking behind draperies and tapestries and looking under the bed. She crossed the room and stood over him, hands on hips, and said, "Have you lost your mind, princeling? It wasn't enough that assassins tried to murder you in your bed? I saved your ass, and this is the thanks I get? You turtle my wine and come straight here so they can have another go?"

One thing you had to say about Lila: she knew how to launch an offense.

Ash just looked at her and said nothing. He was no wordsmith, but experience had taught him that silence was often the winning hand where Lila was concerned.

"Well? What the hell are you doing here?" She held his gaze for a moment or two, as if that might get her a response, then began pacing back and forth next to the bed. "What were you thinking, using magic in the middle of the courtyard? I know you're a rum healer, but you couldn't let somebody else be the hero this one time?"

"If I had, Hamon would be dead," Ash said evenly.

"That's beside the point," Lila said, likely because she knew it was true. "Nobody expects you to sacrifice yourself to save somebody else."

"I'm the reason he got burned," Ash said. "I had a certain obligation to fix him."

Lila stopped pacing and swung around. "What are you talking about?"

"Never mind," Ash said. The less information he divulged to Lila the better, until he figured out her game. "Why are you here? Aside from badgering me, I mean?"

"I'm supposed to ask you if there are any herbs or remedies you might need beyond the standard sort so I can be on the lookout for them."

"I mean, why are you in Ardenscourt? Is this where you've been spending your summers? Cozying up to the king of Arden? You could've mentioned that the two of you were friends."

For a moment, Lila had no comeback. "We're not friends," she said, avoiding Ash's eyes. "I'm here on business."

"What kind of business?"

"None of yours. I'm not accountable to you."

"Who are you accountable to?"

"Myself," Lila said.

"Maybe you're the one that gave me up to the Darians at Oden's Ford."

"Right," she said, staring up at the ceiling. "And then I turned around and rescued you. You know women— changeable as a day in April. Sometimes we just can't make up our minds."

"Maybe you figured you'd collect twice—once from the Darians, for outing me, and once from my mother, for bringing me home."

Lisa went back to offense. "You're not planning to do something rash, are you?"

"Such as—?"

"Such as trying to kill Montaigne. Do you think nobody's thought of that before? Do you think profession- als haven't tried? You're an amateur, sul'Han. Don't let the fact that you're a wizard make you overconfident. This king is surrounded by mages, and he wears a clan-made talisman night and day to protect against magical attacks."

Bellamy was right, Ash thought. Good to know.

"He employs a taster, and takes antidotes against com- mon poisons on a regular basis."

What about uncommon poisons?

"Where does he get the antidotes?"

Lila released an exasperated breath. "I should save

myself a lot of trouble and hand you over to the king. I'm sure he'd offer a rich reward. Instead, I've got to find a way to get you out of here, which won't be easy now that His Majesty is all smitten with you." She began pacing again. "I don't have time for this."

"I missed the part where I asked for your help," Ash said. "Why do you care so much? You don't have anything on the table, as far as I can see. All I want is for you to go about your business and leave me alone."

"I would love to take care of business," Lila muttered. "And I don't need an entitled runaway wizard blueblood princeling mucking it up."

"No problem," Ash said. "Stay out of my way, and I'll stay out of yours."

"Huh," Lila said. "We'll see. You'll find it's hard to stay out of anyone's way in this place."

HOMECOMING

To Jenna's surprise, Karn and his blackbirds didn't bother to bring in a healer to treat the wound just below her ribs. Karn treated it himself, packing it and wrapping her middle in linen bandages. It stopped bleeding almost immediately, and turned icy.

At first, she worried that it wasn't deep enough to kill her, but the way Karn barked orders at everyone told her that he thought it might be. They left her in her bloody fortunetelling clothes, wrapped her in furs, and bundled her into a closed carriage, with three blackbirds and Karn inside, and more up top and riding alongside. It was snowing heavily, and bitter cold.

They'd taken her dagger, but she still had the pendant,

at least. Nobody seemed to notice it in all the fuss about her wound and the magemark. She'd tucked it inside the lining of her coat when nobody was looking. She slid a finger in and touched it now and then, wondering how long before that was taken away, too. With any luck, she'd be dead before they took it.

At first she struggled and kicked, and once almost threw herself out of the carriage while it was moving, but she gradually grew weaker and then slept most of the time, conscious of a creeping chill that gradually took over her body. Karn tried to give her soup, and tea, but she resisted, and he spilled more than he got into her.

It was like she felt every bump of the journey. Once, they had to stop to put runners on the carriage to come through the deep snow. Karn swore and pounded his fist on the frame of the carriage.

She heard soldiers over her head, shouting travelers off the road. She felt the pressure of Karn's eyes, as if by watching her he could keep her from slipping away. As if he could look into her soul, and see what was hidden there.

As her body grew colder, the air grew warmer, moister, and filled with the scent of growing things.

She didn't know how long they were on the road, but finally one day as she lay between sleep and waking she could hear sounds outside the carriage that told her they were in a city. She heard the horses' hooves striking cobblestones, and dogs barking. The familiar stench of coal fires burned in her nose, and people were shouting at each other the way they do when they are packed close together. She heard the sound of temple bells overhead.

It must be almost Solstice, she thought hazily. Perhaps they're taking me somewhere for the holiday. The thought made her smile.

It was a large city, because it was another hour before they clattered across a bridge and into the stable yard at the palace. When they opened the door to the carriage, she could smell horse dung. Or was it the river? She knew she must be in Ardenscourt, the city of her birth. Or, at least, the city where her grandmother had handed her over to the only parents she'd ever known, along with a ruby-hilted dagger and a warning.

She wondered if she would find any answers here.

She was surprised that they would bring a Delphian Patriot this far south to wring answers out of her. Maybe with Clermont gone, they were short of help when it came to torture.

They wrapped her up again and Karn himself carried her into the palace. His face looked haggard, furred with a stubble of beard. On her back as she was, she could see the frowning stone façade stretching above her as she passed beneath it, and the night sky beyond, stained sallow by the lights of the city.

THE KING'S HEALER

Ash had no idea what time it was when they brought in his breakfast, but it seemed that he'd just laid down his head when he was awakened by the bang and clatter.

He took the arrival of the servant as a sign that his audience with the king was scheduled for an early hour, so he reluctantly rolled out of bed. He ached all over, and he still had his cuts and bruises, but he was clean, and alive, and he could see, even in the dim light of the banked hearth. That was something to be grateful for.

Despite his weariness, he hadn't slept well. Lila's words kept running through his head. *You're an amateur, sul'Han. Don't let the fact that you're a wizard make you overconfident.* He'd been ready to attack the king in the barn after Crusher went down, without knowing that he wore a talisman. And then he'd all but lost his temper in the courtyard after healing Hamon.

He'd have one chance at the king, if he was lucky. He had to make it count. Now that he was in the palace, with so many eyes on him, he needed to play it smart.

He washed his face using the basin and the mirror. The sunburned look was fading, and his eyes were a little clearer. He pulled his new boots on, being careful of the gash in the back of his leg. They fit perfectly. He ran his fingers through his hair, roughly distributing it, and he was ready.

Breakfast was porridge and sliced fruit. There was no bread. He supposed the destroyed kitchen might affect meal preparation in the palace for a while. Ash thought of Hamon, wondering how he was doing, and where they had taken him. What had the baker seen? Had they asked him any questions?

Despite his worries, Ash was ravenous, as he always was after a difficult healing, and he ate heartily.

All through breakfast, he gripped his amulet, feeding it the trickle of power that was all he could manage. Soon, he'd have enough to do some real damage.

He was just finishing eating when he heard a commotion in the corridor. His door flew open and six blackbirds poured into the room. They were all mages, all collared, and they seemed to be on a mission. One of them shut the door and put his back against it, while the other five surrounded Ash. He grabbed for his amulet, but two of them pinned his arms before he could touch it.

Panic flickered through him again. Had the Darian brother survived after all? Had they come to take him down to the dungeons?

Worse, had Lila betrayed him?

"Relax, boy," one of them said. "There's no point in fighting it. You'll get used to it after a while." He dug in a carry bag and pulled out a silver collar, inscribed with runes. Ash recognized it as one of the flashcraft collars made by the clans during the wizard wars, now used by Arden to enslave the gifted.

Maybe it was useless to resist, but Ash refused to go quietly into bondage, so it took all five of them to pin him to the floor and fasten the thing around his neck. If he'd had more magic on board, maybe it wouldn't have happened at all. By the end, one of the gifted blackbirds had a bloody nose and another a purpling eye and Ash had a collar around his neck.

He crouched in a corner like a wolf at bay, exploring the thing with his hands. He found the catch, which seemed to be welded shut now. He could feel the engraving under his sensitive fingers. It was a wide piece, and he found he had to keep his head upright or it would bite into his chin or his collarbone.

The blackbirds watched him with varying degrees of

sympathy, depending on how they'd fared in the wrestling match. Some wouldn't look at him at all.

The mage who'd brought the collar extended a hand to help him up. After a moment's hesitation, Ash took it and stood. "How does it work?" he asked. "Does it make it impossible to use magic or what?"

The mage shook his head. "They want to take advantage of magery—that's the whole point. So they need us to be able to do spellcasting. Here at court, the collars prevent us from using attack magic and killing charms. That's the main limitation."

"Do they work on their own or does somebody have to activate it?"

"They work on their own. General Karn has some magemasters who oversee the program and can change the settings when we go into the field."

"What triggers it—the nature of the charm or the intent?"

"Trying to figure out a way around it, are you? Good luck." The mage stuck out his hand. "I'm Marc DeJardin. Call me Marc."

"Adam Freeman." Ash paused. "You're a southerner, right?"

Marc nodded. "There are mages in the south, though the Church of Malthus would like to pretend otherwise. For centuries, we've been able to survive, as long as we keep our heads down and our magic to ourselves. Until

King Gerard found a use for us." He tapped his own collar with his forefinger. "Out in the field, these can be used to track our movements, to control our use of attack magic, and to direct our behavior in battle. They're also used to torture or kill a mage that misbehaves."

"Define 'misbehaves,'" Ash said.

The mage snorted. "A mage who doesn't follow orders, who tries to escape, who fights back. As long as you do what you're told, they pretty much leave you alone."

Ash saw then that the flesh around Marc's collar was thickened, rough, and badly scarred, as if it had been repeatedly burned in the past.

Marc noticed him staring. He smiled crookedly and ran a finger under his collar. "I used to misbehave a lot," he said. "We'd better go. The king is waiting."

They walked back toward the center of the palace, the council chambers and the king's apartments. The guards had to slow their pace to match Ash's faltering gait. Despite the hour, there were many people about, most of them servants. He didn't draw as many stares as before, because now he was clean and clad in the bark brown of the healers. It seemed the king of Arden liked to sort people by colors.

His escorts stopped before a door that looked much like any other, except that there was a brace of the king's guards standing in front. "Prepare to kneel to the king, healer," the outside guard muttered, giving him a rough push through the doorway. Marc followed him in.

He found himself in a small reception room, sumptuously decorated, with tall windows overlooking the gardens. The king sat finishing breakfast at a small table by the fireplace. Eggs and ham, not babies and kittens, as Ash might have expected.

He's just a man, Ash told himself. He can die, like anyone else.

There were four blackbirds in the room, plus Marc. All of them were gifted. He was definitely outnumbered, even if he hadn't been collared. Even if the king didn't wear a talisman.

But you're in the same room with him, he thought. That's a start.

This morning, Montaigne was clad in rather plain clothing, black trousers and a black doublet edged in gold, sturdy boots, his gold necklace with its seal of office. An elaborate dagger was belted at his waist.

"Your Majesty, here is Adam Freeman, collared per your command." Marc took a few steps back, so that Ash stood alone.

Ash went down on his knee before the king. He didn't rise until Montaigne told him to do so. When he did, Montaigne was leaning back in his chair, toying with the hilt of his dagger, studying him.

"You look much more presentable this morning,

healer," he said. "I trust you suffered no ill effects from your night in custody?" This spoken with the bite of sarcasm.

"No, Your Majesty. It was very comfortable," Ash replied, chin up, eyes straight ahead. With some effort, he unclenched his jaw.

Montaigne's lips twitched. "Shall I assume that you were reluctant to take the collar?"

"Do you blame me?"

"A necessary precaution. It shouldn't interfere with your abilities, as long as they are employed in the interests of the crown. Should you stray from that, you will be punished."

"So I'm told, sire."

"Since the clothes appear to fit, ask DeJardin to have another set made so you can wash them now and then."

"Thank you for the clothes, Your Majesty. They are much finer than the ones I had."

Montaigne raised an eyebrow and straightened his lace cuffs. "It appears a night in the palace has improved your manners as well as your appearance."

"I apologize for my behavior last night. I wasn't myself, as often happens after a difficult healing."

The king's eyes narrowed, as if he weren't entirely convinced by this performance. "I am glad to see that you have recovered your good sense." He paused. "I was impressed with what you did with the baker last night. I have a number of skilled healers at court, and I've never seen any of them heal a man so damaged so completely, and without the use of herbs or tonics."

"Herbs and tonics are helpful, Your Majesty," Ash said. "But I hadn't any."

"No. You hadn't." The king pulled at his earlobe. "Mages have been an integral part of our military for years. Until now, I had not considered the advantages of using them in the healing service—selectively, of course. So. I'm offering you a new position, beginning today. I would have you join my guild of healers."

So after weeks of waiting, Ash would finally have the access he'd sought in the beginning. But it came at a price. He brushed his fingers over the collar. It was already becoming a habit. Sometimes he imagined it was cutting off his air.

"Thank you, Your Majesty," he said.

"Merrill is my master healer. He'll put together a kit for you, any supplies you will need, any herbal preparations and tonics you favor. We ought to be able to provide most anything. If there is a specialty item you need, not commonly available in the realm, address it with Barrowhill."

"We've already had that conversation, Your Majesty," Ash said.

"DeJardin will explain what we expect from mages who serve the crown." King Gerard gestured to Marc, standing just behind Ash. "Escort Freeman to the healers' quarters and introduce him to Merrill. Tell him to find the boy space with them."

The healers were housed in a quiet part of the palace that opened onto the service gardens. There was a small library just off the hallway as well, lined with herbals and apothecaries and surgical texts. Ash made a mental note to return there. He had seen more new books to tempt him in two days in the palace than he had seen in the last six months.

As they walked, Marc filled him in. The infirmary served mostly the palace staff and lower level officials whose quarters would not function well as a sick room. The nobility who fell ill usually insisted on being treated in the privacy of their own quarters.

The infirmary was small, but bright and airy, with a tiled floor and whitewashed walls, and six beds lined up against the walls. Everything looked clean, to Ash's critical eye. He found most hospitals to be deadly places, to be avoided at all costs.

Only one bed was occupied. Ash could see the bulk of a large man under the blanket, apparently asleep.

The attendant went to find Master Merrill. While they waited, Ash made a wish list for his healer's kit. It turned out that he had plenty of time. The master, when he finally appeared, was a tall man with thinning hair and a weak chin, clad in the same drab colors as Ash. Although he was not especially heavy, there was something soft and yielding about him, as if he never did any significant physical work. He made no attempt to hide his irritation.

"Now what's this all about?" Merrill looked them over and chose Marc as the one in charge. "I am in the middle of a complicated extraction, and I don't care to be interrupted."

"This is a new healer, Adam Freeman," Marc said, nodding at Ash.

"Healer! I choose my own apprentices, and I don't know this boy." He looked Ash up and down, his face a storm cloud. "Where did you steal those clothes?" Then his gaze fastened on the silver collar, and he made the sign of Malthus. "You've brought me a *mage*?" He poked a finger into DeJardin's face. "I won't have your kind in my service. I'm not in need of any more help, anyway. I've trouble enough with the apprentices I have."

"King Gerard has ordered that Freeman be admitted to the Royal Guild of Healers," DeJardin said evenly. "Do you wish me to carry your objections to His Majesty?"

The commotion had disturbed the patient in the bed. He stirred and sat up, rubbing his eyes. They went wide when they lit on Ash. "Adam! By the Maker, you're here! I can't believe what they've been telling me." It was Hamon.

The night baker stretched out his arms toward Ash, and a big tear rolled down his face. "They say I was dead for sure, and you saved my life. They say you rescued me from the fire, and then you healed me. They say it was a miracle. Come here, my boy, so I can feel of you, for surely you were the instrument of Holy Malthus in this."

Reluctantly, Ash moved to the bedside, and endured the baker's embrace.

Now that Merrill understood who Ash was, he looked even less happy. "You're the stable boy!" he snapped, as if it were an accusation.

Hamon was still babbling. "I remember bringing the oil up from the cellar. I must have let it slip. I just don't remember. But things are going to be different from now on, praise the Maker. I've sworn off it, I tell you. I'm a changed man."

Ash realized that Hamon was blaming himself and his drinking for the fire.

"You'll be fortunate if His Majesty doesn't throw you in prison," Merrill said sourly.

Hamon ignored him. "All day long people have been coming in to see me, to look at my back. I'm famous. And to think I was healed by a stable boy. Wait till they hear that you're working here."

Ash was beginning to understand the source of Merrill's murderous bad humor.

The master fixed Ash with the haughty gaze of a saint confronting a sinner. "From what I heard, it was sorcery." He pointed a warning finger at the baker. "'Tis a poor bargain if you've traded the integrity of your body for the future of your immortal soul." That was when Ash noticed the emblem of the rising sun of Malthus dangling from a chain about the master's neck. So the healer was a churchman, a not uncommon wedding of professions in Arden.

"No, no! It was a blessing, Master Merrill!" Hamon insisted. "I have never felt so close to the faith as I do now."

"It couldn't have been much of a burn," Merrill said, scowling. "It is nearly healed."

"It was monstrous big," Hamon said, leaning forward. "Rolley, he said I was burnt to the bone. He saw it with his own eyes."

"His Majesty would like you to put together a kit for Freeman," Marc said, "and provide a place for him to stay."

"The boy won't need a kit," Merrill grumbled. "He's not qualified to do any actual healing."

Ash was accustomed to working with oversized egos from his time with Master Vega in the Fells. "I know you're busy, Master Merrill," he said, holding up his list. "I just need a few things to get started. I can put it together myself, if you tell me where things are. And I'll be happy to do any necessary extractions, as well."

Merrill snatched the list from Ash. "I don't want a stable boy mucking around in my formulary." He scanned the list and looked up, surprised. "How did you . . ."

"My mother taught me about herbs and medicinals. And I had some training at the academy."

"It will take a while to put this together." The healer seemed resigned to it. "Wait here." He disappeared into the rear.

Ash returned to Hamon's bedside. "As long as I'm here, why don't I take a look at your back. Are you still in any pain?" He thought it better to examine his patient in Merrill's absence.

Hamon obligingly lifted up his shirt and turned his back to Ash. "It's still tender, like a scald, maybe. Not much worse than that."

Ash pushed lightly on the skin and watched with satisfaction as the blood returned. "Have they put anything on it?"

"Some kind of ointment," the baker said, over his shoulder.

Aloe, probably. That's what it smelled like.

"I don't think you'll have any scarring. Make sure you drink plenty of water. Keep a pitcher by your bed and empty four before the day is over. Eat as much as you can. No alcohol at all for now. If it suddenly seems worse, or there's any new drainage, or swelling, any fever, get word to me." Years of training were reasserting themselves. "I'll be here, instead of the stable, from now on."

Hamon nodded solemnly, committing the instructions to memory. Ash hesitated, then said, "Hamon, do you know if they found . . . if anyone else was hurt in the fire?"

He was immediately sorry, because the big man teared up again. "I don't know. I hope not. Nobody told me, if they were." He shook his head sadly. "It's all my fault."

Ash put a hand on his shoulder. "You can't be sure you

had anything to do with the fire. Fires break out all the time, especially in a kitchen, and there were flammables stored in the basement. Maybe you just happened to be in the wrong place at the wrong time."

"Maybe," Hamon said grudgingly. "And you happened to be in the right place. I see you burned your face, rescuing me. I'll pray to Saint Malthus for you, every night." Ash's discomfort grew as the baker went on.

Merrill made them wait another good long time. Finally he returned with a tray and a cloth sack. The tray held numerous small bags and glass bottles. There was also linen for bandaging and small surgical tools.

Ash set the tray down on a table. Then he took the list and ran through the items on the tray, matching them, and putting them into the cloth sack. He uncorked the bottles and sniffed them and tasted some, and opened the drawstring bags, sometimes shaking a bit of dried herb onto his palm. Merrill waited impatiently, clearly annoyed that his new apprentice was rechecking his work. Finally, Ash looked up at Merrill and extended his palm toward him, with a bit of brown, rootlike material.

"This is water hemlock. I asked for chamomile."

Merrill stared at him, his mouth opening and closing. Then he snatched back the bag. "Those blasted apprentices! I'll have their hides for this."

"If you'd like, I can go into the garden and find it," Ash offered.

The healer furiously shook his head. "I'll be back."

"The leaves and flowers, not the root," Ash called after him.

"What's water hemlock?" Marc whispered.

"Poison," Ash replied calmly.

The master healer was quick this time. Ash finished putting his bag together and thanked him.

"We don't have any rooms to spare, boy," the master healer warned. "You'll have to share."

"That's all right," Ash replied. "I'm used to that." Frankly, he would have felt more at ease in the stable than in the palace, between the Darian brother and his hostile new master. "My name is Adam," he added, with little hope that Merrill would ever actually use it.

Merrill ignored him. "You can bring your things over any time. You'll be sharing with Harold and Boyd. I'll expect you to be ready to work this afternoon."

"I don't really have anything to bring. I can start to work now."

"As you wish," Merrill said. "You can start in the garden, since you fancy yourself an expert at telling one plant from another."

AN EARLY MORNING SUMMONS

Ash shared a tiny room in back of the extraction laboratory with two other apprentices, both much younger than him. Harold and Boyd seemed surprised to be teamed with someone who was nearly grown. Over a period of days, as they realized how knowledgeable he was, they began turning to him for guidance when they had a question. Merrill wasn't much of a teacher. He seemed to be threatened by anyone with a smattering of talent or skill.

Ash was happy to help them, but only when Merrill wasn't around.

The apprentices were expected to clean the extraction lab and set up materials for the master healers. When the lab was in use, their sleeping room was almost unbearable because of the odors. So Ash spent very little time there.

Since the healers' quarters were out of the way, it was more difficult to keep track of events in and around the palace. But Ash was just as happy to lay low, in case more Darian brothers came looking for him. After days passed and there was no sign of them, he began to relax a little. It was possible the priest who'd spotted him had kept it to himself, not wanting to share with his brothers.

Ash had hoped that a position in the healing halls would give him better access to the king, but that didn't happen. When he asked Harold and Boyd who took care of the king, they said Montaigne hadn't called for a healer since they'd been there.

"He's never sick?" Ash asked.

"If he is, he don't call on us," Harold said.

The nobility, including the Ardenine thanes, were treated in their own quarters by the master healers. Apprentices often went along to assist, but Ash was never invited. The other healers gave him a wide berth, making the sign of Malthus if he got too close.

Much of Ash's assigned work consisted of cleanup, the harvesting and drying of plants, the chopping of roots and grinding of herbs with a mortar and pestle. Tasks he'd been doing for Taliesin since he was twelve. Sometimes he was allowed to pour off and label extractions after they were made. He suspected that Merrill didn't want to give Ash another chance to demonstrate what he could do.

Once Hamon was released from the infirmary, however, there came a steady stream of servants, soldiers, and minor officials with illnesses and injuries, asking for "Adam Freeman." Apparently now that the baker was on the loose, he was spreading the good news. Master Merrill's annoyance was tempered by the fact that he had no interest in treating the riffraff.

Eventually, a patient was admitted with dysentery, and Ash was assigned to bathe the unfortunate and change his bed. Merrill seemed to delight in finding menial tasks to keep him busy. So, unless the king of Arden needed his toenails trimmed, they were unlikely to meet again.

Ash had retrieved his death-dealing formulary from the stables. He hid it carefully under a stone in the garden and protected it with a charm. He was at a loss for how to use it. He could tamper with the food down in the kitchens, but there was no guarantee any of it would make its way to his target. The king had a taster—those who shared the palace with him did not. Innocent people would die, the kitchen staff would pay the price, and the king would go on living.

The same applied to the herbs and medicinals in the healers' formulary. Unless he could get his hands on an order specifically for the king, he was unlikely to succeed by that route. Taliesin always said that using poison in a crowd was like shooting a bolt into the sky, not knowing where it would land. Anyway, Merrill kept a hawk's eye on Ash, waiting for him to make a misstep. Ash had no doubt that any problem would be laid directly at his door.

One morning about a fortnight after Ash had moved to the healers' quarters, he was setting up and labeling the solvents and diluents using the compounding recipes while the two younger boys gathered materials from the storeroom in the rear. Master Merrill was away and the two apprentices were eager to tell him why.

"Did you hear what happened last night?" Harold said, dumping an armload of herbs onto the table. "With Lady Estelle and all?"

Ash shook his head, distracted. He was counting out measures of willow bark. "No. I didn't hear." Lady Estelle was the king's current favorite, and Harold and Boyd were unrepentant gossips. Ash really didn't care who was carrying the king's chance-child.

"Last night the king all but climbed in bed with a viper."

That caught Ash's interest. "A viper? How could that happen?"

"From all I heard, it was a deathsting adder," Harold went on. "They're only big around as your little finger, but if one bites you, you're a goner."

"A snake was in his rooms?"

Harold shook his head. "Like I said. It was in the Lady Estelle's suite."

Ash abandoned all pretense of working. "Was the king

bitten?" he asked with a spark of hope.

"I don't think so. King Gerard, he ran out of the room, shouting for his guard. Five blackbirds went in and tore the bed apart looking for it, and finally killed it. Lady Estelle and all her ladies, they were hysterical."

Ash sat down on the bed, heart thumping. "How do you know all this?"

"Master Merrill took me with him, to help carry. He thought he'd need help, what with five women all carrying on." Harold was beside himself with delight at being the bearer of such important news, while Boyd looked glum at being left out.

"Master Merrill is treating the king?" Ha! No danger of a cure there.

Harold shook his head, as if Ash were a little thick. "Nah. I told you, the king—it's like he don't believe in healers. I mean the ladies. They was in a frenzy, and we had no lady's tonic made up, so we give 'em enough brandy to put a sapper on his back. Then the King's Guard, they come in, and they have at Lady Estelle and the ladies, asking 'em all kinds of questions. Only they wasn't making much sense by this time, and the Guard, they want us to sober 'em up again." Harold lowered his voice to a conspiratorial whisper. "See, they're thinking the snake was meant for the king."

"Who would want to hurt the king?" Ash might have sounded a little sarcastic, but it went right by Harold and

Boyd. "Do they have any suspects?"

"Well, I don't guess they'd tell Harold if they did," Boyd broke in, eager to participate.

"Well, after the guards left, Lady Estelle and her ladies were all in a panic, because it seemed like the blackbirds thought maybe they was in on it."

"Where was the king all this time?"

"He went back to his suite, far as I know."

Just then, they heard a footstep in the hallway. Boyd and Harold hurried to look busy, thinking maybe it was Master Merrill. But it was Marc DeJardin.

"Freeman, get your kit and come with me. The king has asked for you."

Ash tried to read Marc's face but got nothing. "He asked for me specifically?"

The mage nodded.

Was it possible the king had been bitten after all? With mingled apprehension and anticipation, Ash set his work aside and washed his hands. He retrieved his kit from under his bed. "Wait here," he said. "I need to get something from the garden. Just in case I need it."

Blessedly, they didn't follow him out there. He knelt behind a low wall, lifted the stone, and pulled out his hidden saddlebag. Running his fingers over the packets and bottles inside, he chose two small bottles. The first he tucked it into a pocket he'd sewn into his sleeve. The other he slid into a mesh pouch he'd attached to the inside of his silver collar. Even if he came under suspicion, they were unlikely to take the collar off.

On his way back inside, he plucked a fistful of snakebite weed.

Harold was eagerly filling a visibly uncomfortable Marc in on the events in Lady Estelle's suite.

"You'd best watch yourself, Harold," Marc said. "It seems to me they're trying to keep that whole thing quiet. You don't want the king to hear that you're spreading that story."

It was almost comical, the way Harold's mouth snapped shut and a look of panic crowded onto his face. Almost.

"Can you two finish setting up?" Ash asked his two young colleagues. They both nodded, staring at him, wide-eyed, unsure whether Ash was in trouble or in luck. "If Master Merrill is looking for me, tell him I've been summoned by the king. I don't know how long I'll be." Ash figured he might as well take his time. Merrill would make his life miserable for the next week regardless.

"What's this all about?" Ash demanded as they hurried back toward the center of the castle.

Marc shook his head. "I don't really know, but the entire palace is crawling with the King's Guard. I've never seen anything like it. If what Harold says is true, they're taking the snake episode seriously."

That was certainly true—as they approached the king's apartments, the blackbirds flocked thicker.

"The only other rumor I've heard is about plague," Marc said.

"Plague! Here in Ardenscourt?"

Marc shook his head. "Delphi. Word is that riders came in from the north a few hours ago, blackbirds escorting a closed carriage. Nobody knows anything, also unusual. Maybe some visitor needs healing."

"Why would they bring plague to Ardenscourt?"

"Maybe it's someone really important. That's why it's such a secret."

"It still doesn't make sense." Ash thought of the city, teeming with people, and the consequences if the plague were loosed here with no gifted healers to treat it.

"All I know is, this morning he sent for me early and told me to fetch you, that it was urgent."

This might be the opportunity I've been looking for, Ash thought. Unless they just need somebody to make the beds.

The guards seemed to be expecting them, and admitted them quickly after the usual search. Ash saw immediate signs of heightened security. There were ten fully armed blackbirds inside, along with Montaigne, Lila, and another man Ash had never seen before. An uncollared mage. He and Lila had their heads together over a map spread out on the hearth.

Ash studied the king, looking for signs of illness, but saw none, only evidence of murderous foul humor.

The stranger looked to be the same age as Ash, with a lean, muscular build, hazel eyes, a stubble of reddish beard, and brown hair. His clothing was travel-stained, as if he'd been on the road for days, and hadn't had time to change.

Was this his patient? Ash guessed not. The mage appeared worried, almost agitated, but Ash sensed no physical disorder about him.

When they entered the room, Lila and the stranger broke off their conversation. He leaned forward, hands on his knees, examining Ash with sharp interest.

Should I offer him the secret wizard handshake? Ash thought.

"Lieutenant Karn!" Marc exclaimed. "You're back!"

Karn! Ash all but missed a step.

"Good to be back," the young man said, his gaze flicking to Marc, then back to Ash.

This must be Destin Karn, the Ardenine spymaster. Ash had heard his name during his travels through Arden. The son of Marin Karn, general of the Ardenine armies, he could have been the one behind the attack on him at Oden's Ford.

If so, would Karn recognize him? Tall and red-haired were the descriptors most often applied to Ash. At least now his hair was dyed a muddy brown color.

Just another friend of Lila's apparently. Ash was beginning to feel hemmed in by Lila's friends.

"That will be all, Lila," Gerard said, gesturing toward the door.

Lila looked from the king to Ash, her lips tightening. Ash could tell she was hot to stay. But she curtsied a farewell just the same.

"When you're free, Lieutenant, come see me in the quartermaster's office. I should be there most of the day, arranging for the wagons."

Karn nodded. "Let's talk tonight. I need to get a few things done here before we leave."

Leave for where? Ash wondered. Did this have to do with whatever scheme she was working on?

As Lila departed, Ash knelt, and then rose to his feet. "You wished to see me, Your Majesty?"

"This is the healer I told you about, Karn," Montaigne said, nodding toward Ash. "Have him take a look at the girl if you really think we need a second opinion, but I think you're worrying unnecessarily. Merrill said that she would mend, given rest and a little time. He offered to bleed her if need be."

"I would be pleased to examine your patient," Ash blurted. "If you wish, sire." Ash had a low opinion of Merrill's opinion, and it might be another opportunity to win the trust of the king.

Karn unfolded to his feet and walked toward Ash, moving gracefully, like a cat. "Where are you from?" he said to Ash, his eyes fastening on his collar.

Maybe I should get a decorative scarf to cover it. "Tam-ron," Ash said.

"From your speech, I would have guessed you were from farther north."

Ash stiffened. He should have expected the spymaster would be familiar with the accent. Karn had probably tortured his share of military prisoners. But Ash hadn't realized he still had one. "My mother was from the Fells, but I've never wanted to go. They say there are monsters there."

"There are monsters here, healer," Karn said.

You're right about that, Ash said to himself. "About the patient. Is it plague, Your Majesty?"

"Plague!" King Gerard raised an eyebrow. "Why would you think of plague?"

"They say there's plague in Delphi," Ash said, acutely aware of the weight of the bottle in his sleeve. "I—if it's a concern, I have a tisane that might protect you if taken early. I could make up some now, and—"

"Who told you I came from Delphi?" Karn interrupted, eyes narrowed.

"No one, sir," Ash said, not wanting to involve Marc. Get hold of yourself, sul'Han, he thought. I think this collar is cutting off the blood to your brain. "I heard that travelers had arrived from the north, and I assumed—"

"It's not plague," Karn snapped. "It's a sixteen-year-old girl with a stab wound." He rolled up the map and slid it into its case.

"We need someone who can keep whatever he sees to himself," the king said. "Can you do that, Freeman?"

"Of course, Your Majesty," Ash said. "Thank you for your confidence in me."

"We would be . . . most distressed," Karn said, "if word were to leak out about this, do you understand?" The lieutenant's hand crept to the knife at his belt, making the implied threat explicit.

"I understand, Lieutenant Karn." Ash's curiosity burned hotter. Who was this patient? Why was it such a secret? Had he been chosen for this task because he was considered expendable?

That's when he put the pieces together. This patient—a sixteen-year-old girl—had come from the north in a closed carriage. It was a big secret he needed to keep to himself.

Lyss.

His heart stuttered, and then began to pound. It was like he couldn't get his breath.

Maybe she'd been wounded, taken prisoner, and brought here.

Ash breathed in, breathed out, struggling to still himself. After the attack at Oden's Ford, he knew Montaigne was targeting his family. He knew, and yet he'd whiled away his time in a stable. He should have acted sooner. He should have found a way to stop the king before this happened.

If it *is* Lyss, he thought, I will find a way to save her.

Unbidden, Taliesin's words came back to him. *The time will come when you will wish that you were a better healer.*

"Healer?" Karn tilted his head, frowning. "Is there a problem?"

"No, lieutenant," Ash said, his gut churning. "No problem at all."

IN THE KING'S DUNGEONS

They left the king's apartments with two blackbirds in tow, using the first available staircase to descend to the cellar level. Karn led the way, with Ash in the middle, and the guards behind. They wound their way into the heart of the castle until they came to a stout wooden door sunken into the wall, blackbirds to either side. Behind the door, another staircase descended to a level beneath the cellar.

Ash couldn't help recalling his last visit to the cellars with the bloodsucking Darian priest. "You keep your patients in the cellar?" he said, unable to keep the edge from his voice.

Karn gave him a long, measuring look. "This patient we do," he said, pointing down the staircase. "This way."

At the foot of the stairs, there was another door, a metal one this time, and two more guards before it. The guards saluted the lieutenant, eyed Ash, and ushered them through. The door clanged shut behind them, and when Ash heard the bar being thrown, his suspicions were confirmed. They were in the king of Arden's dungeons.

Claustrophobia settled over him like a shroud. If it *was* Lyss, how could he possibly get her out of here, especially if she was injured? And if these southerners ever became aware of who he was, he would be killed or clapped into the cell next to her. Imprisoned and tortured, most likely. The son and daughter of the queen of the Fells would be worth more alive than dead.

Ash slid a finger under his collar, touched the bottle hidden there. He knew how to get dead if he needed to.

They walked through a dark stone corridor, just wide enough for two to pass abreast, poorly illuminated by torches stuck into niches in the wall. The floor was uneven underfoot, carelessly excavated in some remote age. The air was dank and stale, as if it had been rebreathed so many times that there was nothing nourishing in it.

There were doors to either side of the corridor, with high, barred windows, none large enough to get a man's shoulders through. He heard sounds from some of them, wounded sounds and weeping, the repetitive wailing of the insane. Ash quickly turned away. You can't save everyone, sul'Han, he thought.

The floor sloped downward, and they passed through two more checkpoints with guards. They took several turns until they were in an area where the doors were farther apart, suggesting the cells were larger. Although they were farther underground, the air seemed better there, too. He noticed ventilation shafts driven through at intervals. Most of the cells in this area seemed to be empty.

At the end of the corridor was a large, circular room with a high ceiling and three doors set in the stone around the perimeter. At the far end of the room was a crumbling stone wall, stained and damaged by the wet, layered with fungus. Water trickled off it and pooled on the floor. Ash guessed that meant they were close to the river.

There were two large stone slabs in the central room, leather straps attached with iron rings, stained dark from long use and indifferent cleaning. Wrought metal chains and pulleys and leg irons dangled from the walls. Ash didn't recognize the tools he saw there, but many of them bore an uncanny resemblance to medical instruments. The room stank of old blood, intentional pain, and terror. He took a deep breath, released it in a long shudder.

"Nervous, healer?" Karn gave him a sideways look.

"Feeling the damp is all," Ash said, his mouth ashy with fear. There were two guards stationed outside one of the doors in the far wall, a door with no window. This must be their destination.

If it was Lyss, would she recognize him? He'd changed

a lot in four years, and his hair was dyed brown, and yet—they had been so close, the connection between them so strong that she might.

What if she did, and called him by name?

What if he saw what had been done to her and gave himself away? He could not allow that to happen.

The guards unlocked the door and stepped aside so they could enter.

"Stay outside," Karn ordered the blackbirds. He lifted two torches from sconces on either side of the door and led the way in.

The room was dimly lit by lamps set into niches in the walls. Their light didn't make it all the way into the corners. The cell was roughly twenty feet square, hollowed out of stone, and empty of furniture. The ceiling was higher than in the upper part of the dungeon.

On the far side of the room, a low bed had been set up against the wall. There on the bed, under a pile of blankets, someone was dying. That understanding slammed into Ash like a runaway horse, all but forcing the air from his lungs.

Karn mounted the torches in sconces on the wall at either end of the bed. "Hello, Jenna," he said softly. "We've brought another healer for you."

Jenna. Not Lyss. And when he looked at the girl huddled in the bed, he realized that she was a stranger.

Ash all but crumpled to the floor, his relief mingled

with confusion. If it wasn't Lyss, then who was she?

"Healer?" Karn was eyeing him again like he didn't know what to make of this wobble-kneed mage.

The prisoner watched them warily as they approached, like an animal in a trap. It was a girl, perhaps a little younger than Ash, a rough gray blanket pulled up to her chin. Her hair was tangled and appeared to be streaked with color. It was hard to tell, it was so badly in need of washing.

Her clothes were filthy, too—though they'd once been fine. She wore what looked like boy's breeches and a torn linen shirt stained with blood and only the gods knew what else. A velvet coat lay crumpled up on the floor next to the bed.

Her hands were manacled together, attached to a bolt in the wall by a short chain. The skin at her wrists was scabbed and discolored, as if she'd struggled to get free. Ash's fingers found the collar around his own neck and his stomach clenched with sympathy.

Her eyes, though—they were a striking gold color, clear and piercing, set into a planed face with a rather prominent nose. Raptor's eyes that missed nothing. Undefeated in a place intended to extinguish hope.

She wasn't the kind who could survive long in captivity, even if she hadn't sustained a mortal wound. His heart broke a little.

"The first healer said I'd be fine." Her voice was weak and thready, but there was an element of steel in it. "I thought he was the best you had."

"Merrill said you wouldn't let him come anywhere near you," Karn said.

Smart girl, Ash thought.

The girl shifted on the bed, bunching the blanket in her fists. "Is that what he said? He's a liar then."

"Jenna," Karn muttered, as if frustrated.

"Anyway. He said he didn't need to touch me. He could diagnose me by my aura."

"Blood of the martyrs!" Karn said through gritted teeth. "I'm trying to save your life." He gestured toward Ash. "This one is gifted."

Jenna looked Ash up and down, and something like fear flickered in her eyes. "No," she said, licking her cracked lips. "He's too tall. I don't want a tall healer. Bring me someone else."

She doesn't want a gifted healer, Ash thought. Is she worried that I might actually succeed in healing her? Or is she afraid that I'll ferret out secrets that she wants to keep hidden?

Ash squatted in front of her, setting his kit down beside him, so he could take a closer, appraising look.

Her eyes were overbright, her breathing quick and shallow. Likely her pulse was rapid, too. He could feel a blaze of white-hot magic, centered in her midsection. That must be where the injury was. The girl was not a wizard—she had no telltale glow. Her arms were well muscled, like she worked hard for a living. She'd eaten well, too, at least until recently. Her skin had an unusual reflective quality—it shimmered in the light from the torches as if there were flames under her skin.

"I'm Adam Freeman," he said. "How do you feel?"

Jenna gazed into his face for a long moment. "You are a wolf," she said, her lip curling. She looked up at Karn. "Why did you bring a wolf into the palace?"

That was like a punch to the gut. Once again, Ash tasted fear, like metal in his mouth. Why had she said that? How could she possibly know? The last thing he needed was to be tied to the Gray Wolf line.

"What do you mean, Jenna?" Karn demanded, looking from the girl on the bed to Ash. "What do you mean, he's a wolf?"

"The lieutenant doesn't know, does he?" Jenna said, smirking like a cat with a bird in its mouth. She breathed in sharply, like she was tasting his scent. "Now I have made you sweat, Wolf." She brought both hands up, put her finger to her lips. "Shhh," she said, then slumped back onto her pillows and rolled onto her side, facing the wall, so Ash was staring at her back.

It seemed that his patient had been doing an assessment of her own.

"Well?" Karn shifted impatiently. "Are you going to get to work or not?"

Ash rose to his feet and broadened his stance. "She

needs to be moved upstairs. She needs fresh air and light."

Karn folded his arms and shook his head. "That's not going to happen, healer. You'll have to do the best you can right here."

"At least unchain her, so I can examine her properly. And you need to leave."

"I'm not going anywhere."

"If she can speak to me in confidence, maybe she'll be more cooperative."

"I don't want to speak to you at all," Jenna said to the wall. "Both of you, go away."

Karn looked from Ash to Jenna and back again, as if he were debating whose side he was on. "Why should I trust you, alone with her?" he said finally. "I don't know anything about you."

"The king's word isn't enough?" Ash raised an eyebrow.

Karn just looked at him for a long moment, then said, "Step outside. I need a word with you." He jerked his head toward the door.

As soon as they stepped out into the interrogation chamber, Karn turned, quick as thought, and pinned Ash against the wall, his knife pressed into the hollow of Ash's throat, just below the collar. Ash saw it coming, but he let it happen, because he knew by then that the lieutenant needed Jenna healed and he would not kill Ash to make a point.

"Why did she call you a wolf?" the lieutenant demanded.

"What did she mean by that?"

Ash should have known that Karn hadn't forgotten. He thought of claiming that Jenna was confused, but he had a feeling that Karn wouldn't buy. The lieutenant knew something about his prisoner that made him take her words seriously.

"I'm not going to talk with a knife to my throat," Ash said, meeting Karn's gaze. "It won't make any difference, anyway."

Karn stared at him for a long moment, then lowered the knife and took a step back.

"I think it means she's smart," Ash said. "She wants to die, and she's afraid I might succeed in healing her where Merrill failed. If she can plant enough suspicion to make you pull me off the case, she'll get what she wants."

"She does want to die," Karn said grudgingly. "She stabbed herself. That's why she's so uncooperative. We need to keep her alive at least until—we need to keep her alive."

If she wants to die, Ash thought, then maybe I should let her. But he guessed it wouldn't be wise to say that aloud.

"If you want to keep her alive, then I'll need some answers from you."

Karn frowned, as if he were surprised to hear a healer snapping out orders. "Such as?"

"Do you have the weapon?"

For a few heartbeats, Karn seemed to be debating.

Then, fumbling in his carry bag, he pulled out a dagger in a sheath and extended it, hilt first, toward Ash.

Ash pulled the blade from its covering and looked it over. It was magicked, but the spells used were unfamiliar to him, like a fragment of song from a faraway place. It was still smudged with blood.

"Is this her blood?"

"Hers and . . . and someone else's." Karn cleared his throat.

"Yours?"

"No. One of the guardsmen in Delphi. He's dead. She killed him the night she was—we found her."

"Is that why she's here—because she murdered a guardsman?"

"That's not your concern."

"Where did the dagger came from?"

Karn shook his head. "She had it on her person." He looked like he was going to add something else, then changed his mind.

"How long ago was she wounded?"

"Five days."

"How was it treated?"

"I cleaned it, packed it, and applied a dressing."

Ash nodded. "Good. Did it bleed much?"

"To start with, it did," Karn said, "but it closed up quickly. It's swollen. I think it might be infected. Or something."

Or something. "Has she been eating and drinking?"

Karn shook his head. "Not much."

"All right." Ash handed the dagger back to Karn, who weighed it in his hand.

"Well? Can you heal her?"

"I'm not Merrill," Ash said. "I can't tell without examining her. But I'm not familiar with the magic in the blade. If I had to guess, I'd say it was from outside the Seven Realms."

A muscle twitched in Karn's jaw, but he said nothing.

"Given that, and given the delay in treatment, I'm not optimistic."

"Listen to me." Karn leaned in close. "You say you're a healer, but I know you're a mage, from somewhere to the north of us. Maybe you're working for the king, and maybe you're working for the witch in the north, and maybe you're working for somebody else entirely. Maybe you're a miraculous healer, and maybe this girl is as good as dead. But what you need to understand is that if she dies, it doesn't matter whether the king recommended you or not, it will be our fault, and we will both pay the price."

"I never expected anything less from His Majesty," Ash said. "I'm one of only two people in the empire who might possibly save her life. I'll do my best, whether you're watching me or not, but I might get some helpful information if you stay out here. It's up to you, but I'm going to need all the help I can get."

26

THE WOLF HEALER

So the wolf healer is supposed to be the kind one, Jenna thought, still staring at the wall. The one she might confide in, after holding out stubbornly all this time. They played their roles flawlessly, bad lieutenant and good healer. Then they both went out the door to conspire together.

Perhaps the boy was chosen for his looks. He was tall and well built, with broad shoulders, muscular arms, and large hands, like a young predator coming of age. He wore the same brown clothing as the other healer, but he filled it differently.

He had a long, solemn face, his coppery skin framing deep blue-green eyes that spoke of a mongrel ancestry. His hair was an odd muddy brown, though, which didn't fit with his reddish eyebrows and the bit of stubble on his face.

He was a mage. An aura of power framed him, a diffusion of light more brilliant than Karn's. That and the silver collar told her that he served the monster king. The gifted were never turned to healing, not in Arden. He's probably just another blackbird, someone with a talent for ferreting secrets out of the weak and gullible.

When she glimpsed him out of the corner of her eye, she saw wolves: gray wolves with razored teeth and brilliant eyes, loping across the blue-shadowed snow. His feral scent reminded Jenna of the witch wind that blew down from the Spirit Mountains during the cold moon.

That must mean he's a killer, she thought. He's ruthless. That's all.

She heard the door open, then two sets of footsteps crossing the room.

"Roll over, Jenna," Karn said brusquely, "so I can unlock your hands."

That surprised her enough that she rolled onto her back to look up at him. He reached across and unlocked the manacles from her wrists, allowing them to clang back against the wall. He stood staring down at her for a long moment, as if he wanted to say something, then left again, closing the door behind him.

Meanwhile, the wolf pulled up a stool next to her bed and set a bag on the floor by his feet, making himself at home. "Lieutenant Karn is going to bring some hot water and soap so I can clean out your wound."

She saw no point in objecting, knowing it would do no good.

"Is it all right if I call you Jenna?" he asked.

"If I can call you Wolf," she said.

He scowled, gritting his teeth. "Could you *please* call me Adam?"

"All right," she said. "I will try and think of you as a wolf called Adam."

"So, Jenna," Adam Wolf said, like he just had to try it out. "What exactly happened to you?"

"Why do you care?"

He seemed stuck for a moment. "You're a person," he said finally.

"Well, this person wants you to go away."

"I can't do that," he said. He paused, and when she didn't have a comeback, leaned forward again. "Tell me about the dagger. It seems to be magecraft. Where did you get it?"

"Tell me about your collar," she said, pretending to look up at the ceiling, but watching him out of the corner of her eye. "That's magecraft, too. Does the king have a leash for you as well?"

"It wasn't my idea," the healer muttered, scowling.

"So we have a bond, you and I, both being leashed by the king, and now I'll reveal all my secrets. Is that the idea?"

He shook his head, his jaw tightening as anger rose from him like mist. The wolf was like a tapestry—the surface he presented was calm, tightly woven, but underlain by dark threads of violence. "I don't need to know all your secrets," he said. "Just the ones that will help me do my job."

"For a healer," she said, still pushing, "you have a very dark soul."

He flinched back, as if he'd been caught in a lie, and rubbed the back of his neck. "One of my teachers once told me that healers stand astride the line between life and death. Maybe that's why." He paused, and when she didn't respond, said, "Why are you the king's prisoner?"

"They seem to think I blew up some stuff. And set fire to some stuff. And maybe gave away some secrets." She didn't mean to admit to anything unless she was forced to.

"Why did you stab yourself with your own dagger?"

"It seemed like a good idea at the time."

Adam's lips twitched, and he almost smiled, his eyes crinkling at the corners. It looked good on him. "Why is it so important to them to keep you alive?"

"They don't want me to die before they torture me into naming some names. Then they'll execute me. Which is why healing me is a waste . . . of everyone's time." She stole a look at him. From the stubborn look on his face, she knew he wasn't going to cooperate.

"Thank you for answering my questions," he said politely. "Now. I'm going to examine you. Don't worry," he said, when she shrank back. "This won't hurt. It's not . . . complicated." His eyes met hers, catching and holding. With a slow, deliberate movement, he reached out and took both her hands, his fingers blazing hot against her frozen skin, his thumbs planted on the pulse points of her wrists.

She tried to pull free, but his grip was too strong. She gritted her teeth, steeling herself against whatever magery he would use against her.

At first, she felt only a gentle tendril of . . . something. Like a shaft of sunlight leaking through a canopy of cloud, warming her a bit. Then the channels opened between them, and images flooded through from both sides. Brilliant, heartbreaking, the unvarnished truth. Colliding and entangling and mingling so that it was hard to tell whose was whose, what was real and what was conjury.

She saw wolves again, like gray spirits haunting the twisting streets of a mountain town. Little Maggi, tossed aside like a broken toy. A small, fierce woman with copper skin and green eyes, pacing, smacking her fist into her palm. Riley's eyes, locked with hers, his blood steaming when it hit the snow. A solemn-faced, red-haired boy holding hands with a weeping little girl while grim-faced blue-jacketed guards marched by, carrying flower-decked biers. The deeps of the mine, the scent of damp stone, and darkness as impenetrable as a shroud. A dagger with a dragon hilt, its blade smeared with blood. A fair-haired man lying on slushy cobblestones. The red-haired boy knelt next to him, clutching a pendant carved in the shape of a serpent. Her own father's blood soaking into the tavern floor. The perfect whoosh as the mudback warehouse went up in flames, the bedrock shaking as the munitions inside blew.

A lone wolf with savage, wounded eyes, keeping to the shadows. Scales and claws that glittered in the sun.

She stole a look at the healer. Adam Wolf sat as if mesmerized, lips slightly parted, memories and dreams swimming in the ocean of his eyes, his face changing as each one burrowed into his heart.

He sees it, too, she thought, amazed. He sees me. That had never happened before.

Shared grief and loss, unquenchable rage and vengeance. Familiar. Connecting the two of them in a hundred ways. There was no going back—she'd given too much away. She was vulnerable to him now, but it didn't seem like a bad thing, because he was vulnerable to her.

The wolf was the one who broke it off. He jerked his hands back and stared at her with the most peculiar expression on his face, like he was looking into a mirror and seeing himself reflected back. "What the hell?" he whispered, his voice thick and unfamiliar.

"You tell me, Wolf," she said, blotting tears from her eyes with her sleeve. "What the bloody hell?" She sank back into the bedclothes, trembling. "How . . . was that . . . not complicated?"

Just like that, she was done sparring with the healer. In a world full of villains, she didn't have to know exactly who and what he was in order to know that he was not the enemy.

Adam wet his lips and flexed his shoulders, as if to relieve the tension there. Stole a look at the door as if planning his escape. "What . . . what did you do to me? What does it mean?"

"It means that we are done lying to each other," she said. "There's no point. All right?"

She looked into his eyes, but saw no agreement there, only a new wariness, as if he'd never expected to be ambushed by his patient. And then the shutters closed.

He's scared he's revealed too much.

Didn't you see what I saw? Didn't you? If you know the truth, you have to honor it.

She wanted to shake him, but the conversation was wearing her out. The edges of her consciousness were crumbling away, like the fragile pages of an old manuscript, like wolves breaking away from the pack.

The door banged open and in came Karn with a basin and rags, a fistful of linen strips, and a pot of steaming water. "Am I interrupting something?" he said, looking at the two of them with their heads together. He clunked the supplies down next to the bed.

The wolf blinked at him, as if breaking out of a dream. He gently rocked the pot of water, so it sloshed. "Did you really boil this for ten minutes?"

"Isn't that what you said?" Karn gave them both a pointed look, then went and sat against the wall by the door, so he could watch what went down from a distance.

With Karn in the room, the healer left off questioning her and got down to business. He pulled the pot of water closer, tipping some of the contents into the basin.

"Jenna, I'm going to clean out your wound a bit and see what's going on. Then we'll decide what to do."

"We?"

That brought forth smile number two. Almost. "Are you able to sit up? If I help?"

She nodded.

Gripping her hands again, he gently pulled her upright, turning her so her feet dangled over the edge of the bed. She clutched her bedclothes under her chin, like they were a fort she could hide in. Her head began spinning, and black spots danced before her eyes. She swayed, and he instantly gripped both her shoulders, preventing her from tumbling off the bed.

The healer leaned down so they were nearly nose to nose. The blue-green eyes were framed with long lashes. "Do you want to lie back down?"

"I'll be fine," Jenna gasped. "Just—just give me a minute."

"Then, here. Head between your knees." Gently, he pushed her head down toward the floor. "Breathe." One hand remained between her shoulder blades. She was acutely conscious of the weight of it, the warmth of it, and the pressure of his knees braced against hers.

Eventually, her head cleared enough that she could nod for him to go on.

"Just let me know if you need a break. Once I get this uncovered, you can lie back if you want to."

"Karn!" the healer barked, making her jump. She hadn't realized he'd been speaking so softly. "Jenna's going to need something clean to change into."

"Such as?"

"Bring a loose-fitting man's shirt," the healer said. "Smallclothes. And new bed linens."

It amused Jenna to think of Karn hunting for small-clothes.

The lieutenant went to the door, conversed with the blackbirds outside, and returned to his seat.

"You're still shivering," Adam said. "That's why dungeons are not a good place to treat patients," he said loudly, again for Karn's benefit. "Here. Wrap up in this." He draped the scratchy blanket around her shoulders and she snuggled into it gratefully.

"Now," he said. "Let's have a look." Gently he eased her bedclothes down across her hips and spread a clean sheet over top. Then, quickly, he unwound the bandage that held the dressing in place, pitching it onto the floor. The dressing was stuck to the wound, but he pulled it free so quickly that Jenna had no time to tense up. Maybe it would have been fine anyway—the area around the wound was totally numb, cold, and lifeless.

Next came the wound packing, nasty and foul-smelling, followed by a gout of drainage that the healer sopped up with more rags. That, she felt. That hurt like a stubbed toe. She tried not to show it, but the tears came anyway. He took both her hands now and released his witchery into her. Just as when Karn had tried to interrogate her at the Lady of Grace, it did nothing.

Adam noticed. He leaned close, again speaking softly, so that Karn couldn't hear. "Are you blocking me, Jenna? If so, please don't. I promise, I'm only trying to help you with the pain."

"I'm not a mage. I'm not doing anything. It just doesn't work on me."

"It doesn't really feel like you're blocking me," he said slowly, his eyebrows drawn together in a frown. "More like . . . I'm pouring water through a sieve." He rummaged in his carry bag, found a cloth sack, and shook a fuzzy, gray-green leaf onto his palm. "Hold this under your tongue," he said. "See if it helps."

The leaf was faintly bitter to the taste, but the healer was right—it did help. She felt her body relaxing, floating. The pain was still there, but it was like it belonged to somebody else. That way, it was at least tolerable.

Meanwhile, he gathered up the sheet full of nasty rags and set them aside.

"That was the worst part," he said. "You can lie back now." He washed his hands and dried them on a clean rag, helped her settle into place in bed, and covered her top half with the blanket. He dipped a cloth into the water, wrung it out, and worked some soap into it. Then rolled her bed-clothes back so he could get at the wound again.

His touch was gentle, his movements sure. Though he wasn't any older than she was, Jenna could tell that he'd done this many times before. The way he went about it made an awkward situation bearable.

He washed the wound out with water, several times, then gently probed it with his fingers. It was strangely unsettling to feel the pressure of his fingers under numb skin. He slid a hand under his tunic to grip his jinxpiece and muttered charms. Nothing seemed to happen.

Finally, shaking his head, he sat back. He used his fore-arm to swipe sweat from his face, since his hands were once again covered in blood. "Here's the news," he said. "Healing magic doesn't seem to work on you, meaning I can't repair the damage through wizardry. Unfortunately, you are not resistant to the magic in the blade. It will kill you, if left alone. I'm guessing it won't be pleasant."

Jenna leaned closer. "You could give me a gentle death."

"I could," he said. "But if I treat you, and then you die,

then I'll be in for an ungentle death. I would need more information in order to decide whether to make that trade."

"What are you two whispering about?" Karn demanded.

"She's telling me about working in the coal mines," the healer called back. "How it's not for everybody, but if you survive, you get to keep on doing it."

He's a smart-ass, Jenna thought. I like that in a person.

Karn stood, picked up his stool, and carried it over to the head of Jenna's bed. Then sat again, close enough to listen in.

Adam washed his hands again. Jenna had never seen anyone so keen on hand washing.

"All right, Jenna," he said with a grim smile. "I've got one more thing to try. Let's both hope this works." Taking a deep breath as if bracing for an ordeal, he placed his palm over the wound. She felt the tingle of magic against her skin, then a pulling sensation, as if he were drawing something out of the wound. It felt peculiar, like he was trying to yank her spine out through her navel.

"What are you doing?" she said, pressing herself down into the bed.

"I may not be able to heal what is already damaged, but I can draw the magic out and give you a fighting chance."

She fixed on his face. Adam's eyes were squinted with concentration and sweat beaded his upper lip as if he were calling on all the strength he had. It went on and on, until she felt as if she might turn inside out.

This time, it made a difference. Gradually, the area around the wound warmed as the blood returned. It grew more and more painful as sensation returned as well.

She gasped, and his eyes met hers. "I'm sorry. Sometimes the cure seems worse than the disease."

As her strength returned, hope rekindled, and her will to live burned brighter.

But the healer, he looked worse and worse as she grew better. His skin went ashy, his breathing became labored, his eyes clouded. At one point, he turned away and vomited something vile into the basin. But right away he went back to it, pulling and pulling and pulling until he looked more like the patient than the healer.

"Stop it!" she said. "Healer! That's enough. You're hurting yourself." She gripped his wrists with newfound strength and tried to pull his hands away from the wound. He shook his head fiercely and pressed harder. The silent struggle continued until the healer swayed, slumped sideways, and crumpled onto the floor.

"Karn!" she cried out. Vaulting from the bed, she knelt beside the healer, but Karn was already there.

Swearing, the lieutenant rolled the boy onto his back. "What happened? Did you stab him, too?"

"Shut it," Jenna said. "I think he's fainted." She brushed the healer's hair off his clammy forehead. His eyes were closed, his lids like twin bruises against the pallor of his face, his legs and arms twitching uncontrollably.

Squatting in front of him, Karn slapped him on the cheeks, at first lightly, and then with more force. There was no response.

Jenna gripped Adam's hands, chafing them, wishing she could somehow pull the deadly magic back, but she had no idea how. Reaching into the neckline of his tunic, she pulled out the jinxpiece. It was the serpent pendant she'd seen in the healer's memory. She tried to wrap both of his hands around the pendant, but they fell away as soon as she let go.

No. Nobody else was going to die because of her.

She glared at Karn. "You're a mage. Heal him!"

He shook his head, shrugging helplessly. "I don't know how."

In desperation, she grabbed the water pitcher from a niche in the wall and upended it over the healer's head.

Adam spluttered and coughed, batting at the pitcher with one hand. "I'm all right," he said. "Stop drowning me." He shook his head, spraying water everywhere like a dog. Jenna grabbed up a clean rag and mopped at his face. Now his hand found his amulet and he hung on. "I've just got to learn to pace myself, is all," he said, licking his lips.

"You've got to learn not to do stupid things," Jenna said.

Karn sat back on his heels and looked at Jenna for the first time. "Well, well." He smiled faintly, a smile of relief. "You look better, if he doesn't. You *are* a fine healer, Free-man. The legend lives on."

Jenna sank back onto the bed, her fingers searching out the wound under her rib cage. Though it was still open, it no longer drew her attention like an icy boil, and the skin around the wound was hardening. Her head was clearer than it had been for days, and she was beginning to care that she was filthy. "That's . . . that's amazing," she said. She looked at the drenched healer. "You're amazing."

Then Adam smiled, a full-on, genuine smile that warmed her to the core. Maybe it was foolish, maybe they looked like a pair of loons, grinning at each other in a dungeon cell. Maybe it would be all ashes and regret tomorrow, but she couldn't help smiling back.

TO THE KING'S HEALTH

By the next morning, Ash had nearly recovered—physically, at least—from his healing of Jenna. He had a depleted amulet and a major magical hangover, which wasn't improved by the tongue-lashing he received from Master Merrill for leaving his post the day before.

"What do you mean disappearing yesterday and leaving all of your work for Harold and Boyd to do?" Merrill demanded. "They couldn't do some of the calculations, so the proportions were wrong, and we had to throw out an entire batch. Do you have any idea what that costs?"

Ash stared at him in dull disbelief. "Didn't they tell you where I . . ."

"You are answerable to me," Merrill fumed. "I don't

care what else you had to do, you need my permission to leave your work area."

Ash wasn't long on patience to begin with, and what little he had was quickly draining away. "The king summoned me. I didn't think it was wise to say no."

That made things worse, especially when the master healer noticed the condition of Ash's tunic, which was draped over a chair. "Is that blood on your tunic? Were you performing surgery? By the great saint, you are not qualified! If His Majesty doesn't understand that now, I'll make sure he does before the day is out."

"You do that," Ash said. "You go right ahead and talk to him. Make your case. Let me know how that works out for you." And he pushed past the master healer and into the compounding area.

All morning and into the afternoon, Ash couldn't keep his mind off Jenna Bandelow with the golden eyes and kindled skin. It was as if their minds had been joined, however briefly, when he'd tried to examine her. It would be a long time before he recovered from that.

He picked over the images Jenna had shared with him. Hurtling down into a coal-hole in a huge iron bucket. A bridge exploding, too far away to hear, the pieces sparkling in the sunlight before landing in the river. The king of Arden on a platform, looking down on a sea of roughly dressed miners, a little girl struggling in his grip until he broke her and flung her aside. A name scrawled on the side of a building. Flamecaster. A battered building with a sign over the door: Fletcher's Tack and Harness. A warehouse in flames, sending sparks high into the winter sky.

Ash had played at murder in the summers, returning to the sanctuary at Oden's Ford the rest of the year. If what he'd seen was true, Jenna had been a fighter, and survivor, nearly every day of her life. She put him to shame.

If he could believe what he'd seen. Perhaps her gift was the planting of lies that mimicked the truth. Truth or not—he did believe it. When he'd asked her what it meant, she'd said, *It means that we are done lying to each other.*

But he'd never agreed to that. He had a lot to lose by telling the truth.

Maybe she knew the truth already. She'd spotted him for a wolf, after all, as soon as she saw him. After all these years away, did that mean he was still a wolf under the skin?

She'd mucked around in his mind. What else had she learned about him that she might reveal under interrogation? Would he end up regretting that he'd saved her life?

No. He didn't regret it—he couldn't. That had been his mission since his father's murder—to heal the innocent and punish the guilty.

It was as if they'd shared a lifetime during that brief connection. The only other person who knew him that well was his sister Lyss. And he'd changed so much that she didn't really know him anymore.

Had Lyss changed as much as he had?

One thing he knew—Jenna Bandelow was dangerous. He'd saved her life—now he should just stay away from her.

But he couldn't. Every time he thought of her, his heart accelerated and his gut clenched with longing. He'd been alone for so long. Though he'd walked out with girls at school, he'd kept his mind and emotions under lock and key. Had he really been so hungry for a different kind of connection that he'd completely lost his footing?

It wasn't like she'd shown any sign of being smitten with him. If he made a move on a patient, chained in a dungeon, it would just seem creepy.

Don't lose your head, sul'Han. Remember what you're here for. As his father always said: the hunter who can't keep his eyes on his target goes to bed hungry. Remember that feeling you had when you thought Lyss was the one locked in Montaigne's dungeon. The best way to help Jenna Bandelow was to kill the king of Arden—sooner rather than later.

All morning and into the afternoon, Merrill's foul mood continued. Harold and Boyd disappeared after the setup, so Ash cleaned up the lab afterward. Then he was assigned to change all the beds in the infirmary, although no one had slept in them. By the time he'd finished, the place had emptied out. Even Merrill had given up finding him jobs to do and disappeared.

"You survived, I see."

Ash looked up to see Lila standing in the doorway of the infirmary.

"Barely," he said.

"You do look like scummer on a slab." She came forward, into the room, peering around to make sure nobody else was in there. Then she perched on the edge of one of the prep tables. "So who was it who so desperately needed your skilled healing hand?"

Ash shared an edited version of what had happened the night before, still wary of handing Lila anything that might be used against him.

Lila listened, head cocked, swinging her legs.

"Her name is Jenna Bandelow?"

"So I'm told," Ash said.

"She's from Delphi?"

Ash nodded.

"Why is she important? Is she a blueblood, or—?"

"She's a coal miner."

"A coal miner?" Lila sat forward, her hands on her knees. "Seriously? So what does the king want with a coal miner?"

"She says they suspect she's a saboteur back home, and they're going to try and make her give up her friends."

"Is she a saboteur?"

"Maybe," Ash said. "Probably."

"Well. How's it looking? Do you think she'll survive?"

"I think she has a good chance, now," Ash said.

Lila chewed her lip, like she wanted to say something, but couldn't quite get it out.

"What?"

Lila raised both hands. "Never mind." She slid down from the table. "I actually came here to fetch you to the Great Hall."

Ash eyed her suspiciously. "Why?"

"Did you know that it's Solstice?"

"Solstice? Really?" Ash stared at Lila, ambushed by a flood of memories. Celebrations of Solstice in Fellsmarch, wizard lights decorating the evergreens on the palace grounds, taking the sleigh up into the mountains to cut pine roping and fir, wassailing the trees in the palace gardens, breaking open the Solstice crackers at dinner, releasing magical illuminated birds that fluttered around the room. His father's dramas in the Great Hall that rivaled those seen in any large city.

And later, Solstice at Oden's Ford, when the Temple choirs sang on the quad, and speakers from all the temples proclaimed the good news of the returning sun.

Lila grinned. "I thought you might have overlooked it. I came to get you. They're serving wassail in the Great Hall, and we are invited to drink to the king's health."

To his good health or bad health? "Thanks for coming to get me. Just . . . I need to get something from my room. I'll be right back."

In his room, Ash stood on his bed to retrieve a thin leather sleeve that he'd slid behind the crown molding. Inside, he'd hidden a needle painted with black adder. Anyone pricked with it would be unlikely to know he'd been stung until much later. When it was too late.

Ash slid it into the pouch under his collar alongside the bottle he'd hidden there the day before. Slinging his healer's bag over his shoulder, he rejoined Lila. "Let's go," he said.

She eyed the bag. "Do you ever stop working?"

"I'm going down to see my patient afterward," he said.

The Great Hall was crowded with servants and soldiers and the petty nobility, many of them already deep in their cups. There were huge wassail bowls at either end of the room, and fruits and nuts and cakes and pastries. Many of the servants were decked out in unusual finery, having left off the uniforms of Arden for a day. Apparently this was-sailing custom was a long-standing tradition. Ash found it interesting how different people looked when they wore the clothes they chose themselves. Almost unrecognizable. He was still wearing drab healer colors, since he didn't really have any other clothes.

The wassail was thick and potent. Someone had tacked up sprigs of mistletoe in every doorway, and many were taking advantage of it.

At the center of the hall, a small dais had been con-structed, layered over with evergreens and white and gold ribbon. Up on the platform stood a table centered with two large gold chalices. That must be where the royal family would preside over the festivities and drink to the return of the sun.

Ash worked his way in that direction, hoping to get access to the stage before the king arrived. But when he went to mount the steps, a brace of blackbirds blocked his way. "That up there is for the king and his family," one said. "There's plenty for you lot at the ends of the hall."

Ash loitered next to the dais, nursing his drink, waiting for another opportunity. Finally, a stir at the far end of the room announced the arrival of the king and queen and their entourage, clad in their holiday finery, a riotous bouquet of color. The procession was surrounded by perhaps four dozen blackbirds, armored and grim, no doubt the result of the recent attempt on the king's life.

Whoever this competing would-be assassin is, he's making my job a lot harder, Ash thought.

The contrast between glittering armor and glittering jewels and silk and gold and taffeta was striking. Under the pikes of the guardsmen, the crowd parted like water before the prow of a great ship, closing behind the royal procession like a wake.

Montaigne was clad in cloth of gold. Queen Marina was dressed all in white, her gown a stunning contrast to her dark hair and complexion. Her trailing sleeves were edged in white ermine, uncommon here in the south. Ash studied her with interest. He rarely saw the queen, who almost never left her apartments. She seemed ill at ease, and kept her eyes on her feet, moving cautiously as if afraid of a misstep.

With them was a handsome, dark-haired boy, near Ash's age, perhaps a little older, wearing a circlet of gold, and a younger girl, maybe a seven-year, whose hair had been arranged in soft ringlets.

"That's Prince Jarat, heir to the throne, and Princess Madeleine," Lila murmured. She'd found him in the crowd.

Both royal children had inherited something of their mother's beauty, though their complexions favored their father's. The boy had a stingy-looking mouth and his father's glacial blue eyes.

Ash planted himself by the steps where the royals would pass by, carefully palming his needle. But an impenetrable wall of black uniforms kept him from getting to within arm's length of any of them.

When the royal family reached center stage, a servant filled jeweled cups from the two gold chalices—one for the adults, and another, perhaps less potent brew for the children. Marin Karn stood to the right of the dais, and a foot or two below, covered in the military glitterbits appropriate to his rank. Ash looked around the room, finally spotting Destin Karn in the galleries, scanning the crowd for trouble. For once, he was wearing the black of the royal guard, a dress sword belted at his waist.

When everyone on the stage was served, Montaigne and his queen lifted their cups. As was traditional, they would drink first. "To the great good health of the servants of this household, and the noble houses that are our strength! To the health of the nation, and glory to the great saint!"

And the assemblage lifted their much less elaborate cups and cried, "To the great good health of their majesties, King Gerard Montaigne and Queen Marina, and their royal highnesses, Prince Jarat and Princess Madeleine!"

That was when a servant standing next to the chalice swayed and crumpled to the floor.

There was instant pandemonium up on the stage. Marin Karn batted the cup from the king's hand. It landed, rolling, splattering steaming wassail everywhere, until it disappeared over the edge. The royal children set their cups down with a thunk, their faces pale and frightened. The blackbirds surrounding the stage formed a prickling wall around the dais and blocked all the exits to the hall.

But Queen Marina tilted her head back and drank greedily, three huge gulps, before Father Fosnaught wrenched the cup from her hands and handed it off to a blackbird. Then he gripped her wrist and thrust his face into hers, haranguing her about something.

"Who was that—the one that fell?" Ash whispered.

"That was the king of Arden's taster," Lila said. She pulled him into a corner and got in his face. "Do you know anything about this?"

"What do you mean?"

"No doubt they'll search all of us. You're not . . . carrying anything you shouldn't be, are you? If so, give it to me and I'll get rid of it."

"Besides an amulet?" Ash touched his amulet, in the process returning his sting to its sheath. "Do you think I'm stupid? Only a fool would use a fast-acting poison on a target with a taster. The taster goes down before the king gets it into his system."

Lila blinked at him, as if surprised by this display of logic. "What about the viper?" she persisted. "Were you responsible for that?"

"I may be good with animals, but until I can teach a snake to bite the right person, I wouldn't use one to try and kill someone. Either this would-be killer is an amateur, or someone wants to put the king on his guard." Ash watched as Merrill forced his way through the crowd to kneel at the taster's side.

And that's when the queen collapsed. Her ladies surrounded her, fluttering like birds. Merrill abandoned the taster and knelt by the queen's side.

"Blood and bones," Ash muttered, debating. He hated to leave the queen in Merrill's incapable hands. There was no escaping the hall, anyway.

You can't save everyone, sul'Han. That was becoming his mantra.

And suddenly, somehow, Destin Karn was there, in Ash's face. "Come with me," he said, gripping Ash's arm, "and see to the queen." The lieutenant seemed unaccountably agitated. Maybe he was worried that if the queen died, he would get the blame for not somehow preventing it.

"Master Merrill's handling it," Ash said. "I'd rather not butt in. He's furious with me already, and I'm still a little shaky from—"

"Listen to me, healer," Karn said. "The queen is the kindest, most compassionate—the only truly decent person in this entire court. You are going to come with me, and you are going to heal her if you can, understand?"

"All right," Ash said. "Let's go."

"That's what you get for being so damned capable," Lila called after him.

DEATH'S DOORSTEP

The crowd parted to let Ash and Karn through. He climbed onto the dais to find Merrill waving a pomander under the queen's nose. "Stay back and give Her Majesty some air," he cried.

Montaigne leaned against a marble pillar, guards on every side, arms folded across his chest. His eyes were like chipped ice, fixed on Destin Karn. There would be no getting close to the king now.

"That poison was meant for me, Lieutenant. How could you let this happen, when there has already been one attempt on my life. You knew there was an assassin in the palace." He gestured angrily, the stone on his right hand glittering. "Apparently he has the run of the place."

"Nobody leaves this room without being searched and questioned," Karn said. "The kitchen staff are being interrogated as we speak. We will find out who's responsible."

Ash knelt beside the queen. She lay on her back like a princess in a story, her skin pale as porcelain, her breathing shallow and ineffective. There was a blue tinge around her lips and fingernails.

"Go tend to the taster, boy," Merrill snarled. "I'll handle this. I've been treating the royal family for years."

"Then they are lucky they are still alive," Ash murmured. "I should let you treat the queen, and when she dies, you'll reap the consequences. But I've taken oaths. I can't do that. Now get out of my way."

"Merrill!" Lieutenant Karn said, planting a hand on the master's shoulder. "Do as he says, by the king's command."

The look Merrill gave him was pure poison itself. The healer rose, straightened his tunic with great dignity, and crossed the dais to where the taster lay, neglected.

Ash sent up a prayer for the taster, then turned back to Queen Marina. Using his thumb and forefinger, he slid back her eyelids and did not like what he saw.

He looked up at Karn. "Bring me the cup she drank from."

Karn did as he was told.

When he handed Ash the wassail cup, Ash sniffed at it. Sniffed again. There, amid the cinnamon and clove and rum, he smelled something familiar.

Gedden. Made from a fungus that grows on yew trees, it was easy to find throughout the Seven Realms. There was no time to lose.

He rummaged in his kit, came up with a small brown bottle, thrust it into Karn's hands. "One part powder, one part water, cook over flame until it dissolves."

Karn glanced over to where Merrill was hunched over the taster, but watching them. "Perhaps Master Merrill—"

"No," Ash said, recalling the water hemlock incident. "Whatever you do, don't get him involved. Do it NOW!" he roared when Karn hesitated. "Are you going to wait until she is dead?"

Ash turned back to the queen. Her breathing was already slowing. Soon she would forget to breathe, her heart forget to beat. The poison was abroad in her body, hunting down the spark of life so it could be extinguished. There was no easy way to call it back. The best he could do until Karn returned was to support her breathing and keep her heart going. He leaned close, feeling the whisper of her breath against his cheek, the thread of her pulse in her wrist. When her heartbeat faltered, he pressed both hands against her chest and used flash to compress and release the heart.

It seemed to take forever, but finally Karn was back, with a bottle of warm, murky liquid. Ash sniffed at it, nodded, and said, "Good. Now sit her up as best you can." He felt Lila's presence behind him. "Each of you, take an arm and hold her steady."

Tipping her chin up, Ash poured half of the preparation into her mouth. "If you can hear me, Your Majesty, please swallow."

He wasn't sure if she heard him or not. He massaged her throat. She coughed and choked a little, but he managed to get most of it down. They waited. For an awful moment, she lay still and cold. Then she took a deep breath. Released it. Took another. The color returned to her pallid cheeks. Her breathing strengthened, and her heartbeat, too.

Karn and Lila both breathed out, as if they had been holding their breaths.

"Good work, healer," Karn said softly, not bothering to hide the relief in his voice.

Ash held up the bottle with the remaining antidote. "Give this to the taster," he said.

Lila cleared her throat. "He's dead," she said. "You may as well give her the rest of it."

Ash turned back to the queen. "Your Majesty," he murmured, stroking the damp hair off her forehead. "Can you take a little more?"

She opened her dark eyes and smiled at him, as if she would know him anywhere, as if they were old friends under the skin. "I had the most wonderful dream," she whispered. "I dreamed that I had died."

VISITING HOURS

It's one thing to be locked in a dungeon when you're nearly dead, and it doesn't matter much where you are. But Jenna was feeling better, and getting restless.

Though she'd worked underground for half her life, she was a person who needed to see the sky, even briefly, every day. She wanted to feel the wind in her face and breathe in all the scents it carried. Not that there weren't smells in the king of Arden's dungeon—she just didn't like any of them. She needed a bath. She didn't even want to be with herself.

Jenna was still manacled to the wall, but Karn had given her a longer chain, maybe convinced that she didn't intend to hang herself. So she used the extra bit to pace back and forth, burning off energy and trying to build her strength back up. If she had the chance to escape, she wanted to be ready.

She'd slid her pendant out of the lining of her velvet coat and had hidden it between two loose stones in the wall. She was tempted to put it back on, but worried that it would be discovered.

She was hungry, too—starving, in fact, like her body knew that it had fasted for a week and was making up for lost time. She had no way to mark the time, but it seemed forever since anyone had brought her food.

That wasn't the only thing she was hungry for. She'd hoped the healer, Adam Freeman, would have come back to see her by now.

She was drawn to him in a way she hadn't been since Riley, back when she was just a lýtling, and easily smitten. It's not easy to muster up a romance when you're cold, and exhausted, and dirty most of the time. It didn't help the cause that she'd been walking the world as a boy ever since Riley died.

Besides, after Riley, she'd realized that love was just a setup to get your heart broken.

So now she was locked in a dungeon, dirty as a miner on a bender, and she was falling for the enemy's healer, who might be a wolf. Maybe she hadn't learned much after all.

Wolf, she repeated in her head, like a besotted farm girl. She really should stop calling him "healer" and "Wolf," but Adam Freeman didn't sound right, somehow, and so she had a hard time saying it. Even when *he* said it, it sounded like a lie.

She was getting tired of the tight circle she could make around the bed. She scanned the room. The torches were mounted high on the wall. If she stood on the bed, she might be able to reach them.

Then what? Play with them? They wouldn't burn hot enough to melt her shackles.

Still, for something to do, she climbed up on the bed and stretched up high, reaching, feeling the pull in the wound in her belly . . .

She heard somebody fumbling at the door and dropped like a rock, hitting the bed hard. Was it the healer? Her heart accelerated.

But, no. The door swung open to reveal Destin Karn with a goblet in one hand and her jeweled dagger in the other.

Oh.

"What was that noise?" His eyes flicked around the room.

"What noise?"

"Just now."

Jenna gave him a look like you might give a lýtling who's making up stories. "I didn't hear it."

Karn crossed to the bed and pulled up a stool, resting the blade across his knees. At least the blade was clean now.

He raised the goblet. "Happy Solstice, Jenna," he said. He took a long drink.

"Is it really Solstice? I didn't know."

Karn raised his glass again. "May the sun come again."

"Where is my wassail?" she asked, eyeing his.

"You need to be careful, drinking wassail around here," Karn said with a wink. His slow, deliberate speech said that he'd definitely been drinking, though he wasn't stumble drunk.

"I'll chance it." When he didn't respond she said, "What about something to eat?"

Karn furrowed his brow. "Are you hungry?"

"Nobody's been down here all day," Jenna said. "So, yes, I'm hungry."

"Oh," he said. "I'm sorry." He seemed to think that handled it.

Jenna gritted her teeth. "Why are you here?"

"I need to ask you some questions," he said, "now that you're feeling better."

Jenna's empty stomach clenched. This was what she'd worried about, all along—that if she survived, she'd be put to the question. He'd brought nothing with him save a cup of wassail and the dagger, but there was a whole array of torture tools just outside her door.

"Look," she said, "I'm not who you think I am."

"Who do you think I think you are?" Karn said.

It took a while to hack through that word tangle. "You

think I'm one of those Patriots, but I'm not. I worked in the mines and made a little coin on the side telling fortunes. Me and my da—we just tried to keep our heads down and stay out of trouble. Yet you came into my father's tavern and you killed him."

"It was an accident," Karn said.

"Well, he's just as dead as if you did it on purpose, isn't he?" Jenna was having a hard time reining in her temper, partly because she was guilty and her father was innocent, yet he was the one who had died.

Karn waved this away. "Anyway, I'm not here about the Patriots."

"You're not?"

He shook his head. "I'm here about you."

Fear lay like a stone in her belly. "Look, if you think you can get drunk, come down here and—"

He shook his head. "No," he said flatly. "Tell me what you know about the symbol embedded in your neck."

And that was how the truth she'd been beating away with both hands found a place to roost. "This is really about the magemark?"

"Yes," Karn said. "It is."

"Then you probably know more than I do," she said, exploring it with her fingers. "You've seen it, I haven't."

"Were you born with it?"

"As far as I know. It's—it's like a birthmark. Or maybe a curse."

"A curse?" Karn leaned forward, eyes narrowed. "What do you mean?"

Jenna didn't know much, so she saw no reason not to spill it. "All I know is what I've been told," she said. "My parents adopted me from an old woman who said she was my grandmother. She said they should hide the birthmark, because people would kill me because of it."

"What people? And why?"

"She didn't say."

Karn scowled, like he was angry with her dead grandmother for not leaving clear directions. "Have you seen it anywhere else—the symbol, I mean? Or seen anyone else with a marking in the same place?"

"No," Jenna said, "but I haven't really been looking."

"What was your grandmother's name?"

"I don't know."

"Where was she from?"

"She never said, I guess, though my da said she sounded like a foreigner."

Karn rolled his eyes. "Your parents adopted a baby and they didn't ask a single swiving question?"

"They must've asked when my name day was, so they could celebrate when it came around," Jenna said. When he kept shaking his head, she said, "Look, they'd waited a long time to have a baby. They were getting up in years. Maybe they figured beggars can't be choosers. Or they might learn something they didn't want to know."

"Have you ever been to the Northern Islands? Or Carthis?"

Jenna shook her head. "I'm not even sure where that is."

"Perhaps your family was from there? Or maybe they traveled there?"

"Why all these questions about places I've never been? Are you sure you have the right person?"

"Why is the Empress Celestine looking for you?" Karn snapped the question out, like it would catch her off guard.

Jenna felt like she was wading in deeper and deeper, with nothing to hang on to. "Who is Empress Celestine?"

"Empress Celestine is the empress in the East. She rules the Northern Islands and Carthis," Karn said. "Or most of Carthis. So. What is her interest in you? And don't tell me you don't know, because I don't believe you."

"I don't know what to say, then. I never heard of her, and I had no idea she was interested in me. If she's the one looking, then why don't you ask her?"

"That," he said, wincing, "would not be a good idea." He held up the dagger. "Where did you get this?"

"My grandmother gave it to my parents. She said it belonged to my mother."

"What's your mother's name? Where is she now?"

"I don't know her name, and she's dead. Both my parents are dead."

"Really," Karn said skeptically. "Let me fill you in. This weapon of yours is from the Northern Islands. It is carried by Empress Celestine's bloodsworn warriors."

Jenna stared at it, then looked up at Karn. "But . . . you acted like you didn't know anything about it before, when the healer—when Freeman was trying to treat me."

"What I've been told is that nobody survives a cut from a bloodsworn blade. Sharing that would have served no good purpose."

Jenna swallowed hard. "Oh." That explained why Karn was so desperate to get her to Ardenscourt—because he thought she was going to die.

"So. It seems that Freeman is very good at what he does. Now," he said, as if he'd backed her into a blind alley, "would you like to change your story?"

"Not unless you want me to make something up." It was like she was in class at the temple, and she hadn't done her work.

"Celestine tends to seek out the powerful. So what makes you powerful, Jenna? What does she want from you?"

Karen's rapid-fire questions about things she knew nothing about were getting on her nerves. "Think about it, Lieutenant," she said. "If I were powerful, do you think I'd be locked up in somebody's dungeon?"

"You are resistant to magery," he said.

"I didn't know that until you tried to spell me."

"Do you have other gifts as well?"

"Nothing that an empress would cross the ocean for."

"Such as . . ."

Jenna sighed. "I see things that other people can't. Like, you know, visions. Sometimes I see hints of the future. Sometimes I see a person as they really are. Or I see the truth when you tell me a lie."

Karn shifted on his stool, as if he found that last bit unsettling. "What else?" he persisted. "Even if it seems trivial."

"I have good hearing and a sensitive nose. I can see farther than anyone I know, even in the dark." She hesitated. "I heal up quick, whether it's a cut or whatever. And—and I don't burn."

"What?"

"Just what I said. My skin turns heat and flame. Even when I was little, I could snuff out a lantern with my fingers or pull a pan out of the oven bare-handed."

Karn didn't seem impressed. "How is that helpful?"

"It's helpful to a blaster," Jenna said, "or a baker."

Karn gripped the chain that bound Jenna's wrists and jerked her in close, so they were eye to eye. "Do you think this is some kind of joke? I don't think you understand just how precarious your situation is," he hissed. "The empress is hunting you, and we need to know why before she finds you."

As it sometimes did, the truth tapped Jenna on the shoulder. "Who's 'we'?" she said. "The king doesn't even know you're down here, does he?"

Karn stared at her for a long moment, his face gone stony as the Fellsian escarpment. He pushed to his feet, reached high, and pulled down one of the torches. "You're resistant to flame, are you?" He thrust the torch into her face and she flinched back, startled. "Prove it."

Jenna raised her manacled hands to shield her face. "I don't know what you're trying to—"

"I said prove it!" He jabbed at her again, and this time she closed both hands around the flaming head of the torch and held on until she smothered it out. By then, the end of her sleeve had caught fire, and she had to bat it out against her side.

"Look what you did," she said, examining the charred cuff. "I only have the one shirt, and you—"

"Blood of the martyrs," Karn whispered. "I never meant you to—let me see your hands." Karn gripped both her wrists and examined the palms of her hands. He sucked in a breath and looked up at her, eyes wide with relief or surprise or both. "They're not blistered—they're not even red." He tapped her hand with his fingertip. "It feels like they're armored."

"That comes and goes," Jenna said, pulling free. "I don't know why you keep asking me questions when you don't believe any of my answers."

At that moment, the door banged open and they both turned, startled. It was the healer, Adam Wolf, his arms full of packages. He froze in the doorway, staring at the two of them, apparently clasping hands.

"What the hell is going on?" He spoke quietly, but his voice was laced with steel and there was a darkness at his center that she'd not seen before.

"Freeman," Karn said. "This is a surprise."

"Obviously," Adam said. He set his packages down at the head of Jenna's bed and turned to face Karn, his body balanced and ready for action. He did resemble a wolf in a way—one who had chosen his prey and was considering the kill. "Well? What are you doing here?" He took a step toward Karn. "I told you that she needed rest. You couldn't let this wait for even a day?"

"Careful, healer," Karn said with icy calm, though one hand found his amulet. "Don't lose your head and do something you'll regret. I needed to question Jenna today, because I'm . . . it was now or never. She may be your patient, but she is our prisoner."

"But I'll get the blame if she has a relapse." Adam sniffed the air, then took another good look around the room. "What's burning?"

"One of the torches went out," Karn said, shooting Jenna a warning look as he relit the torch and set it back into place.

Ah, Jenna thought. The lieutenant doesn't want the healer—or the king—to know what he's been up to. Well, then. Her da always said that when somebody offers an unexpected gift, it was bad manners not to take it.

"Don't be too hard on the lieutenant, Wolf," Jenna said. "He came to tell me that he's arranged for a bath, some books, and a transfer out of the dungeon into an actual room."

Jenna couldn't say who looked more surprised, Karn or Adam.

"Really," Adam said, looking at Karn narrow-eyed. "That's . . . difficult to believe."

By then, Karn had his sharp's face back on. He smiled crookedly, acknowledging the deal. "The bath and the books are no problem. But the transfer may not happen until after I get back." Karn scooped up the dagger and got off a bit of a bow. "Jenna. We'll speak again." With that, he went out the door.

SOLSTICE
CELEBRATION

As soon as Karn walked out, Adam pulled the door shut
and swung back around. "Are you all right, Jenna?" he
said, his eyes glittering in the torchlight.

"I'm all right."

"He didn't hurt you? When I walked in, I could've
sworn that Lieutenant Karn was threatening you."

Jenna decided not to share the part with the torch. She
saw no good coming from it. "No," she said. "Not really.
Karn seemed eager for answers, but he didn't get rough,
if that's what you mean. Maybe he's been told not to hurt
me."

"It's hard to imagine King Gerard coming up with a
rule like that," Adam said, claiming the stool.

Jenna hesitated. "I got the feeling that Karn was down here on his own account, like the king didn't know he was interrogating me and . . ." She trailed off, distracted by a delicious smell. "Is that food in there?" she said, eyeing the healer's packages.

Adam nodded. "I brought you some from the Solstice celebration. Do you feel up to eating?"

Jenna snatched up one of the parcels and sniffed at it. Roast beef. Sharp cheddar cheese. Freshly baked bread. She was practically drooling on it. Ripping away the cloth, she took a large bite.

The healer stared at her, surprised, then loosed one of his rare smiles. "You seem to be feeling much better," he said. "Better than I could have hoped, considering the way you looked yesterday."

Jenna nodded, not wanting to talk with her mouth full. She swallowed, then said, "I am much better. I've always been quick to heal, but you—you work magic."

"Maybe," he said, hunching his shoulders like praise made him uncomfortable. "I'll want to take a look at that wound in a bit." He watched her eat for a while then said, like a dog returning to a bone, "What kinds of questions was he asking? Karn, I mean."

"That's what surprised me. He said he wasn't here about the Patriots."

"Patriots?"

"The ones in Delphi fighting King Gerard. I thought

that was what it was about—that they thought I was doing spying and setting fire to things. But, no, he kept asking me about an empress." She watched the healer carefully, to see if he knew about the empress already, but he looked as ambushed as she had been.

"What empress?"

"Someone named Celestine, from Carthis. Or the Northern Islands. Have you heard of her?"

He shook his head. "No. All I know about Carthis is, you know, pirates. And that wizards—mages, I mean—came from the Northern Islands. Besides the pirates, the storms are so bad on the Indio these days that we never get ships from there anymore."

"Karn said this Celestine was hunting me, and he wanted to know why, and what the magemark on my neck meant, and all about my family. He seemed tweaked that I couldn't help him."

Adam mulled this over. "Does he think you're the empress's long-lost daughter or what?"

"Karn doesn't know what to think. He knows more about the dagger than he let on, though. He says it's the kind carried by the . . . by the bloodsworn warriors who serve the empress. He said that nobody survives a cut from those blades."

"I knew it was magicked, I just wasn't familiar with the enchantments."

By now Jenna was licking her fingers, having finished

off the meat and cheese. "Do I smell a peach?" She looked pointedly at Adam's bag.

Smiling and shaking his head, Adam pulled a ripe peach out of his bag and held it out to her. Jenna snatched it and bit into it, the juice running down her chin.

"Merciful Maker," she said. "We never get these in Delphi."

"Save room," Adam said. "I brought sugar cakes and wassail, too."

"Wassail?" Jenna leaned forward, making no attempt to hide her excitement. "You brought wassail?"

The healer unwrapped another bundle to reveal fancy Solstice cakes, and set them next to her on the bed. Then he handed her the flask and a cup.

"Ah," Jenna said. She expertly uncorked the flask with her teeth and poured, then wound her fingers about the cup and closed her eyes, breathing deeply. "Everybody makes wassail his own way. Cinnamon. Cloves. Hard cider." She took a sip. "Rum," she added.

"It's strong," he warned her.

"Good," she said, and drained the cup. Adam stared at her as she picked up a sugar cake and bit off a corner.

"I'd go easy on that," he said. "Poison and alcohol don't mix."

"I disagree," Jenna said. "This is just what I need. My da owned a tavern. I used to make the wassail on Solstice, and on the Day of the Dead. He always said I made it best."

She paused, lost in wistful memory for a moment. When she focused in on Adam again, he seemed to be staring at her lips. Which made her stare at his, and wonder what it would be like to . . .

Stop it. You've probably got peach juice running down your chin and that's why he's staring. She mopped her sleeve across it, just in case. Now he probably thinks you were raised in a barn.

She refilled her cup, trying to cover her embarrassment. "Are you feeling better?"

"I am," Adam said, taking a swallow from the flask. "It always takes a while to recover from a healing. Believe it or not, I'm faring better than usual, since I couldn't use magic to heal you."

Jenna frowned, confused. "Isn't that what you did?"

"It's a subtle difference. In most people, I can use magic to close up a wound or cure an infection or minimize pain—to treat disorder of whatever kind. In your case, that didn't seem to work. But what I could do was remove the toxic magic that was causing damage, because that wasn't part of you." He paused, grimacing. "I'm sorry. Sometimes I don't know when I've crossed the line from a conversation into a lecture."

"No, it's all very . . . interesting," Jenna said. "You do seem like you've had a lot of practice, and some schooling, too, which surprises me. When I first met you, I took you for a soldier."

"A soldier? Why a soldier?"

"Because the king of Arden uses his mages to kill people, not to heal them. Plus, you have the body of a soldier." She reached out and squeezed his muscled arm, then quickly let go, flustered. "I mean, you didn't get those muscles stitching up wounds or mixing potions."

"I don't do much of that around here. I scrub a lot of floors, I'm a demon with a mortar and pestle, and I've been shoveling a lot of horse dung, too."

"There's never any shortage of that," Jenna said.

The healer laughed. "No," he said. "Especially not at court." He tipped back his head and drank again, his long throat jumping as he swallowed. "Now," he said, setting the flask aside and pulling his healing kit closer. "Before I drink too much, I want to take a look at that wound."

Jenna sat on the edge of the bed, her blanket draped around her hips. She lifted her shirt up, out of the way.

Adam leaned forward, reaching around her to unwrap the linen. Her skin prickled at his closeness, the warmth of his breath, the scent of soap that she was beginning to associate with him. Looking at the top of his head, she could see a faint line where the natural red of his hair met the brown dye. She resisted the temptation to trace it with her fingers, to let him know she wasn't fooled.

I know you, Wolf, she thought. Even though you try and keep your secrets.

Adam pulled the linen away and set it aside. Jenna's skin

pebbled as the air hit her bare middle. Then she felt the warmth of his hands under her rib cage as he examined the wound. Her heart began to thump so hard it seemed he would notice.

She fought a sudden urge to slide off the bed and onto his lap, wrap her legs around his middle, and—

Stop it! Still. That idea, once kindled, was hard to put out.

Think of something else. Name the saints of the Church of Malthus—that would kill anybody's desire.

Fortunately—or unfortunately, the healer's mind was on other things. "Blood and bones," he muttered, sitting back. "That's impossible."

"What?" Jenna said, breaking out of her fog. She craned her neck, trying to see.

"Your wound is all but healed. Overnight." He looked up at her, his expression bewildered, as if expecting her to explain.

"Well, they said you were a damned good healer, Wolf," Jenna said.

"I'm good, but I'm not that good." Adam shook his head, biting his lower lip. "The area over the wound is hard, like—like armor. Or scales. I've not seen anything like it."

"That always happens when I get hurt," Jenna said. "It . . . crusts over like that at first, then goes back to normal." She shrugged. "Strange."

The healer ran his fingers over the wound. "I don't see

any reason to wrap it up again. It's better protected than anything I could do." He pulled a jug of water from his kit and warmed it between his hands, then washed the area and allowed it to air-dry. When he finished repacking his kit, he set it between his feet, but made no move to leave. He seemed to be wrestling with himself.

"What?" Jenna leaned forward so she could look into his face.

"Would it be all right if I took a look at your magemark?"

"Why not?" she said with a sigh. "Everyone else has." She turned half sideways, scooping her hair up and arching her neck so he could see. He sat next to her on the bed and leaned in close to look, brushing his fingers over the symbol, raising instant gooseflesh.

"Can you feel that?" he asked.

She nodded. "Maybe I'm just used to it, but it feels like my own skin."

"I've never seen anything like this," he said. "Like . . . like metal and jewels set into the skin. Did you have an injury there in the past?"

"It's been there as long as I can remember," Jenna said. "I've tried to—to pry it off, but it's as permanent as any other part of me."

"Do you know what the symbol means?"

"Everybody keeps asking me, and I don't know. Based on what's happened so far, I'd say it means trouble and bad luck."

"And you were born with this?"

"So I'm told."

The healer was studying her, eyes narrowed, rubbing his chin, as if she was a puzzle that he couldn't work out.

"What?" she said, brushing at herself, thinking maybe she'd dropped something.

"Why are you telling me all this?" he asked bluntly. "You don't know me. Why should you trust me?"

Jenna could tell that he was asking himself the same question—if he should trust her. He's a wary wolf. As well as lonely. I wonder why.

She reached out and took one of his hands in both of hers, feeling the buzz of connection between them. "You're wrong. I *saw* you yesterday. I saw the red-haired boy and the man lying dead in the snow and the gray wolves." When he said nothing, doubt trickled in. "Are you saying that you didn't see me?"

When he stiffened and shifted his eyes away, she knew that he had.

So she pressed him. "What did you see?"

He breathed in, then released the words bottled up inside. "Too much," he said. "Enough." He paused. "Those—those images I saw." He stopped, cleared his throat. "The little girl, and the boy, and the king of Arden . . . were they true?"

"They were true," she said, a catch in her voice. "The boy—his name was Riley. He was fifteen, and I was twelve."

"I'm sorry, Jenna," Adam said softly. "I'm sorry that happened."

She turned to face him. "I punched the king in the nose," she said, fierce tears leaking from her eyes. "He bled, and bled, and bled . . ." She trailed off. "That was the beginning. I've been fighting back ever since."

"Since twelve?"

"Do you think I wasn't a grown-up, after that?"

"I see your point."

"You've had losses, too," Jenna said. There was a question buried in there, but he didn't take the bait.

"Yes," he said. "I suppose I'm still walking that line between life and death, trying to choose which side I'm on."

"I want you on my side, healer," Jenna said.

"And . . . I want to be," he said. "It's just . . ." He searched her face. "How do you ever really know a person?"

Jenna ran her fingertips over the back of his hand, tracing the veins. "Not everything is a lie, Wolf," she said. "Sometimes you have to believe what you see."

His head came up, as if she'd startled him. Leaning forward, she slid her arms around his neck and kissed him on the lips. For a moment, he resisted, then surrendered. It was a long time before they broke apart.

31

THE EMPRESS'S GIFT

It was becoming an ordeal—getting in to see the king. After only three days away in Baston Bay, the change in procedure was striking. Lila and Destin submitted to the pat down, the interrogation, the magery—all before they even entered the small council chamber. The mage on duty, Marc DeJardin, scowled as he rooted through the crates full of flashcraft.

"More chains for the enslaved, Barrowhill?" he said when he'd finished.

"You may not approve, but it's a living," Lila said. "Somebody has to do it, so it might as well be me."

DeJardin didn't seem impressed by that logic.

The blackbirds hoisted the crates and carried them into

the hall, Lila and Karn following behind.

The usual suspects were ranged around the conference table—Marin Karn, Michel Botetort, and Gerard Montaigne. They all wore grim expressions, and the tension was thick as thistle and just as prickly. Whatever they were discussing, it seemed to be bad news, and General Karn was the one in the hot seat. They had no intention of sharing, though, because they quit talking as soon as Lila and Destin walked in.

Destin seemed to pick up on the mood in the room as well. His gaze flicked from face to face, resting on his father's the longest.

Well, Lila thought, as she and Destin took a knee, at least we've brought some show-and-tell.

"Your Majesty," Destin said "Barrowhill and I are pleased to report that our operation in Baston Bay was a success. In fact, the results have exceeded our wildest dreams."

I don't know about that, Lila thought. My dreams are pretty wild.

Destin chose an item from each of the crates and set them on the table for display. A collar, a talisman, and an amulet.

Lila had never seen General Karn display any spark of excitement or enthusiasm, but now he came damned close before he tamped it down. He picked up an amulet, which lit up brightly when he touched it. He set it down again quickly and said, "What's the count?"

"One hundred and thirty-three collars," Destin said. "Fifty-four talismans. One hundred fourteen amulets."

"It's a pity you weren't able to get more talismans," the general said, mopping at his face with a handkerchief. "That's what we really need."

It's a pity you're such a heartless, ungrateful bastard, Lila thought. This time, blessedly, she kept it to herself.

"How were you able to secure so many at once?" Botetort asked, showing no desire to examine the loot.

"We intercepted a shipment of old flash on its way from the Southern Islands to Chalk Cliffs," Lila said. "This is more than a thousand years old."

"What was it doing down south?" General Karn asked. "They have no use for flashcraft. They drove out their mages a long time ago."

"It was hidden down there by the copperheads at the end of the Wizard Wars, when they knew they'd lost," Lila said. "They didn't want it to fall into enemy hands. It's been there, forgotten, ever since. Somebody tipped them off, and they decided to ship it back home, so to speak."

"How did you find this out?" General Karn persisted, seeming intent on poking holes in her story.

"Lila has relatives in the Southern Islands who keep her informed," Destin said.

"That's convenient," the general said.

"Very impressive, Lieutenant Karn, Lila," Montaigne

said with a twitch of a smile. "Now, more than ever, this could spell the difference between victory and defeat."

General Karn shifted in his seat.

What's going on? Lila thought. Did somebody die while I was out of town?

There came a pounding at the door. One of the idling blackbirds opened up and spoke briefly with someone outside.

"It's the principia, Your Majesty," the blackbird said. "He says it's urgent."

"Everything these days is urgent," the king said. "This had better be. Show him in."

Cedric Fosnaught, the spiritual leader of the Church of Malthus, swept into the room in a flurry of self-importance. "Your Majesty, I am so sorry to interrupt," the prelate said. "However, a ship has arrived in the harbor from the Northern Islands. The commander came ashore to inform us that he represents the Empress Celestine."

Empress who? Lila thought. But the others wore stunned looks that said they were familiar with the name. What else have I missed? she thought. She was usually better informed than that.

"This ship is here?" the king said in a low, fierce voice. "At the river docks?"

Fosnaught nodded. He reached inside his robes, pulling out a rolled parchment and a velvet bag. "He gave me a message to you from the empress. And a token of her esteem." The prelate extended the parchment and the bag toward the king.

Montaigne eyed them warily. "Hold those for the moment," he said. "Botetort, tell the staff outside to send for Freeman."

"Freeman?" Botetort looked from Montaigne to Fosnaught, who appeared as unhappy as the thane. "But what would he—?"

"Do it," the king said.

Fosnaught opened his mouth as soon as the door closed behind Botetort. "Your Majesty, please indulge this loyal subject's concern in the matter of the healer," he said. "Is it really wise to—to—" His gaze fell on the Karns, and he seemed to be trying to rework what he meant to say. "—to introduce unfamiliar magery into the room? Especially a mage who has had such a brief tenure here?"

The king's lips tightened into a thin line. "The boy has demonstrated more talent in his brief tenure here than many who have been here at court for years."

Hmmm, Lila thought. Maybe I've underestimated the runaway princeling. He seems to have charmed the king, at least.

Eventually, Ash arrived, with Botetort watchdogging him, having run the gantlet outside. He bowed to the king. His eyes flicked from Destin to Lila, narrowing when they lit on the crates of flashcraft. "You asked for me, Your Majesty?"

"Fosnaught, give the items to the healer, so that he can examine them for curses, enchantments, and poisons."

All at once, the principia seemed more than eager to drop the empress's gifts into Ash's hands.

Ash set the velvet bag on the table. He cradled the parchment in his hands, closed his eyes, and murmured charms over it. He looked up at the king, tapped the seal with his finger, and said, "Would you like to examine the seal, Your Majesty, in order to verify its authenticity before I break it?"

Montaigne leaned forward, careful not to get too close, and scanned the seal. "It seems to be in order," he said. Ash broke the seal, unrolled the parchment, and ran his fingertips over the ink, murmuring what sounded like gibberish to Lila. Then nodded, as if he'd made a decision. "Good news, Your Majesty," he said. "It is safe. If there were curses present, I have disabled them." He handed the parchment to the king, then turned his attention to the velvet bag.

Meanwhile, the king scanned the empress's message quickly, then thrust it at Destin. "She knows. The bloody empress knows we've found the girl. She wants to make the exchange as soon as possible."

"But . . . that doesn't make sense," Destin muttered. "How could she possibly know?"

"She's a bloody sorceress," the king snarled. "A witch. Maybe she sacrificed a virgin or a goat. How would I know?"

"She's a witch?" Fosnaught looked betrayed. "Commander Strangward never mentioned that."

Destin read, tracing the script with a finger. "'I understand that you now have the magemarked girl in your possession. I have sent Commander Strangward with an array of gifts, including a powerful weapon that will ignite terror in the hearts of your adversaries. This will be evidence of my good faith.'" He looked up. "What's all this about a weapon? Did you see it, Fosnaught?"

The cleric shook his head. "It's still on board his ship."

"She promised us an army of mages," General Karn said, snatching the parchment from his son's hand and reading it over himself. "What makes her think that we would be satisfied with a weapon?"

"It takes time and resources to move an army," Destin said. "The empress might have been unwilling to undertake it without knowing for sure that the girl is the one she is seeking."

"What would you know about armies?" General Karn growled.

The general never misses an opportunity to take a shot at his son and heir, Lila thought. I wonder why.

Destin met his father's sneer unflinchingly. "Given that the empress learned of the girl's presence here so quickly, I think we have to assume that she has agents right here in the capital."

"Agents that *you* should have ferreted out before now."

"Lord Strangward is eager to meet as soon as is conveniently possible," Fosnaught said, as if eager to reclaim the stage. "He says that any time after dinner would suit him."

"Tonight?" Montaigne snorted. "He shows up here unannounced and demands an immediate audience with the king of the Realm?"

The cleric's mouth twisted, as if he tasted something sour. "He appears to be . . . unschooled in court manners, Your Majesty. From his appearance, I would have guessed him to be a horse savage. Or a pirate."

"He'll just have to wait," the king said. "Tell Strangward we'll meet with him tomorrow in the Small Hall."

Fosnaught cleared his throat. "Tomorrow is the Feast of Saint Malthus."

"The day after tomorrow, then," Montaigne amended.

"Lord Strangward would prefer that we meet on board his ship, so that he can display the weapon, which is down in the hold."

"If he thinks that I am foolish enough to get on board a ship with a pirate, he is sadly mistaken," the king said. "I don't mean to be carried off to the Northern Islands and held for ransom."

"Your Majesty," Destin said. "Could we perhaps meet in your pavilion at dockside? That would be close to the ship, and yet would allow us to meet on our home ground."

"I see no reason to meet this barbarian halfway,"

Montaigne said. "He should be happy that I am meeting with him at all."

His liege men looked at one another, as if each hoped that one of the others would speak up. They want this deal to go forward, Lila thought, whatever it is.

Strangward might be unschooled in courtly ways, but the king has no practice at diplomacy, either. He's used to getting what he wants by force.

"Your Grace," General Karn said. "We need that army, we need the funds, and if the empress is offering a fearsome weapon, we need that, too, especially now."

"It is your failures that have put us into this position, Karn," Montaigne said. "Don't forget that."

"It could rekindle enthusiasm for the war in the Thane Council," Botetort said. "We have nothing to lose and much to gain by hearing what the barbarian has to say."

"It's a wise leader who keeps his eyes on the ultimate goal—uniting the Seven Realms under Ardenine rule, and in the grace of the true church," Fosnaught said. "We know that you are the kind of strategic thinker who takes the long view, even if it involves dealing with . . . witches. At least until we get what we need from her."

The king looked from one to the other, a muscle working in his jaw. "Spare me the flattery, gentlemen," he said. "Very well. We will meet in the Small Hall. Fosnaught, tell Pettyman to arrange for housing for Strangward and his crew outside the—"

"He prefers to stay on board his ship, Your Majesty," Fosnaught said. "He does not want to inconvenience you or impose on your hospitality."

"Is that so?" the king said. "If true, that would be a first. Lieutenant Karn, tell Pettyman to arrange for new quarters for the girl, inside the keep, but on one of the upper floors, in the tower."

"It's already in process, Your Majesty," Destin said.

Montaigne swung toward Ash, who still seemed to be studying the contents of the bag, though Lila suspected he was listening closely. "How's the girl's health?"

Ash looked up. "She is doing remarkably well, sire, to have suffered such a serious wound," he said. "I would, however, recommend that you wait another week before—"

"See that she's in good shape by the day after tomorrow," the king said.

"Yes, Your Majesty," Ash said.

Well, Lila thought, at least the princeling seems to be learning when to give way.

But he wasn't finished. "Your Majesty," Ash said, "would you like to hear more about the empress's gifts?"

The king seemed to have forgotten all about the velvet bag. "Yes, of course," he snapped. "What is it?"

"There are no enchantments," Ash said, weighing the bag in his hand. He pulled a silver platter toward him and emptied the contents onto it. "If I've counted correctly, this bag contains fifteen large diamonds. If they are real, they would be of a very high value."

Montaigne eyed the diamonds greedily. "You have examined them? They are not poisonous or cursed?"

Ash shook his head. "They are not."

"Good," the king said, scooping them back into the bag and sliding them into his doublet. "I will examine these further at my leisure."

"The diamonds are impressive, Your Majesty, but they are not the most precious of the empress's gifts. This is." Ash displayed a small ceramic bottle inscribed with runes.

"What is it?" the king asked.

"Living silver," Ash said. "Very rare, very valuable. Here, let me show you." Uncorking the bottle, he poured a small amount onto a ceramic plate. It formed small silver globules that rolled around in a mesmerizing way. Ash poked it with his finger and the droplets shimmered and danced.

What the hell is he up to? Lila thought. She craned her neck to get a closer look.

"That's remarkable," the king said, looking smitten. "But . . . what is it good for? Can it be molded or hardened like ordinary silver?"

"Not unless it is married with other metals," Ash said. "But that would be a waste. It is most valued for its magical qualities. When burned or heated, it releases white magic."

The king was extending his hand toward it, but now he

drew back. "White magic?"

"Bear in mind, I'm no expert," Ash said. "All I know is what I've read in the old manuscripts. In the Northern Islands, it is used as a kind of talisman. Its vapors protect against evil. It is particularly abhorrent to snakes, assassins, and other malevolent creatures."

Fosnaught made the sign of Malthus. "Your Majesty," he said. "It is the grace of God that protects us against evil. I can't imagine that the use of such agents would be consistent with—"

"Where was the grace of God when some villain put a viper in my bed?" Montaigne said. He turned back to Ash. "How is it used?"

"Some sprinkle a few drops on a pomander and carry it with them. Others use a small lamp or diffuser and let it burn all night so that the vapors accumulate during sleep. When used in that way, it has been known to cause some irritation to the eyes and throat, but most sources say that it is relatively minor, and well worth it, given the protection it affords."

Lila had never heard of liquid silver or white magic, but then she didn't run in magical circles. "Have you heard of that?" she murmured to Destin. He shook his head, frowning.

"Why should we trust you, healer?" General Karn glared at the silver puddle suspiciously. "How do we know that's not some kind of poison, or black magic?"

"The general is right," Fosnaught said, looking thrilled to have an ally. "Here in Arden, we have used sorcery in very careful, tightly controlled ways to the glory and in the service of the great saint. It is best not to proceed too quickly down this road lest we go astray."

"I understand, Father Fosnaught. These days one can't be too careful." Ash carefully scooped the living silver back into the bottle, restoppered it, and slid it inside his carry bag. "Is there anything else you wanted me to clear, Your Majesty?"

"Not so fast," Montaigne said, putting up a hand and giving Ash a narrow-eyed look. "You want the living silver for yourself—admit it, Freeman."

Ash wet his lips. "I only thought that, since you would rather not risk it, that I would—"

"Do you think I'm a fool?"

Ash hastily dug out the bottle and held it out to the king. "Please. Take it. I never meant to presume that—"

"If you think it's safe, then why don't you demonstrate for all of us," General Karn said.

Blood and bones, Lila thought. Now the princeling has backed himself into a corner, and there's no way to get him out. But she had to try, even if it meant taking her life in her hands.

"Your Majesty," Lila said, hoping to change the subject. "I'm sorry to interrupt, but before Lieutenant Karn and I go, I wondered if you might want to choose a new talisman from this old flash collection."

Irritation flickered across the king's face. "Why would I want to do that?"

"Well, since people say that old flash is the best, so—"

"I'm happy with what I have," Montaigne said, waving her away and turning back to Ash. "Well, healer? The general makes a good point."

"He does, Your Majesty," Ash said. "I am happy to oblige." He picked up the bottle, uncorked it, tipped back his head, and sipped. His lips were silvered when he lowered the bottle. They all stared as he pulled his handkerchief from his pocket and blotted it away. "I don't recommend drinking it, as it's not the best use of a precious element. But, as you can see, it is perfectly safe."

The king smiled. "I am convinced, healer. And therefore, I will keep the empress's gift for myself."

"As you wish." Ash bowed. "Careful," he warned, "it's heavier than you think." He put the bottle into the king of Arden's hands.

A LITTLE BAD JUDGMENT

Jenna dreamed she was back at the Lady of Grace, in her Lyle Truthteller guise, with the scent of coal fires and mutton stew in her nose and the laments of a mediocre minstrel in her ears. Behind the bar, her father stood, alive again. She felt the pressure of his anxious eyes, always waiting for her to disappear.

Across the table, in the client chair, sat Adam Wolf, his hair an honest red.

Jenna shuffled and reshuffled the cards, once losing hold of them so that they scattered across the battered wood like rose petals. She and the healer both reached for the cards, and their hands collided. They yanked their hands back like they'd been burned.

Jenna scooped up the cards, stacked them, and slapped them down on the table in rows. One by one, she turned them over, arranging them like puzzle pieces.

"You will meet a girl," she said, "who will bring heartbreak and trouble into your life. A thousand times, you will curse the day you met her."

"No." The healer raked the cards from the table and onto the floor. "I won't accept that." He reached across the table and took her hands. "We have a future. I know we do. Now tell me a different truth."

The scene dissolved, and she was looking into a pair of golden eyes, eyes just like her own. Fierce, hypnotic eyes in a jeweled setting, but the light in them was going out. There was a pain in her shoulders as if she carried a weight too heavy to lift. The stench of rotten meat filled her nostrils and burned her eyes. The floor rocked gently under her.

Flamecaster. We are trapped in a dark place, and we cannot see the sky.

The back of her neck prickled and burned. She extended her arms, and saw glittering scales where her skin had been, her nails growing into claws. She breathed in the scent of prey, then realized that something furry was crawling across her knee. Swearing, she sent the creature flying into the darkness, burning like a shooting star. It squealed once as it hit the wall, then went silent. She hunted for it, her wings hitting the walls on all sides, following her nose to fresh meat. She was starving and yet she could not find food. She screamed in frustration.

Light blinded her. It must be the Skins who had imprisoned her. She gathered herself, found her flame, roared a challenge. She might be weak, but she could still make a kill. Then she caught a familiar scent and knew.

It was the wolf.

She heard shouts outside the door, banging, someone fumbling with the latch. The scent of burning fur and flesh slowly faded, along with the remnants of the dream as she remembered where she was.

She was no longer in the dungeon. She was in new quarters, high in the king of Arden's tower, with a window overlooking the river.

The door burst open, and the wolf was across the room in a few long strides, kneeling next to her so that he could look into her face and take her hand in his. "Jenna? What is it? What's wrong?"

His voice and his scent, more than anything, anchored her back in her body.

"It was nothing. A dream." She took a deep breath, then let it out. The wind from the river stirred her hair, bringing with it a memory of fish and salt water and the not-too-distant sea. She'd fallen asleep reading in the chair by the window, the one place where she could see the sky.

Adam drove off the blackbirds who had swarmed through the door on his heels, saying, "It was just a dream."

When they'd left, he turned back to her. "You're shaking." He pressed the back of his hand against her forehead. "No fever." He stood, and ignited a lamp on the table with the tips of his fingers.

While his back was turned, Jenna examined her hands and arms in the moonlight. They looked perfectly normal—no claws, no scales. She breathed a sigh of relief, then thought, Are you losing your mind?

"I dreamed I was back in the dungeon and there was a rat and—and I was going to eat it," she blurted.

He turned, hands on hips, and raised an eyebrow. "I know you're always hungry, but that's setting the bar pretty low. I'd have brought you some more food, but they told me you'd just had supper."

She shook her head, her cheeks heating with embarrassment. "No, no, it's not that. You know how you just . . . have stupid dreams sometimes."

"You're right," he said, his face clouding. "Sometimes we do have stupid dreams."

He pulled a chair in close and sat, so they were almost knee to knee. "I'm glad to see that Lieutenant Karn came through. I didn't realize that you had moved upstairs until I went to the dungeon and you weren't there." He looked around. "This is much better."

And it was. The room was small, being high in the tower, with curved walls. The furnishings were plain—a bed with a thick straw mattress and plenty of quilts and coverlets. A stand with a pitcher and washbasin. Two chairs. A screen in the corner to hide the chamber pot. A hearth with a crackling fire, and a window—a barred window, of course, but a window nonetheless.

"It will do, I suppose," she said, mimicking some of the finer guests at the Lady. "The servants are surly and the food marginal. But there is a view of the harbor."

He laughed. "I'm guessing this is where King Gerard keeps some of his more valuable political prisoners."

To be fair, it was larger and finer than the rooms at the Lady of Grace. Still, it seemed crowded with Adam in the room, especially now that she no longer wore the armor of filth and illness. At every moment, she was acutely aware of his position and the distance between them.

He was looking at her expectantly, and she realized that he was waiting for her to say something. "Ah . . . as you can probably tell, Karn made good on his promise of a bath and a change of clothes."

"You do look different," he said, studying her through narrowed eyes. "I'm not used to seeing you in a dress."

She tugged at her bodice self-consciously. "This one's a little tight across the—it's a little tight, but the seamstress said she'd bring something made-to-measure tomorrow." Sucking in a quick breath, she stumbled on. "I'm not used to dresses. I've been playing a boy for four years, nearly all the time, so it feels odd not to be wearing breeches."

"I had no idea your hair was so many colors," Adam

said. "Copper and gold and silver and amethyst. It's almost . . . metallic. I've never seen anything like it." He reached out and fingered it, and gooseflesh rose on her back and shoulders.

"Now you know how dirty it was. My da always said that when I was a baby it looked like I stood on my head on a painter's palette and spun around."

Gaaah. Shut your mouth. She'd never learned to flirt—she'd had no practice at it. Besides, flirting seemed too lightweight a term to fit what was happening between them.

A prickling heat crept up from her shoulders and into her face. The memory of their kiss hung between them like forbidden fruit. Everything they said or did seemed charged with meaning. Desire crouched in the room with them like an awkward guest.

Now what? Where do we go from here? Do we back away or go forward? Maybe Adam felt the same pressure, because he seemed to be groping for something else to talk about.

"What are you reading?" He reached for the book on her lap, picked it up, and leafed through it. "*Alencon's History of the Realms*? We read that at school. Highly subversive." He cocked his head. "Karn brought this?"

He's stalling, she thought. There's something he doesn't want to tell me.

When he handed the book back, she set it aside. After another siege of silence, Jenna reached out and took both his hands, looking for a clue. The only image that came to her was that of a ship, hazy-looking, shrouded in mist, more like somebody's idea of a ship.

"I dreamed I read the cards for you," she said.

"And?"

"And I predicted I would bring heartbreak and trouble into your life," she said.

"Too late," he said, staring down at their joined hands. "Heartbreak and trouble got there ahead of you."

"You may as well tell me what's on your mind," she said, releasing his hands. "What's the news? Am I to be executed? Sold into slavery?"

The look on the healer's face said she wasn't far off the mark. "An emissary has come from the Empress Celestine," he said. "She's the one Lieutenant Karn was asking you about. Apparently, she's offering to trade a sack of diamonds, a mysterious weapon, and an army for you." He paused, looking around the room again. "That might explain the sudden hospitality. Montaigne doesn't want to be accused of trading in damaged goods."

"Then he's damned lucky you're so good at what you do." Unable to sit still, Jenna stood, crossed to the hearth, and poked at the fire with a stick. "Why would somebody I don't even know be offering that kind of swag for me?"

"There's to be a meeting in two days," Adam said to her back. "Maybe we'll find out then. I wanted to warn you ahead of time."

"Good," Jenna said, staring into the flames. "We'll get it sorted out before this goes much further."

When he didn't reply, she turned back to face him. Adam was chewing his lower lip, his face all-over dread, as if trying to decide whether to keep delivering bad news or leave her in the dark.

"You're wondering if I'm stupid or naive or both," Jenna said. "I'm neither." Settling down on the thick rug in front of the hearth, she patted the space beside her. "Sit with me, Wolf."

Just for a heartbeat, she thought he wouldn't come. But then he did, crossing the room and dropping to the floor beside her. He sat, his thigh pressing against hers, one knee up, the other leg extended straight out in front of him.

She arched her back, wriggling a little, enjoying the heat and the crackle of flames while she tried to work out what to say.

"This is an argument I used to have with my da all the time. He was the kind who saw disaster waiting around every corner."

"See? He was right," Adam said, fussing with his collar, as if it pinched.

"He was right . . . after sixteen years," she said. "We spend so much of our lives waiting to be ambushed by heartbreak. Why couldn't we be ambushed by joy? Anything's possible, right?"

"Anything's possible," Adam said, staring up at the

ceiling, a muscle working in his jaw.

"Take a wolf, for example," she persisted. "If he's got a thorn in his foot, he's miserable and snappish, like a person would be. Once you take it out, does he worry it's going to get infected, or he's going to step on another thorn?"

"No." Adam shifted his body, the friction between them sending her heart into a gallop.

"Does he cut off his paw to make sure it doesn't happen again?"

Adam snorted, his lips twitching. "No."

"Does he beat up on himself because he was careless, or he took the shortcut through the bramble?" She shook her head. "No. He moves on. He enjoys the fact that he's not in pain. He doesn't know what's coming—whether he'll bring down a fellsdeer or break his leg and freeze to death, but he recognizes that he doesn't know. But people—we act like we do. We write that bad ending before we even get there."

"Isn't that what makes us human? The ability to look at the present and predict what's likely to happen?"

"But we're really not all that good at it, are we?"

"No," he said.

Jenna rested her hand on his thigh and heard his startled intake of breath. They both looked at it, a pale starfish against his dark breeches.

"Take me, for instance."

Startled, he looked up. "Excuse me?" he said hoarsely.

"By most standards, I've had a miserable life. Orphan, raised in Delphi, forced into the mines at a young age. Marked for death since birth."

He eyed her, his brow furrowed, as if waiting for the punch line. "So? How does that—?"

"And yet, dozens of times, I've been ambushed by joy and beauty in the most unlikely places. Things I would have missed if I'd been preoccupied by pain. A sunrise over a slag heap. Ham for breakfast when I didn't expect it. A song that goes straight to the heart." She ran her fingers along his thigh, feeling his muscles tighten under her hand. "Maybe it's primitive, to live in the moment, but there are advantages. For instance, I never expected to be ambushed by love in a dungeon."

Jenna turned toward him, coming up onto her knees so they were at eye level. She looked into his face, reading the heat and hunger in his eyes.

"Me, neither," he whispered. Sliding his arms around her, pulling her in close, he kissed her.

It was even more intoxicating the second time, and the third. Then she lost count as his fingers tangled in her hair and he pressed his body against hers. It was all lean, hard muscle, and it fit in against hers just right.

Then he kissed her throat, and her mouth again, long and sweet. It hit her like a gulp of stingo, running down into her middle and kindling a flame there. She caught his lip between her teeth, nibbling it gently, then tipped him backward so that they were lying flat on the rug.

She wrapped her arms around his neck and devoured him with kisses—his lips, his neck above the silver collar, that place just behind his ear. She slid her hands under his tunic, walking her fingers down his spine to the hollow at the base. He kissed her lips, her throat, the tops of her breasts, then crushed her to him, cradling her backside with his large hands. His fingers set off little explosions when they touched her skin that had nothing to do with magery.

She sat up then, one knee to either side of him, and fumbled with the laces on her bodice. She had no skill at it, though, and before she got far, he caught her wrists, pulling her hands away.

"Jenna," he said, looking dazed, like he'd stood too close when a deep mine charge went off. Despite the desire in his voice, there was a "no" there, too.

"Let go, Wolf." She shifted, pulled, trying to free herself. She could feel his body respond, and that made matters worse.

"You don't understand," he said. "I've been here too long already. The blackbirds. They could come in at any moment."

"Damn the blackbirds." She was strong, but he was stronger. It was like a cruel joke. The more she struggled, the hotter she burned, and the harder it was to let him go.

Finally, he rolled her over so she was on her back and he on top, sitting astride her. He pinned her hands to the floor and looked down at her, breathing hard, like he'd been running a race.

"You are . . . making it . . . really difficult to do the right thing," Adam gasped. "You know that, don't you?"

"This is the right thing," Jenna said, arching her back so she pressed up against him.

With that, he straightened his arms and his weight came off her as he levered himself to his feet, putting the chair between them.

Jenna hung her head, cheeks burning. "I'm sorry," she said. "I—I only—"

"Don't be sorry," Adam said, his hands clenching the back of the chair, his eyes glittering in the firelight. "This is the right thing. It's just not the right time. I don't want it to be like this—" He gestured, taking in the tower room. "Hasty, and furtive, under constant risk of interruption."

She knew he was right, but still, she couldn't help saying, "If not now, when? What if this is it, and we never—" Her voice broke. She tried again. "What if we look back and say, If only . . ."

He crossed the room to her and gripped her shoulders, his eyes darkening to the color of the deepest lakes. "I promise you, Jenna," he said, his face fierce with purpose, "this is not it. I will find a way to—"

She pressed her hands against his lips. "No promises, healer." She pulled his head down and stopped the promises with kisses.

PLAYING THE KING'S GAME

Was the king burning his "gift" of living silver or not? That was the question. For all Ash knew, the vial he'd given the king was rolling around in a drawer somewhere. He'd shot his poison arrow into the air, but he didn't know if it would hit a vital spot, and whether it would be soon enough to allow him to keep the promise he had tried to make to Jenna.

He'd reviewed the telltale symptoms in Taliesin's leather-bound book. Tremors, mental and emotional impairment, skin changes. Montaigne didn't need to die from it—only feel poorly enough to call on Ash for treatment so he could finish the job.

Though he watched the king carefully, he saw nothing

promising. Montaigne remained astonishingly, annoyingly healthy.

Meanwhile, Ash kept adding to his arsenal of easily hidden, easily deployed, easily explained assassin's tools. Fortunately, many of the medical tools in his healer's kit were dual-purpose. Shivs, scissors, scalpels—these were all edged weapons that could be used on either side of the line. A garrote was threaded through the hem of his tunic. He still had the sting under his collar, ready to deploy, if the opportunity presented itself.

All he needed was the smallest of openings to make sure of him, but the multiple attempts on the king's life had put him on his guard, and it was challenging to get anywhere close to him. Ash wished the competition would either succeed or get out of the way. At least there hadn't been any more tries since the wassail incident—that he knew about, anyway. Give it another year or two, and the king might grow careless again.

That was a problem. He didn't have a year or two, he had a day. Now it was the Feast of Saint Malthus, on the fourth day after Solstice, and the king's meeting with the empress's emissary was scheduled for tomorrow. He toyed with the idea of killing the emissary instead, but the Carthians stayed on their ship, out of reach.

Instead, Ash found himself in the queen's bedchamber, trying to prevent the king of Arden from undoing his hard work. He'd been called in because Queen Marina had wilted while her attendants were trying to dress her for the annual Saint's Day dinner. She lay back in bed, dark hair spread across the pillows, her usually dusky skin nearly as pale as the sheets save for the places where blue veins showed through.

She's skin and bones, Ash thought. She has no reserves.

Montaigne paced back and forth, ablaze with all the badges of his office, his boots clicking on the stone floor. He was in a dangerous mood, even for him. "Can't you give her something, healer, to get her through this? Every thane in the kingdom is here. Rumors are flying that the queen is dead. They need to see her alive and well." He paused. "Especially now."

The low flame that had burned inside Ash ever since his father's death blazed up.

This is the man who declared war on the Fells when my mother refused to marry him, Ash thought. They'd been at war ever since. She'd paid a high price. They all had. But it could be Raisa lying here, being dithered over like a side of beef with no agency of her own.

No, he thought. She wouldn't have lasted this long. One or the other of them would be dead. Ash was beginning to recognize just what his mother the queen had accomplished in keeping this southern tyrant out of the Fells.

"There's just one problem, Your Majesty," he said through his teeth. "The queen is alive, thank the Maker, but she is not well. What she needs is rest, and quiet, and good, nourishing food. Not a public ordeal."

"We cannot have people think it is a simple matter to murder a sovereign. That would send the wrong message."

"What kind of message would it send, Your Majesty, were the queen to collapse during dinner?" Ash said in a barely civil tone. "If tongues are wagging now, that would only make matters worse."

"It's your job to make sure that doesn't happen," Montaigne said.

"Never mind, healer," the queen said. "The king is right, of course. I need to be there." She propped up on her elbows and nodded to her ladies, who carried several dresses to the bedside for Marina to choose from.

Ordinarily, when the queen was indisposed, as she often was, Lady Estelle would step in as hostess. The king of Arden saw no reason to keep his mistresses hidden away. But Estelle was dead—killed for the crime of hosting an assassination attempt on the king. Wittingly or unwittingly. Hence the current crisis. The king needed to make show.

"I want my queen by my side at dinner," the king said. "Why is that so difficult to understand?" He ripped a dress from the hands of one of the queen's ladies and thrust it into Marina's face. "Put this on. And drink a measure of rum, if that's what it takes to put a little color in your cheeks. Our guests are already seated, and I don't like to give them time to conspire together in my absence."

The queen sat frozen in her bed, holding the dress up like a shield.

"I told you to get dressed, you stupid slut of Tamron. Are you deaf?"

"Your Majesty, please," Lady Argincourt, one of the queen's ladies, murmured, gesturing at the crowd of black-birds in the room. "If you could give the queen a little privacy?"

"I want to see you downstairs in less than fifteen min-utes," Montaigne said. "Freeman, you will attend the queen in the dining room to handle anything that might arise. And find something other than that bloody healer brown to wear. Having a healer hover over her would also send the wrong message."

"Of course, Your Majesty," Ash said.

Signaling to his blackbird guard, the king strode from the room, leaving Ash with two questions: Would he at long last get close enough to the king to do some actual damage? And where could he possibly get hold of dinner clothes in the next fifteen minutes?

When he was sure the king was gone, Ash turned back to the queen. "No rum, Your Grace," he said. "Not while your liver is still recovering from the poison. I suggest small beer or tea."

"Tea suits me well, Master Freeman," the queen said.

"Good," Ash said. "And, finally—would any of you know where I could find some suitable clothes in a hurry?"

Fifteen minutes later, Ash was shadowing the queen into the state dining room. Somehow, Queen Marina's ladies had managed to scrounge up some black breeches and a doublet in green velvet and leather that fit—more or less. Happily, he had a fine silver collar to go with.

It had been a long time since he'd worn anything resembling court garb. It felt like he was wearing a costume.

As soon as they crossed the threshold, Ash could tell that something was wrong. The tension in the room was as thick as day-old porridge and the room was lined with more blackbirds than was usual, even these days. The main course had been served, but most of the plates looked to be untouched. The women in the room were staring down at the table as if they hoped they could disappear.

All eyes were fixed on a tall muscular thane with a bristle of gray hair and a black eye patch. He stood at the end of the table nearest the door, surrounded by a handful of men-at-arms. He was the kind of hard-bitten soldier who looked out of place in civilian clothes. Next to him stood a much younger edition of the thane, maybe twelve or thirteen, this one in mudback brown.

As they walked in, the queen seemed to tap some hidden reservoir of strength. Her spine straightened, her chin rose, and she smiled brilliantly when the guests rose to greet her. She walked the length of the room with great dignity and took her place beside the king. Ash followed a few steps behind and stood against the wall behind the royal couple, staring at the barricade of blackbirds between him and the king.

No opportunity there, Ash thought.

Montaigne kissed Queen Marina's hand, turned to the other guests, and said through gritted teeth, "I know you'll join with me in toasting Her Majesty's good health."

This was met with a murmur of good wishes and a few raised glasses, but it didn't change the mood in the room. It looked more like a standoff than a dinner party. Marin Karn, for instance, looked like he could chew rocks and spit out gravel.

"Sit down, Lord Matelon, and eat," the king said. "This is the Saint's Day. It is not the appropriate time to discuss the state of the war. We will take it up when the Thane Council meets."

"You have not called a council in months, Your Majesty," the eye-patched lord said. "Instead, you seize property and treasure from your loyal bannermen to fund this never-ending grudge match."

A rumble rolled around the table, mingled protest and assent.

Reliable royal ally Michel Botetort stood as well. "I beg you, Arschel, let's defer this."

"I agree," General Karn said. "I've not yet had the chance to brief His Majesty on . . . recent developments."

"Then by all means, Karn, let us brief him now,"

Matelon said. He scanned the room. "I believe we have a quorum."

"Perhaps the ladies should leave the room," the king said, eyes glittering, his hand on his sword, "so that we can speak plainly."

"Perhaps they should," Matelon said.

The women rose in a rustle of silk and brocade and left the room. All except the queen. "I will stay and hear what you have to say, Lord Matelon," she said simply.

Matelon shrugged. "If you like, Your Majesty." He turned to the boy. "My son Robert is a corporal stationed at Delphi. He has a report to offer. Corporal?"

Robert was so nervous that the paper in his hand was shaking. "D-Delphi has fallen, Your Majesty."

Delphi! Ash struggled to maintain his street face while he scanned the room for reactions. If he was any judge, Marin Karn, the king, and Botetort, at least, already knew.

The king waved an impatient hand. "Rumors are always flying about this or that disaster. I have heard a rumor about Delphi, and we are in the process of investigating."

"It is more than a rumor, Your Majesty," Lord Matelon said. "Go on, Corporal."

Robert stood ramrod-straight. "I spent the Solstice holiday at temple church, on leave from my posting at Delphi. While I was there, we received a message from my brother—from Captain Matelon's headquarters north of the city. Shall I read it?"

"Go ahead, Son," Matelon said, resting his hand on the boy's shoulder.

Robert cleared his throat and read. "'A miners' riot has turned into a full-blown rebellion, supplemented with what appear to be Fellsian Highlanders from the north. The rebels now control the mines, the heights, and the town, and our headquarters is under attack.'" Robert swallowed hard. "'As it is unlikely that reinforcements from temple church can arrive in such time and in such numbers as to change the outcome, I recommend against risking more troops until a sufficient force can be deployed to assure a decisive victory. Captain Halston Matelon, Commander, His Majesty's Army, Delphi.'"

The entire room had gone silent with shock.

General Karn spoke. "It sounds to me like Captain Matelon is making excuses for his poor performance."

Blotches of color blossomed on Lord Matelon's cheeks. "Explain, General," he said.

"First off, everybody knows that the northerners never poke a toe south of the Spirit Mountains," General Karn said. "Even if they decided to change their tactics, only a fool would attempt to bring a force through the Spirit Mountains at this time of year. The passes have been closed for a month."

"Perhaps," Matelon said, biting off each word, "the witch queen has decided to spend the winter in the south this year. Perhaps her mages melted all the snow with sorcery. All I know is that, from the beginning of this damnable war, every assurance we have received, every prediction that has been made, every report that victory is at hand has been wrong."

Montaigne directed his response to the entire room. "As many of you know, Lord Matelon's support for the war and his loyalty to our person have been lukewarm for some time. Which leads me to wonder—could this be part of a larger conspiracy? Multiple assassination attempts here in the capital, while Matelon's son betrays us to the rebels in the north."

Why is it, Your Majesty, that when things go wrong, it's always somebody else's fault? Ash thought.

"Your Majesty," Matelon said. "I have provided unflagging support through twenty-five years of war. No one has contributed more troops or treasure to this effort. People are suffering and starving throughout the empire. Now, it appears, I have sacrificed my eldest son. And for what? Control of a small realm infested with sorcerers and savages whose major exports are things we do not need. Enough is enough. I am done."

"Are you saying that you will not submit to the command of your sovereign, anointed by God?"

"I am saying that I am tired, and I want to go home and mourn with my lady wife, and see to my estates, which are sorely in need of attention." The thane inclined his head, then turned and strode toward the door, attended by his men-at-arms and his son.

"Go home if you like," Montaigne said, "but your lady wife is not there."

Matelon froze mid-stride, then turned to face the king. "Explain yourself," he said.

Montaigne spoke to the entire hall. "In view of events in Delphi, I have taken the precaution of sequestering the families of my Thane Council members in keeps far from the northern border. That way none of you will have worries about their safety, and all of you will be able to focus on winning this war."

At this, the thanes around the table pushed to their feet, many of them with their hands on their swords. It was a vicious move, even for Montaigne.

"And yes," Montaigne said, "that includes the ladies who have just left the hall."

The doors to the dining room swung open, and blackbirds flooded into the room, most of them collared mages. They took up positions all around the perimeter.

"Do note that I don't expect you to carry the entire weight of this new effort. I have initiatives underway that should provide some relief from the demands of this war, in terms of levies of money and men. I just ask for a little . . . forbearance."

If I killed the bastard now, Ash thought, none of these lords would lift a finger to stop me. But then they'd turn around and execute me, because, you know, precedent.

He'd have to wait a little longer. Since he'd met Jenna, it had become increasingly important to survive.

"Now," Montaigne said. "I would ask you to remain in your city houses until the end of the month. By then, I should have some good news for all of you. You may go—all except Lord Matelon, who will remain here as our guest during our inquiry."

By then, the thane and his men-at-arms were nearly at the door. He turned to face the king. "With all due respect, Your Majesty, I decline." He turned, a blade in each hand, and cut the throats of the blackbirds nearest to him. His men formed a circle around their lord, prickling with swords. They drove a wedge through the King's Guard and out the door.

The banquet was, for all intents and purposes, over. The king hurried from the room, insulated by a crowd of guards, while Ash accompanied the queen back to her quarters.

Ash's skin prickled with a growing unease. The fall of Delphi and a possible civil war might be good news for the Fells, but it would make Ash's job that much harder. An embattled king would be harder to get at than before. Prisoners didn't usually fare well within a kingdom in chaos. And the rebellion of the thanes would make a potential deal with the empress of Carthis more appealing than ever.

THE EMISSARY

When Ash arrived at the king's Small Hall for the meeting with Strangward, the room was already crowded. Pettyman, the king's steward; Jerome, his new taster; and far too many blackbird mages were already on hand.

The hall was a smaller, more intimate version of the throne room, adjacent to the king's privy chamber. Montaigne even had a throne of sorts, an elaborate chair on a raised dais, so he could look down on those around him.

Pettyman knew how to find that sweet spot where hospitality and politics met. He'd refreshed the Solstice greenery around the mantel and doorways, and laid a modest display of food and drink out on the sideboard. Jerome was in the process of tasting it under the watchful eyes of Fleury and Marc DeJardin.

It was a waste of time. Ash knew by now that the king wouldn't touch it anyway. Montaigne had always been paranoid, but he'd grown worse after the assassination attempts. His personal guard searched his bedchamber each night before he locked the door. No morsel passed his lips without being trialed on the taster—multiple times. He constantly complained of headaches, tremors, and rashes, but refused Ash's offers of help.

Could the king's symptoms be a signal that Ash's plan was working? He didn't know. It would help if he knew whether the king was using "white magic," but he didn't want to draw attention to the living silver by asking about it.

Ash and Jerome were spending lots of time together these days. Ash had become the equivalent of the king's magical taster—assigned to keep a constant eye out for magical threats, scrutinize visitors, and be ready to leap into action in the event of sudden illness or another attempt on the king's life.

Ash would have been more than happy to allow any rival assassin to do the honors, but it hadn't happened yet. With the arrival of the emissary, he knew that time was running out—for Jenna, anyway. A handful of people would be coming together with the Carthian delegation to decide Jenna's fate like brokers at a slave auction.

Ash took a deep breath, forced himself to unclench his

fists, to loosen his muscles, to lean against the wall as if he had nothing to lose. He hadn't survived this long by being stupid.

Speaking of the slave trade, Lila and Destin Karn arrived together—of course. Ash fingered the collar around his neck. Since the delivery of the crates of flash-craft, Ash's last illusions about Lila had disappeared. Lila would go anywhere and do whatever it took in order to make some coin. If she thought she was going to take him back to the Fells and collect a reward, she was in for disappointment.

Now that Lila and Karn were experts on magical devices, they'd been called in to offer an opinion on the "weapon" Commander Strangward had brought.

Or maybe the king was just lonely. General Karn was in the field, deploying his forces in the path of a possible attack by Arschel Matelon and his allies. Matelon was on his way to his fortress at White Oaks, calling in his ban-nermen along the way, getting ready for a fight.

I wonder if my mother knows the consequences of her claiming of Delphi.

Maybe that was the plan all along.

It seemed like he was learning more about his mother at a distance than he ever had at home.

While little Karn made plans with the blackbirds, Lila drifted over to where Ash stood.

"You're not even tempted?" she asked, nodding at the

spread along the wall, a blackbird standing guard at either end.

"I just ate," Ash said, "and I don't care for herring."

"You know what I mean."

"No, I don't," Ash said, showing his teeth in a smile. "But help yourself if you're hungry. The king's not going to touch it, not after it's been sitting out."

Apparently, Lila wasn't hungry, either, because she didn't chance it.

The king arrived soon after that, with Botetort. The king was well turned out in black and silver, but he looked a bit under the weather. The skin on his cheeks appeared chapped and he repeatedly rubbed his forearms, as if they itched. His hands tremored a bit until he clasped them together on his lap.

Ash bent his knee to the king, then rose, studying his face. "Are you well, Your Majesty?"

"Never better," the king snapped. "Did you scan the room?"

"I did, and found nothing suspicious," Ash said.

Greenberry, the chamberlain, appeared at the door. "The principia, Father Fosnaught, is here with the delegation from the Northern Islands, Your Majesty," he said. "Shall I show them in?"

"By all means," Montaigne said. "Let's get this done."

The first man through the door was massive, broadshouldered, a mountain of a man. His hair was the color of burnt honey, braided and twisted into locks. He wore a loose linen shirt, tucked into trousers, a baldric and belt over top. He wore his wealth on his wrists and around his neck—a random assortment of gold cuffs and chains and pendants. A light cape was thrown over all, and it seemed to change colors in the light from the torches. No weapons were in evidence—the delegation had been relieved of them outside.

I wonder if the empress is as impressive as her emissary, Ash thought, eyeing him.

There were six of them in all, none of them wearing any kind of uniform. They were dressed in clothing in various colors, of a comfortable style similar to that worn by the emissary. Men and women dressed the same, resembling sailors more than anything else. Their one consistency was that all of them displayed wavelets of tattoos covering their arms. Ash guessed that must be the signia of the empress. Most were fair-skinned, but colored by long hours in the sun, their hair ranging from a shade like bleached linen to corn silk to light brown.

All of the men were clean shaven. Some had longer hair drawn into thick side braids, while others were more closely shorn. Both the men and women wore more jewelry than was fashionable in Arden. Most wore earrings, others bangles or elaborate belt buckles.

What kind of people were they? Ash studied them closely, looking for clues. Fosnaught's description of them as horse savages or pirates seemed to fit. Not encouraging. Carthian pirates had a ruthless reputation, and they would sail off with Jenna unless Ash could find a way to prevent it.

When the group stood in front of the king, Fosnaught cleared his throat to introduce them, but the Carthian emissary seemed oblivious to protocol. He stepped forward and said, in Common, "I am Teza Von bin Miralla, Sworn Sword of Tarvos. May I present Lord Evan Strangward, Emissary of the Empress Celestine, ruler of the Northern Islands, the Desert Coast, Carthis, Endru, and Anamaya, and True Source of Tarvos." Standing aside, he gestured toward a young man who had been lost in the pack until then.

"That's the emissary?" Lila murmured, as if unimpressed.

"Don't underestimate him," Ash said, eyes narrowed. "They're all wizards of some sort, but I'm guessing that he's by far the most powerful of the lot."

Though clearly the Carthians were gifted, their auras seemed different from what Ash was used to. Western wizards glowed a cool bluish-white. Strangward's aura came closest to that. He lit up the entire room with a brilliant white glow. Each time he gripped his amulet, which was often, it was as if the lights dimmed. The other delegates glowed a faint red, like dying coals.

Are they different kinds? Ash wondered. Or is it just that Strangward is more powerful than the others?

The emissary wasn't as tall as Ash, but looked to be about the same age. He was wiry more than muscular, and of a more slender build. He wore a loose linen shirt under a close-fitting leather jerkin that buckled up the front. His roomy breeches were tucked into soft knee-high boots. His swordbelt was cinched around his waist, the scabbard empty. He was less decorated than the others, save a gold earring in one ear and his amulet, boldly displayed on the outside of his clothing. The fact that his nose had been broken at least once saved him from being too pretty, with his glittering fair hair, feral green eyes, and finely planed face.

"I'll bet he's someone the girls like to look at," Lila murmured.

I'll bet they do more than look, Ash thought.

Ash had never been to the Northern Islands, and yet there was something familiar about the emissary's voice and features. Perhaps he'd met some wizard who was a throwback to an earlier time.

Montaigne was studying the emissary with a faintly bemused expression, but whether it had to do with Strangward's youth or his manner of dress, Ash didn't know.

Fosnaught continued with the introductions. "May I introduce His Majesty, Gerard Montaigne, by the grace of the Maker King of Arden and Tamron, and ruler of the New Empire of the Seven Realms."

"Your Majesty." Strangward inclined his head enough

to be polite, though probably not as much as protocol demanded in a meeting between an emissary and a king. "It is a pleasure to meet you at last. We have looked forward to engaging with Arden, and with the rest of the Seven Realms. This is such a pretty, green place." There was something hungry about the way he said it that raised the hair on the back of Ash's neck.

The emissary spoke Common well, though with an unfamiliar accent. Which made sense, since as far as he knew, Ash had never met anyone from the Northern Islands.

"Welcome to Arden, Lord Strangward," Montaigne said. "I trust you had a fair weather crossing."

"Yes," Strangward said, lips twitching, as if at some private joke. "I nearly always do."

Fosnaught gestured toward the others. "This is Lord Botetort, speaker of the Thane Council, and Lieutenant Destin Karn, who is with the King's Guard."

Strangward's gaze flicked over each person as they were named. Then he turned to look at Lila and Ash, who stood off to one side. "You left out these two," he said, pointing.

"Those two are . . . ah . . ." It was clear that Fosnaught had no idea how to describe their role in this meeting.

Destin Karn came to the rescue. "This is Lila Barrowhill, an expert in weaponry and logistics. Adam Freeman is a member of our Royal Guild of Healers."

"Do you anticipate that there will be a need for a

healer?" the emissary asked, looking around, as if to spot the afflicted. "Or do you always keep one standing by?"

"Freeman is here to answer any questions that might come up about the health of the girl," Karn said.

The emissary cocked his head, studying Karn. "You are a mage," he said. "Aren't you?"

Karn seemed unusually skittish for some reason. He looked to the king for guidance, received none, then said, "Yes, Lord Strangward, I am."

"And so are you," Strangward said to Ash. "How curious." He turned back to Montaigne. "I had not expected to see mages made so welcome at court. You see, I had heard that you burn the gifted in Arden. I am so relieved to learn that I was misled."

For a long moment, nobody had anything to say. Ash bit his lip to prevent amusement from crawling onto his face.

Finally, Father Fosnaught cleared his throat. "We are people of faith, Lord Strangward, and well aware of the dangers of demonic influence. In certain situations, in which certain mages violate the tenets of the church, they are examined by the Hand. If found to be corrupted, they are cleansed by the flame."

"Cleansed?" Strangward raised an eyebrow.

"Cleansed," Fosnaught repeated. When Strangward kept looking at him, as if puzzled, he snapped, "We burn them."

"And so then they are dead?"

"But cleansed. And, therefore, saved."

"Fascinating," Strangward said, rubbing his chin.

Fosnaught fondled the keys to the kingdom that hung at his belt. "What religion do you practice in the Northern Islands, if I may ask?"

"In the east, the empress is the religion," Strangward said. "She is not one to share power, not even with the gods." He turned back to Ash. "Why is it that you—and these guardsmen—wear metal collars? Is it a mark of rank, or personal fashion, or do you belong to a particular tribe that—?"

"That's enough!" Montaigne roared, having reached the end of his patience. "If you would like, Emissary, we can assign one of our clerics to explain to you some of our customs," he said testily. "My time is limited, however, and I would like to proceed to the main topic of this meeting, that is, an agreement between the empress and ourselves." He gestured to a grouping of chairs. "You may sit."

The emissary sat, thrusting his legs out in front of him, but his companions remained standing. "Forgive me," he said. "Where I come from, it often takes several days of tay drinking and storytelling to get down to business. I can see that your habits are different, and clearly much more . . . efficient."

The emissary had an oddly formal and self-deprecating manner of speaking, and yet hidden in every line was a rather sharp point.

Fosnaught, Botetort, and Karn sat as well. Lila and Ash remained standing, while Montaigne stayed where he was, on the dais, with his guard of blackbirds around him.

"I appreciate your seeing me at what must be a busy time, given the events in the north," Strangward said.

Montaigne's eyes narrowed. "What events?"

"The loss of Delphi must have been a blow, given its importance as a source of iron and steel."

"News travels fast, it seems," Montaigne said, pretending to straighten his cuffs.

"Bad news, especially. That's the way of the world, I'm afraid."

He's laying the groundwork for a better deal, Ash thought, with grudging admiration. You need us, is what he's saying.

"Delphi is a miserable place to campaign in the winter," Botetort said. "We'll clear out the rebels when the weather warms."

"Of course," Strangward nodded politely. "Unfortunately, the northerners do not seem to mind the cold." He sighed. "So much trouble with the Fells." The words were delivered carelessly, but the smile had bite.

"If the witch queen has captured Delphi," Montaigne said, "she won't hold it for long. War is a constant series of advances and retreats."

"I agree," Strangward said. "In that sense, warfare is like the course of true love. You've been knocking on this queen's door for a good long time, yet she will not open the gate."

Blood and bones, Ash thought. Strangward knows that my mother spurned Montaigne's offer of marriage a quarter century ago. He's done his research, and he is not afraid to go for the throat. Poking the king of Arden is a dangerous game.

But perhaps Strangward was dangerous, too. There was something that lay beneath his calm and undecorated exterior, some elemental power that rippled the surface like a serpent swimming in a quiet pond. Strangward bled confidence, as if he knew that, despite his almost frail appearance, he was the deadliest predator in the room.

What would that mean for Jenna? If this is the emissary, what must the empress be like?

"Your point is . . . ?" Montaigne's voice penetrated the ear like slivers of ice.

"My point is, perhaps we can help . . . move things along."

"We had specifically discussed an army," Montaigne said. "While your personal guard is no doubt highly skilled, six soldiers will hardly suffice."

"The empress worried that the sudden appearance of a foreign army would be poorly received in the absence of an agreement," Strangward said. "Celestine will want to see the magemarked girl before she makes that kind of commitment. If she is the one the empress is seeking, make no mistake, the army will come." Strangward leaned forward. "Now. You refer to her as a girl. How old is she?"

"Perhaps sixteen or seventeen," Karn said.

"Ah," Strangward said, his face unreadable. "Is she gifted?"

Karn shook his head. "No. At least . . . not in the usual way."

"Meaning?"

"She is not a mage." And then, as if realizing he should make a better pitch, added, "However, she may have other gifts that have not yet . . . made themselves apparent."

Ash frowned. Karn was not his usual smooth self. His face gleamed with sweat, and he kept fingering his amulet and looking from the king to the emissary as if unsure who his audience was.

The king shifted restlessly in his seat, looking more and more annoyed at Karn's clumsy attempts to make the sale. "Given that the empress was the one who asked us to find the demon-marked girl, perhaps *you* should tell *us* why she is of value," Montaigne said.

Evan Strangward sat back in his chair, putting the tips of his fingers together. "The empress does not share her motivations with me. She is, however, a collector of sorts, with an appetite for the arcane and the exotic." He paused again, tilting his head, so the light caught his golden earring. "Perhaps that's all it is."

Ash struggled to keep the revulsion off his face. Jenna

was being discussed like she was a rare piece of art, to be put on display.

"You expect me to believe that your empress is willing to trade an army for a tavern wench with a blemish?"

"Before too much time passes you will meet Celestine in person," Strangward said, and to Ash's ears, it sounded like a threat. "It is likely that all of your questions will be answered then. In the meantime, when may I see the girl?"

"Why not now?" Montaigne said. He nodded to Greenberry. "Tell Fleury and DeJardin to fetch her."

OFF TO MARKET

Two servants—Treece and Nettie—came early to ready Jenna for market. They brought a made-to-measure dress in purple silk shot through with silver and gold. They helped her into it, which was a good thing, because it fit like a dandy's breeches. At least the skirt flared enough that she could walk.

"Purple is a good color for you," Treece said.

"The gold matches your eyes, my lady," Nettie said.

Jenna didn't argue. She sat numbly while they fussed with her hair. It took them a long while, and they argued quite a bit. She guessed that they weren't top-shelf when it came to chambermaids, but good enough for her. Her hair had been mostly under cover for the past four years, so she wasn't exactly up to the minute on style. In the end, they pinned it up on the top of her head like a princess in a fairy tale.

"I look like a Solstice cake," Jenna complained when they were finished.

"Well," Treece said, "everybody likes Solstice cakes."

Nettie couldn't figure out why Jenna wasn't more cheerful, since she was getting all dressed up. "Look at this, my lady," she said, displaying a necklace of amethyst and pearls. "Lovely, in't it?" When she went to fasten it around Jenna's neck, she sucked in her breath and fingered the magemark on the back of her neck. "That's lovely, too," she said. "It's like you've got a permanent brooch on."

That was one way to think of it.

When they decided she was ready, an escort of blackbirds took her downstairs. She thought she was going to meet the emissary right then, but instead they took her to a tiny room on the main floor, not much more than a closet with a single bed and a washstand and mirror.

"This is the gentleman butler's quarters," DeJardin said, pausing in the doorway. He was the kindest of the king's blackbirds. "It's right next to the king's suite. We'll come get you when it's time."

Jenna wondered where the gentleman butler was. There was scarcely room to pace, so it was good she'd brought a book along.

She opened her book, but it was hard to concentrate.

She didn't even know what to worry about, because she had no idea why an empress would put out a warrant on her.

Flamecaster!

Jenna flinched and looked around. The room was as empty as before.

I starve in the dark.

"Where are you?" she whispered to the empty room.

Nothing.

Don't be a loon, Jenna thought, refocusing on the page. She'd been seeing visions all her life. Voices—that was new.

Flamecaster. Help me.

"Shut up," she hissed. Maybe that was a long-term effect of the poison. It made you lose your mind.

The door to the room slammed open, and Jenna jumped. It was DeJardin and Fleury.

"Who're you talking to?" Fleury demanded, looking around.

"Nobody," Jenna said.

Fleury scowled, but he couldn't exactly argue the point.

DeJardin bowed his head, as if she were a lady, and he was her escort to a party. "It's time to go, my lady." He leaned closer. "Take courage."

The room, as he'd said, was right next door. As soon as she walked in, she was smacked by a dozen sensations. The scent of food and greenery, sweat and salt water. Her heart stumbled when she spotted Adam against the wall in green velvet, his expression grim, his eyes like twin bruises. Next to him stood a young woman in a blue overdress and dark skirt, someone Jenna didn't know. Also Destin Karn, a crow of Malthus, a richly dressed thane, and the king.

The king! She took a second look. The image was still there. In place of the king's head was a grinning skull.

Her heart began to thump. What did it mean? Was it because the king was so often the agent of death? Or did it mean that Montaigne was not long for this world? She prayed with everything she had for the latter.

She struggled to focus on the rest of the room. Facing off with the Ardenines were a half dozen exotically dressed foreigners. All glowed as red as a toper's nose except for one: a fair-haired mage with a cocky look and a blue-white aura.

Karn ushered her forward, his sweaty hand between her shoulder blades. "This is Jenna Bandelow," he said, "the girl with the magemark."

Karn didn't bother to introduce anyone to Jenna, but the fair-haired mage walked toward her, smiling, hands extended, so she guessed he must be the emissary.

"That's close enough," Adam said, planting himself between them. Jenna hadn't even seen him coming.

The stranger stopped an arm's length away, looking amused. "I thought you were the healer," he said to Adam. "Are you the chaperone, too?"

"I'm the king's expert on magical threats," Adam said.

"Creating them or preventing them?"

"Both. You can look, but don't touch."

"Ah," Strangward said. "Good to know the . . . parameters." He stepped past Adam until he stood face-to-face with Jenna, two scant feet away. "I am looking, healer," he called over his shoulder. "Not touching." He refocused on Jenna. "I'm Evan Strangward, Emissary of Celestine, Empress in the East," he said.

Jenna said nothing, just stood, clutching her skirts to either side. Should she say she was pleased to meet him when she wasn't?

Strangward nodded gravely, as if acknowledging a greeting from her. "I'm told you have a magemark on the back of your neck. May I see it?"

Feeling as trapped as a butterfly pinned to a board, Jenna looked around the circle of faces, at grim-faced Adam Wolf, and sweating Destin Karn, the blackbirds with their weapons, the scruffily exotic Carthians, the king and the thane and the mages. Every eye was fixed on her.

She remembered her conversation with poor Riley on the way to the mines years ago. She'd told him that her magemark meant that she was powerful, and destined for great things. She didn't feel powerful now. How did a coal miner from Delphi end up here?

"No," she said, swallowing hard, claiming the only power she could.

The king motioned impatiently to his blackbirds, and as they moved toward her, the emissary said, "Please, Jenna."

Jenna looked up in surprise. There was something in Strangward's green eyes—something that might have been sympathy.

"All right," she said, swallowing hard, "as long as you say please." She turned, bowing her head so he could get a good look. She felt the burn of his scrutiny, the slow release of his breath in a sigh, as if this confirmed something. Was that good news or bad news?

"Thank you," he said, taking a half step back. "What have you been told about the mark?"

She turned to look at him. "That I would be hunted and killed for it," she said.

The emissary's lips tightened. "Anything else?" he persisted.

"No."

"Are there any other markings on you?"

"A few scars is all," she said. She lifted her chin. "What does the empress want with me?"

"I don't know," Strangward said.

Jenna studied him, trying and failing to conjure up an image. He wasn't exactly lying, but— "You're afraid of her, aren't you?" she said.

"Anyone who is not afraid of the Empress Celestine is a fool," Strangward said. He turned back to the king. "I should like to interview the girl in private," he said.

Jenna was afraid to look at Adam. She could scent his rage and frustration from across the room.

"You can do that after the trade is made," Montaigne said. "If it is made. We still have not seen this weapon we've heard so much about."

"Very well," the emissary said. "Let's go see it. Who is coming?"

What was it about this girl that made her important? Lila still didn't know. True, she was striking, with her brilliant, multihued hair and golden eyes, but her features were not classically beautiful. She'd not had a close look at the marking, but it likely wouldn't have helped anyway. Lila was no scholar, after all, and even the scholars seemed stumped. From what everyone said, she had an unimpressive, random collection of gifts.

So what explained this empress's fixation on her? True, you could never tell what random person or thing a blueblood might obsess about. Or was this some kind of massive hoax? If it was, Lila couldn't see the point.

She'd know more after seeing the empress's weapon. Lila was among a handpicked trio that boarded the emissary's sailing dinghy to travel out to the main ship for a look—Destin Karn, Botetort, and Lila. She guessed Ash would have liked to come, but he was not invited, and the girl, Jenna, was returned to her cell.

The king of Arden, of course, remained on shore with

his guard. You could call us the expendables, Lila thought.

Strangward cast off the line and leapt aboard, while the big man, Teza Von, raised the sail. They worked well together, as if they'd done this a thousand times before. This was the oddest team of diplomats that Lila had ever seen.

The emissary touched his amulet, the sails filled, and off they went, even though they were traveling in the opposite direction than they had before.

Destin was still jumpy as a cat. Finally, he found a spot on a bench and sat there, knee bouncing, gripping his jinxpiece.

What's with you? Lila thought.

Botetort stood at the rail, staring out at the waves. He showed no inclination to chat with a pirate, so Lila filled the void.

"You seem to be a skilled sailor," Lila said, looking up at the taut sails.

"I was raised on a ship," Strangward said, squinting his eyes against the spray.

"You must have been a useful person to have around."

Strangward laughed. "To some people, maybe. To others, not so much."

"Is this the first time the empress has gone looking for someone with the magemark? Or does she keep an entire stable of such people?"

Strangward looked away. "No. She does not keep a stable of such people."

Lila couldn't help thinking that the emissary's words were carefully chosen.

Then again, he was an emissary.

They were coming up alongside the vessel. The sails slackened, and Von caught a line tossed down to them from above. A ladder followed, the iron rungs clanking against the side of the ship.

Here, in the main channel, the wind picked up, and the climb from the waterline to the lowest deck was terrifying. Botetort, especially, seemed relieved to reach the deck.

"This way." Von and Strangward led the way aft, and Lila did her best to map out the layout of the ship in her mind.

"How many crew does it require to sail her?" she asked.

"With a good crew, six or eight's enough to handle her," Von said. "If you need gunners, boarding parties, and galley staff, it'll be more. Here we are."

By now they'd reached amidships. They gathered around, while Von and Strangward unlatched a hatch and wrestled it open. Strangward peered into the opening, then nodded, as if satisfied. "It's down here," he said. Grabbing up a lantern, he unrolled a rope ladder over the edge. Lila heard the *plop* as it hit bottom.

When he went to climb down, Von gripped his arm. "My lord," he said in a low, worried voice. "Please. Let me go."

"Nonsense," Strangward said. "You'd likely get stuck in

the hatch." When Von didn't release him he said, "*Let go*, Von. I'll be fine."

Von let go and the emissary disappeared down the ladder.

"Are you coming?" Strangward called up when he'd apparently reached bottom.

They looked at one another. Nobody seemed eager to be first. Lila peered over the edge, into the hold.

The emissary stood below, looking up at her, hands on hips. He'd set the lantern on a table, illuminating the entire space. And, next to him, on the floor, lay a dragon.

"Blood of the martyrs," Lila breathed. Stepping over the edge of the hatch, she turned, gripped the ladder, and began to descend.

"This is the weapon we promised your king," Strangward said when Lila stood beside him. "The most powerful predator of the natural world."

It was smaller than Lila would have expected a dragon to be, armored with jeweled scales that glittered in the lamplight. Its eyes shown brilliantly, set on either side of a handsome face—eyes that seemed familiar, almost human. It had stubby horns on its head, and wicked claws on all four feet. One wing was folded tightly against its back, while the other drooped, like a tent with broken poles. It appeared to be torn in places.

Lila studied the beast with mingled fascination and fear. Razor-sharp spines marched down its back, all the way to the end of its tail. Its tail was coiled around it, occupying most of the floor space. Flame trickled from its nostrils. It wore a heavy collar around its neck, engraved with runes. It was connected to a heavy chain, bolted into the wall.

It looked up at Lila with a spark of interest, then seemed to dismiss her and rested its head on its claws again.

The space was entirely lined with brick and tile, which was blackened in spots, like the lining of a malfunctioning furnace. A pile of half-eaten rabbit carcasses lay in one corner, and the entire hold smelled of rum and sick and rotten meat.

Botetort was the next down the ladder, followed closely by Destin. When the thane spotted the dragon, he took a quick step back and gripped the hilt of his sword. "Is . . . is that what I think it is?"

"That depends on what you think it is," Strangward said.

Lila couldn't help liking the emissary's style. Whether she'd keep liking him remained to be seen.

Destin stared at the beast with disbelief. "That—that's a Carthian sun dragon," he said, shooting a look at Strangward. "Isn't it?"

Strangward nodded.

"But . . . it is my understanding that dragons are not real," Botetort said.

Strangward looked from the dragon to Botetort. "I assure you, this dragon is absolutely real. Touch it if you like."

Botetort made no move to do so. "It smells vile down here," he said. "Like a piss-pot in a bawdy house. Do dragons always stink like that?"

"We were anchored crossways in the current and I think it's a little seasick," Strangward said. "It's been closed up down here since we sailed."

Botetort nudged a washtub with his foot. "It smells like rum. Is that what it drinks?"

"Rum keeps it calm," Strangward said. "It seems to like it."

"I suppose that would put a fire in its belly," Botetort said. "Do dragons really breathe flame, like the legends say?"

Strangward rocked his hand. "Sometimes."

Lila squatted in front of the dragon. Its eyes were glazed, its breath coming fast.

"I wouldn't get too close," Strangward said sharply.

"It's not trained?"

"This one is not quite training size," Strangward said. "But once you begin, they catch on quickly."

Lila looked from Strangward to the dragon. This emissary's more nervous than he lets on. It's like he's not entirely sure what this dragon might do. Is it because it's a young dragon, and untrained? Or are they always that unpredictable?

"How old is it?" Destin asked.

"I'd say six months to a year. I don't know for sure,

since it was captured in the wild. But they grow fast. It's nearly doubled in size since we sailed. We had to bring a young one. It would be impossible to transport a full-grown dragon."

"Why? How large can they get?"

"Double the length of this ship."

"Truly? They get that big?" Botetort's eyes gleamed.

Before long, this dragon will be too big to get through the hatch, Lila thought. Even now, it would be tight.

"Is it a male or female?" she asked.

"I don't know," Strangward said. "Dragons are like some people—it's difficult to tell without close examination."

"How long has it been locked in the hold?" Destin asked. "Shouldn't it get some fresh air?"

"The ship is made of wood, Lieutenant. Would you give a dragon the run of a wooden ship?" Strangward patted the tile wall with the flat of his hand. "If our deal goes forward, it will have plenty of room to roam here in the wetlands."

"I'm trying to imagine how dragons could be used in warfare," Botetort said, rubbing his chin.

"Here's an example," Strangward said. "One problem you have in fighting the northern forces is that the mountains are a formidable barrier. Another problem is the distance you must travel to get to the enemy. A full-grown dragon could fly over the mountains, destroy a city, and be back in Ardenscourt in time for supper. It would no longer be necessary for you to send your soldiers north, year after year."

The thane looked from the dragon to Strangward. "You have seen this with your own eyes?"

"Where I come from, the sight of a dragon will send any army fleeing for their lives," Strangward said. He turned toward the ladder. "It's crowded down here. If everyone's had a look, perhaps we could continue this conversation back on shore." He hurried all of them back up on deck. Von seemed visibly relieved when Strangward emerged from the hold.

Back in the palace, they reassembled in the presence chamber so that they could make their reports to the king. Lila noticed that Ash lurked nearby. When he heard about the dragon, he abandoned all pretense and moved in closer.

"Have you used them for reconnaissance work?" Montaigne asked Strangward.

"They can see long distances, and in the dark, so even the young ones would be suitable for that sort of thing," Strangward said.

"Can they understand orders?" the king asked. "Can they tell the difference between enemies and allies?"

"Dragons are the most intelligent creatures I have ever encountered," Strangward said. "They are much brighter than most people I meet." He smiled a feral smile. "I have no doubt that they could make that distinction."

Lila thought of the collar the dragon wore in the hold.

It faintly resembled the flashcraft collars used here in the south. "Can dragons be controlled using collars, in the way that mages can?"

"With dragons," Strangward said, "it's more a matter of knowing how to train them."

Something about the way he said it reminded Lila of a barker at the fair.

Maybe the king thought so, too, because he motioned to Destin. "Lieutenant," he said, "can you verify the truth of what the emissary is saying?"

Destin licked his lips. "Your Majesty," he said, "as a diplomat, Commander Strangward is protected by a certain—"

"No worries, Lieutenant," Strangward broke in. "Truly. I don't mind." Smiling, he extended his hands toward the spymaster.

Destin took a breath, released it, then took hold of the emissary's hands. He looked straight into the diplomat's face. "Are you telling the truth, Commander Strangward?"

"Always, Lieutenant Karn," Strangward said. "Or, at least, as often as possible."

"Do you mean harm to the king, or the empire?"

"No," Strangward said.

"Is this dragon as powerful as you say it is?" Destin whispered.

"If anything, I have underestimated its potential."

"Can they carry soldiers? Or supplies?" Botetort asked.

"I've not seen that," Strangward said, "but they are certainly strong enough. I suppose you would need some sort of harness. Or a saddle."

Botetort turned to Lila. "Would you be able to procure something suitable? Clan-made, perhaps? Something that combines the control of a collar with the practicality of a saddle?"

"I could . . . look into it," Lila said reluctantly. "Though, since my sources have had no experience with dragons, I imagine that it would take time to work up a design."

Destin turned to the king. "Was there anything else you wanted me to ask, Your Majesty?"

"No, Lieutenant," Montaigne said. "I am satisfied."

Destin held on to Strangward's hands a moment longer, then released his hold and stepped back.

But Lila wasn't done. She took a quick breath, knowing she had to tread lightly. "I am concerned about the health of the dragon we saw today," she said. "It seemed . . . listless."

Out of the corner of her eye, she saw Ash sit up straighter.

"Dragons eat large meals, and then sleep for long periods in between," Strangward said. "The dragon you saw made a fresh kill immediately before we sailed. He will get progressively more . . . lively."

"What do dragons typically prey on?" Lila asked.

"They are meat eaters, so they'll eat pretty much anything large enough to catch their interest."

"Including people?" she persisted.

"They have been known to eat people, yes," Strangward said.

"Would you be able to supply more dragons, if we needed them?" Botetort asked.

"I know where to find large numbers of dragons," Strangward said. "More than you'll ever need."

There were nods all around. This is too easy, Lila thought.

Strangward must have sensed that, too, because now he moved to close the deal. "So. Here is what I propose. We will leave the dragon with you, and take the girl back to the Northern Islands with us. If the empress determines that she is the girl she is looking for, our armies will arrive in time for the marching season in the north. If you find the dragon to be useful, we can make arrangements to supply more."

Montaigne shook his head. "I'm sorry. That is not acceptable to us."

Strangward went perfectly still. "It's not acceptable? In what way, Your Majesty?"

"We were promised an army for the girl," Montaigne said, "and we do not intend to give her up until we get one. We've given you the opportunity to examine the girl and determine if she is the one you are looking for. If you believe she is, inform the empress and return with the army, and we will make the trade. If you are interested in establishing trade in dragons, I suggest that you leave the dragon here so that we can evaluate its potential usefulness to us."

Strangward gazed at the king for a long moment. When he spoke, his voice had an edge to it. "So. The dragon and the diamonds stay with you and we leave empty-handed? That hardly seems fair."

"You've learned a lesson, then—one you should have mastered long before now," Montaigne said. "Life isn't fair."

"I'll make a note of that, Your Majesty," Strangward said, his jaw tight. "I am certain this lesson will be of great use to me going forward. In truth, I have little interest in establishing a trade in dragons. I'll report your requirements to Celestine and we will see what she decides." He inclined his head slightly. "Gentlemen. And lady. Thank you for your time."

With that, the delegation from the Empress in the East walked out, leaving behind their last vestige of protocol.

"Arrogant savage," Montaigne said.

Lila glanced at Ash. His eyes were closed, his face slack with relief. Lila frowned. Was he relieved that Arden would not have a dragon at its disposal? Wasn't a dragon preferable to an army? Or was he just happy with the delay?

"Your Majesty," Botetort protested, "a girl for a dragon? It seems to me that there is little risk to us in such an agreement. The empire is swarming with women, but with a dragon we could fly all the way to Fellsmarch and burn the wolf bitch to a crisp." Clearly, Botetort envisioned himself as just the hero to do that.

"I have examined the girl," Destin said, "and I have not been able to identify any qualities that would match the value of a—"

"Enough!" Montaigne stood, trembling with rage. "I have made my decision. We may not see the girl as valuable, but the empress clearly does, and that is all that matters. I will not allow a shipload of unwashed pirates to conduct a bait and switch. When the empress sends me an army, we will do business, and not before."

STRANGE
BEDFELLOWS

When Ash left the royal apartments, he headed straight for the stables. Though he was officially working full-time in the healing halls, he found that sometimes hard physical labor was the only treatment for the anger and frustration that accumulated at court. And right now he needed that sort of relief.

Grabbing up a pitchfork, he proceeded to pitch dirty hay out of the nearest stall and into the aisle, not particularly careful about where it landed. He mucked out a half dozen stalls, until the muscles in his shoulders and arms burned, and he was soaked in sweat.

All the while, his mind boiled like a mud spring. What could the empress of a faraway island realm possibly want with Jenna? All of the possibilities seemed bad. Besides, any Ardenine alliance with a realm known for powerful magic spelled bad news for the Fells.

"I thought you were out of the stables," someone said behind him.

Ash knew without turning around that it was Lila.

"Every now and then, I get in the mood to shovel horse-shit. You're welcome to help."

"We need to talk."

"No. You *want* to talk. There's a difference."

"This thing—this agreement—can't go forward."

"Maybe it won't," Ash said, digging into the dirty hay. "You heard the king. Maybe he and the empress will never come to terms. Which is fine by me."

"I think they will, eventually. Unless something happens to stop it."

Ash finally turned around to face her, leaning on his pitchfork. "What do you care? There's money to be made either way. Dragon harnesses, specialized clothing for dragon riders, dog collars for Carthian mages—the possibilities are endless."

"The last thing we need is another army mixing in," Lila said. "The situation is bad enough as it is."

"*We?* I don't know whose side you're on, but I'm pretty sure it's not mine. How do you think all those collars, talismans, and amulets are going to be used?" Ash's voice rose. "I'm not interested in getting involved with any of your schemes."

"Shhh," Lila said, looking around. "I don't think you want to share that with the entire stable yard."

"We're done here, anyway," Ash said, resuming his forking. "Now why don't you just go about your business, and I'll go about mine. That was our agreement, remember?"

"You're wrong about me," Lila said. "I've not been straight with you, and that's why we need to talk—someplace we won't be overheard."

Something about the way Lila said this caught Ash's ear—and made him turn around again. She looked and sounded serious as plague. It was like the smooth-talking, hard-drinking, unscrupulous slacker he knew had been swapped out for somebody else.

"All right," he said. "We can go into the tack room. Nobody will be in there this time of day. But I'm warning you—you'd better not be wasting my time."

As Ash had expected, the tack room was deserted. Rolley would be at dinner, and it was too dark to be out riding this late at night at this time of year. Ash hung the lantern from one of the saddle racks and sat down on a trunk, arms folded, prepared for smoke and mirrors.

Lila settled onto the bench that centered the room, raked her hand through her cap of curls, and squared her shoulders. "First off," she said, "my name is not Lila Barrowhill. It's Lila Byrne. Amon Byrne is my father."

As usual, Lila's first move set Ash reeling like he'd been

clubbed over the head. He didn't know what he expected, but it wasn't that. Amon Byrne was the captain of the queen's Gray Wolf guard. The queen of the Fells, that is. His mother.

"Close your mouth, sul'Han," Lila said, sounding more like herself. "You look like a beached fish."

He scrambled for something to say. "I know Byrne's a widower, but I don't recall any children except for Simon."

"Simon was the oldest, then my brother Silva," Lila said. "My mother died in childbirth with me. Simon stayed on with our da, and me and Silva went to live with my mother's relatives in the Southern Islands."

When Ash took a closer look, he could see that it was possible. Captain Byrne's wife had been a Southern Islander, with dark skin and curly hair. Lila had inherited that, but her eyes were gray like her father's. Ash had guessed she was a mixed blood, but it had never occurred to him that it was this particular mix.

"I guess you could say that this apple fell pretty far from the tree," Lila said with a crooked smile. "I never saw much of my da until I went to live with some cousins in Baston Bay when I was ten. They were smugglers, though they called themselves traders, and they had ships that ran up and down the coast. My da would visit my aunt Lydia in Chalk Cliffs sometimes, and I'd take a ship up and see him. Not often; I was kind of mad at him, to tell you the truth."

"How come you were mad at him?"

"My mother was dead and he was busy saving the queendom, so he never paid too much attention to me until Simon died. Then he couldn't figure out how to fit a square peg like me into the plan."

"What do you mean?"

"I was like this massive joke played on my father. I'm not good with stupid military rules, and I had no head for schooling. The things I was good at—like smuggling and role-playing and sailing and deal-making—he had no use for. Still—one thing you can say about Captain Byrne—he is persistent. He just kept calling in his markers, sending me back to Oden's Ford, trying to hone this bit of bad metal into a sword. I was damned tired of it."

Much as Ash hated to admit it, his and Lila's lives had parallels. They'd been war orphans from the start.

"Then you ran off to Oden's Ford. Well, at first they thought you were dead or captured, but your friend Taliesin ratted you out."

"*Taliesin* told them?" Just one more club to the head.

"You think you know a person, right? She wanted your mother to know you were still alive, but she talked her into letting you stay at Oden's Ford."

"So the queen knew I was there all along." A couple of minutes into this conversation, and Ash already felt beat up. Questions swirled through his mind. "Why didn't she—why didn't she ever . . . reach out to me? Or drag me home?"

"The queen doesn't confide in me," Lila said. "But I think she was worried that any contact with you might put you at risk. Ardenine spies are everywhere." She glanced around again, as if to make sure none had slipped into the room. "Except for a few key people, everyone in the Fells thinks you're dead."

"Does Lyss—does my sister know?"

"I don't know," Lila said. "She was pretty young, wasn't she, when you ran off?"

When he ran off. That's exactly what he did. "Yes," he said. "She was."

"By then Captain Byrne was beginning to realize that I could actually be useful. Maybe my name will never be up on the brag board in Wien House, but Oden's Ford is a great place to chat up assholes like Tourant. Being a smuggler is great cover for traveling around the Realms."

"You were a spy?"

"Among other things," Lila said vaguely. "My da asked me to keep an eye on you—from a distance, since following you around would just draw attention to you. I wasn't hot for the job—the last thing I wanted to do was nanny a runaway princeling. If King Gerard found out where you were, it wouldn't do any good anyway, and I'd get the blame." Her gaze was frank and unblinking. "I finally agreed, but I negotiated summers off to do my own thing. It turns out I worried for nothing. Watching over you was an easy job until, you know, this year. After the death crows came, I decided I'd better take you home, but you didn't cooperate."

Good thing you didn't know what I did with my summers, Ash thought. "What are you doing here? Still nannying?"

She shook her head. "I've been working on a long-term project with a friend of mine. We're becoming major suppliers for the Ardenine army."

"That seems to be going well," Ash said drily. He rose and paced back and forth. "So you sold them a boatload of flashcraft. You don't think that was going a little overboard when it comes to winning their trust?"

"It would be," Lila said, "if the flashcraft worked as intended."

Ash swiveled to face her. "Why? What's wrong with it?"

"Let's just say that it was custom work."

"But . . . I thought you said it was old flash."

"My friend Rogan is a rum clan flashcrafter. He is very good at reproductions."

"All along, then, you've been working for the Fells."

Lila nodded.

"Why didn't you tell me that before? I would have been at least marginally more polite."

"To be honest, I thought of you as an amateur—a spoiled, entitled, runaway princeling bent on revenge who would get caught and then complicate and compromise my elegant scheme. I figured the less you knew, the better."

"I hate it when you sugarcoat things," Ash said. "If you had access to the court, why cook up an elegant scheme? Why not just assassinate Montaigne?"

"Damn! Why didn't I think of that?" Lila slapped her forehead.

"I'm serious."

"What makes you think I haven't tried?"

"That wasn't you with the gedden weed and the—?"

"No." Lila rolled her eyes. "The thing is, I never inherited the Byrne gene for martyrdom. I enjoy life too much to want to spend it on gutter-swiving Montaigne. How do I know Prince Jarat will be an improvement? From what I've seen and heard, he probably won't be."

"At least maybe he won't be hell-bent on murdering my family," Ash growled. "So. Why did you suddenly decide it was time to have a heart-to-heart with me?"

"Because an alliance between the Northern Islands and Arden will dilute the effect of the project Rogan and I have been working on for three years. And because the loss of your father as High Wizard makes us more vulnerable to magical attack than before. Lord Bayar has stepped in, but—"

"Bayar is High Wizard? Really?" Micah Bayar and his father had been rivals, if not outright enemies, for years. Whether intended or not, the grudge had been passed along to Ash.

"You really need to get out more, sul'Han," Lila said, looking amused.

Ash had been in a bad mood since the meeting with Montaigne, and being blindsided like this didn't improve things.

"So stop it. Kill the king. Kill the emissary. Launch an invasion of the Northern Islands. There are so many options."

"The thing is, I need your help."

What could a spoiled, entitled, runaway princeling possibly do for you? Ash thought it, but he didn't say it out loud, because then he would sound like one.

"What kind of help?"

"You're not going to like it," Lila said, shifting her eyes away.

"That doesn't surprise me. Go on."

"The simplest way to prevent the deal from going forward is to eliminate the girl."

"As in kill the girl."

"Yes." Lila had the grace to look sheepish.

"And you want me to do it."

"You still have access to her, right? You're likely the only person who could do it and get away with it." She leaned forward, speaking fast and persuasively. "Look at it this way, healer. If not for you, she'd be dead. So, in a way, you're just undoing what you did."

"Breaking what I fixed."

"Exactly," Lila said, looking proud that she'd come up with that.

"You can find a way to justify anything, can't you?"

"Look, it's the only way to kill the deal without giving everything away."

"Without giving your scheme away, you mean."

"Well, yes," Lila said. "Plus, we survive. It's all good."

"For everyone but Jenna."

"Do you think it's better to send her off to the Northern Islands? Have you heard the expression 'fate worse than death'?"

"You need to get out of the habit of thinking of me as stupid," Ash said. "I'm not going to help you kill Jenna, and it's not because I'm naive."

"If I went to her, and I told her what the stakes are, what do you think she would say?"

That was when Lila crossed the line.

In a heartbeat, Ash had her pinned up against the wall. She tried some cagey moves, but got nowhere. "You will not go near her, do you understand?"

Lila stared at him, an incredulous look on her face. "Blood and bones. How could I of missed that? You're not stupid, you're in love!"

"Just because I won't sign on to whatever plan you come up with doesn't mean I—"

"I can't believe it!" Lila crowed. "He has a heart after all."

"You're not improving your chances of winning me over," Ash said. "Just so you know. If you want my help, you're going to have to come up with a different plan."

37

A PLEDGE AND A PROMISE

When Ash arrived at the tower room that night, the posted guard had been doubled. Whether because of Jenna's demonstrated market value or mistrust of the pirates, it was getting more and more difficult to get in to see her. Just another sign that time was running out.

When he finally gained entry, she was sitting, looking out the window, a book lying forgotten in her lap. She'd changed out of the dress she'd worn to the interview with Strangward and into the one she'd worn the day before. She'd pulled her hair free, too, and it hung softly around her shoulders.

When she turned and saw him, she launched out of

the chair, the book thunking onto the floor. They came together like two magnets slamming home. Ash could feel Jenna's wildly beating heart through his velvet and her silk. It was like kisses were oxygen and they'd been drowning.

Or they were about to drown.

Finally, she broke away and held him out at arm's length so she could look him over. "What's that?" she asked, pointing to the bottle he carried.

"It's wine," he said. "To celebrate some good news." He set the wine jar and two cups down on the table next to her chair.

"So," she said, "what's the news? Wait, don't tell me—the king is dead."

There was something in her voice that caught his attention—some private knowledge or intuition. He hadn't told her about his attempts to poison Montaigne. He didn't want to get her hopes up, and she'd told him not to make promises, after all.

He studied her a moment, then said, "Not yet. We're celebrating for two reasons—first, Arden and Carthis were unable to come to terms. Montaigne is demanding his army before he hands you over. That buys us a little time."

"I'll drink to that," Jenna said, pouring them each some wine.

"It might just be a temporary setback," Ash warned.

"Remember my rule? Savor the moment." She raised her glass and they toasted.

"Secondly, have you heard that Delphi has fallen?"

Jenna was swallowing down some wine, and she all but choked on it. "F-fallen? To who?"

"The Patriots have retaken the city. They've booted the mudbacks out."

Jenna set down her wine, gripped his elbows, and danced him around the room in a kind of impromptu upland reel, her bare feet thumping on the stone floor. "Come on, Wolf," she said, when his feet didn't move fast enough, "put the wine down and dance with me!"

Ash did his best, and, finally, they collapsed into the chair, gasping and laughing.

"Say it again," she said fiercely. "I want to hear it again."

"The Patriots have retaken Delphi," Ash said. "They've dealt the Ardenine army a crushing defeat."

"Oh," she said, smiling. "I'll bet the bonfires are still burning on the hills. I wish I could be there to see it. Fletcher must be in a world of joy." Gradually, her smile faded and the melancholy crept back into her eyes. "There are so many people who didn't live to see it. Maggi, and Riley, and my da . . ."

He cupped her face with his hands. "Remember what you said—that worrying about the bad times can ruin what should be the good times. So celebrate. Celebrate without regret." He kissed her, then poured them each another cup of wine.

"To the Patriots of Delphi, both the living and the

dead," Jenna said, raising her cup in a toast. She drank deeply, then stared into space, turning the cup in her hands. "There it is again," she murmured.

"There's what?"

"*Flamecaster.* I keep hearing that name in my head."

"What do you mean?"

"Ever since that emissary arrived, I've been hearing voices. It sounds like someone crying for help, saying 'Flamecaster! Help me!'"

"Flamecaster." Ash frowned. "Wasn't that your street name in Delphi?"

Jenna nodded. "I . . . picked it because I was always setting fire to things and blowing things up."

"Is that new? The voices?"

She nodded. "It's always been images before."

"Could it have something to do with the fighting in Delphi? Maybe your gift is letting you know about somebody in trouble."

She shrugged. "Or I'm losing my mind. Anyway. Tell me about the emissary's weapon."

Ash took a fortifying gulp of wine. "I didn't actually see it myself, but I'm told that it's a dragon."

"A dragon?" Jenna's voice rose. "But . . . there's no such thing?" She said this in the form of a question, as if she were no longer sure what was real and what was fantasy.

"That's what I thought, too," Ash said. "But Lord Botetort saw it—he was all excited about it, in fact, and he has the imagination of a slug."

"How big was it?"

"They said that it was the size of a horse, but, you know, built differently. Strangward said it was young, and not fully grown—that a fully grown dragon would be too big to transport by ship." He paused. "It's being kept in the hold, and Lila said that it looked like it was sick."

"It was sick?" Planting her feet on the floor, she leaned forward, her hands on her knees. "What do you mean? What was wrong with it?"

"I'm just going by what Lila said. She said it was listless. Strangward said that it was fine, that it always sleeps a lot when it's had a large meal."

Jenna pressed the heels of her hands against her temples, as if her head was in danger of splitting apart. She seemed to be getting more and more agitated as the conversation went on.

"Are you all right?" Ash said. "What's the matter?"

"I don't know," Jenna whispered, fingering the mage-mark on the back of her neck. "It just seems like there's something about dragons, something I should remember. Something that's burned into my bones." Her eyes were glazed, her breathing quick and shallow, and Ash guessed that images were flying through her mind.

He waited until her eyes refocused a bit, then said, "Could you have foreseen that the empress meant to trade a dragon for you? Is that why it's familiar?"

She shook her head. "I don't know. Anyway. What does the king want with a dragon?"

"What he really wants is an army of mages," Ash said. "That's what the empress promised. Strangward is trying to persuade the king to accept a dragon as a kind of down payment or deposit so he can take you back with him. He claims that dragons could be useful in the war, to carry soldiers, and incinerate cities, that sort of thing." It was an effort to keep his voice matter-of-fact. "Botetort was convinced, anyway. He was practically salivating, asking if he could have more than one."

"What did Lieutenant Karn have to say about the dragon? Did he see it?"

Ash nodded. "He saw it. He didn't say much, either way." He paused. "What did you think of Strangward?"

"He's such a mingle and a mix, he's hard to read. My gut tells me he's dangerous, he's scared, and he's telling a big, big lie."

"I don't believe him, either," Ash said, "but he brought a big sackful of diamonds to prove he was in earnest."

She rubbed her chin. "I wish I could get my hands on him."

"What?" Ash's stomach clenched.

She grinned at him. "Easy there, Wolf. Sometimes I have to touch a person to get a reading." She paused. "So—what do you think? Is this going to happen?"

Ash shrugged unhappily. "He's gone to a lot of time and

trouble to get to this point. The empress must really want this deal."

"There's a solution," Jenna said. "What if I died before the exchange is made?"

"What? No!" Ash felt a twinge of guilt, recalling his conversation with Lila. "That is not a solution."

"Think about it," Jenna said. "The only thing worse than the king we have now is a king with a dragon and a whole new army."

"No one is asking you to—"

"You don't need to ask. I'm volunteering," Jenna said. "Thousands of Patriots have died, fighting for freedom. It's a chance to do my part." Her voice trembled a bit.

Ash cast about for options. "What if the dragon dies instead? Then Strangward has nothing to trade."

"No," Jenna said, lifting her chin.

"I don't like it either, but when it comes to a choice between—"

"Look," Jenna said. "If the dragon dies, it just delays things. The empress can always ship over another one. Besides, from what you said, Montaigne is really looking for an army. What we need to do is prevent Montaigne from forming an alliance with this empress, whoever she is."

"A delay would help," Ash said. "With a little time, the king could die. Or you might escape."

"That's a prayer or a wish," she said. "It's not a plan."

"Give me another suggestion," Ash said. "Something a

little more creative than self-sacrifice."

She studied on it a while, and then her eyes lit up. "You said that the emissary's ship is here, in the harbor?"

Ash nodded.

"What if we blow it up, and put the blame on Arden?"

"We?" Ash raised an eyebrow. He reached up and tapped his collar. "And this would happen how? I'm out of commission when it comes to attack magic, remember."

Jenna rolled her eyes. "It's not all about you, healer. I'm no wizard, and I've been blowing things up for years. I can tell you what you'll need, and how to do it. You probably wouldn't want to use magery anyway, if we want to blame it on Arden."

Yes, Ash thought. I am in love with this girl.

He heard Taliesin's voice in his head.

It's the worst thing in the world, to risk yourself by loving someone. At the same time, it's the best thing in the world—and worth the risk.

Jenna's mind was elsewhere. "Do you know someone who can get black powder, fuses, and the like?"

Ash nodded, thinking of Lila. "I do."

"I'll make a list then. But you have to promise me something."

"Promise you what?"

"You'll free the dragon if you can."

Ash pressed his lips together to prevent words from spilling out, but Jenna saw.

"You're wondering why I have this fixation on a dragon I've never met?"

"The thought . . . did occur to me," Ash said carefully.

"The dragon didn't volunteer," Jenna said. "Anyway, I just—I can't help feeling that I—that it's going to be important, going forward." She looked up at him. "Can you trust me on that? I'm not asking for a contract. All I'm asking is that you try."

Ash swallowed hard. "I'll do what I can." He paused. "Have you thought about what might happen to you if the deal falls through? It's not like the king is going to set you free."

Jenna shrugged. "I'm from Delphi. I should have been dead a long time ago."

"Some things are worse than death," Ash said.

"Then give me an out." She held out her hand and wiggled her fingers.

"That again?"

"No, healer. This is different. I don't want to die. I want to live. I want to hear the bells in the temple church in Delphi, ringing out the victory. I want to hike into the Spirit Mountains and speak to witches and faeries. I want to sail over the ocean, all the way to the horizon and beyond. I want to go all those places I've never seen, except in books. I want to fly—"

He raised both hands. "All right," he said, "but, remember, I—"

"I want more of this." She pulled his head down and

kissed him soundly on the lips. "And this." Sliding her hands under his doublet, under his shirt, finding the bare skin, she lay back in the chair and pulled him down on top of her, wrapping her legs around him.

"I have plans for you, Wolf," she growled, biting at his ear. "I don't intend to die any time soon."

"I believe you," he said hoarsely.

An hour later, by the temple bells, they still lay tangled together in the chair, their clothing in definite disarray.

There is a lot can be done in a chair, Ash thought. Maybe we can just live in this chair from now on.

"I'd better go," he mumbled against her shoulder.

Jenna yawned and snuggled in closer. "This is scandalous, you know, that we've spent so much unchaperoned time together."

"Are you complaining?"

"No!" she exclaimed, with such fervor that he laughed. "It's just—in Bruinswallow, I think we'd be considered married, and I still don't know your real name."

Ash searched her eyes, brushing her lips with his fingertips. "Do you really want to know? Because I'll tell you."

She returned his gaze for a long moment, then shook her head. "It can keep. I rather like Adam Wolf. When this is all over, you can take me to meet your mother."

"I'll do that," he said, realizing that he wanted them to meet.

She grimaced. "She'll probably hate me."

"You're wrong," Ash said. "She'll probably like you

more than me." He took her face between his hands and kissed her nose and her eyelids. Then gently freed himself, straightened his clothing, and buttoned up.

She wrapped up in a quilt, found paper and a quill, and wrote him a list. Then told him exactly what to do with the items on it.

Ash slid his finger under his silver collar and brought out a tiny packet made of cloth. He held it up for her inspection. "This contains two berries, known as baneberry. A single berry will kill you within minutes."

She stared at it. "You've had this all along?"

"You never know when you might face the sudden need to die," he said. "Or for someone else to die."

Jenna eyed the packet. "Is it—is it painful?"

"Would I choose something painful?" Ash snorted. "I'm told it's quite pleasant." He showed her the cords attached to the packet. "This ties in place, inside your clothing. Any questions?"

She was looking at him, head tilted, questions crowding into her eyes. "More secrets, healer?"

He shrugged. "We are trading secrets, I believe. Just remember to take it with you if you change clothes."

"I'll remember," Jenna said. She dug into the little bag and extracted one of the berries. "Keep this," she said, holding it out to him. "I only need one."

"I have plenty," he said.

They kissed. And kissed again.

Finally she broke away and said, "I have something for

you, too." She crossed to the bed, reached under the straw ticking, and retrieved something. She took his hand and dropped it into his palm, closing his fingers over it.

He opened his hand and looked at it, poking at it with his other hand. It was a pendant on a chain, both corroded by the passage of time. "What is this?" he said.

"It was my father's," she said. "It's all I have of his."

"Jenna," he said, his voice thick. "You can't give me this. Why are you—"

"I want you to have this, for luck," she said. When he shook his head, she said, "I *want* to give it to you. If I keep it, sooner or later they'll take it away."

"But . . . what about you?" Adam said. "What will you do for luck?"

"I have you, healer," she said. "That's all I need. You can give it back to me when I see you again. Now kiss me again, and go."

So Ash did. Pausing in the doorway, he said, "See you soon."

"Thank you, healer," she called after him. He looked back at her and she was sitting cross-legged in the chair, hands resting on her lap, palms up. There was something in her eyes that sent a shiver of apprehension through him.

It was hope.

38

ON THE WATERFRONT

Ash was already sorry he'd brought Lila along. She'd been raising objections and complaints ever since he'd shared the new plan.

"Couldn't you have picked a less miserable night?" Lila grumbled as they navigated the twisting streets of the harbor district of Ardenscourt. She swiped rain from her face with her sleeve and hunched her shoulders.

"I don't know how much time we have," Ash said. "Strangward could decide to sail with the morning tide."

"Strangward seems to be tight with the weather gods. Maybe he knows we're coming, and he ordered this up special."

The hair prickled on the back of Ash's neck. No. How would he know?

"Do you really think the empress will blame this on Arden?"

"It seems plausible, doesn't it? Arden sinks their ship and steals their dragon so they don't have to come to terms."

"That doesn't work if what you really want is an army," Lila pointed out.

"You don't have to come with me," Ash said. "I only brought you along because you're good with a knife. And got us the uniforms. And the explosives."

Lila snorted. "Sorry I'm not pulling my weight."

"This may not be your idea," Ash said doggedly, "but it's what we're going to do."

"Is it? Are you really going to start playing the prince card after all?"

"Don't start in about my mother the queen, because I don't want to hear it."

"All right, then, as your peer and absolute equal, I can't help thinking this is a really bad idea." Thunder crashed, and Lila flinched. "Will this stuff even work when it's wet?" She patted her backpack.

"Jenna says it will."

"How did she get to be such an expert on explosives?"

"She worked in the mines."

"At least tell me you've changed your mind about the dragon."

"I made a promise," Ash said.

"So break it. You break promises to me all the time."

"Maybe the dragon could help us in the war."

"And maybe we could set fire to Fellsmarch and hope it spreads south." Three more strides and she said, "I say, bring back the old, hard-hearted Ash."

When Ash said nothing, Lila muttered something else that he couldn't quite make out.

"What did you say?"

"I said I should have drugged you and dragged you back to Fellsmarch when I had the chance."

"I'm the one with the drugs, remember?"

"Ha."

"Anyway, since when have you—did you hear that?" Ash spun around, his hand on his amulet, staring back down the street. He glanced at Lila, who somehow had a knife in each hand. They both looked and listened.

"I guess it was the rain or the wind," he said finally, thinking, It's never the rain or the wind when you want it to be the rain or the wind.

"Probably," Lila said, the knives disappearing. "Or Lieutenant Karn and the real King's Guard, out for a stroll." She took another long look before she turned and trudged on, shoulders rounded under her heavy rucksack. "What do you know about ships, anyway?"

"Not much," Ash admitted. "Breaking into a ship can't be much different than any other burglary."

"Except for the part where there's no place to run if you get caught, or if somebody blows up the ship. Or if a dragon decides to roast you like a chestnut."

"You can swim, can't you?"

"Of course I know how to swim. But have you smelled the river?" Lila wrinkled her nose. "It's a cesspool. I'm not planning to do any swimming tonight, just so you know."

"Are you really going to whine the whole time?" Ash buckled his blackbird cloak over his collar and pulled the hood up.

"There's no reason both of us have to go," Lila said abruptly. "I'll handle it. You stay here."

"Give it up, all right? If anyone stays behind, it's going to be you. Otherwise, we stay with the original plan: You deal with the explosives. I'll deal with the dragon. That way we can be there and gone in no time. If you're spotted and questioned, we're the harbor patrol, remember. We saw something suspicious, like somebody boarding their ship."

"And that's why we're carrying canisters of black powder. Got it."

On reaching the docks, there was one piece of good news: at some point, Strangward's ship had raised anchor and was now tied up at the wharf, maybe to load supplies for their departure. Once again, Ash thought he heard something, soft footsteps or maybe the creak of planks behind him. He turned, scanning the length of the dock. He saw nothing, and heard nothing beyond the slap of water against the pilings and the clank of rigging against masts.

It was near midnight, and there was just a single light burning in the wheelhouse. The crew quarters were dark and silent, the gangway was drawn up, and the ship was shrouded in a shimmering layer of what appeared to be greenish ice.

Ash stood staring at it, hands on hips.

"What's that?" Lila whispered.

"I don't know," Ash said, "but I think it means keep out."

"Can't you do something?"

"Maybe." Closing his hand on his amulet, Ash sent a tendril of magic forward. When it collided with the barrier, the ice vaporized into a poisonous-looking cloud that was carried away by a stiff wind blowing upriver. He continued until the near side of the ship was clear.

They waited for someone to sound the alarm, but there was nothing. The ship appeared to be deserted.

"What do you think?" Ash whispered.

"Looks like a trap to me," Lila said glumly.

Ash threw a line over the rail and used it to pull a rope ladder up and over. Then waited again. Nothing.

"I'll go up first, take a quick look, and then signal to you," Lila said. Sliding the backpack over her shoulders, she scrambled up the ladder to where she could peer over the rail. Apparently satisfied, she vaulted over, turned, and motioned to Ash to come ahead. Then she disappeared.

Ash ascended the ladder, climbed over the railing, and

dropped to the deck on the other side. He pulled up the ladder so that it couldn't be seen from the wharf, then hurried amidships, where the hold was.

The hatch was secured by a chain and padlock. Ash melted the chain and removed it, then wrestled the hatch open. The stench from below hit him like a physical blow.

We're too late, he thought, heart sinking. The dragon's already dead.

He knew he should be relieved. Instead, he felt a keen sense of loss. And not just because he hated the thought of facing Jenna with the news. If he survived the night himself.

Dropping the ladder into the darkness, he climbed down, using his fingertips to kindle his torch.

The dragon lay at the rear of the hold. Its head was down, resting on its forelegs, and its eyes were closed and crusted, like it hadn't opened them in a while. Even its scaly armor seemed dull. Rabbit carcasses lay untouched in the corner, which accounted for some of the smell. A trickle of vapor from the dragon's nostrils was the only visible sign of life, but Ash sensed that a spark still burned deep within.

"Hey," Ash murmured. There was no response. Ash reached out with his mind, trying to make a connection, but the mind behind the eyes was murky and muddled, impossible to read, or to communicate with.

"What's wrong?" he asked. "Are you sick?"

For a moment, he could have sworn the dragon understood. It turned its head, and looked into Ash's eyes, like a plea for help. Then it rested its head on its forelegs.

He eased closer until he could reach out and touch the dragon's shoulder. It was dry and cool. But maybe that was the way it was supposed to be. He pressed his fingers against the side of its neck and felt a pulse, thready and weak. Truth be told, Ash knew nothing about dragons. But his healer's instinct told him that this dragon was close to death.

Was it sick because it had been penned up inside the hold too long? Had it been taken away from its mother too soon? Or had it lost the will to live? Who wouldn't, in this environment?

"I'm here to help you if I can," Ash said. "I'm going to try and get you out of here." The dragon didn't stir, didn't open an eye.

Taking a deep breath, Ash sent magic in, exploring in totally unknown territory.

The dragon was cold, cold, cold until he neared its head. It got warmer and warmer until he reached the area around the collar, which was blistering hot, feverish with power.

What was going on? Was the collar leaking magic into the dragon? Or was it preventing it from flowing into the rest of its body? Ash ran his finger over the dragon's collar, feeling a familiar tug. Ash touched the collar around his own neck—the one that prevented him from accumulating enough flash to do mischief.

The sensation was the same. The collar around the dragon's neck must serve the same purpose—to collect flash and to keep the dragon from fighting back.

Ash touched the dragon's collar again, sliding his finger between the collar and the dragon's scales. He could find no opening, no catch. It seemed to be as permanent as his own.

Could a lack of magic be what was making it sick? If so, elemental flash might be the cure. Experimentally, he pressed his palm against the dragon's head and fed a little flash into it.

Nothing.

He fed it a little more.

The dragon shuddered and opened his eyes. They glowed like amber in the murky hold.

"Does this help?" Ash fed him more flash.

The dragon nudged Ash with its nose, pressing against him like a cat. The message was clear. More, please.

Ash complied. This time, the dragon lashed its tail against the floor.

It seemed to be helping, but Ash doubted he could produce enough flash to make up for what the collar was sucking away. He had to find a way to remove the collar.

Just then, the light trickling through the hatch was

blotted out. "Ash! You down there?" It was Lila, her voice oddly shrill.

"Yes. I was just—"

"We've got to go. Now. All hell's broken loose. Bring the dragon and come on."

Ash could hear other noises. It sounded like fighting.

"I can't bring the dragon, but maybe if I—"

"Then leave it and come before they—scummer!" Lila swore. She slid through the hatch, pulling the trapdoor closed after her. For a moment, she dangled from it by one hand, then dropped to the floor, crying out in pain when she landed.

"What's going on?" Ash said. "Is there—"

"Shhh!" Lila looked up at the ceiling. What sounded like a dozen pairs of feet pounded overhead, the sound receding as whoever it was raced toward the bow of the boat.

"They'll be back," Lila said.

"Who's they?"

"It's those miserable bloodsucking priests," Lila said. "A whole pack of them. They must have sniffed you out somehow. They've killed everyone else on board, as far as I can tell."

That was when Ash noticed that Lila was favoring her right arm. When he moved the torch closer, he could see that her sleeve and the side of her jacket were sodden with blood.

"You're hurt," he said. It was an ironic turnaround from the night he'd first met the Darians, back in the dormitory at Oden's Ford.

"It's just a scratch, but thanks for noticing." Lila squinted into the darkness. "If we could find a way to fasten the hatch down, maybe they won't find us. Or at least they'll make a lot of noise trying to get in and draw the blackbirds."

It's a rare day, Ash thought, when a person actually *wants* to attract the attention of the King's Guard of Arden.

Ash looked around. There was the washtub full of rum, some putrefying dead rabbits, his healer's kit. A sick dragon. Nothing much to work with.

"If not for this bloody collar, I could at least give them a warm welcome," Ash muttered.

Lila stared at him. Licked her lips. Looked shifty-eyed and guilty.

"What?"

"I think I can help you with that." Digging into her carry bag with her good hand, she pulled out a small silver object. "Turn around so I can get at your collar."

"What's that?" Ash asked suspiciously, turning around.

He could feel her fumbling at the back of his neck. "It's a . . . it's a sort of a key."

"A key."

"To open the collar." Lila was obviously struggling to operate the device with one hand.

"You have a key to open mage collars," Ash said in a flat, deadly voice.

"Well, it stands to reason that there would be keys," Lila said brightly. "Otherwise, there would be no way to get them—bloody bones!" Growing impatient, the dragon had nudged Lila's leg, startling her. She flailed backward, ending up on her butt on the floor, nearly eye to eye with the dragon. The key landed next to her with a soft clank.

"Shhh!" Ash hissed, looking up at the ceiling.

"That—that—it—"

"It's all right," Ash whispered, stepping between Lila and the dragon. "It's not in any condition to hurt you." He hoped. He scooped up the key and handed it back to Lila. Knelt and took a closer look at her face. Don't you dare pass out until you've unlocked my collar, he thought, but didn't say it aloud because he didn't want to give her any ideas.

He turned around so that she could get at the back of his neck. She fumbled with the collar again. Finally, he heard a soft click, and the collar slid forward a little. Ash gripped it on either side, pulled the halves apart, and dropped it onto the floor. Experimentally, he tilted his head one way, then the other. He fingered his amulet. It was like the floodgates burst open, and magic torrented in.

Above their heads, Ash could hear voices, startlingly close. "The scent is stronger right around here." A cold finger of fear ran down his back when he realized that they were scenting his blood.

He turned to look at Lila, who was by now propped against the wall, eyes glazed with pain.

Squatting next to her, he began to unbutton her jacket. She took hold of his wrist with her good hand. It was slippery with blood. "No," she said. "I'm all right. Save your strength. You're going to need it."

"Shut it," Ash murmured, gently pulling free. "I'm just going to see what's going on. I might be able to slow down the bleeding." He decided to keep her talking. "How'd you do with the explosives?"

"The ship's all wired and ready," Lila said. "For all the good it does us."

"Could you set it off from here?"

"No."

"I'm not saying now. I'm saying if it comes to that."

"I'm not blowing up this ship with you on it. I promised my da I'd keep you alive, and I mean to keep that promise."

"Why didn't you tell me you had a key before now?"

"Well," Lila said, "I didn't have a key, not at first. By the time I got one, I was afraid you were going to get killed in an unsuccessful attempt on Montaigne. Or you were going to get caught and ruin my plans."

"Thank you for the vote of confidence."

"So. As long as you had the collar on, I knew you couldn't use attack magic to do it. I'm just glad they never traced the snake and the poison back to you."

"I *told* you. That wasn't me." Ash had continued working, and by now he had exposed the wound, a ragged cut that had bounced off her collarbone and into the shoulder. "Good news," he said, releasing a sigh of relief. "It's bleeding like a champ, so the risk of dying from poison is just about zero."

"Hooray," Lila said.

"If it makes you feel better, you were right. It was a bad idea to come here." Ash pressed his fingers into the wound, trickling in magic. He had no time to do any diagnostics, but given the location of the wound, the blade was unlikely to have hit anything vital. Still, he had to stop the flow of blood, or Lila would bleed out.

A minute, two minutes, and the flow slowed to a seep. She could live with that. He took off his cloak and laid it over her to keep her warm.

Something bumped Ash's shoulder. He turned, and it was the dragon again, looking at him rather plaintively.

"Look," he said, "you're going to have to wait your turn. I've got way too many patients, and vampire priests trying to get in, and—"

He stopped talking and looked up. Somebody was fumbling with the hatch. Ash stealthily rose to his feet, stretched, gripped the handles, and hung on. The hatch lid moved a little, so that he could see light around the edges, but whoever was outside was unable to lift both Ash and the hatch, and it stayed closed.

"It must be locked," one of the priests said, pounding on it, the way people do for no good reason. Did he really think that if they were down there, they were going to answer the door?

"He must be down there," a second voice said. "We've searched everywhere else, and the demon's stench seems to be coming from here." The hatch rattled again.

"I'm lead on this, remember," priest number one growled. "We all agreed that I'm to be first to bleed the demon mage."

"I didn't agree to that," priest number two retorted.

"You were there," priest number one said.

"That was days ago. If you wanted first blood, you should have cut one of the other mages."

"They aren't the same," priest number one whined. "There's something different about them. Foreign-tasting."

"We'd better decide before the others finish with the ones in the cabin," a new voice said, "or there'll be all of us sharing."

"You are not in on this, Robert," said priest number two. "Why don't you go back and see how the others are doing? Maybe they'll share."

The squabbling continued, growing more heated. At least they'd left off yanking at the hatch, but Ash knew it couldn't last forever. He found the collar and retrieved some of his smaller weapons, secreting them on his person.

Not that he was likely to live long enough to use them, but still.

His flash was building, but it was like he was trying to stopper multiple holes in a crumbling dike. There was no way he could hang on to the hatch, heal Lila, and see to the dragon as well. He needed some help.

Which gave him an idea. Quietly, he let go of the handles, knelt, and began running his fingers over the floor.

"What are you doing?" It was Lila, her voice barely a whisper.

"Looking for the key. Ah. Here it is." He held it up triumphantly, then looked it over. It was hinged, two half circles that seemed to fit together to form a tube. "How does this work?"

"This doesn't seem like a good time to—"

"I'm going to free the dragon," Ash said.

"Oh, I see. This situation isn't bad enough, so you're going to try and make it worse."

"I know what I'm doing," Ash said. "The dragon can be a distraction."

"A distraction. Right. Being burned alive would distract me from my other troubles." She rolled her eyes. "You're just hoping it will set the ship on fire and then it'll blow."

Well, he was hoping that. Just a little. "Lila. I need to know now."

"All right, fine. It fits on to the collar. Once you close

it, slide it along, and when you hear a click, you've reached the latch. If you pull on the collar, it should come apart at that spot."

Ash eased up next to the dragon. Its golden eyes were fixed on him, pinning him like a serpent's. "Let's try this," he murmured. He released a little flash into the dragon, to placate him. Then, slipping his fingers under the metal collar, he managed to slide the key under. He brought the two halves together, then attempted to slide it along the collar. It just barely fit, and it slid in fits and starts. He worked it around the dragon's neck, slowly, listening hard. Finally, he heard a click. Gently, he pulled on the two sides of the collar, and it came apart in his hands.

He was out of time. Metal scraped on metal as the hatch shifted. Light poured in. Ash leapt to grab the handles. He hung on, but this time the priests seemed to have found a way to work together. Ash found himself rising with the hatch until he was looking into the hooded face and fanatical eyes of a Darian brother. Multiple blades sliced at him frantically. He let go and fell back into the hold. He heard the crash as the priests toppled backward and the hatch landed on the deck above.

He looked over at Lila. Her eyes were closed. The dragon lay quietly alert, watching him as if to see what he would do next.

Now we're in for it, Ash thought. He touched his amulet. Not enough. Not nearly enough. Though if he fried the first few who came through the hatch, that might discourage the rest for a while.

Where's the bloody King's Guard when you need them? he thought.

Guarding the bloody king, no doubt.

If he set fire to the ship, would the charges go? He tried to remember what Jenna had said about that. All right, sul'Han, would you rather burn to death, be blown to bits, or have a bunch of fanatics suck you dry?

Ash gripped his serpent amulet, the one that had belonged to his father, and waited for the first vampire priest to come through the door.

39

THE DEVIL'S BARGAIN

Jenna lay awake in her tower room, listening to a thunderstorm roll in from the northwest. The wind howled, lashing against the walls. Rain thundered on the tile roof, and she could hear it splattering from the mouths of the gargoyles to either side of her window. Thunder crashed, reverberating through the stones of the castle, and lightning glared through the barred window, creating crazy, shifting designs on the walls.

A change in the weather, Jenna thought, for better or worse.

She propped up, looking around her chamber, reorienting herself. She'd not slept soundly since she'd been moved from her dungeon room. It was ironic, since this bed was more comfortable, and was not infested with vermin, and she didn't have to worry about rats coming out of the walls.

Well, maybe that last part wasn't entirely true. This palace was swarming with human rats, and they might be coming for her before long.

Every time she closed her eyes, dreams, images, and memories swarmed through her head.

That voice, pleading for help. *Flamecaster. We are dying.*

She was flying over a coastline, where the turquoise sea met white sands and buff-colored cliffs. The wind tore at her hair, she slitted her eyes against the wind and . . .

No. It wasn't the sea, it was Adam Wolf's eyes, dark with desire, and the taste of his kisses; it was his embraces, all long limbs and gentle, knowledgeable hands. It was the scent of his skin and the thud of his heart.

It was the way he haunted those borderlands between life and death, dark and light, pain and pleasure, and how he selflessly healed other peoples' wounds while he kept his own hidden away.

Gerard Montaigne, the demon who held her fate in his hands. Maybe. And Evan Strangward, who struck an odd chord of memory in her. Why did he seem so familiar?

Tonight, Adam would put their plan into motion. It hadn't happened yet—otherwise the palace would be buzzing like a kicked-over beehive. It satisfied her spirit of anarchy—the notion that she could strike one last blow against the king of Arden, whether she landed it herself or not.

Sliding from her bed, she padded in her bare feet to the window. The wind had driven the rain through the narrow windows of her cell, making puddles on the floor. She shivered. The nightshirt the healer had given her was gone, replaced by a silk nightgown that reached nearly to her ankles. At least her legs were covered now.

She leaned on the broad stone windowsill, staring out through the grille of metal, thinking that, what with the sound of the storm, she was unlikely to hear an explosion down at the wharf. Please, she thought, though she wasn't one for praying. Whatever happens, let Adam be all right.

She heard a faint noise in the corridor and whirled, staring at the door, heart thumping. It sounded like a grunt of surprise and pain, followed by a thud as a body hit the floor. As she watched, the door eased partly open, spilling the light from the hallway into her room.

Who would have reason to sneak into her room at this time of night? Surely not the king or his minions. Was it a rescue? A kidnapping? Some kind of ambush?

She looked around for weapons, grabbed up an oil lamp and waited, scarcely daring to breathe, until the door swung open the rest of the way.

First in the door was a huge man with a long braid on one side of his head. She recognized him—he'd be difficult to forget. He'd been with the Carthian delegation in the king's presence chamber. The Carthian scanned the room, sword in hand, before stepping aside to admit the others.

There followed four more, three men and a woman, who took their places just inside the door to her room, as if standing guard. And, finally, Evan Strangward, wearing a knee-length coat over his clothes.

Definitely not a rescue, then.

Strangward turned and spoke hurriedly to someone out in the corridor. Looking through the doorway past him, Jenna saw that it was Destin Karn. Karn nodded at whatever the mage had said and pulled the door shut.

Had the king changed his mind about the interview Strangward had requested? If so, why was this happening in the middle of the night? And where were the blackbirds?

Strangward stood, feet braced apart, hands on hips, and studied her. She felt self-conscious, standing there in her nightclothes, the wind whipping her gown around her legs, wishing she had a robe to put on. She tried not to look at her rumpled bed.

Jenna raised the lamp. "Stay back," she said, "or I'll use this." It probably wasn't a very effective threat against a mage with a sword.

"Jenna," he said. "I apologize for the late-night visit, but we are running out of time. Your king has forced my hand."

Not my king, Jenna thought. "What do you mean?"

"I had meant to take you back with me and so have the time to find out more about you. From the looks of things, that might not happen."

Jenna stared at him, her mind racing. Did that mean that the deal was off? Adam had said they hadn't come to terms. There was something furtive about Strangward's expression and the way he kept looking at the door. His guard stood clustered, fondling the hilts of their curved swords, their bodies rigid with tension.

"Does the king know you're here?" Jenna said, taking a shot in the dark.

Strangward shrugged, rubbed his nose, and said, "No. He doesn't."

"You're not afraid that I'll scream and bring the guard running?"

"That's possible, but not too likely," Strangward said. "We've dispatched the guards outside your door. Since this is the only occupied room in this tower, I doubt you'll be heard, especially with the storm going on. All in all, it seemed a tolerable risk." He gestured toward her, an invitation. "Would you like to give it a go? Screaming, I mean?"

It's not like she would feel any safer with Montaigne's men in the room. At least this way, she might learn something useful.

"No," she said. "I suppose not."

"Good," he said. "Shall we sit?" He gestured toward the chair by the hearth.

She was just stubborn enough that she sat on the edge of the hearth rather than in the chair.

Touching his amulet, Strangward kindled the logs in the fireplace with a gesture, then sat down on the hearth as well, a few feet away from her.

"If certain people knew that it was this easy to slip into the palace uninvited, the king would have been dead a long time ago," Jenna said.

To her surprise he laughed, long and hard. "You really don't like him, do you?" he said, wiping at his eyes.

Jenna breathed in through her nose. He had a wild scent about him, like sunlight and rain in the dust, and storms coming in from the sea. It was familiar, like a taut line that connected the two of them together.

They couldn't possibly have met before . . . could they?

"Have you ever been to Delphi?" she asked, extending her hands toward the fire, warming them.

"No," he said, leaning back against the fireplace and crossing his legs at the ankle. Although he must have been in a hurry, he made a show of making himself at home. "I have not. Why do you ask?"

"I keep wondering if we've met before."

He tilted his head, studying her. "Strange. I was thinking the same thing. Your eyes are memorable. Like cat's eyes."

"So I'm told," Jenna said.

"Perhaps," he said, "we met in a dream."

"I am not a dreamer," Jenna lied. "You said you wanted to talk to me. What about?"

He sat up then, uncrossed his ankles, and planted his feet on the floor, a signal that he was getting down to business. "Let me see the magemark again."

Jenna gathered her hair into her fist, lifted it away from her neck, then turned her back so the emissary could see.

He reached out and put his hand on her bare shoulder, turning her a bit more. The fingers of his other hand, warm and dry, stinging with magic, traced the pattern just below her hairline. She shivered, feeling the gooseflesh rise under his hand.

"Hmm," he said.

Now he closed both hands on her shoulders, and she felt a whisper of power as he sent it into her. She knew he was trying to use magic in order to get the truth from her, just as Karn had done. She gritted her teeth, but put up with it, thinking that if he learned something, he'd share it with her.

"You're not a mage," he said finally, sounding surprised.

"I'm not a mage," she said, rolling her eyes. "Didn't Karn tell you that? I would have told you that, too, if you'd asked."

"What kind of magic do you have, then?"

"What makes you think I have magic?"

"The empress is hunting you for a reason. Since she's greedy for power, I assume that you have something she wants."

"I'm not going to apologize for being just an ordinary

person. To tell you the truth, I haven't been all that impressed with the gifted people I've met so far."

"No," Strangward said, shaking his head. "There's got to be more to you than that."

"Has it occurred to you that I'm not the one the empress is looking for? That I'm just a girl with a birthmark who has nothing to do with any of this?"

"That may be," Strangward said, "but I can't take that chance. If you tell me the truth, I might be able to help you, depending on what the truth is."

Jenna's anger rekindled. "You'll help me? Before you came along, I didn't need help."

He frowned at her, as if confused. "What have I done?"

The anger that had been simmering in Jenna came to a full boil. "I had a life," she said. "It was a hard, desperate life, but it was something. Your mistress set the king of Arden to hunting me, and I lost my only family, my home, and my livelihood in the space of a month. Since then, I've been chained in a dungeon. Forgive me if I'm not eager to accept your offer of help."

"I am sorry about what's happened to you," Strangward said. He stood and paced back and forth. "I know what it's like to be hunted."

Through the window, Jenna heard the bells in the temple tower strike one.

"My lord?" The tallest of Strangward's companions nodded toward the window and raised his eyebrows.

"I know, Teza. I just need a little more time." Strangward came back and sat down on the hearth, letting his hands drop between his knees. He took a deep breath, then said, "Tell me about your relationship with the Empress Celestine."

"I am sick and tired of answering the same questions over and over," Jenna said, her voice rising. "Why don't you ask one of the other dozen people who've asked?"

The emissary raised both hands, as if to fend her off. "I am sorry for that. But I just want to make sure—make very sure—that we haven't missed anything."

She shivered, and it wasn't just the draft from the window. There was something about the way he said it—something told her that there was a lot riding on the answer.

Abruptly, he gripped her hands again and sent more power sizzling into her. "Why is the empress looking for you? Tell me." Finally, he let go and muttered, "This isn't working, is it? You really are resistant to magic." He said it like he was confirming something he'd been told.

But now images swirled through her mind, spinning so rapidly that she couldn't fasten on any one of them. She pressed her hands to either side of her head, as if she could trap them somehow.

What was it? It was so damned frustrating.

"My lord," the man called Teza said again. "We cannot stay much longer if we're to catch the tide."

Strangward nodded then, as if resigned. He squatted in front of Jenna, so he could look her in the eyes. "Are you telling me the truth, Jenna?" he asked quietly. In a last-chance kind of way. "You really don't know why the empress is so desperate to find you? This is really important to both of us."

"No," she said, "I don't know. I wish that I did. I'd hoped that you would explain it to me. I suppose we'll just have to . . ." Her voice trailed off. She'd heard another voice, deep in her mind, stronger than it had been before.

Flamecaster. I come.

"Lord Strangward, a moment," Teza said, motioning him closer. Strangward stood and crossed to where his liegeman waited near the door.

"I know this is hard for you," Teza said in a voice that Jenna shouldn't have been able to hear. "If it must be done, let me do it."

"It is not fair for me to ask you to do this task for me," Strangward said. "You've risked your life, you've lost so much already. I'll do it myself."

"But I'm volunteering, my lord. You know that I'm good with a blade. It will be a quick, kind cut. She won't feel it, I promise."

Jenna's heart began to thump. She was no lamb, waiting patiently to be sacrificed. Easing to her feet, she grabbed up the oil lamp from the hearth, sprinted toward them, and flung it at the two of them. It shattered on the floor at their feet, spilling burning oil over the floor and the two men.

Flamecaster.

Jenna bolted for the door, leaping over a puddle of burning oil. She grabbed the door handle and yanked at it. Someone—Strangward or Teza—seized her arms and shoulders, dragging her back. They slipped in the oil and fell. The back of her head slammed into stone, and lights exploded behind her eyes. She heard screaming, someone calling her name, the door opening and closing. She smelled burning flesh, and wondered if it might be hers.

At that moment, one of the images Strangward had given her finally came into focus. It was a silver-haired woman, standing next to a fiery crater. She held a struggling child in her hands, dangling him over the flames. And then, as Jenna watched, horrified, she let him go.

She propped up to find that there was flame all around her. The draperies were ablaze, and the tapestries smoldering, stinking of burning wool and lanolin. Flames burned ceiling-high between her and the door. There would be no escape that way. She saw two charred bodies, but nobody else. The rest must have fled, and left her here to burn.

She guessed her skin must be charred as well, because it felt oddly numb. She looked down, and saw that her arms were encased in glittering scales, her hands replaced by claws. It reminded her of the way her wound had looked when it began to heal. The scales were gold and silver and copper—all the colors of her hair.

She screamed, but the sound was lost in the inferno.

I'm addled by the smoke and the blow to my head, Jenna thought. I've got to get to fresh air. Crawling on her hands and knees over broken glass, she made her way to the window, where the wind still howled through the grate, only now snow swirled into the room, and hailstones the size of marbles clattered on the floor. She huddled under the window, her arms wrapped around herself, waiting to burn to death. And then it occurred to her that she didn't have to wait.

She'd tied the packet the healer had given her inside her bodice, so it hung between her breasts. She caught a claw under it and lifted it out, but then could not manage to untie the string with her hands the way they were. She bit at the string, then tried to rip apart the cloth bag. As she did so, the berries fell out, landing somewhere on the floor.

She groped with her clawed hands, but couldn't find them by feel or by scent. She screamed, a harsh cry of despair and frustration that echoed around the room. There came an answering cry from outside the tower, a cry that resonated inside her.

She thrust her face into the wind, into the clean, cold air, slitting her eyes against the bits of ice. Pressing her claws against the marble, she cried, "Flamecaster!" and heard the beating of wings.

DEATH BY DRAGON

Ash cut the throat of the first priest who dropped through the hatch. He didn't need flash for that. He stopped the heart of the second, which didn't take much. With the third one, though, there wasn't time for finesse. Ash immolated him before he hit the floor. It felt good, to be using attack magic again, as if he were using muscles he hadn't stretched in a while.

Then something struck him hard, on the shoulder, sending him flying into the wall.

It was the dragon; it was trying to open its wings.

"Not down here," Ash hissed, scrambling to his feet. But by that time, one of the priests had dropped into the hold and stood facing Ash, his blade in his hand, so fixed on his target and the scent of blood that he didn't seem to notice the dragon.

"Prepare to die, demon," the priest said, drawing his lips away from yellowed teeth stained with blood. It was the nightmare in the dormitory room all over again.

The dragon can be a distraction. That's what he'd told Lila.

Ash pointed over the priest's shoulder. "Look out for the dragon," he said.

"If you think I am so foolish as to—aaaaiiiieeee!"

Ash dove out of danger as the dragon lashed his tail, the spikes impaling the oblivious priest, then smashed him against the wall to either side. Ash covered Lila with his body as tiles shattered all around them, the shards littering the floor and biting into his exposed skin.

Death by dragon. That hadn't been on his list of possibilities.

More priests were wedged into the hatch, all of them trying to get through at once. The dragon sent flame torrenting into them, wave after wave, and the screaming began.

The noise was deafening—the shrieking of the priests, the dragon's primal cries of rage and fear. Ash's eyes burned as he breathed in the stench of sulfur and charred flesh.

Well, all right, Ash thought. Maybe freeing the dragon wasn't such a good idea. Especially since there was no way any of them could get out of the hold.

Then again, it *was* a great distraction. And he was enjoying watching those meetings between the dragon and the priests.

The dragon roared, a battle cry. His legs bunched under him and he launched, smashing through decking, sending what remained of the priests flying in all directions. Another scream of rage and it was gone, leaving a charred hole behind.

Rain poured through the shattered deck, sending steam rising where it hit burning wood and bodies. It turned out there was a way out for a dragon. And, now, for them.

"Let's go," Ash said, giving Lila a hand up. "I don't think we want to stay and find out if dragon flame can set off explosives."

They climbed over and around mounds of rubble, passing through the hole where the wall of the hold had been, moving forward until they found a stairway. Lila cried out once or twice when she bumped or jostled her arm, then pressed her lips tightly together as if to prevent its happening again. Once on deck, they hurried aft to the gangway. Ash didn't think Lila could manage the rope ladder.

The dock was swarming with blackbirds, who must have come running at the sight of the burning ship. Ash scanned them, looking for someone that he knew, and spotted Marc DeJardin. He and Guy Fleury were busy wetting down the docks and hurrying masters to their ships so that they could get underway and out of danger.

FLAMECASTER

"Marc!" he called from the deck. "Barrowhill is hurt. She needs a healer right away."

Marc motioned to a handful of wide-eyed healers, standing by for orders. Ash was pleased to see that Harold and Boyd were among them.

"Harold, Boyd! Get over here!" They hustled forward, bursting with importance, pleased and proud at being chosen out. When Harold recognized Ash, he said, "Master Adam, why are you wearing a guardsman's cloak?"

"I got cold," Ash said. "And so did Barrowhill. She's been stabbed, and I know I can count on you to take care of her until I get back."

"I'm all right," Lila hissed. "I need to take care of the—you know—"

"I'll handle it," Ash said. Turning back to the apprentices, he said, "It was a four-inch blade, entry between the collarbone and the right shoulder. I've stopped the bleeding, on the outside at least. Apply a dressing and bandage, then immobilize the arm and fashion a sling. Keep her warm and keep her quiet. Make sense?"

They nodded in unison, ignoring Lila's grumbled protests.

"Check her pulse and breathing every few minutes. I'll be right back." He handed Lila off to the two of them.

"Where are you going?"

"I'm going to check for any other survivors on board." And kill them.

He caught Marc's arm. "Move everyone away from the ship, as far away as possible. Don't let anyone else get on board. The way it's burning, I wouldn't be surprised if it explodes."

Without waiting for a response, Ash jogged back up the gangway. He searched the main deck from bow to stern, wishing he knew how many priests had boarded to begin with so that he could account for them all. There were three Darian bodies scattered around the hatch opening, and one priest near death, broken and badly burned, who Ash had to finish. He made himself climb back down into the hold, where he found three more dead. In the crew cabin, two of Strangward's mages lay crumpled on the floor, sucked dry. That was it.

There was no sign of the dragon, nor Strangward, Von, and the rest of his crew. They must have disembarked before the attack began. Where could they be? Where else would they go in Ardenscourt? He'd had the impression that the emissary didn't mean to stray far from his ship.

He recalled the conversation in the presence chamber, the expression on Strangward's face when the king refused to make an immediate trade. Was it possible he'd decided to go after Jenna himself? If he had, would he know where to find her? Possibly. Somehow Strangward had known that Jenna had been found and had come to collect her. He must have an informant at court.

The longer Ash thought about it, the more convinced

he became that wherever Jenna was, that's where he would find Strangward. And he needed to find them right now.

Before Ash returned ashore, he took one more walk around the ship, lighting the slow fuses that Jenna had recommended. From what he could tell, Lila had done her job well. He hoped they would both survive long enough for him to tell her so.

41

FLAMECASTER

The wall of the tower room shattered, sending shards of stone flying, all but burying Jenna. She struggled to free herself from the cairn of stones. Blood poured down into her eyes from a cut on her scalp so that she could scarcely see. When she finally staggered to her feet, the wind caught her, nearly toppling her, and needled her face with sleet and cold rain. Her arms and legs were still covered with armor-like scales.

Every time I think things can't get any worse, they do.

She found herself standing on what remained of the tower—a platform littered with rubble. Everything above her head was gone, and only one wall remained of what had been her tower cell. She cowered against the wall, shivering, mingled blood and rainwater splattering on the stones under her feet. Had the tower been struck by lightning, or a typhoon, or what?

At least the rain was putting out the fire.

She heard another screaming cry, and a furious beating of wings. She looked up, just as an enormous beast stooped down on her, claws extended, its huge wings blocking out the sky. Instinctively, she crouched, so as to make a small target, closed her eyes, and covered her head with her arms, waiting for its razored claws to sink into her flesh.

Instead, she heard a splash as it hit the deck next to her. She cracked her eyes open to see it skidding across the wet surface of the platform, flapping furiously to keep from sliding off the edge. It managed to stop at the far side, balancing on the edge. Once stable, it turned back toward her, straightening its crumpled wings.

Then it came to her, what she was seeing. It was—it must be—the empress's dragon. Ash must have managed to free it. And then it had come straight here to kill her. Scummer.

It was about the size of a large horse, with huge feet and a massive head, like it wasn't fully grown. It had large, golden eyes set on either side of its face, horns, and claws that left long gashes in the wood floor.

Its back was armored with two rows of sharp spines, running from just behind its shoulders to the end of its tail, which was so long that it hung over the edge of the building. It seemed to grow larger and larger as it came toward her, flame and smoke fuming from its nostrils.

I guess I can *still* find a way to burn to death, Jenna thought. But she was too dull-witted and dizzy to fight back. Or even to move.

When it was within a few feet of her, it stopped and cocked its head. *Flamecaster?* The word sounded inside her head, a question mark at the end. Understanding flooded in. It was the voice she'd been hearing since the emissary's arrival.

I'm either dead or dreaming, she thought. But sometimes you just need to go on with it.

"Flamecaster," Jenna repeated. "Is that your name? Have you been looking for me?"

It inched forward, head bowed, and bumped its nose timidly against her knee. She rested her clawlike hand on its head, feeling its hot breath on her bare toes, the scent of char and flame mingling in her nose. She tried to remember what she'd heard about dragons, besides the fact that they are made up. Did they eat people?

"I'm Jenna," she said, as if it wouldn't eat her once they were introduced.

She could feel the push of the dragon's mind, as if it were seeking an opening that it knew was there. Finally, something came through clearly. It was more an image in her mind than a word.

Jenna.

"That's right!" she said. "You're just a lýtling, aren't you?" she murmured, scratching behind its horns. It nudged her like a cat, wanting more, but a dragon is not a cat. She ended up flat on her back, with the dragon looking down at her, all shamefaced, its golden eyes wide with alarm.

Jenna hurt.

"You don't know your own strength, do you?" she said, forcing a smile to reassure it. She managed to sit up, resisting the temptation to close her eyes and let the rain fall on her face. She was shaking, teeth chattering, fighting off waves of dizziness.

Help?

At first, she thought he was asking for help, but then she realized that it was offering help.

"I wish you could help," she said, blotting at her eyes. "I dropped my berries and I can't find them." She knew she sounded like a loon, but she couldn't seem to form a sentence that made sense.

Berries? Flamecaster said eagerly. *Want food?*

Jenna laughed, stroking the dragon's head. She looked down at her own arms. Her scales were fading now that the fire was out, and her hands were losing their clawlike appearance. It was as if she armored up only when she needed that protection.

All right, then, she thought. Tally up another gift, you bloodthirsty bastards.

First it was fire, and now ice. She was freezing in the wind and sleet, clad only in her thin silk gown. Flamecaster's body burned with a hot, dry heat that was just what she craved. Jenna pressed herself against him in an effort to warm herself. She could hear his heart beating, and hers began to beat in time.

The dragon shifted, sliding his body under her, gripping her arm and rolling a little so that she ended up lying on top of him, just forward of where the spines began, her face pressed against his muscled neck. She wrapped her arms around his neck and tightened her knees around his body. It was like hugging a wood-burning stove, only more intimate, somehow.

"Thank you," she murmured. "That's much warmer. It really—"

Now fly.

Claws rattled against stone as Flamecaster charged forward and launched from the tower with Jenna clinging to his back.

Jenna screamed, and kept on screaming, her voice mingling with that of the dragon. At first it was all terror, but soon became a cry of ferocious joy. They soared out over the castle close. The city beneath them was as small as a child's toy village left out in the rain, with poufs of smoke from many chimneys.

Squinting her eyes against the rain, she looked back at the ruined tower, which resembled a charred and broken tooth. Take that, you gutter-swiving, murderous, black-hearted devil. She tightened her knees against the dragon's sides and whooped.

So this is what heaven is like, she thought. Who knew?

They were over the harbor now. Below, she saw a ship with broken masts and a hole in the side. It looked tiny from so high above. Could that be the emissary's ship? Though badly damaged, it was still afloat.

Chains and stinging collars. Dark, stinking hole. Enemies.

"Yes," Jenna whispered, pressing her cheek against Flamecaster's neck. "Enemies."

They were some distance east of the river when they were buffeted by a shock wave and an earsplitting series of booms that sent Flamecaster spinning sideways, flapping madly until he could regain his balance. Jenna looked back toward the city and saw that the ship had exploded, leaving chunks of burning debris floating in the water and little else.

Adam Wolf had come through. If the emissary and all his friends hadn't burned to death, she hoped that they had returned to their ship in time to blow up with it.

Jenna thrust her face into the rain and wind and screamed with a savagery she'd never tapped before. That was when she realized that they were losing altitude, despite the dragon's efforts to keep them aloft. Jenna wasn't heavy, but she was likely too much weight for a young dragon to carry. Especially one that was injured.

She leaned down to where she thought his ear might be, and said, "Flamecaster. Find a place to land. I don't want us to fall." He beat his wings, achieving a shallow glide. Flying east.

She fell asleep, and dreamed of Adam Wolf. Stay safe.

She didn't know how much later it was when they landed. She jolted awake as they bounced, then bounced again, and came to a sliding stop.

They were on a beach. The rain had stopped, but the sand was still pockmarked from the recent storm. A few stars had shaken off the clouds and glimmered overhead. To the west, the moon was rising, gilding a path on the breast of the ocean.

Jenna had never seen the sea. She blinked, scraping her wet and bloody hair out of her eyes, and drank it in, her heart full to bursting. When she finally looked down at herself, the scales had disappeared. She hurt all over, especially her head. She was hungry and ferociously tired, but she was alive.

Flamecaster was obviously exhausted, too. He lay, head on his forelegs, already sound asleep. Jenna crawled into the warm shelter of the dragon's body and closed her eyes again.

42

BACK AT THE CASTLE

Ash knew it wouldn't be easy to convince Lila to stay behind while he returned to the castle to look for Strangward. He sidestepped the issue by avoiding the conversation altogether. He used the rope ladder at the bow end of the ship to descend to the wharf. He spoke briefly with Marc, telling him that he'd found no survivors on board, and reminded him to keep people away from the ship until the fires burned out.

The storm was still raging with a ferocity Ash hadn't seen since he came south. Even with his blackbird cloak, he was soaked through before he'd gone a block. He was halfway up Citadel Hill when he heard it—a thunderous boom behind him. He swung around in time to see the second explosion, and the third. A fireball rose from wharfside, raining burning debris over the warehouses and taverns near the docks. Ash was glad it was raining, making it less likely that the buildings would catch. By the time the last of the charges went off, the ship was engulfed in flames.

"Sail *that*, Strangward," Ash whispered. And then, "Thank you, Jenna." He couldn't wait to see her face.

When he caught his first glimpse of the keep, he nearly stumbled. The tallest of the towers—the one that housed Jenna's new quarters—was broken, a large bite having been taken out of the very top. How would that have happened in the short time he'd been away?

He hurried on. Though it was the small hours of the morning, the streets grew more and more crowded as he approached the close. He began seeing chunks of stone-work and masonry lying about, bits of the demolished tower. One woman was sweeping grit and stone from her stoop in the rain, her face set and angry.

"What's going on?" he asked her.

"A demon smashed into the tower and knocked it half down," she said. "I was asleep, mind you, so I didn't see it. People said it lit up the whole sky, it burned so bright."

"A demon?" Ash stared at her. "Did they say what it looked like?"

"It had wings and a long tail. It looked like a flying snake. Or a dragon."

"A dragon," Ash repeated numbly.

"Aye," the woman said with the sort of grim satisfaction some people have when they've been proven right. "It must've been sent down here by the witch in the north, to punish us." She made the sign of Malthus and continued sweeping.

"Was anybody hurt?" he asked, his heart sinking.

"You'll have to ask them that know more," she said, nodding toward the keep.

The dragon he'd freed had flown straight to the castle. Was that the purpose of the emissary's visit—to carry out an attack on Arden from the inside?

And Ash had helped make it happen. He'd launched a new kind of arrow into the sky without knowing where it would land.

Within the close, blackbirds milled about, their hands on their swords as if they anticipated another attack at any moment. Some of the officers seemed to be questioning witnesses. Ash approached one of them. "What's going on?" he said.

"There was an attack on the castle. Maybe a bomb thrown from a catapult, we don't know."

"Was anybody hurt?"

"I dunno for sure. I been outside the whole time. Somebody said they found a couple bodies up near the top, where the break is."

"Who was it?" Ash said hoarsely. "The bodies, I mean?"

The blackbird shrugged. "I guess they couldn't tell, they was burned so bad."

"Thank you," Ash said. Fear and despair welled up in him like vomit. "I'll go look for myself."

A few of the nobility with quarters in the castle close had gathered in the Great Hall, which likely seemed safer than anywhere out on the grounds. In one corner, Father Fosnaught was holding a prayer service for a rapt audience, most on their knees on the stone floor.

Ash spotted Botetort, standing with a small group of retainers, issuing orders. He drifted close enough to hear.

"Beauchamp. Take five men to Brightstone Keep and stay there. Warn the steward to keep the children inside and the livestock in the riverside pastures so they can keep an eye on them. We've sent messages to Middlesea and Baston Bay to put them on alert, but the last thing we need is stories about dragons and witches spreading through the countryside. Granger and Larue have escorted the prince and princess to safety in the countryside until we see what's what."

"Lord Botetort," Ash said, joining the group. "What's happened? Is anyone in need of a healer?"

Botetort gripped his elbow, hard, and pulled him aside. "We are not entirely sure," he said, speaking low and fast. "It seems that the dragon escaped from the emissary's ship and attacked the keep. We don't know whether it was an accident or part of a plan, and if it is a plan, who is behind it."

"Where is the emissary?" Ash asked.

"Nobody knows. He seems to have disappeared. The bodies of two of his guards were found in the tower, in the"—he lowered his voice—"in the cell where the mage-marked girl was being kept. Where they had no business being."

Why were they in the tower at the time of the dragon attack? Had they called it there somehow?

"And the girl? What about her?"

"We haven't found her. Her body could be up there somewhere, buried in rubble. Or she might be lying anywhere within a mile of the keep. The beast hit right at the level of her room."

Had the empress meant to murder Jenna all along? Or had Strangward been ordered to kill her if they hadn't come to terms?

Ash felt the pain of remorse like a knife in his gut. If she's dead, then it's my fault, he thought. It didn't matter that King Gerard, Strangward, and the empress had all played a role—that did not diminish his own guilt. It was his father's death all over again.

Only this time, the king of Arden was within reach. Maybe.

"The king and the queen? Are they safe?" Ash struggled to keep the menace out of his voice.

Fortunately, Botetort didn't notice. "Neither were hurt in the attack. King Gerard seems badly shaken, which I suppose is understandable."

"I'm sorry to hear that," Ash said. "Perhaps I can give him something that will settle his nerves." In a permanent sort of way. "Do you know where he is?"

Botetort shook his head. "I don't know. If you do find him, I hope you can help him." He paused, choosing his words carefully. "He's not been himself lately. We need strong leadership at a time like this."

"I understand, my lord," Ash said, turning away.

Ash climbed the steps into the tower, two at a time. It had been nearly empty while Jenna was in residence there, and now it appeared to be completely deserted. There were few signs of damage until he reached the floor below Jenna's rooms. Here it looked like there had been one of the earthshakes he'd heard were common along the southern coast. Walls were cracked, and some seemed near collapse. As he climbed the next flight of steps, he could hear the wind whistling through up above.

When he emerged from the stairwell, he found nothing but ruins. The tower walls were gone on three sides, and everything above Jenna's floor was missing. Some of the furniture was still there, although it was charred and burned. It resembled a child's dollhouse, where the sides have been peeled away so you can look into the rooms.

"Jenna!" he shouted, the wind whipping the word away as soon as he released it. "Jenna, it's Adam." If there was a response, he didn't hear it.

The rain had churned ashes and cinders into a black soup. As Ash crossed the floor, glass crunched under his feet. He found two bodies against the remaining wall, burned nearly beyond recognition. When he looked closer, bits of braid and jewelry told him that they were the emissary's guard.

Ash walked the room in a miasma of grief and rage, forcing himself to search methodically. He found charred scraps of fabric in purple silk—the dress Jenna had worn to the meeting with the emissary. He tucked the fragments of silk inside his shirt for safekeeping.

The iron bed frame remained, though the bedclothes were a soggy, blackened mess. And on the table next to the bed, a lump of charred leather and water-soaked paper. Her book.

I wonder if she finished it? He blotted tears from his eyes, recalling what she'd said on their last night together.

I want to live. I want to hear the bells in the temple church in Delphi, ringing out the victory. I want to hike into the Spirit Mountains and speak to witches and faeries. I want to sail over the ocean, all the way to the horizon and beyond. I want to go all those places I've never seen, except in books. I want to fly—

He slipped his hand inside his coat, fingering the battered gold pendant she'd given him. It looked like a piece of a mariner's compass. He remembered what she'd said.

You can give it back to me when I see you again.

When you love someone, that catches the attention of the gods, who punish you.

He walked to the edge and looked out over the city. Where would Jenna's body have landed, if she'd been thrown from the building by a dragon?

It made no sense that a dragon would kill her. He'd always heard that dragons loved beautiful things.

I should have killed it when I had the chance, but Jenna wanted it freed.

Ash heard a slight sound behind him, like a boot crunching into glass. He began to turn, reaching for his amulet. But it was too late. A hard push between his shoulder blades, and he was falling, over the edge and into space. Desperately, he grabbed at the air, and his hands fastened on a pair of gargoyles—drain spouts on either side of a window. He dangled from the spouts until his toes found a bit of a ledge to dig into.

The wind was howling, and the stone was slippery from the rain. Ash was afraid to move for fear of losing his hold and falling the rest of the way.

He looked up, blinking away rain, to see Gerard Montaigne standing over him. He resembled some avenging spirit in a cautionary tale, silhouetted against the roiling clouds, with his cloak whipping in the wind.

The king knelt, reached down, and yanked Ash's amulet over his head; the serpent amulet his father had given him. Ash was helpless to stop him.

Montaigne tossed the amulet over his shoulder. Ash heard the clank as it hit the stone floor.

"So, Adam Freeman," the king said as if he no longer believed in the name. "I see that you are uncollared once more. How could that have happened?"

Ash couldn't think of any answer that would be helpful, so he said nothing at all.

"I am wondering why it is that, ever since you arrived in Ardenscourt, I've had one piece of bad luck after another."

Ash judged the distance between them. He shifted his feet, seeking more secure footing. With a better base, he might be able to push up and grab the king's ankles. He'd fall, but he'd take the king with him, and just now that seemed like a worthwhile trade. Especially with Jenna gone.

But if he missed, or lost his grip . . .

When Ash said nothing, the king continued on. "Fires in the kitchen, snakes in my bed, poison in the wassail, and now dragons on the tower. Truly, I am beginning to feel like a target."

Keep him talking, buy some time to think. "Maybe it's time to make your peace with the Maker," Ash said. "To take a close look at your life so far, and—"

"Do not dare to defile the Maker's name!" Gerard thundered. "You are not worthy!"

. . . but don't rile him up enough so he ends it now.

Ash hung there silently, as if chastened.

"I was forced to dispose of my beloved Estelle," Montaigne said, back to icy calm. "I loved her, but once I realized that she had been corrupted, she had to be sacri-ficed." He paused, as if gathering his thoughts.

Ash had left most of his arsenal of poisons with the dis-carded collar. But not everything. Keeping a tight hold on the gargoyle with one hand, he slid the other into the pocket of his cloak, groping until he found what he was looking for—the sting in its leather sheath. Using his teeth, he pulled the sheath away.

"But that is nothing, nothing next to these recent calam-ities. The thanes were already mutinous, always whining about paying for this holy war against northern witchery. Then Delphi falls to a mob of coal miners, ships explode in the harbor, and a dragon attacks the castle itself. That's when I knew."

"That's when you knew what?" Ash said.

"That's when I knew that you were responsible."

"Well," Ash said, "much as I'd like to take credit for all of that, I can't see how you think I'm to blame." Well, maybe for those last two things, but he wasn't going to bring that up.

"Your name is not Adam Freeman," Montaigne said, triumphantly, "is it?"

Ash looked up at him. Suddenly, he was eager to face the king of Arden in no other skin than his own. "No," he said, "it's not."

"How long did you think you could fool me?"

"Long enough to kill you, I hoped."

"It should have been obvious." Montaigne shook his head. "I can only think that the Breaker clouded my eyes. That first night, when you came walking out of the flames and raised the baker from the dead, I should have known. That was unnatural. Then you insinuated yourself into the healing service so that you could get to the girl with the magemark."

"You were the one who asked me to treat her," Ash said.

"I was blinded by sorcery. Otherwise, I would have known. But tonight, I will do what I should have done in the first place." He paused, as if to build suspense. "I will kill you."

Fragmented thoughts swirled through Ash's mind. This doesn't make sense. Why wouldn't he try to keep me alive and hold me hostage? Or break my mother's heart by torturing me to death?

Maybe he'll send the pieces home in a box, the way he did with Hana.

"You are going to lose," Ash said. "I don't care how many of us you kill, we will never surrender. You will pay for murdering my father, and my sister, and you will pay for Jenna. You never should have picked a fight with the Gray Wolf queens."

But the king didn't seem to hear him. "Behold your redemption, demon!" The king thrust a stoneware jar into Ash's face.

That was the opening he needed. Ash jabbed the sting into the king's forearm. Gerard didn't even notice.

Ash withdrew the needle and let it fall. He released a long, shuddering sigh. There. It was done. Finally.

"Behold your redemption, demon!" the king repeated, apparently miffed at the lack of response.

"What's that?" Ash asked.

The king rocked the jar. It sloshed. "This is oil." He smiled. "The only way to kill a demon is by burning."

Ash couldn't help wishing the poison he'd used was faster acting.

If wishes were horses, even beggars would ride.

Montaigne was mumbling to himself. "I should have known. But I didn't, not at first." He refocused on Ash. "You see, I thought your kind had red hair."

Ash blinked at him, confused. He was the only one in his family with truly red hair. "What do you mean, 'your kind'?"

"Demons."

"Demons?" Ash stared at Montaigne. "Hang on—you think I'm an actual demon?"

"It's my fault, for agreeing to use mages in the war, and so violating the Maker's laws," Montaigne said. "I had become convinced that one has to use witchery against witchery in order to win. But now I know that all I did was open the door to sin and depravity. That's the thing about demons—you have to invite them in. I should have listened to Father Fosnaught and burned you that first night. From tonight forward, everything changes. I will send the Hand into every corner of the empire and cleanse it of every tainted person. It begins with you."

Raising the jar, he dumped it over Ash's head, managing to splatter it all over himself as well. He tossed the jar over, then stalked to the inside wall and yanked a torch from its bracket.

He returned to the edge, his face monstrous in the light from the flames. "By the great saint!" he said, raising the torch with both hands. "Die, demon!"

But the torch never came down. Instead, someone grabbed the king's torch arm and jammed it down so the burning head ignited his clothing. Montaigne screamed and stumbled forward, his arms and legs pinwheeling wildly as he toppled over the edge. Ash flattened himself against the tower wall to avoid being struck as the king screamed past him like a falling star. The screaming ended abruptly when he hit bottom.

"Die, demon," Ash murmured. Cautiously, he raised his head and peered up to see someone looking down at him.

"Are you all right?"

Ash was momentarily speechless. It was Queen Marina, dressed in a nightgown, her hair caught into a long braid. She looked very young.

"Are you all *right*?" she repeated, a little impatiently. "We may not have much time."

"Y-yes," Ash croaked.

She dropped a rope over the side. "Grab hold of this carefully, please, and wrap it around your waist. The last thing I want is to lose you when you've held on for so long."

He grabbed hold, despite his oil-slicked hands, and walked up the side of the building until he could slide over the edge on his belly. He lay there, gasping, for a moment, then rolled over and sat up.

Queen Marina dangled his amulet in front of him. "I believe this is yours?"

Ash practically snatched it out of her hand and dropped the chain over his head, grateful to feel the weight of it again. Oil dripped from his hair and down his neck.

He crawled to the edge and looked down at the crumpled body of the king. He'd landed in an inner courtyard, and no one seemed to have noticed yet. He would have thought his enemy's death would be more satisfying, but all he felt was mingled grief and relief. Grief for those who had died too soon. And relief that perhaps this chapter was over.

Marina came up beside him, looked down, and shuddered. "Thank the Maker he's dead," she said, her voice trembling. "I was beginning to think he was immortal."

"But . . . how did you—" Ash couldn't seem to complete a coherent sentence.

"I've been his favorite target for years," Marina said,

fussing absently with the ties at the ends of her sleeves. "I kept thinking that someone would kill the loathsome bastard for me. If it happened soon enough, I might be named regent over Prince Jarat. I'm used to biding my time. But lately . . . lately the king had started in on Madeleine. I knew the time would come that I would no longer be able to protect her.

"So. A year ago, I decided to kill the king myself. It had to be in a way that would not be traced back to me." She smiled crookedly at Ash. "I'm a Tomlin. You'd think I'd be good at this sort of thing, but it turned out to be harder than I'd thought. The snake seemed perfect, but—" She shrugged. "I'm truly sorry about Estelle. I didn't mean for her to be the one to pay for it."

Ash remembered what he'd said when he and Lila had discussed it, when she'd tried to blame it on him. *Either this would-be killer is an amateur, or someone wants to put the king on his guard.*

"What about the wassail? Was that yours, too?"

She nodded, shrugging.

"But—why did you drink it, if you knew that it was poisoned?"

"That was a low point," she said, wincing. "I was beginning to think I'd never be rid of him. When I saw that the king wasn't going to drink it, I decided to drink it myself. If I survived, it would direct suspicion away from me. If I died, I wouldn't have to live with that bastard pretender any longer. You are too skilled a healer, I'm afraid."

Ash recalled what Montaigne had said just before the Feast of Saint Malthus. *You stupid slut of Tamron.*

"What happens now? Do you think they'll suspect you?"

She shook her head. "It's unlikely. Everyone in Arden thinks of me as the king's doormat. Plus, the king has been growing more and more erratic these past weeks. After the attack, he seemed clearly unhinged—I've never seen him like that. No one will be surprised that he took his own life."

"That may have been the effect of the living silver," Ash said.

Marina frowned. "What do you mean?"

"That was supposedly a gift from the empress," Ash said. "I slipped it in with the diamonds she sent to the king. It's a mercury compound that comes from some of our hot springs up north. When heated, it releases a deadly vapor. I told him it was white magic, that it could be used to keep away demons if he burned it all night. If it didn't kill him, I hoped that it would make him sick enough that he would come seeking treatment from me."

Marina laughed. "How many assassins does it take to kill a king?"

"And so, your son will come to the throne?"

She bit her lip. "He will. I only hope that he'll accept some guidance from me." She gestured toward the stairwell.

"I think you'd better be on your way. They'll be up here before long to find out what happened. Give my greetings to your mother the queen. Tell her I'll never forget the way she looked at her name day party—so beautiful and strong and confident. She has always been something of a role model for me."

Ash had been making for the stairwell, but now he turned back toward her. "You know who I am." He was all but numb to surprises by now.

Marina smiled. "I've known since Solstice. Despite opinions to the contrary, I am not stupid."

PARTING OF
THE WAYS

In the days following the attack on the palace, Ash barely slept. He scoured the city for any sign of Jenna, alive or dead. He questioned people who had collected souvenirs in the streets—chunks of stone and roof tiles, along with other bits of debris. Some had been wakened from their beds when the dragon smashed into the upper floors of the palace—twice.

Not long after, some saw it careening away from the castle close, flying east, toward the sea. Rumors flew—that the dragon had incinerated entire villages along the way; that an army of dragons was assembling in the mountains north of Delphi; that the witch queen had been seen driving a carriage pulled by dragons through the sky; that dragons had attacked ships at the wharf and destroyed one of them.

The official story—that the damage had been caused by a bomb planted by Fellsian operatives—gained little traction.

Destin Karn was put in charge of an investigation into the king's death, which wrapped up quickly. He found no evidence of foul play. The official verdict: a tragic accident while the king was assessing damage to the palace. The unofficial cause of death: suicide. Ash tried to meet with Karn several times, but Karn seemed to be avoiding him.

He knows something, Ash thought, but it was too risky to push, considering his own role in the scheme of things.

The queen made a lovely and gracious widow. In the days immediately following the death of the king, she issued a number of quiet pardons and executive orders. Among those, that Adam Freeman had been uncollared in recognition of his service to the crown.

Ash and Lila watched Jarat's coronation from the gallery. It was spare and rather rushed, as coronations went. No doubt Jarat didn't want to give the restive thanes time to organize an alternative. The heir looked every inch a king as he presided at the feast afterward—tall, dark-haired, handsome. Father Fosnaught sat on one side of him, Lord Botetort on the other, Botetort's daughter next to him. The queen and the princess were seated halfway down the table. General Karn was still in the field, jockeying with Lord Matelon. And Destin Karn was out of the city.

Security was extremely tight. Tasters tried every course before the new king dug in. Some things hadn't changed.

Ash and Lila had already packed up their things and moved into an inn outside the castle close. Lila's excuse was that she was heading back to the Fells to collect more goods for smuggling. Ash had made up a story about a position with a healer in Bruinswallow. No one was happier to see Ash go than Master Merrill.

"That's a smart move, boy, to gain some more experience before you practice in a challenging setting like this. Hard work is the path to improvement. Out in the countryside, the need is great and the standards not so high."

Ash nodded, as if filing away wisdom. "Perhaps, when I have more experience, I could come back to Ardenscourt and—"

"No!" Merrill blurted. He collected himself. "Training takes time, and I've spent all the time on you that I can spare."

Harold and Boyd, at least, were sorry to see Ash go. Boyd gave Ash a knife with a carved handle, and Harold gave him a book he'd stolen from the healers' library. Ash ignored their hints that they'd like to come along.

"You both really have come a long way," Ash said. "If you'd like to learn more, you might consider the healers' academy at Oden's Ford."

"Oden's Ford!" Harold said, wide-eyed. "That's for bluebloods."

"Oden's Ford is for everyone who wants to learn," Ash

said, shouldering his healer's kit. "Good luck."

Their last night in Ardenscourt, Ash and Lila shared supper at the inn, making plans for departure.

"You're really coming back with me?" Lila said, blotting her lips. "You're not going to drug my wine and abandon me at a campsite, are you?"

Ash shook his head. "It's time I went home." He slid his hand inside his shirt, where Jenna's pendant hung next to his serpent amulet. Both represented losses.

"What changed your mind?"

"Spending time in Arden has awakened my patriotism, I suppose."

That was part of it, but the truth was more complicated. Four years ago, he'd run away and left his mother and sister on their own to deal with his father's death. For four years, he'd done as he liked, rationalizing that he was doing his bit for the queendom, never considering what they might want or need from him. He'd been selfish, and a coward, and losing Jenna seemed like a penance for that.

Maybe he'd deserved it. But not Jenna. He'd intended to take her home before her death. Now going home seemed like the right thing to do. He had a lot to make up for, if that was even possible.

Sometimes home is where you need to go for healing.

Time would tell whether Arden under King Jarat would change its warlike ways. Meanwhile, there was work to be done at home.

"Are you sorry you didn't get to kill Montaigne all on your own?" Lila asked.

Ash thought about it, then shook his head. "I wanted him dead, I'll admit. I think the world is a better place without him. But I'm beginning to realize that revenge is never as satisfying as you think it will be. Sometimes there's a high price."

The irony didn't escape him. If he hadn't come to Ardenscourt to kill Montaigne, he'd never have met Jenna. He'd never have fallen in love with her, and maybe she would still be alive.

"We did manage to quash any chance of a deal between Arden and Carthis. That's something."

"That's something," Ash said, turning his mug between his hands. It might be something, but it felt like nothing.

"There are a lot of loose ends, though. The dragon, for instance."

Ash shrugged. "I'm thinking it might be dead. It was heavily armored, but, still—to crash through the stone wall of a castle like that. It must have been badly injured. Maybe it hid away somewhere to die." He paused. "Strange."

"What's strange?"

"Animals usually have more sense than that. It's only humans that tend to bang their heads against a stone wall."

"I wonder if we'll ever find out why the empress was so eager to get hold of Jenna."

"Sometimes I wonder if the empress wasn't just made up,

a story Strangward told in order to get what he wanted."

"Which was?" Lila raised an eyebrow.

"I don't know," Ash said.

"Any news about—"

"No."

"Is it possible the Carthians kidnapped her? I mean, two of them were found dead in her room. And Strangward's gone missing, too."

"Anything's possible, but even if I knew for sure that's what happened, I wouldn't know where to start looking."

"I'm sorry about Jenna," Lila said, her eyes dark with sympathy. "If you want to stay on longer, and keep looking, I'm good with that."

Ash shook his head. "Something would have turned up by now," he said. "Even though it was the middle of the night, somebody should have seen something."

"Remember what I said, back at Oden's Ford? About hope?"

Ash frowned, trying to remember. "While I try and treasure up every word that comes out of your mouth, I can't—"

"Hope is the thing that can't be reined in by rules or pinned down by bitter experience. It's a blessing and curse." Lila raised her glass. "To hope."

"To hope," Ash said. They clanked.

"Now," Ash said, "let's go home."

EPILOGUE

In another tavern, far away in the port city of Spiritgate, Evan Strangward killed time, nursing an ale and playing nicks and bones with himself. He'd glamored his appearance, so that to any but his stormsworn guard, he wore the brown skin and straight black hair of a traveler from We'enhaven.

He shivered and turned up the collar of his coat. He sat close to the door so that every time it opened, the raw wind from the Indio howled in. He'd chosen this seat on purpose, so he wouldn't miss anyone coming and going.

He'd been too long in these wetlands. He would be glad to go back to the sunbaked land he called home. For multiple reasons.

He heard familiar footsteps, and turned. It was Teza. Just Teza. It was what he'd expected, it was what he'd demanded, in fact, but he was still disappointed.

"My lord," Teza said, shoulders slumping in relief. "Thank the Maker."

Evan smiled. "Ah, Teza, I can't imagine that the Maker is looking after the likes of me. I've not seen any sign of it so far." He stood, opened his arms, and they embraced.

"Destin didn't insist on coming with you?" Evan asked, reclaiming his seat.

Teza shook his head. "He said he could be of more use to you in Ardenscourt."

"Not if he's dead."

"He says he has no plans to be dead, my lord." Teza settled into the empty chair.

I don't want him to be of use to me, Evan thought. I want him to forget about me. I want him to kill that monster of a father, leave Arden, and find a house by the sea.

I want him to be happy.

"The plans we make are not the problem," Evan said. "It is the machinations of others. Did you give him the money?"

Teza shook his head, handing over a small pouch. "I tried. He refused it."

Again, Evan wasn't surprised, but he was disappointed. He signaled for the server.

"You've lost weight," Teza said. He looked travel-worn and hollow-cheeked himself.

Evan rolled his eyes. "It never takes you very long to start in nagging. It's this rich wetland food. We'll be fine once we get back to salt pork, way bread, and rations of rum."

"When you were late," Teza said, "I—I didn't know what might have happened."

"I usually travel much faster by sea than you would by land, but I ran into trouble in Middlesea, and I had to sail farther north to make a landing."

"The empress?"

Evan nodded. "The entire port was infested with Cele's spies. I think she's planning to come find the girl herself. Everything points that way. I'd hoped to sail from there, but it was too risky."

"We need to be gone before she arrives."

"I suspect she'll land at Baston Bay. She's one to go straight for the heart."

The server arrived tableside. "Two ales and two lamb pies," Evan said.

"My favorites," Teza said, smiling, as the server hustled away.

"Were you able to arrange for a ship?"

Teza nodded. "She's a two-masted schooner. No match for *Sun Spirit*, but she'll do, I think."

"How many of the stormsworn did we lose?" Evan asked. "Can we crew a schooner?"

"We lost Ephraim and Trey on the ship," Teza said. "Plus the two in the tower."

"I don't like to hire casual crew. They ask too many questions, and talk too much after. I'll just have to make do with what we have." He paused. "Could Des tell you anything more about what happened down at the harbor?"

Teza scowled. "It's like someone spilled a box of puzzle pieces and none of them fit together. Ephraim and Trey were in the pilothouse. They had stab wounds and slashes all over their bodies, and, apparently, bled to death before the explosion. In and around the hold, there were seven dead priests."

"Priests?" Evan rocked back in his chair, resting the heels of his hands on the edge of the table.

Teza nodded. "Most were badly burned. It looked like they tried to go down into the hold and somehow the dragon got out of the collar and flamed them. Then escaped."

"Hmm. Doctrinal differences, no doubt."

"My lord?"

"The church flames mages, and dragons flame priests."

"Oh. I see, my lord."

Evan sighed. Destin would have understood immediately. Teza was willing, but Evan's humor usually went right over his head.

"It seems that somebody who knew what he was doing used explosives to blow up the ship." Teza set his bag on the table and opened it. "Destin found two collars in the hold. There was this one." He held up the collar they'd used on the dragon. "And this." He handed over another silver collar in a smaller size.

Evan tapped the runes etched into the silver. "Why is this familiar?"

"According to Destin, this is the collar that the healer wore."

Evan looked up, puzzled. "The healer?" Had he met a healer?

"The collared mage at the meeting. The one responsible for 'magical threats.' Speaking of threats, you'll find some interesting enhancements to that." He pointed his chin at the neckpiece.

"Ah." Evan saw what Teza meant. The collar was typical of flashcraft, except for the tiny bottles and pouches attached to the inside. "Something tells me that these are not medicinal." He shook his head, bemused. "What would he have been doing on my ship? We barely spoke."

"Someone wanted to prevent us from making a deal with Montaigne," Teza said.

"More likely, they wanted to prevent the empress from making a deal with Montaigne," Evan said. "Could it have been agents from the Fells?"

"That's the common opinion," Teza said. "The entire countryside is in a frenzy of superstition. The churches are packed. They think the wolf queen is going to send more dragons swooping down on them."

"One day I'll have to meet this demon queen and see if

she really eats babies for supper." Maybe I'll sail north, he thought, instead of east.

"Just wait until they meet the empress."

"I hope they don't," Evan said, his smile dying away. "I hope I'm wrong." He cleared his throat. "Any word on who killed Montaigne?"

"Rumor has it that he killed himself. He was despondent over recent events, and went a little crazy."

Evan snorted. "If true, it would be the first good deed he's ever done. But I don't believe it. Somebody finally got to him." He raised his glass. "To dead Montaigne," he said softly.

Teza raised his own glass. "To dead Montaigne." They clanked. "See? It wasn't a complete disaster. Montaigne is dead, and we prevented the empress from getting hold of the magemarked girl. That's something."

"But Jenna Bandelow is dead, too, and we don't know any more than we did before. We don't even know what her gift really was." Evan brushed his fingers over the back of his neck, tracing the symbol embedded there. Different from Jenna's, and yet somehow connected, rooted in the same magic, the same history.

"You didn't kill the girl."

"She'd still be alive if I hadn't intervened."

"Maybe not for long. In any event, we couldn't risk leaving her there for the empress to find. We couldn't chance an even more powerful Celestine."

The food came. Evan waited until the server moved away again, then leaned in, pitching his voice low. "Why does my life count for more than Jenna's? She was smart and brave, Teza! I think we would have been friends. It seems like we should be allies. It's one thing to kill someone because they know too much. It's another to kill someone because they can't provide the answers you don't have yourself."

"What do you think Cele will do when she finds out the girl is dead?"

"What she always does. She'll go back to hunting me. Maybe I should just get it over with and arrange a meeting."

"No!" Teza said, too loudly. He looked around. Several people were staring, but they hurriedly returned to their meals. "Look," he said softly, "no one can fault you for trying to survive."

"No one but me," Evan said. "I always put the ones I love at risk." He paused. "It's getting late. Let's finish up so you can walk me down to this ship you've found. We'll need to be ready to catch the tide."

ACKNOWLEDGMENTS

Change is good, right? Maybe. But it's never been easy for me. I'm not the girl who leaves, I'm the girl who's left behind. And yet, here I am, launching a new series with a new publisher.

Fortunately, in the small-world tangle that is publishing, some good things continue, and others come around again. My new series is set in the familiar world of the Fells, where you still don't want to be one of my characters.

I continue to benefit from the wise counsel of my agent, Christopher Schelling, who has managed to scrub every vestige of Ohio from his skin and from under his nails but who still houses a huge Midwestern heart. Thanks to my foreign rights reps, Chris Lotts and Lara Allen, who decipher the indecipherable.

The team at HarperCollins has given me such a warm welcome. I am beginning this new journey with an old friend, senior editor Abby Ranger. I first worked with Abby at my previous publisher, Hyperion. Abby knows how to sound those chords that are in your heart already. There are very few suggestions she makes that don't resonate.

I've been extraordinarily fortunate in my covers throughout my career. Thanks to designer Erin Fitzsimmons and illustrator Sasha Vinogradova, the winning streak continues with a spectacular cover for *Flamecaster*, full of pizzazz and glitterbits. Senior art director Amy Ryan oversaw the cover process, dealing patiently with ephemeral demons in the artwork and adding sparkle at every stage.

The publicity, sales, and marketing staff are critical in bringing my work to the attention of readers. Thanks to publicist Lindsey Karl, the marketing team of Nellie Kurtzman (another familiar face!) and Jenna Lisanti, and associate publisher and senior vice president of sales Andrea Pappenheimer. They have all made me feel like a visible fish in the publishing pond.

As always, thanks to my husband, Rod, the most responsive webmaster ever; my sons and other early readers; and all of the other writers who offer critique, support, commiseration, sage advice, and the occasional glass of wine. I raise my glass to all of you.

THE SEVEN

THE QUEENDOM
of the FELLS

Shivering Fens

Hallowmere

Rivertown

Eastgate

Dyrnnewater R.

Westgale

Demonai
Camp

Hanale

LEEWATER

Delphi Rd.

Swansea

THE KINGDOM of
TAMRON

Fetters Ford

Tamron R. (West branch)

Tamron R.

TAMRON FOREST

Malthus
Shrine

Tamron
Court

Tamron Rd.

West Rd.

Harbor Rd.

Oden's
Ford

South Rd.

Sand Harbor

South Gate

SOUTHERN ISLANDS

Bruinsport

BRUINSWALLOW

REALMS

FROZEN SEA

Grey Lady

THE VALE

Invaders Bay

Wizard Head

Fellsmarch

Chalk Cliffs

Marisa Pines Camp

Firehole R.

Fortress Rock

Marisa Pines Pass

Way Camp

Hunter's Camp

Queen Court

Alyssa Plateau

The Harlot

Spiritgate

Delphi

KINGDOM of ARDEN

Heartfang Mtns.

Middlesea

North Rd.

Temple Church

Ardenswater

Bittersweet Keep

Ardenscourt

East Rd.

Baston Bay

THE INLAND OCEAN

Ardenswater

Heartfang R.

Bright Stone Keep

Bitter Springs R.

Watergate

Gryphon

The Cl

The Wastes

WE'ENHAVEN

Hidden Bay